Praise for the Novels of Lesley Kagen

The Resurrection of Tess Blessing

"How wonderful it is to spend time inside Lesley Kagen's creative mind. In *The Resurrection of Tess Blessing*, Kagen deftly illustrates her gift for blending the serious and the funny, the light and the dark. With a touch of magical realism, she once again creates a story that's as hopeful as it is poignant. As a reader, I feel safe in her hands."
— Diane Chamberlain, international bestselling author of *Necessary Lies*

"Kagen's talent shines in this wholly original and richly imagined story where unbearable heartache is softened with humor and a touch of magic."
— Beth Hoffman, *New York Times* bestselling author of *Looking for Me*

"Read *The Resurrection of Tess Blessing*, but don't read it in public because it'll yank the emotions out of you. You'll laugh, you'll cry, and by the end you'll be Tess Blessing's best friend."
— Cathy Lamb, bestselling author of *What I Remember Most*

"*The Resurrection of Tess Blessing* is Lesley Kagen at her finest, magically weaving together a tale of poignant regrets, powerful aspirations, and forgotten dreams through Tess, a woman who is really a bit of each of us. By traveling this journey with Tess we are shaken, uplifted, and transformed."
— Pam Jenoff, bestselling author of *The Winter Guest*

"Confronting her own mortality, Tess Blessing, a lifelong list maker tackles the only to-do list that matters: healing fractured relationships, and empowering the children she fears she will leave behind. Poignant, funny, and searingly wise, *The Resurrection of Tess Blessing* will stay with you long after you turn the last page."
— Patry Francis, bestselling author of *The Orphans of Race Point*

"*The Resurrection of Tess Blessing* is helmed by the most interesting narrator I've read in ages. She and her gifted author, Lesley Kagen, lead us through heartbreaking, humorous, compassionate twists and turns until we find ourselves on the other side, wiser but also, appropriately, resurrected and blessed. It is a journey I was delighted to take."
— Laurie Frankel, bestselling author of *Goodbye for Now*

"I was hooked from the get go. Tess Blessing's story is quietly inspiring. With faith, hope, grace, and humor, she shows us how to keep moving forward in the face of fear, uncertainty, and pain . . . put one foot in front of the other and call in your oldest friend."
— Julia Pandl, bestselling author of *Memoir of the Sunday Brunch*

The Undertaking of Tess

"A tender yet big-hearted coming-of-age story filled with heartbreak, secrets, and humorous observations of the convoluted adult world through which two young sisters must navigate."
— Beth Hoffman, *New York Times* bestselling author of *Looking for Me*

"Heart-rending, yet humorous and filled with hope, *The Undertaking of Tess* is a rare treat from an author who truly knows how to create unforgettable characters. Readers who loved Kagen's *Whistling in the Dark* will adore Tess and Birdie in this delightful novella."
— Sandra Kring, author of the national bestseller *The Book of Bright Ideas*

"A bittersweet coming-of-age-in-the-fifties story that'll have you crying one minute and laughing out loud the next. Kagen's ability to capture children's deepest emotions never fails to impress."
— Bonnie Shimko, award-winning author of *The Private Thoughts of Amelia E. Rye*

Good Graces

"*Good Graces* deftly dwells in '60s Milwaukee. Through her preteen narrator, Sally O'Malley, [Kagen] evokes the joys, sorrows, and complexities of growing up."
— *The Milwaukee Journal Sentinel*

"Kagen does a remarkable job of balancing the goofiness of being an eleven-year-old with the sinister plot elements, creating a suspenseful yarn that still retains an air of genuine innocence."
— *Publishers Weekly*

"For all the praise garnered for *Whistling in the Dark, Good Graces* more than lives up to its predecessor."
— *School Library Journal*

"A beautifully written story. . . . You will weep for and cheer on the O'Malley sisters . . . [and] immediately miss them once the last page is turned."
— Heather Gudenkauf, *New York Times* bestselling author of *Little Mercies*

"Moving, funny, and full of unexpected delights. . . . Kagen crafts a gorgeous page-turner about love, loss, and loyalty, all told in the sparkling voices of two extraordinary sisters."
— Caroline Leavitt, *New York Times* bestselling author of *Pictures of You*

Tomorrow River

Winner of the Wisconsin Library Association Outstanding Achievement Award

"[A] stellar third novel. . . . Kagen not only delivers a spellbinding story but also takes a deep look into the mores, values, and shams of a small Southern community in an era of change."
— *Publishers Weekly* (starred review)

"The first-person narration is chirpy, determined, and upbeat. . . . Shenny steals the show with her brave, funny, and often disturbing

patter as she tries to rescue herself and her sister from problems she won't acknowledge."
— *Mystery Scene Magazine*

"*Tomorrow River* . . . [and] the charming genuine voice of Shenny . . . is impossible to resist."
— *Milwaukee Magazine*

"An excellent, moving story, very well written, and one that will linger in your thoughts long after you've finished it."
— *Historical Novels Review*

"This book is packed with warmth, wit, intelligence, images savory enough to taste—and deep dark places that are all the more terrible for being surrounded by so much brightness."
— Tana French, *New York Times* bestselling author of *Broken Harbor*

Land of a Hundred Wonders

A Great Lakes Book Award Nominee

"Kagen's winsome second novel offers laughter and bittersweet sighs."
— *Publishers Weekly*

"A truly enjoyable read from cover to cover . . . . Miss Kagen's moving portrayal of a unique woman finding her way in a time of change will touch your heart."
— Garth Stein, *New York Times* bestselling author of *The Art of Racing in the Rain*

"I've been a Lesley Kagen fan ever since I read her beautifully rendered debut, *Whistling in the Dark*. Set against the backdrop of the small-town South of the 1970s, *Land of a Hundred Wonders* is by turns sensitive and rowdy, peopled with larger-than-life characters who are sure to make their own tender path into your heart."
— Joshilyn Jackson, *New York Times* bestselling author of *Someone Else's Love Story*

"Gibby hooks the audience from the onset and keeps our empathy throughout. . . . Her commentary along with a strong supporting cast make for a delightful historical regional investigative tale. [Gibby] is a "shoe-in" to gain reader admiration for her can-do lifestyle."
— *The Mystery Gazette*

"Lesley Kagen has crafted a story that is poignant, compelling, hilarious, real, and absolutely lovely."
— Kris Radish, author of *Gravel on the Side of the Road*

Whistling in the Dark

The Midwest Booksellers Choice Award Winner

"Kagen's debut novel sparkles with charm thanks to ten-year-old narrator Sally O'Malley, who draws readers into the story of her momentous summer in 1959. The author has an uncanny ability to visualize the world as seen by a precocious child in this unforgettable book."
— *Romantic Times Top Pick*

"Innocently wise and ultimately captivating."
— *The Milwaukee Journal Sentinel*

"I loved *Whistling in the Dark*. Living with the O'Malley sisters for the summer is an experience that no one will forget."
— *Flamingnet* TOP CHOICE Award

"One of the summer's hot reads."
— *The Chicago Tribune*

"The plot is a humdinger . . . a certifiable grade-A summer read."
— *The Capital Times*

"The loss of innocence can be as dramatic as the loss of a parent or the discovery that what's perceived to be the truth can actually be a big fat lie, as shown in Kagen's compassionate debut, a coming-of-age thriller set in Milwaukee during the summer of 1959."
— *Publishers Weekly*

The Resurrection of Tess Blessing

LESLEY KAGEN

Published by SparkPress, a BookSparks imprint,
A division of SparkPoint Studio, LLC
Tempe, Arizona, USA, 85281
www.sparkpointstudio.com

All company and/or product names may be trade names, logos,
trademarks, and/or registered trademarks and are the property
of their respective owners.

Printed in the United States of America.

ISBN: 978-1-940716-55-8 (paperback)
ISBN: 978-1-940716-56-5 (e-book)

Cover design © Julie Metz, Ltd./metzdesign.com
Cover photo © Arcangel Images at arcangel.com
Author photo by Megan McCormick/Shoot the Moon
Photography
Formatting by Polgarus Studio

This is a work of fiction. Names, characters, places, and
incidents either are the product of the author's imagination or
are used fictitiously. Any resemblance to actual persons, living
or dead, is entirely coincidental.

For my eternally loved son, Riley Orion

"Everything is determined, the beginning as well as the end, by forces over which we have no control . . . we all dance to a mysterious tune, intoned in the distance by an invisible piper."
— Albert Einstein

"It is the nature of grace always to fill spaces that have been empty."
— Johann Wolfgang von Goethe

"If there ever comes a day when we can't be together, keep me in your heart, I'll stay there forever."
— Winnie the Pooh, Alan Alexander Milne

While Others Leave Her Side,
I Never Will

My Tess is a sly one. Quite the little actress. When called upon to do so, she can appear to be a concerned citizen . . . a capable mother . . . the confident wife of the president of the Chamber of Commerce. Appearing ordinary is one of her best talents. As long as nothing unexpected blows up in her face, which, of course, life being the minefield that it is, is about to.

Morning winter sun is streaming through the four-paned kitchen windows that overlook the white picket-fenced backyard of the darling red-brick colonial in Ruby Falls, Wisconsin, population, 5,623. There are three of us gathered around the distressed pine kitchen table that's been passed down through the Blessing family for generations—forty-nine-year-old, Tess, her lovely eighteen-year-old daughter, Haddie, who has returned to the roost to spend the Christmas holiday, and me, who has always been and always will be, but remains unnamed, for the time being. The man of the house, Will, has already left for the day. He's busy seating the breakfast bunch at Count Your

Blessings, the popular Main Street '50s-style diner that he inherited from his father upon his passing. Tess's other child, Henry, a junior in high school, remains upstairs wrapped in his *Star Wars* sheets. Like most fifteen-year-olds, the boy believes the world revolves around him.

"Just a nibble?" Tess asks her daughter.

When the gifted photographer struggling through her first year at Savannah College of Art and Design turns her nose up at the French toast her desperate mother prepared with her secret ingredient—tears, Tess can barely keep herself from pounding the top of the pine table and asking yet again, "What did I do wrong? How can I make this better? Please ... please let me in." She swallows the questions back because she knows from experience that Haddie'll only change the subject, at best. Worse, she'll get angrier than she already is.

Tess sets her gaze out of one of the kitchen windows and locks on the solitary snow angel I watched her create last night while her family remained snug in their beds. Others may leave her side, but I never have, and never will. We are bound together not only in this life, but for all time.

Most of what you think you know about "imaginary friends" is probably inaccurate. We're a much more complicated lot than the way we're often portrayed in books, movies, psychological articles, and such. For instance, not once have I heard it mentioned what an important part readiness plays in our relationship. Nor have I seen it noted how we are imbued with whatever qualities our friends need the most, which depends upon at what point in their lives we are called into what is known on our side as, "Service." The profound spiritual component in our friendship has never been touched upon either. Even the term, "imaginary friend," is nothing more than a handy phrase a psychiatrist came up with to describe the indescribable and put the inexplicable in its place.

Since Tess has had quite a bit of prior experience with an IF—a nickname we like to call each other sometimes— I'm not anticipating that she'll put up much of a fuss when the time comes for us to connect again. (*At Last.*) While I can't know exactly when that momentous occasion will occur—that's entirely up to her—I can feel it drawing nearer. Hoped it might happen last night when I was perched on the faded green Adirondack chair under the weeping willow tree in the Blessings' backyard watching her swish her arms and legs back and forth in the snow. (Wearing just her ancient cows-sipping-*café-au-lait*-on-the-*Champs-Élysées* nightie on the chilliest night yet this winter proved that she needs someone to lean on sooner rather than later.)

Because I know every thought and feeling she's ever had, as Tess sets the French toast Haddie had rejected on the floor next to the family's beloved golden retriever, Garbo, I can hear her telling herself—I'm gonna do it again tonight. Not just once, I'll make a dozen angels.

And on January 17, 1999, after the dawn smudges peach and blue across tomorrow's horizon, she'll rise from her bed, slip on her worn-to-the-nub green chenille robe, and pad downstairs to get things going in the kitchen like her world hasn't cracked wide open and the contents spilled. And before Haddie takes off for an eight-mile run,

Tess'll wish her a perky good morning, offer her a cup of freshly squeezed orange juice, and not mention the life-shattering news she's about to receive. My friend will put on the smile she keeps close at hand, point out the kitchen window at her newly created flock, and say, "Look! Angels have come by to say halo!" with the hope that her daughter will be tickled by the corny joke she'd thought was hilarious when was she was ten 'cause Tess would do and say just about anything to recapture the closeness of those days.

Angel shmangels. How many times did I tell you not to have children, Theresa? Yours barely speak to you and look what they did to your figure and. . . .

If you're thinking that's me talking mean like that to Tess, well, you'd be wrong.

That there is the unrelenting voice of her mother that she hears in her head even though the gal's dead.

When Louise Mary Fitzgerald Finley Gallagher passed on last year, instead of leaving her eldest daughter a 1940s bureau with a couple of missing porcelain handles or linen hankies with swirling lavender initials, she left Tess her remains, a heart full of pain, and her head full of criticism.

I'm not sure where Louise is in her celestial education at the current time—upon the death of her body, her soul moved from the living room to the school room where she will be held accountable for her actions and be given the opportunity to learn from her mistakes—but while she was still on Earth that self-centered woman did indelible damage to my friend that I hope to heal when she allows me in. I have a couple of ideas on how to remove her thorny mother from her side, but have yet to come up with anything to stick in the hole to staunch the bleeding. (Not yet, anyway.)

Tess sets the washed fry pan on the yellow-and-blue kitchen counter, wipes her hands dry on the seat of the bulky gray sweatpants she wears to conceal the blubber she's put on in her efforts to show Haddie how much fun eating can be, checks the clock above the stove, and looks for the black purse that holds her good-luck totems—a hanging-by-a-thread copy of *To Kill a Mockingbird*, remnants of her children's baby blankets, and her daddy's Swiss Army knife that fell out of his pocket that fateful day on the boat. She doesn't go anywhere without that lucky purse.

"I've got an appointment this morning," she tells the girl whose photographs are so remarkable for one so young that *National Geographic* has shown interest in hiring her as an intern next summer. "Why don't you call me when you're done shooting at the Nature Center? Maybe we could—"

"What kind of appointment?"

"No big deal. Just my yearly mammogram."

"Does it hurt?"

Tess lays her cheek atop her daughter's head and breathes deeply. Her natural aroma has always been earthy. Like she'd grown the child not in her womb, but her garden. Haddie's hair is really something too. Not a deep red like her mother's, but a daisy yellow like Will's used to be, and the child was blessed with eyes that are a paler shade of blue than Tess's that are almost navy. "Nothin' to worry about, honey," she reassures. "Cancer doesn't run in the family. Mammograms are just part of the program when you get to be—"

"Uh-huh," her daughter says as she ducks away from her mom's lips.

My friend has been raked over these coals so often that she's grown used to and accepts the rejection, but that doesn't mean she doesn't try everything she can to change it. She's sure that if she could only figure out *why* Haddie is so angry with her, she would get better and they could go back to the way they used to be. Inseparable.

Tess wonders if it's because of the way she reacted when she was first informed that her daughter planned to attend college at the Savannah School of Art and Design. Was that it?

She can't deny that she was far from thrilled that Haddie meant to fly off and leave her in her contrail. When the acceptance letter was waved in her face, Tess freely admits she said, "Georgia?" like it was the one on the Black Sea. (She also failed to hide the excruciating ripping sensation she was feeling that was not dissimilar to the eighteen-hour back labor she'd endured during the child's birth.)

But . . . once she'd gotten over the shock, hadn't she tried her hardest to be supportive of Haddie's desire to test her wings the year before she left?

Unfortunately, due to the losses she had experienced as child, the profound sense of abandonment Tess was experiencing was almost impossible to contain. Even though she's normally highly skilled at keeping her true emotions secret—she's successfully hidden her severe emotional problems from her children and the rest of the world her whole life—it was pretty damn obvious that she didn't mean it when she threw kisses and hollered, "Go get 'em, baby!" on the mid-August afternoon that her husband and daughter pulled out of the driveway in the packed-to-the-roof green Taurus her parents had given their overachieving, artistic child after she'd graduated with the highest grade-point average ever recorded at Ruby Falls High.

So, of course, when the homesick freshman called begging to return home sixteen days after her arrival in Savannah—"Mommy, please . . . I made a mistake. I miss you . . . I'll eat whatever you want. Please, please come get me," Tess didn't think twice. She scribbled a late-night "Be Back Soon, xoxo" note to Will and Henry, and off she and Garbo drove to save Haddie from her freedom.

She made it as far as Zionsville, Indiana, when the doubts she'd been wrestling with forced her to pull into an abandoned truck stop. Under the fluorescent lights, she finally admitted to herself that as much as she wanted to bring her girl back home, if she did, she'd be acting as selfishly as her own mother had. She cried herself dry, and then called Haddie to tell her in a barely used firm voice that she was sorry, but, "You need to stick it out."

Is that why she's mad? Tess wonders. She thinks I wasn't there for her when she needed me most? She takes another stab at connecting with Haddie before she leaves for her appointment. "Maybe we could get a little lunch today?" In the good old days, shrimp egg rolls followed by chicken chow mein used to be her daughter's favorite. The number-four special would be out of the question, but maybe she could talk Haddie, who appeared to know the caloric content of every food ever created, into a lettuce wrap. "Wong Fat's?"

On her daughter's generous lips even disgust looks good.

What did you expect? Louise snipes in Tess's head. *You just invited a kid with an eating disorder to lunch at a place that has FAT in its name. Theresa ... Theresa ... Theresa ... could you be a worse mother?*

I wish my friend could shout back, *Yeah, I could be you!* but at the present time, she doesn't have the confidence to speak back to her mother, nor bury her either.

Tess tries again. "Do you want to ... ?" She almost asked Haddie if she'd like to go to the mall instead. That would've been another mistake. Her girl used to adore shopping, but she won't try on flouncy dresses or frilly blouses anymore. She'd grab armfuls of pretty things off the racks, but once they hung in the dressing room, she would collapse in tears after she stripped down to her panties and saw her "grossness" reflected back in the store mirror. "What about ... ?" Haddie adores illness movies. If she could find one about a young woman suffering with anorexia or bulimia she'd be in hog heaven and expect her mother to wallow in it with her. "We could watch a Lifetime movie tonight."

"Whatever."

Sensing that she's hit yet another conversational dead end, Tess clears the rest of the breakfast dishes and slogs down the basement steps to turn off the TV that Will and Henry left on last night. When she steps back into the kitchen with her arms full of their leftovers, Haddie shudders at the greasy popcorn bowl, empty pop bottles, and gooey candy wrappers.

"Thanks for rubbing it in," she growls as she stomps past her mother toward the staircase.

Tess calls after her, "I'm sorry . . . I'm stopping at the grocery store after my appointment. Do you need anything?" but she leaves the house uncertain if Haddie heard her before she slammed the bathroom door shut behind her.

A Passed Life

As Tess backs out of the driveway in the dinged-up '83 silver Volvo she refuses to sell because she brought her children home from the hospital in it, she's thinking about her family. It's not just Haddie that she's having such a hard time with. She's no longer the star of Henry's or Will's lives either. On good days, she figures she has a supporting role, on the not so good ones, she fades into the scenery. Her carefully considered words are nothing more than background noise. Mommy Muzak.

On her drive down Chestnut Street, she passes homes similar to hers, good-sized and over a hundred years old. Tess envies their rock solidness, their ability to withstand the onslaught of time. When was the last time she and Will strolled beneath the old-fashioned streetlights after the children turned in for the night? A month? Two? She'd made him laugh, and they'd shared stories of their day. When the time for words was over, Tess got a hooded look in her eyes and began to softly singing "their" song—*Hernando's Hideaway.*

"I know a dark secluded place. . . ."

Will knew that place too, and he took his wife of almost thirty years into his arms and they tangoed back to the ancient oak tree that he'd carved their initials into the same way his father had his mother's. He pressed Tess against the rough bark and cupped her breasts in his hands, laid his lips against hers with insistent tenderness until she felt him rise to the occasion.

They hadn't made it up to the bedroom.

After circling for a few minutes, Tess spots an open space in nearby St. Mary's North Hospital lot and pulls in. She bustles toward the pneumatic doors, but once inside, she stomps her feet for an inordinately long time on the long black mat to loosen the snow trapped in her boots. She's telling herself that she's just being courteous, but she's stalling. Her fear of hospitals, a.k.a. "gigantic petri dishes," is one of many.

"Good morning!" an elderly volunteer says to Tess as she dawdles into the hospital lobby.

The greeter is wearing a white blouse with a bow and gold button earrings. The shiny label on her chest says— *I'm Vivian*. Now, some folks might find her overly arched penciled eyebrows and caked pancake makeup pathetic, but Tess thinks Vivian looks valiant, and nothing like Betty Davis in *What Ever Happened to Baby Jane?* Though if her arm was twisted, she'd have to admit there *are* some similarities around the lips.

Since she has had prior mammograms at the sister hospital of one of the biggest and best in Milwaukee, she knows where she's going, but she steps up to the desk and asks, "The Women's Center?" because she doesn't want anybody to feel as unneeded as she does.

"Down there, dear," Vivian says as she points to a hall

on the left with a knobby-knuckled finger. "Have a nice day!"

Tess wants to wish her the same, but the cinnamon toast she'd gulped down for breakfast had begun to ball up in her throat when Vivian's hair spray hit her nose. It was Aqua Net.

Sense memories are the strongest, so even though Tess puts up her dukes, it's more out of habit than hope. If she successfully overpowers the feelings that are barging into her brain, it'd be the first time she's won the battle against the enemy that has attacked her thousands of times since the third of June, 1968, the day it first jumped out of the shadows of her mind to have its way with her.

Barely nineteen years old at the time and already a year out of the house and on her own, Tess had picked up a pack of Juicy Fruit from the corner drugstore and was returning back to her efficiency apartment on Milwaukee's Lower East Side when out of the blue, she broke into a shiny sweat. Her heart began beating like a war drum, and her breathing came in staggered, fast bursts. For no apparent reason—a madman wasn't charging at her with a knife, nor had a car jumped a curb and come careening her way—she was experiencing the kind of gut-wrenching fear she'd only feel if both the above were true.

When she tried to run from the invisible enemy, she found her legs were no longer able to do their job. She slid down Pizza Man's front window onto the hot sidewalk where she sat immobilized physically and mentally, unsure if, or when, whatever was happening to her would stop. Passersby took her for just another stoned hippie grooving on the day and gave her the peace sign. She should've found this highly amusing, but it appeared that whatever had her in its grip had also snatched away her strongest coping device, her sense of humor, and that riled her up even more.

When the panic eventually lessened its hold, Tess made it back to her tiny apartment above the bike shop terrified that whatever it was that had struck her down had followed her home. She spent the next two days rolled in a ball on the apartment floor convinced that she was losing her mind. As her mother and stepfather were not what one would call helpful, and she had no friends other than her equally emotionally unbalanced younger sister, Birdie, and the hairy strangers she smoked pot and listened to Jimi Hendrix with every so often in the alley behind the bike shop, she had nowhere to turn but inward, so she pulled herself together and did what she often did to find answers to life's perplexing questions.

Cautiously, she proceeded to the neighborhood library.

She bypassed the medical books because she'd only briefly considered that what she was experiencing was physical in origin. The shortness of breath, the weakness, the cramps, and the sweating had dissipated once the attack was over. She was convinced that her problems had to be in her head, the same way they were in Birdie's, so she made a beeline to the library's self-improvement section. Nowadays it's jammed with books about her condition, but it was slim pickings back then. All Tess could find in the stacks was a diet bestseller that mentioned how coffee put people on edge and sardines might give people nightmares, so she switched to a bland diet that consisted primarily of dry cereal and toast points.

But after changing her eating habits failed to keep three more attacks at bay, she decided that *where* she had experienced the fear must've been the trigger, and she composed one of the many lists she's made throughout her life to keep her on track:

BAD PLACES

1. The sidewalk in front of Pizza Man.
2. The Melting Spoon.
3. Baker's Drugs.
4. The laundromat.
5. The library.

SOLUTIONS

1. Walk on the other side of the street.
2. I never liked the bossy waitresses at the Melting Spoon all that much.
3. Stand out front of the drugstore and ask people with nice faces to buy Maalox for me.
4. Wash my clothes in the bathtub.
5. Read *To Kill a Mockingbird* for the fifty-first, fifty-second, fifty-third time, etc.

Tess followed her instructions and was making do, until an insidious wave of terror swept her out of her balcony seat at the Oriental Theatre during a showing of *Easy Rider*. She stumbled down the darkened aisle with the realization that on top of everything else she'd given up to protect herself, she'd no longer be able to go to the beloved movies that had been one of her only means of escape since her sister's and her Saturday matinee days. Almost penniless, alone, and suffering from an agonizing mental illness, she almost threw in the towel that night. If that sweet old lady hadn't pulled alongside her on her frantic dash down the East Side streets and told her, "It's awfully late for a girl to be out on her own. Can I give you a lift home, dear?" Tess might've jumped off the North Avenue Bridge.

(A friend in need is a friend indeed.)

Since Tess spent most of her time and energy coping with her out-of-control fear, holding down a job had become almost impossible. She'd had to quit answering the phones at Evelyn Wood Reading Dynamics when she developed claustrophobia and could no longer stand being cooped up in a bus or an office. Waitressing at Vince's Grill didn't work out either. She was overwhelmed by happy chatter. Thank goodness for the HELP WANTED sign she spotted in the window of an Arthur Murray Dance Studio. (I might've had something to do with a position opening up.) She applied and got the job.

A lover of musicals since childhood—the ones starring Shirley Temple and Ginger Rogers were her favorites—she picked up the dances quickly, especially loved the tango, and really took to the place. After a few months of working all the hours she could and saving most of her paycheck, she enrolled in two classes at nearby University of Wisconsin-Milwaukee. Along with a singing class—Tess had long ago set aside her desire to win the talent portion of Miss America, but dreamed of performing off

Broadway—she also signed up for Psychology 101—Tess desperately wanted to be sane, and would be thrilled to not end up in an institution.

Her quest for higher learning started out with a bang, but during the course of the semester, she was forced to come to terms with a few heartbreaking realities. Her desire to sing didn't match her God-given abilities, so appearing in musical comedies two blocks over from The Great White Way was out. And by the fifth psych class, she had to admit to herself that she had more in common with the "abnormal" cases the professor shared with the class then she'd ever imagined.

Since there wasn't much she could do about her propensity to sing flat, she vowed to put what little energy she had into solving her emotional problems. She called for an appointment at the university's counseling center. That took enormous courage on her part, because the first time she'd paid a visit to a professional years ago didn't work out so hot.

After the accident that claimed her father's life, young Tess was unable to eat sloppy joes, her daddy's favorite. She acted up at school. Got mouthy with Father Ted during catechism class. Told him that *if* it was true that God was all-powerful, he was also a flaming asshole. "Or maybe that's the Holy Spirit," she cracked to her fifth-grade class.

Even her mother, who had her delusions-of-grandeur nose stuck up so far in the air that she was barely aware of any life growing below her waist, noticed that something was off with her firstborn. She told Tess, like she was doing her a big favor, "I scheduled a series of meetings with Father Ted to save your soul, and I met a psychologist tonight at Lonnigan's—that's someone who deals with head cases. We've got an appointment with him tomorrow."

On the drive to the doctor's office, the widow Finley reminded once again, "Remember to call me Louise, and not *Mom* or *Mother* or *Mommy*. Like I keep tellin' you and your sister, unless we want to end up in the poor house, I need another husband. No man wants to take on another man's children. I gotta catch one, reel him in, *then* break the bad news about the two of you." She instructed Tess to take the wheel of the old woody station wagon with the broken muffler, undid another button on the beige blouse she'd bought for the occasion, and checked her Aqua Net-sprayed hair in the rearview mirror. "So don't act stupid or shocked when you meet the doctor. He's not from around here. He's an Indian."

Tess had always admired Indians, and not knowing there was any other kind other than Tonto, she was sorely let down when Dr. Mukhar Rajagee—not a psychologist the way her mother thought he'd mentioned over drinks in the noisy bar, but a podiatrist—greeted them in his waiting room wearing Hush Puppies without beads, and smelling not like maize, but some other food that made her eyes water.

After the doctor inspected Tess's little feet and gave her a pair of ill-fitting insoles, he said something about "karma" and "a past life," but she thought he'd said something different because he had a foreign way of talking. She spent a lot of time that summer wondering exactly how many "caramels" she'd need to consume to get back her "passed life," which, while not perfect, was a whole lot better than the one she had now.

And here she was almost nine years later to the day, showing up almost an hour early for the appointment with Dr. Glenn Ganges, a balding, fisherman-knit-sweater-wearing psychologist at the university's counseling center. A man so extraordinarily ordinary-looking that she thought she'd have a hard time picking him out of a lineup unless he was smoking his pipe, which was one of those meerschaums.

Dr. Ganges asked about her childhood and proved to be a good listener, but she needed more than a shoulder to cry on. She needed him to diagnose and treat the unbearable feelings that she was experiencing ASAP!

"Am I crazy?" she asked him at the onset of the third session.

The shrink, who Tess had begun to envision as a sea captain, leaned back in his swivel chair with a confident, snaggle-toothed smile. "No, no, of course not," he replied in his preternaturally calm voice. "You just need to relax."

"I'm sorry." She was sure she'd heard him wrong. "Did you say I just need to *relax*?"

When he nodded, her laugh had all the conviction of a sit-com soundtrack. "Could you please be a little more specific? I mean . . . what's wrong with me? Does it have a name?"

Ganges preferred not diagnosing this early in the process, but his client's desperation *was* compelling. He drew deeply on his carved white pipe and released a cloud of swarthy-smelling smoke—unbeknownst to Tess, he saw himself as a sea captain too. One who hunted down mental illness. With a vengeance—and asked her, "Are you familiar with the term *shell-shocked*?"

She bowed her head like she was considering his question, but what she was really doing was checking for his degree out of the tops of her eyes. She wanted to make sure he'd graduated from a school of *psychology* and not *podiatry*. (Momentarily reassured when she discovered his diploma, that soon changed when she realized it was hanging next to a painting of a red sailboat getting tossed about by storm waves without a safe harbor in sight.)

Tess asked, "Don't only ex-soldiers get shell-shocked?" She'd seen plenty of John Wayne and Audie Murphy war movies during her growing-up years. And there was the caretaker at the cemetery, her friend, Mr. McGinty, who had a difficult time being around the living after he came back from bayoneting Nazis. "Like the crew-cut guys around campus who scream '*incoming*' and dive to the ground when they hear a car backfire?" She didn't admit that she jumped out of her skin around sudden loud noises as well, but Dr. Glenn somehow picked up on that. She could see it in his wise sea-faring eyes.

"The symptoms aren't always combat-related," he explained. "Any life-shattering event, such as physical or emotional abuse, or death of a significant loved one can trigger . . . ," he sounded like he was reading out of the most recent edition of the *Diagnostic and Statistical Manual of Mental Disorders,* "depression, panic attacks, paranoia, hypervigilance, phobias, and flashbacks."

Being more than familiar with the list that he'd rattled off, Tess wasn't alarmed, she was filled with a beautiful, horrible relief. If he knew what she had . . . what was that famous saying? "Half the battle of fixing a problem is identifying it?"

"So . . . you can . . . um . . . cure this, right?" she asked.

Ganges didn't say he could, or he couldn't; he passed her a box of Kleenex, settled back into his swivel chair, and said, "Why don't you tell me more about your relationship with your father and sister today?"

Not wanting to appear uncooperative, she dabbed at her tears, curled her legs up beneath her, and proceeded to tell the note-taking doctor how on a lovely August afternoon a few weeks short of her tenth birthday, her father, Edward "Eddie" Finley, borrowed a motorboat from a pal at Lonnigan's where he worked tending bar. Tess's younger-by-a-year sister, Robin Jean, who'd been nicknamed Birdie due to her low birth weight, large eyes, and tiny-boned frame, had made it clear early on that she didn't care for fishing, so she wasn't out on Lake Michigan with them that day. (Non-swimmer Tess was terrified of deep water, so she shouldn't have been bobbing around in that boat that afternoon either, but she adored her daddy and would do anything to spend time with him.)

Father and daughter whiled away the hours in the record-setting summer heat talking, fishing, and laughing that fateful afternoon. When "Good-time Eddie," who was known far and wide for his funny bone, stood to reach for a worm out of the tin can to thread Tess's hook, he comically pretended to lose his balance, but then due to the heat of the day and the consumption of more than a few bottles of Pabst Blue Ribbon, he grew dizzy and lost his balance. On his way down, he conked his head against the outboard motor and tumbled over the side of the boat named *The High Life*.

Her daddy loved practical jokes of all kinds, but he absolutely adored the ones that scared you before they made you laugh. Like, when he jumped out of the girls' bedroom closet, or when he put a hunk of raw meat under their bed on Halloween. That's why after he fell into the lake, Tess swallowed back the water from his splash and wasn't worried at all. Her daddy was an excellent swimmer who took his jokes very, very seriously, so she was ready for him to stay underwater longer than Houdini before he popped back up. She was doubled over in laughter while she waited for him to resurface with a sputtering, "*Gotcha!*"

Her mother, Louise, called the police when they didn't show up by suppertime. The sun had already set by the time the lake patrol showed up to comb the waters for the missing girl and her father. They found and rescued Tess, and began their search for Eddie early the following morning, but a few days later, they gave up any hope of resurrecting him.

With a pencil poised over his pad, Dr. Ganges interrupted Tess's story to ask, "You do realize that you couldn't have saved your father, correct?"

She remained flat faced.

"Was there a memorial service for him?"

She nodded.

"Did you and your sister attend?"

"No."

The psychologist scribbled like mad on his yellow pad. "Were you later given the opportunity to tell him goodbye?"

Tess gave him an eerie smile. "Every day."

Thanks to the Veterans Administration, which had supplied a cheap coffin and a simple stone free of charge, her daddy was buried in the backyard of the Finley sisters' Keefe Avenue house. Mind you, her father's *actual* bones were not interred; they're still lying undiscovered at the bottom of Lake Michigan not far from a freighter that sank in 1822. And I don't mean the Finley sisters' *actual* backyard, but the grounds of Holy Cross Cemetery that butted up against their property.

Louise's adamant refusal to allow Tess and Birdie to commemorate their daddy's passing was somewhat a sign of the times, but also a harbinger of the punitive anger she felt toward her husband for leaving her with two small girls to raise and less than a hundred dollars in the bank.

Not attending the pretend funeral Mass and the burial wasn't quite as vital to Tess for she had borne witness to her father slipping into his watery grave. She knew her daddy was gone forever, but Birdie? Not being in the boat that afternoon nor having the opportunity to play a part in the normal end of life rigmarole—hearing folks praise Eddie Blessing from the altar lectern, grieving for him into their hankies, and meeting up at the cemetery to throw pink carnations on the coffin that held only memories— left the already delicate girl at odds, to say the least.

Their mother's family, the Fitzgeralds, had never played a part in the sisters' lives. Louise had an older brother named Virgil who'd run off when he was sixteen to join the Navy and was never heard from again. Her father died in the second World War, and her mother, a bitter woman whose name was Faye, passed a few years ago of complications from a bladder infection, so during the weeks following their father's demise, the sisters had only their beloved Gammy and Boppa. Tess and Birdie wanted more than anything to spend time with their grandparents in their stone house in the country, but due to a combination of their mother's contentious relationship with her husband's family, and the grief that had taken a toll on the elderly couple, their comfort was not forthcoming, not for a while anyway. Eddie, their youngest, was the second child they'd lost. They had another son who lived in the area, but "The Professor," was quite a bit older, and didn't appear to want much to do with his family.

So the Finley girls—or the "Finley Ghouls," as they were known in the neighborhood on account of their unusual hobby, which essentially was death—were left to their own devices. After they cleaned the house as directed by their mother, they'd sit on the back porch of the Keefe Avenue house that was just yards away from the black iron fence that ringed the cemetery. They'd while away the hours of the hot August days playing Cat's Cradle or Candy Land on the wooden steps, but never Go Fish! because that was just too sad.

Tessie would always work their conversations back to their father's death. She had to, for something alarming had developed. Birdie was refusing to believe that their daddy was gone forever, which was so weird on top of all her other problems. She would drift off in the middle of chats, had a hard time grasping reading or time-telling, and barely understood what was happening in the movies at the Tosa Theatre. Tess grew so worried about her that she'd had to come up with another of her never-ending lists to help her deal with the situation:

TO-DO LIST

1. ~~Talk Mom into letting Birdie and me go to Daddy's pretend funeral.~~
2. Convince Birdie that Daddy is really dead so Mom doesn't send her to the county insane asylum.
3. If #1 and #2 don't work out, find Daddy's pretend grave in the cemetery when Mom isn't around so Birdie can say goodbye to him once and for all because seeing really is believing.
4. Decide if I should confess to the cops about murdering Daddy.

Feeling like a broken forty-five, Tess told her sister once again on one of those Candy Land-playing, back-porch afternoons, "Daddy's dead."

"No, he's not."

"Yeah, he really is."

"Is not."

"Okay," Tess said, "if you don't believe that Daddy is at the bottom of the lake then where is he?"

"Boca Raton."

Tess stopped on her hop over to the Candy Cane Forest. "Boca . . . what?"

"Boca *Raton*," Birdie said like her sister was deaf and dumb. "It's a city."

"Oh, yeah? Where is Boca Raton a city?"

"Florida."

Tess, who always got A's in geography said, "Where'd you hear that? School?"

Birdie said, "Nope," and gave her a wisenheimer smile because she rarely knew something that Tess didn't. "I heard about it at the drug store. There's a picture postcard taped on the side of the cash register and the man on the front of it is Daddy! He's holdin' up a huge silver fish with a pointy nose and wearing a blue shirt. Mr. Dalinsky told me it says, "Greetings from Boca Raton! Wish you were here!""

Tess thought, *Oh, boy.*

Birdie drew another card because she didn't like the one she'd gotten. "They looked really hard for three days and they didn't find Daddy in the lake," she said very full of herself.

"Yeah, but just because they didn't find him," Tess said, "that doesn't mean that he isn't down there."

"Doesn't mean that he is, either."

"But that doesn't make sense, Bird. If Daddy *is* still alive, after he fell outta the boat, why didn't he just get back in? And why didn't he just come home?"

"He wanted to," Birdie said wistfully. "But he couldn't because he got am . . . am . . . am—"

"His arms got amputated?"

Birdie flapped hers up and down. She did that sometimes when she got frustrated. "He didn't get back in the boat because he got am . . . am . . . amnesia."

Tess thought, *Double, oh, boy.*

Even though the pine box that had been sunk in the cemetery was empty, Tess felt sure if Birdie could only *see* the grave and her daddy's tombstone it would help her accept his death. It might even stop her from yelling out in her sleep and wetting the bed, which is why Tess swore to herself then and there that she'd start looking for her father's pretend grave in the cemetery the following day.

She stopped, blew her nose, and told Dr. Ganges, "What's the point of going all over this again?" Sharing the stories that ran through her mind on a continual loop didn't feel healing, it was like picking at a scab. "Couldn't you just give me a drug to make me better? Something to erase the memories, or help me," she made air quotes, "relax?"

"I could refer you to a prescribing physician, but drugs will only mask your symptoms," he said, because he couldn't very well tell a woman in her state that there was no real known cure for what she had other than exposing it to the light of day and learning how to manage it. "The best way to get to the bottom of your problems is by talking about them. We'll need to dive deep."

She could feel his genuine concern and appreciated it, but his diving deep suggestion reminded her of the old television program *Sea Hunt*—a very touchy subject indeed—and she never returned to Dr. Ganges's office.

So, other than comparing notes with her younger and even-more-mixed-up sister, Tess rose every morning hoping for divine intervention even though she didn't believe in that sort of thing by that time. Imagine her surprise when not one, but two miracles were eventually sent her way. William Blessing. And Dr. Charles Drake.

Shortly after she met and fell madly in love with Will when he showed up for lessons at the Arthur Murray

Dance Studio, he told her she was hilarious, but everybody had always told her that. "You're a funny kid, Tessie," her father used to say.

"And all those voices and impressions you can do . . . you should be a comedian!" Will had said. "Like one of those girls on *Saturday Night Live*. Like Glenda!"

"Gilda," she corrected.

"Right!"

The idea of being funny for money clicked with Tess, and after researching the subject, she found that one of the best formal training grounds in the country was The Second City in nearby Chicago. The two-hour, twice-weekly round-trip to the improvisation and stand-up classes was horribly challenging given her fear of travel, but she thrived on the laughter and the thought of how proud her father would be. Socially awkward, she also felt more at ease around the other comedians, who tended toward instability as well. One of the other stand-ups did a bit about her Woody Allen look-alike shrink. She called him, "A real *mensch*." Tess didn't know what a *mensch* was, but she liked the sound of it, so she got his name and made an appointment hoping that he might do her more good than the university psychologist had.

Turned out Dr. Charles Drake was indeed a good man who could be counted on. An added bonus was the fact that his office was on the ground floor of a building located on Chicago's *Miracle Mile*. (I arranged that.) Besides coming up with a more modern name for what was troubling Tess—post-traumatic stress disorder—Dr. Drake proved to be much more useful than Dr. Ganges in others ways as well. He didn't look like he wanted to harpoon her for one thing.

The mild-mannered, middle-aged psychiatrist explained to Tess during one of their many sessions, "If too many traumas happen too close together, the mind can't process them. Feeling under siege, it shifts into high gear to protect a person against further damaging experiences. It appears that your father's death, your mother's indifference, and your tumultuous childhood has become more than you can integrate."

Dr. Drake also assured her early on that she would not spend the rest of her life in a padded room eating ice cream with her fingers. And that the probability of the scenario she feared the most more than likely would never happen. "Yes, that *could* happen," the good doctor stated, but the chance was slim that a tubercular-looking man would hitch up his oily jeans, gob on the floor of a nearby Mobil station's bathroom, rub his overly moisturized hands together whilst muttering to himself, "There she is, that redhead, Tess Blessing. I'll wait until she goes in to the mini-mart to buy a Three Musketeers bar, then I'll grab the Coke can out of her car and slip in some of this curare I carry with me at all times. She'll never know what hit her."

Over the years that she saw him, Dr. Drake didn't only help Tess examine her struggles through brilliant analysis, he taught her what an important role her sense of humor played in transcending her pain, different relaxation techniques, how to recognize when she was in danger of being overtaken by PTSD rage, and they'd worked together to reduce her phobias from fourteen to eleven. They parted ways only when the both of them agreed that her panics, flashbacks, depressions, and other symptoms had quieted down to dull roars.

So other than managing her emotions, and the day-in-and-day-out problems, her life proceeded mostly without incident. Tess married, bore her children, tended a beautiful home and garden in a darling town, enjoyed waitressing at the family diner, and was generally in good physical health. But . . . isn't this how it always goes? Right about the time you dare to get comfortable enough to lower your guard, something unexpected jumps out at you and screams, "*Gotcha!*"

Got Something in My Pocket

After checking in at the front desk of St. Mary's North Hospital, Tess makes herself uncomfortable in the waiting room. She picks at the stack of magazines on the side table with the tips of her fingers, left hand casually placed over her mouth, breathing shallowly in order to avoid inhaling any germs until she accidentally brushes against the *National Geographic*. If Haddie accepts the internship the magazine has offered after she graduates, she'll pack up her cameras and travel to exotic locales to photograph ferocious beasts. Maybe even headhunters, or cannibals with arrows dripping with curare.

God only knows what kind of foreign diseases they'd be carrying, Louise whispers to Tess as she scrounges in her lucky purse for her antibacterial wipes.

"Theresa Blessing?" a woman who looks similar to greeter Vivian calls out, or maybe it *is* Vivian, when humans get to be a certain age they can be as hard to tell apart as newborns. "Good morning. I'm Ginger Baestock, director of the Women's Center."

Tess says something cute about Fred Astaire, and then the two of them chat about the storm in tonight's forecast and how fun that'll be for the kids who received sleds for

Christmas as they walk down the institutional hallways lined with pastoral prints to give them a little pizzazz. When they reach a door marked Mammography, Ginger ushers her in, nods toward a stack of green paper gowns on the metal counter, and tells her that it was nice to meet her and that someone will be in shortly.

Tess changes into a gown and passes the time paging through a seven-month-old *Glamour* magazine. Just like her younger sister had, her 110-pound daughter wants to emulate those starving-for-dollars models. My friend hadn't made Haddie self-conscious about her weight the way Louise had Birdie's when she called her, "Tubby-tubby-two-by-four" and "Two-ton Robin," so it was a shock when she first learned of her daughter's disorder on their way home from an art show in Madison two summers ago. One of Haddie's shots of Garbo sailing through the air with her Frisbee in her mouth had won best in state.

Ice cream had always been a go-to treat, so Tess suggested they stop at Dairy Queen. She ordered a Coke, but instead of asking for her usual hot fudge sundae, Haddie backed away, pushed through the scruffy end-of-the-day kids and the end-of-their-rope parents, and fled out the door.

Tess shrugged, and said to the counter woman, "Teenagers," and ordered the sundae anyway.

When she returned to the car, it was to find her then-seventeen-year-old daughter huddled up in the passenger seat, her hands cradling her face, and her blue ribbon splotched with tears. This was not an immediate cause for alarm. Haddie wept everyday about one thing or another.

She was having trouble with her skin, her hair was falling out, and . . . she was so fat!

It had been a long day that had gotten under Tess's skin in more ways than one. She grew more anxious in crowds like the one at the art show. It'd been exhausting to not only deal with her panic, but hide it from her daughter. Keeping her problems on the down-low was Tess's most important parenting policy. She couldn't let her children know that she was nuts. Wouldn't let Haddie and Henry down the way she and Birdie had been let down by their mother. And on top of all the usual stuff she dealt with on a daily basis, another problem had been thrown into the mix. She and Will had been fighting about the loan he'd taken out to build the party room at the diner. They'd had another knock-down, drag-out fight that morning.

Tess was in no mood for any adolescent guff.

"Eat. You'll feel better," she said as she wiggled the hot fudge sundae under Haddie's nose.

She pushed the cup away and gagged out, "I can't, Mommy."

Tess thought it a strange choice of words. "What do you mean you *can't?*"

When her daughter lifted her face . . . there it was. The same haunted look that had come over her Birdie when she'd begun to struggle with her eating.

"Good morning!"

Tess's sad ruminations are interrupted when a lovely young woman with luxurious dark hair secured atop her head with enamel red chopsticks bustles into the mammography room. Tess is glad she's of the Asian persuasion. She feels more comfortable with people of color, the darker the better. (She thinks it's because the non-white set their expectations a lot lower, which gives them something in common right off the bat, but in actuality, it's a little more complicated than that.) "I'm Rhonda Lee. You know the drill. Let's do the left one first." She smoothes down Tess's breast like she's petting a finicky cat, then twists the knobs that'll lower the Plexiglas. "Deep breath and hold," she says before she runs and hides behind a wall that she comes out from behind a few seconds later. "Other side."

Tess is doing what's asked, but in a robotic way. She's not aware of it, but she's dissociated, which is a defense mechanism she uses sometimes when the going gets tough. (It's something like unenrolling from an organization whose practices you don't approve of. Thing is . . . you're the organization.) Her mind is not engaged in the screening, it's running off one of her many To-Do Lists in her head. After she's finished up here, she needs to head to the grocery store to pick up broccoli for Haddie, who will eat it steamed and torn into pieces that make Tess think of guillotined leprechauns. The usual pepperoni pizza for Henry, and Garbo was low on Milk-Bones. Nothing special for Will. He'll grab something at the diner; he's been doing that on Wednesday nights. Coming home late too. "Busy," he tells her. "With what?" she asks. "The books," he tells her.

After putting up with her for almost thirty years, had Will finally grown sick and tired of her and all her problems? Because he rubs his finger under his nose when he lies, Tess knows he's not doing the books on

Wednesday nights. She's fairly certain that he's doing Connie Lushman, the hostess at Count Your Blessings, who also happens to be his former fiancée that he dumped almost thirty years ago soon after he met Tess.

The mammography technician checks her Hello Kitty watch and says, "Got what I need. Back in a few minutes. Wait to get dressed," and rushes off.

Tess rummages around in her purse for a pen. She's made To-Do Lists her whole life, but she's stepped them up lately because her everyday memory has grown worse. "The Change" has hit. She found her car keys in the refrigerator yesterday, which was fine, because she wasn't sure where she'd parked her car.

Unable to find a piece of paper, my friend rips a piece off the bottom of the paper gown, which causes her breasts to peek through the crack. She thinks back to when they'd first begun to bud, and how she would sneak into the bathroom, lift up her nightie, and get to work. Fiercely pressing her palms together—an exercise she'd watch buxom Debbie Drake perform on her TV show—she'd chant, "I must, I must, I must increase my bust. I must . . . I must . . . I must." She runs her finger across the pale stretch marks that beam out from her nipples like a kindergartener's version of the sun. Like the ones her children drew when they still thought their mom hung the moon and the stars.

Rhonda Lee must've made a stop in the ladies' room, because when she returns, Tess can smell mouthwash—Listerine—and newly applied deodorant—Secret. Spring Breeze. (Like most people with PTSD, my friend has a nose like a hound, German shepherd hearing too, both of which enable her to sniff out danger either real or imagined.) She waits to be assured that everything looks great, but instead, Rhonda Lee, who's already late meeting Laurie from physical therapy to dish on the new resident in radiology over coffee, says grumpily, "We have to take a few more pictures of the right one."

"But—"

"Maybe you moved or didn't hold your breath long enough."

The need for a redo would be a red flag to most women, but Tess puts it down to either a tech error or glitch in the machine. Like she told Haddie this morning, "Nothin' to worry about, honey. Cancer doesn't run in the family."

She's back working on her new To-Do List when not Rhonda Lee, but the head of the Women's Center glides back into the room a few minutes later.

"Please dress and come into my office," Ginger Baestock says in a voice that is not as carefree sounding as it was on their walk to the exam room. She's making Tess feel like she's a dozen eggs being inspected for cracks. "It's two doors down on the left."

This *is* concerning. This has never happened before and Tess isn't equipped to deal with things that have never happened before. As she wrestles on her bra, it finally crosses her mind that they might've found something in her right breast that's not supposed to be there, but only fleetingly. Even in her bleakest, most-depressed times, she has not once imagined having breast cancer. Too far-fetched. More out of line even than that curare foolishness she has not entirely shaken off. So she decides that Ginger must want to talk to her about something else. The bill? Will has been so preoccupied. Had he forgotten to pay the health insurance premium?

She's embarrassed by her husband's potential oversight when she sets herself in the proffered tweed chair on the other side of Ginger's shiny gray desk. A translucent breast paperweight—a snow globe without the fun—sits atop a stack of charts next to pictures of two children in golden frames. "What's up?" she asks.

"Dear?" Ginger extends her age-spotted hands toward her. "I'm afraid there's no easy way to tell you this."

Tess agrees, these types of moments are always uncomfortable. She doesn't want to hold hands with Ginger. She says, "I know. I'm sorry. My husband has been so busy. I'll make sure he gets that insurance payment out today."

"I don't think. . . ." Ginger regroups. "We've found something in your right breast."

Certain that a mistake has been made—you read about that happening all the time in hospitals—Tess gives old Ginger, who must've mixed up the results of her mammogram with another patient's on account of her failing eyesight, a deadpan look and says, "Huh." (Wait for it.) "It's probably just a piece of Juicy Fruit. I heard that stuff never really gets digested."

"How about we take an ultrasound to make sure?" the head of the Women's Center says with a pained smile as she reaches behind her and slips a rust-colored cardigan across her narrow shoulders.

Unnecessary testing—you read about *that* happening in hospitals all the time too. Tess grasps her lucky purse to her chest. "I'm sorry, I can't right now." She doesn't want to embarrass Ginger by pointing out her mistake. "I need to go grocery shopping and . . . how about I call for an appointment?"

"As long as you're here . . . ," Ginger says as she puts a firm arm around her shoulder.

A young man with a wind-swept look that had Tess wondering if he'd sailed to work this morning is waiting for them in a room down the hall. "Hi," he says. "I'm Carl." He's wearing a lab coat and oddly, the same old-fashioned cologne her husband likes—English Leather. Shouldn't he be wearing Old spice? she asks herself.

After Carl helps her onto the table and dims the lights, he smoothes a cool gel over her right breast, and proceeds to rub a wand up and down and all around. He's not looking directly at her, but at an image that's come up on his computer. It reminds Tess of an Apollo lunar landing.

"Look," she says as she points at a glob on his screen. "Feel free to correct me, you're the expert, but I'm pretty sure that's Neil Armstrong."

Carl is kind enough to grin, but his eyes remain riveted to the screen until he switches off the machine and hands her a few tissues to remove the gel. "Good luck," he says.

She thanks him, and is shrugging down her gray T-shirt when Ginger pokes her head through the door a few minutes later. Per her suggestion, Tess follows her back to the office where she's positive Ginger is about to offer her a butterscotch out of the pretty crystal dish she has on her desk before she tells her with an apologetic smile, *Sorry to have wasted your time. It was a false alarm. But I'm so glad we went ahead and did the ultrasound anyway, aren't you? Better safe than sorry.*

But the head of the Women's Center doesn't offer Tess a piece of candy when she sits down across from her. She says, "I'm sorry, but I'm afraid the mass looks very suspicious." Ginger opens a drawer and removes a thick packet that she slides across the desk. "I know this is a lot to take in. This literature will be helpful. Is there someone I could call for you?"

Tess brings her thumbnail to her mouth.

Only riffraff bite their nails, Louise barks in her head.

Tess lowers her hand and says, "No offense meant, but is there a doctor I can talk to?"

Ginger, who had grown concerned over Tess's blasé reaction to the diagnosis, appears relieved by the question. (She has no idea of how terrified she is, that's how great my friend is at hiding her feelings.) "Certainly," she says as she quickly steps out of the office to search for a physician.

Tess forces herself to look down at the top pamphlet in the packet Ginger had given her. A woman with a pageboy is gazing up gratefully at a Marcus Welby look-alike. It's unclear which one of them is wondering:

Breast Cancer . . . Now What?

Told you there were a coupla stupid questions, her mother pipes in.

"Dr. Blankenship," Ginger announces when she returns moments later with a svelte man who's raked his hair like a Zen garden. "Our radiologist."

Tess is sure the doctor must've said hello and something else nice, but all she heard was, "We can't be positive it's cancer without a biopsy, and we don't have the necessary equipment here. They'll have to perform it at St. Mary's City Hospital."

When Ginger passes Tess a card with the information she'll need to set up the biopsy appointment, her fight-or-flight response kicks in. Her heart begins beating against her ribs, her breath comes in gasps, her stomach cramps, and courtesy of the extra adrenaline coursing through her bloodstream, she possesses enough strength to beat the hell out of Ginger and the radiologist with one hand tied behind her back. Or . . . she could run for her life.

She wisely chooses option two. "Thank you . . . nice to meet you both, but I gotta. . . ," she tells them as she flees out the office door, down the hallway, and out the hospital doors to the safety of the old Volvo, her home away from home.

"Cancer?" comes out on frosty breath. "But. . . ."

She knows more about malaria than she does breast cancer. She's gonna die? What about the children? Unable to process the tsunami of thoughts and feelings, she reminds herself to breathe. She's in a full-blown, thought-ceasing panic, but on some level she knows she needs to restore equilibrium before she goes off the deep end. Crying would help, but she doesn't do much of that. No, when the chips are down, Tess Blessing sings.

"I've got something in my pocket that belongs across my face. I keep it very close at hand in a most convenient place," she wails in her flat voice on the way out of the hospital lot. "I bet you'll never guess it if you guess a long, long while. So I'll take it out and put it on, it's a great big Brownie smile."

Hard to Swallow

"Fear of the marketplace" is the technical definition of agoraphobia, which is a pretty good handle considering that a grocery store is one of the overstimulating places people like Tessie find extremely difficult to cope with. There are stacks upon stacks of multicolored packages and smells that don't go together like German potato salad and Lysol, shoppers shoving around squeaky-wheeled carts, music without soul, and so many decisions to make.

Sure, the news has hit my friend hard, the way it would any woman, but she is not like other women, is she. She can't go running home to her husband's loving arms due to their current lack of closeness. She'll not tell the children either. Nor can she find comfort in her religious beliefs since she doesn't believe in God anymore. And since she has avoided people most of her life because she was too frightened that they'd discover how "abnormal" she is, she has no close friends other than her sister, who she currently does not have a relationship with.

After Tess arrives in the parking lot of Olsen's Market, she reminds herself not to get ahead of herself. If she gives in to the overwhelming fear she's feeling, her already traumatized mind will automatically categorize the Market as a danger spot and she'll never be able to shop here again.

"Don't flash back. Don't panic," she's chanting. "Get out of the car." She thinks she can manage that, but only if the woman in the tan minivan parked next to her stops throwing off one of *those looks*—nose elevated and nostrils flared as if she's gotten a whiff of something beneath her. Her hair is done up like Tess's mother's too, in one of those neat French twists. Is she hearing Muddy Water's *I Just Want to Make Love to You* and wondering why as well?

It's your cell phone, you nitwit, her mother grouses.

Tess rifles through her lucky purse and flicks a half-digested lemon drop off her cell phone. It's Haddie. She takes a deep breath, puts her Brownie smile back on, and says, "Hi, honey."

"Where are you?"

"Olsen's. Do you need anything?"

"Broccoli. And frozen yogurt. Make sure it's the absolutely no-fat kind." She doesn't give her mother a chance to respond before she adds on, "You there? Can you hear me?"

Tess could ask the same of the girl who starved herself until she vibrated with hunger, or foraged through the pantry and stuffed herself sick. After everyone else turned in for the night, Tess would lie in the dark and listen for the creak of the bathroom door down the hall and the dull clunk the toilet seat made when it hit the tank knowing that Haddie was about to dig up the food she'd stashed in her stomach like it was loot from a robbery.

Tess went to Will for advice, but he rarely has much to

add to a conversation. When had that changed? Or had it? Because there was a constant stream of chatter going on in her head, she'd found his tight-lipped stoicism both sexy and calming when they'd met, but what starts out as a virtue in a marriage can often take a turn for the worse, can't it. His contributions to the discussions of their daughter's disorder were to offer either a sad look, a scratch of his head, or a suggestion that Tess handle it.

Lord knows, she tried. Resorted to everything a mother with a daughter in imminent danger would. Reason, bribery, begging, threats, magazine articles, talk shows, throwing out the bathroom scale, taking away privileges, and fear-inducing doctor visits. When nothing seemed to do a bit of good, she finally told Haddie, "If you don't want to talk to Dad or me, you *have* to talk to someone who can help us figure this out." Therapy with Dr. Drake had helped *her* slow her skid over some of the most treacherous patches. "I'll find a shrink."

"I don't need your help," her daughter said with a snarl. "I can find someone myself."

Tess was only partially relieved that the burden of figuring out what was going on with her daughter would no longer fall entirely on her shoulders. Since she'd consulted a multitude of practitioners over the years—one suggested that meditating on blue crystals would cure her panics, and another, an elderly Scottish gentleman she called McShrink, insisted that lying naked on his tartan couch would be a wonderful metaphor for baring her soul—she was well-aware of the pitfalls. Sorting through the feelings of a vulnerable person is akin to locating the right wire to snip when defusing a bomb, and if Haddie chose the wrong therapist, she could be picking shrapnel out of her already-wounded psyche for years.

Tess *needed* to make sure that her daughter was in good hands. The only way to do that was by getting up close and personal with the woman Haddie had found in the Yellow Pages, so she insisted on accompanying her girl and her hostility to the third therapy session at psychologist Frieda Klein's office on Milwaukee's Lower East Side. Tess was familiar with this part of town. Her first apartment above the bike shop was right around the corner. She'd been ambushed by her inaugural anxiety attack just down the block. The university where she'd consulted with Dr. Ganges was a half mile north. The area had been gentrified some over the years, but when she parked the Volvo in front of a busy tattoo parlor next to a natural food restaurant, the aroma of pot and patchouli still lingered in the air.

Seated below a University of Oshkosh counseling degree that hung on the wall next to a half-dozen pictures of cats and a tie-dye quilt, Tess got things rolling during the therapy session in the smallish office on the ground floor of the converted Victorian house.

"Haddie and I use to be so close," she told Frieda Klein.

The Birkenstock-wearing counselor gave her one of those cloying therapeutic smiles and replied, "Hmmm . . . maybe a little too close?"

Tess had no idea that there was such a thing as too much love, because there isn't, and she was ticked as hell that the counselor had told Haddie there was. It was too late to stop the barely bridled rage racing up her neck on its way to her mouth, so she did what she'd been taught to do by Dr. Drake if she found herself in this kind of situation. She ran out of the office before she could shout something raw and ugly two inches from Frieda's face.

On the drive back home, Tess carefully suggested that they seek the advice of another clinician with more traditional training. "Someone with a little less *ommm* and a lot more—"

"Frieda predicted you'd say that," Haddie trumpeted.

"Oh, yeah? What'd she do? Throw the I Ching?"

When the flashback fades, Tess finds herself in Olsen's floral department sitting legs akimbo at the base of one of the elaborate displays. Because she doesn't experience the passage of time the way most folks do—the past and present flow more like a watercolor and less like a sharp-edged oil—she's unsure exactly how long she's been breathing in the smell of the greenery. It can't have been too long because . . . is that Haddie shouting out of the cell phone, "Mom? Mom?"

"I'm here, honey." She rubs the cell phone across her chest. "Sorry, bad reception. Anything else you want me to pick up besides the frozen yogurt, the absolutely no-fat kind," she says. "How about . . . ," hot fudge sundaes used to be her favorite, "some low-cal whipped cream and—?"

"How about another mother?" Haddie hisses out before their connection goes dead.

All too aware of what is expected, newly diagnosed and further disheartened Tess knows she shouldn't be sitting on the floor in Olsen's Market. She's gotta get a grip before one of the Ruby Falls ladies notices her.

When she moved into the Blessing family homestead shortly before she and Will had gotten married, neighborhood women had asked her to join them for tennis and PTA meetings, but because of her unpredictable condition—she could panic at any time and lose control of not only her mind, but her sphincter muscle. She would literally become scared shitless—she had to keep the gals at arm's length. The women misinterpreted Tess's fear as snobbery, her being part of one of the oldest families in town and all. Will had always been okay with her lack of social graces, even found it chest-beating charming that she's so dependent on him, but lately the newly elected President of the Chamber of Commerce has been stressing the importance of getting along with the townspeople. "Maybe you could at least try to be a little more ¨outgoing?" he'd recently requested.

The way his vivacious sweetheart Connie Lushman is? Louise suggests.

"Tess?"

Someone *had* noticed her sitting amongst the flower containers and potted philodendron that she'd tried to use as camouflage. Stan Olsen. She peeks out of the leaves at the man whose tummy is swollen past the top of his black Dockers pants looming above her. The owner of the market is on Will's bowling team—The High Rollers, which was so similar to *The High Life* that it never failed to bring back the day her father drowned.

"What's up?" Stan asks winded. "You okay?"

Tess gives him her standard, "Oh, sure. I'm great," because she discovered early on that while their hearts might be in the right place, folks really rather not know how she's *actually* doing. She can't tell Stan that she's unbecoming whatever it was she'd become fifteen minutes ago. If she exposes her private parts like that, he'll rush off in the other direction and might even call Will to report that she's acting "unusual" in his store. Again. "Just felt a little faint. I skipped breakfast. Sorry for causing a gawkers' block."

Gossip mongering is an honorable hobby in a town as small as Ruby Falls, so nosy shoppers are slowing down their carts, or pretending to peruse the nearby gift-card carousel.

The proprietor, who prides himself on his outstanding customer service, asks Mrs. Blessing loudly enough to impress the flock of gathering ladies, "Should I grab you something out of the deli? Cole slaw? Roast beef? They're on special today."

She says as she gets to her feet, "No, thanks. Really. I'm good," but Stan doesn't seem to be buying that. So she tries to signal him that the conversation is over by staring down at the rest of the list that she'd written on the piece of paper she tore off the hospital gown:

TO-DO LIST

1. Buy broccoli.
2. Make sure Haddie gets the help she needs from a better therapist.
3. Set up a vocational counseling appointment for Henry.
4. Convince Will to love me again.
5. Get Birdie to talk to me.
6. Bury Louise once and for all.

7. Have a religious epiphany so #8 is going to be okay with me.
8. Die.

Tess steals a glance at Stan. He hasn't budged. Sure that she only turned him down because he hadn't offered her the right food group, he nudges his tortoise-shell glasses back to the bridge of his nose with his middle finger, which is something she'd seen him do when the other High Rollers were putting pressure on him to make a crucial spare. "How about something sweet instead?" he says. "The bakery made cream-filled coffee cake this morning. I know it's your favorite." He reddens, like he took her love of the pastry personally. "My treat."

"Thank you, Stan, that sounds wonderful, but please, don't bother," she says. "I'm feeling much better now and oh, goodness, look at the time! My family is probably worried sick about me!"

Fat chance.

Down on Her Knees

As usual, Will has gone all out. Sunday dinner is a Waldorf salad, rosemary roasted chicken, broccoli in a cheese sauce, and mashed potatoes without one lump.

As Tess and her family pass the heaping bowls back and forth in the chandeliered dining room that she'd decorated in pale greens and peaches, she's considering how Will's self-esteem is drawn from the same font as his father's, and his father's before him, as far back to the days when one of the Blessing men was anointed "Cookie" on a wagon train that broke down on the Missouri Trail.

Feeding folks is not only the way her husband makes a living, it's how he demonstrates his love and devotion to his family. After Haddie got dumped the day before prom, he told her, "Awww . . . let me fix you a grilled cheese with tomato sammy." And when Henry came home after a soccer game red-faced over a botched goal, Will wordlessly whipped together a pepperoni pizza. And down at the diner? Buttons just about pop off his vest when he swings by his customers' tables to soak up their compliments. "Hey, those pigs in a blanket were fantastic! And the mock chicken legs! You outdid yourself tonight!"

Tess breathes in the smell of the pink carnations—the perfect funeral flower—that her husband had set in the center of the dining room table, and imagines her impending ceremony. It would be lavish, of course. Will is a Blessing, after all, a descendant of a founding family known for their big-hearted generosity. The extravagant coffin he'd select would be lowered into the ground after a well-attended Mass. Afterwards, when the mourners return from the cemetery to gather at the house, someone he has known all his life will wish him yet again their sincerest condolences. He'll thank them with his gap-toothed smile and one of his business-as-usual trademark winks, point over their shoulder toward the dining room at the heirloom silver bowls overflowing with Gramma Blessing's potato salad and trays stacked with cold cuts and Depression glass plates piled high with cakes and homemade pies and lemon squares. *Have you had a chance to check out the tuna-noodle casserole?* the widower would ask one of the mourners. *It's outta this world.*

Unlike Will, Tess's eroded sense of worth is stoked by her family, and only her family. Occasionally she misses the buzz she got from working the clubs in Chicago and riffing with the other comedians backstage, but she cut back on appearances after Haddie was born, and gave up the gigs completely after Henry's arrival. She doesn't for a moment regret making that decision. And no matter how strained things are between them now, she knows that they love her too. If she dies from this cancer, which she's positive she will, her babies, her always audience, will miss her. They'll feel abandoned. The same way she and her sister had after their daddy had slid into his watery grave.

She wonders as she cuts into her perfectly cooked chicken breast if Haddie and Henry will haunt Ruby Falls' Evergreen Cemetery the same way she and Birdie had haunted Holy Cross in Milwaukee on those humid mid-August afternoons after their father had drowned.

After Tess had mostly convinced her fragile little sister that—"Daddy's not in Boca Raton. He didn't swim there or anyplace else. He's dead, Bird, you gotta face the music"—she hunkered down to conquer the remaining item on her To-Do List—number three. She needed to find their father's pretend grave so Birdie could say goodbye to him once and for all. She didn't anticipate it would take too much longer because it had become a whole lot easier to sneak into the cemetery after their mother got a nine-to-five job at a local hat shop—Turner's Toppers—once they'd run out of money. And now that she wasn't flying solo anymore since Birdie was accompanying her on the search, she felt their odds were even better.

She had just finished pointing out to her sister that their daddy's bones wouldn't be in the grave when they finally visited it, but something else would be. "A lot of people die and it takes a little while for St. Peter to sort out the good from the bad things they did before he can open the Pearly Gates or send them to Hell, so his soul will still be down there waiting its turn," Tess said. "We should start right around here today." She took a few steps toward a part of the massive cemetery that she hadn't scouted out yet. "S'awright?"

When she didn't hear her sister laugh the way she usually would at her Señor Wences impression, she turned around to see why not. Birdie was standing still and looking back at the black iron cemetery fence they'd just come over. Her lips were moving and she was smiling her head off like she was talking to her sister, only she wasn't.

Afraid she might've gone as blind as Helen Keller, Tess trotted back, held up three fingers, and said, "Count 'em." Birdie did, so her eyes were working fine, so what the . . . ? Terrified that their mother was just itching to send her unusual sister to the county insane asylum, Tess pinched Birdie's ear, just a little, to let her know that she wasn't goofing around. "No talking to yourself. That's not allowed."

Birdie swatted her hand away and giggled. "I'm not talkin' to myself, silly. I'm talkin' to Bee."

"Talkin' out loud to bees is also not allowed. Same goes for flowers, rocks, houses, cemetery fences, and . . . and just about anything else but dogs, people, and God is not a good idea. I'm warning you, Bird." She got her by the shoulders and squeezed. She hated to scare her sister, but a girl had to do what a girl had to do. "If you keep this up, they're gonna throw you in the snake pit."

Birdie shook herself free and said a little too uppity for Tess's taste, "For your information, I'm not talking to *bees*. I'm talking to . . . ," she spun around, "her." She pointed at absolutely nothing. "Her real name is Betsy Elizabeth, but she said I can call her *Bee*. She's my new friend."

Tess thought—*Oh, boy,* and was unsure if this was a good thing or a bad thing. Probably bad. Seemed like everything was since their daddy died. She briefly wondered if Birdie had been hitting the bottle. Like that guy in that movie they saw who had a very tall, imaginary rabbit named Harvey for a best friend. She did ask to stop by Lonnigan's a lot. Had Birdie been sneaking up to the bar without her?

Tess took a step closer to get a whiff of her breath. It smelled like cherry Pez and nothing like Daddy's after a long shift at the bar, so that was good, but knowing that didn't solve the problem. Birdie was still talking to somebody who wasn't there.

Tess asked her in a very ho-hum way, like this sort of thing happens every day, "So . . . you and your friend are the Bird and the Bee?"

Her sister nodded and smiled.

Tess couldn't help it, she laughed. The Bird and the Bee? That hit her funny bone. She said, "That's rich," and was sure that their daddy would've told her the same thing. "Does she talk back to you?"

"A course!"

Tess didn't want to hurt her delicate feelings, so she didn't point out that it was weird to have an "imaginary friend." She told her, "I think it's neat that you've got ah . . . a new pal, but we gotta keep Bee a sister secret, okay?" The girls had many. "Don't tell *anybody*. And you have to be really careful not to talk to her in front of Louise." She took Birdie's hands in hers, thought about how Daddy sometimes called her sister his "Little Dream Boat," and made sure to look her straight into her light-blue eyes so she didn't drift off. "If she finds out she might. . . ." She couldn't tell her that their mother would sign her up for a padded room. "She won't let you play with Bee anymore."

"I know, Tessie," Birdie said in her teeniest voice. "Bee told me that already."

Shortly after getting the "imaginary friend" situation straightened out the best she could, Tess had another surprise in store. She spotted their daddy's pretend grave two down from the Gilgood mausoleum! She wanted to shout, "Holy shit!" and pull Birdie in that direction, but before she had the chance to, Louise, who wasn't supposed to be home from the hat shop for hours, called for them off the back porch and the girls went into panic mode.

It wasn't until later that night that they got the opportunity to sneak out of the house and climb the cemetery fence again. Tess could hardly contain herself as she led her sister beneath stormy skies toward the pretend grave she'd seen earlier that day. When they were greeted by a swarm of fireflies that, according to Birdie, Bee had summoned to light their way, they dropped to their knees in awe.

Edward Alfred Finley
Rest in Peace
Born September 2, 1931 – Died August 1, 1959

Tess is brought back to the here and now by B.B. King singing *When My Heart Beats Like a Hammer*. She and Will are R&B enthusiasts with an impressive record collection they enjoy listening to on the retro hi-fi they'd found at a garage sale.

With his silver hair and gray eyes, her husband looks

fetching sitting across from her at the dining room table in a pin-striped, powder-blue shirt that she doesn't remember buying him. He's slicing up a cherry pie with a perfect crust and talking about Norm "Stingy" Harris who is so famous around Ruby Falls for his cheapness that he's become part of the town's folklore. Will drops a scoop of vanilla-bean ice cream on the plate next to the pie, passes it to Henry, and says, "I heard from one of the ushers at Mass this morning that Stingy dropped a Dairy Queen coupon in the collection plate."

Tess hears her family laughing the way you hear music in a passing car—the beat, not the melody. She's worrying about how the children will cope when she kicks the bucket, but she's not concerned about Will. He's already distanced himself from her, so he'll do just fine after the cancer kills her. The man who was voted Mr. Popularity in high school will have everyone in town to console him, including former Prom Queen, Connie Lushman. They'll probably marry quickly. The same way Tess's mother had after her father had passed.

The widow Finley bumped into Leon Gallagher at the Clark gas station on North Avenue after she had a flat tire on her way to work at the hat shop. Leon knew the owner and he was doing him a favor that day by pumping gas and cleaning windshields because the regular guy, who was known as "The Peeker" by the children in the neighborhood because he spent too much time around the restroom window, hadn't turned up for his shift. Mr. Gallagher, a thin man with small feet and hands and a melting jaw line, asked the gorgeous Louise out to dinner and a movie that night, even after she'd accidently let it slip that she had two mouths to feed. A few months later he married their beautiful mother and moved her and the girls away from the cemetery house to an upper duplex off 66th and Center Streets to "Get a whole new start," and to be closer to his job at the American Motors factory where he worked on the assembly line making Ramblers.

As you'd expect, Tess and Birdie were beside themselves about leaving the home that held cherished memories of their daddy, but were relieved to find they didn't hate their stepfather as much as they thought they would. The girls, in fact, welcomed an additional target for Louise's volatile moods. Also in the plus column, Leon had a job, so their mother could quit hers, which made her slightly more pliable. And the duplex was near enough to their old neighborhood that the sisters could still ride their bikes to their usual haunts—Holy Cross Cemetery, Dalinsky's Drugstore, the Tosa Theatre, and the Finney Library. They would attend a different Catholic grade school—Blessed Children of God—which was good by them since things hadn't gone too smoothly at St. Catherine's due to the "Finley Ghouls" love of the dead and Tess's increasingly delinquent behavior.

During the muggy summer nights in the new neighborhood, the sisters would sit outdoors on the stoop and listen to the shouts of the kids up the block playing nightly neighborhood games without an iota of desire to join in. Ghost in the Graveyard seemed pretty dull considering what they'd been through, and they had each other, and Birdie had Bee, and they were fine with playing their usual games, watching TV, and pedaling up to the cemetery and movie theatre every Saturday and the library twice a week.

When, "You ain't nothin' but a hound dog," came drifting out of their next-door neighbor's window on one of those summer nights—they were always playing Elvis over there—Mrs. Hauser laughed at her husband, Gary, who could do a pretty good impression of "The King" after he hoisted a few at a church shindig.

Birdie stopped picking at the scab on her knee, cocked an ear, and said, "That song always makes me miss Jane Russell."

"Yeah, me too," Tess said as she handed her the Kleenex she always kept in her pocket to mop up the blood that'd stream down Birdie's leg. "Jane was a good dog while she lasted."

Leon's pet, an affectionate black Labrador retriever he'd named after his favorite movie star, had also made him more palatable. The dog had puppies a month after the wedding, and Louise, who could be whimsical at times, appeared delighted. But around six weeks later, the girls returned from a trip to the library to find that their mother had sold the black babies to a pet store and given Jane Russell to the pound. "Too much shedding," she snapped at the girls.

Tess told Birdie at the time that their mother wasn't telling them the whole story, and she was right. Louise needed cash to pay off a debt. Her new husband shot craps after work and he'd lost a bundle to an overly-muscled fella name of Tiger Hardesty, who was threatening to break his right arm, which would make it impossible for Leon to bring home the bacon.

After the streetlights popped on, which was their signal

to head back into the house, Tess told Birdie, "It's movie day tomorrow." She rode their red Schwinn to check for the new features at the Tosa Theatre every Friday because she enjoyed movies so very much. But sometimes her sister didn't want to go to the matinee. She didn't care for the movies set in outer space. It was hard enough for her to follow stories about people with regular names, but if you threw Dr. Zarkov and Ming from Mongo at her, that was just asking for trouble. "Something called *To Kill a Mockingbird* is playing."

Birdie thought about that as they climbed up the last of the duplex steps. "Sounds like one of those animal-dying movies like *Bambi* and *Dumbo*. Okay."

On the three-block walk back home from the neighborhood theatre the following afternoon, the girls took turns kicking a rock and agreeing hands down that *To Kill a Mockingbird* was the best movie they'd ever seen. And how next to their daddy, Atticus Finch was the best father. Tess, who'd been profoundly and forever affected by the film, said, "Finch even sounds like Finley! That's got to be some kind of sign!"

Birdie kicked the stone hard and replied with a wistful, and what would turn out to be a prescient smile, "But the name of it reminds me of me, just me."

When the flashback fades to black, Tess finds herself yearning for her little sister, uses her napkin to dab at her welled-up eyes, and drags her attention back to her family at the dinner table. Will and the children have stopped talking and are looking at each other bemused. Familiar with her internal interludes, but unclear about their origin, they roll their eyes at one another when they catch her drifting off. Eventually, one of them would make a, "Houston, we have a problem," or "Find any life on a distant planet?" quip.

This time, it's fifteen-year-old Henry, who says with a laugh, "Hey, Kevin!" (Spacey.)

That's something mother and son have in common. A love of movies. Tess isn't, but Henry is also a gifted writer. His scathing movie reviews for the school newspaper are not so popular with the teachers, but the students of Ruby Falls High eat 'em up. Hadley looks more like her dad, but her red-headed son bares a strong resemblance to his mother except for his height. Tess is pretty sure who he got his length from, but there are other parts of her son that remain a mystery. A potboiler. She absolutely adores the boy. Even though he isn't much fun to be with most of the time now, she thinks, no, she *knows* their hearts are a matched pair that have been temporarily separated. When she folds the laundry and cannot find its mate, she's sure it'll eventually turn up in the most unexpected place to be reunited with its other and she thinks of Henry.

"Take your time reentering Earth's atmosphere," he tells her with a winning smile. "I'll clear."

Since getting her teenage son to help around the house is nearly impossible, she knows that after Henry walks the dishes to the sink he'll ask her for money.

You're a doormat, Louise says disgusted.

Haddie scoots her chair back from the table and tells her dad again, "Delicious." He acknowledges the compliment with a show of his impressive dimples because she's licked her plate clean. She won't eat for her mother, but she binges for her father. Will can't face the truth, but

Tess knows that their daughter will stick her fingers down her throat the minute she gets the chance.

What did I do wrong? my friend wonders for the umpteenth time.

When the nurse had brought the impossibly beautiful Haddie into the hospital room for her first breast-feeding, Tess was shocked at the ghastly error in judgment she'd made. This helpless innocent was depending on her, a messed-up woman with no experience in loving and nurturing a child. "I've changed my mind," she cried. "I can't . . . please give her to someone who can take care of her."

The seasoned nurse muttered, "The blues," and showed Tess how to fasten Haddie onto her nipple, which is where she kept her until she became so chubby that no one would dare question the fact that she'd been taking care of her properly, not even her.

Allowing her to nurse too often and for too long, was that how I screwed up? Tess asks herself as she walks her daughter's plate to the kitchen sink. (She believes that her sister's eating disorder was the result of Louise's bad mothering, and if A=B and B=C, then she has failed as well, but her logic couldn't be more off. All sorts a things figure into a child's makeup. Bad mothering plays a part, but so do brain chemicals and friends and television shows and destiny and wiring and even past lives. A soul is a quilt stitched of many patches.) As she turns on the hot tap water to rinse the dinner dishes, she wishes again that Birdie, a veteran of the Battle of the Bulge, would return her e-mails. Tess misses her so much, and her strangely wise little sister might even be able to help undo the damage she believes she's done to Haddie.

The diner is open seven days a week, so Will is leaving to attend to business. "Cheerio," he says as he breezes past Tess on his way to the mud room. He leaves an unfamiliar aroma in his wake. It isn't his usual English Leather, but some other high-school cologne. It reminds her of beer cans, and making out in the backseat of muscle cars to an eight-track tape of *Rubber Soul*. Was it Jade East? Had his *amour* Connie Lushman given it to him? Is that the scent Will wore when they were going steady?

The thought of losing him suddenly strikes fear in Tess's heart, so when her husband calls out from the backdoor, "Later," she shouts out a desperate, "I love you!" and he answers breezily, "Yeah, you too."

When Haddie grabs the Volvo keys off the rack above the desk a few minutes later and disappears on Will's heels, Tess doesn't ask where she's going. She's too afraid that she'll tell her that it's anywhere she isn't.

Henry hops up on the kitchen counter next to the sink and asks, "How about stakin' me ten bucks? The guys are getting together tonight to play Texas Hold 'Em." His goal in life is to become a professional poker player like Phil Ivey or Wisconsin's own, Phil Hellmuth. (He's planning on legally changing his first name to the obvious at a later date to increase his odds.)

Tess dries her hands on the checkered dish towel, takes her wallet out of her black lucky purse, and slips a twenty into the back pocket of Henry's jeans. Figuring he owes her one, she steals a hug after he hops down from the counter. She tells him, "Have fun." He'll receive his learner's permit next month, but tonight he'll ride his ten-speed bike to his big-time, high-stakes poker tournament. "Wear your helmet."

Once she finishes tidying up the kitchen, she switches the light off above the stove, and heads toward the mud room. Seems like the house, and the dog, are the only ones who want to talk to her anymore. The radiators clank. The grandfather clock in the front hallway ticks. A creak here, a longer creak there. Garbo's nails click on the wide-plank wood floor as she follows Tess out to the garage where she retrieves the cancer pamphlets that Ginger had passed across her desk that afternoon. She'd hidden them under the car's floor mat for safekeeping.

Her stomach jackknifes on her way back into the house and she dashes to the powder room off the kitchen. Kneeling in front of the toilet, she thinks of her daughter and how much time she spends worshipping the bowl. Her already-fragile girl wouldn't be able to handle the thought that her mother could be dying. Same goes for Henry. Beneath his crusty boy exterior, he's mushy. So like she promised herself earlier, she'll not tell either of the children about the cancer.

Is that a crown of thorns appearing on your head, Mother Theresa?

After the rest of her dinner comes up in three more heartfelt heaves, Tess collapses against the cool white tile wall and stretches her legs out to make room for Garbo's warm, bicycle seat head. She shows her golden retriever the pictures in the brochure and says, "Try not to worry, but some doctor is gonna stick a needle into me in a few days and take something out that he'll use to predict my future, which I'm sorry to inform you, dear girl, isn't looking too rosy."

Garbo licks her mistress's salty cheek and backs out of the powder room. She'll return with her Frisbee. It's their usual after-dinner routine.

Tess rinses out her mouth, opens the door off the den that leads to the expansive deck out back, and flips on the flood lights. She looks past her recently created flock of snow angels and flings the Frisbee with all she's got. When a panting Garbo returns, my friend crouches down, picks up the toy, and says with appreciative pats, "Oh, my goodness, that's a magnificent duck you've retrieved!" It's a fill-in-the-blank running joke between the two of them that's based on the holiday calendar. "I'll clean it and we'll cook it up for Easter dinner!"

Another wave of nausea hits when Tess realizes that she may not be joining the family around the antique dining room table to enjoy Will's honey-baked holiday ham and sweet-potato casserole. The spring robins building nests in Henry's birdhouse, the yellow daffodils that always bring Haddie to mind, and the unfurling lilac bushes alongside her garden that are a tribute to her beloved Gammy might be lost to her too.

Will I be around to plant my garden on Mother's Day the way I always do?" she wonders as she rushes back to the powder room. Or will I be the one getting planted?

Erroneous Assumptions

Downtown Milwaukee whizzing past the car window reminds art-appreciating Tess of a sporty Leroy Neiman painting.

Will hadn't gotten around to doing the work he needed to do on the used Taurus they'd bought Haddie for graduation, so instead of him driving her back to school as originally planned, her parents dropped her at the airport to catch the flight back to Savannah. She'd given her dad a clenching goodbye, but she felt like a slab of cement between her mother's arms.

Tess's breath makes a frosty patch on the passenger window of her husband's perfectly restored turquoise-and-white '57 Chevy on their trip home from Billy Mitchell Field. She uses her fingernail to create a heart and draws an X through it.

She still hadn't told him yet about the suspicious mammogram. She'd planned to last night. She'd slipped into the lacy nightie with the slits in all the right places hoping that after Will returned home from the diner, they would make passionate love. Afterwards, with her head resting on his chest, would've been the perfect time to deliver the news. But as she listened to him stripping in their dark bedroom, she smelled the usual French fry oil and his father's famous meat loaf, but she also got a whiff of something womanly that didn't belong on her man—Connie Lushman's Tabu, so she rolled up in a ball and pretended to be asleep.

When Will leans forward to crank the car radio up, the sun catches his tarnished hair that seems darker around his temples. Is he trying to spruce himself up for Connie? Tess knows she should confront him instead of torturing herself like this. She's thought about doing so many times over the past month. She even cruised by the diner this past Wednesday night to see if the Chevy was in the lot, or parked in front of Connie's house, but after years of managing her PTSD, if there's anything she knows it's her limits. She couldn't discover for sure that on top of dying, she was being cheated on. She might lose control and kill one of them. Probably Will.

When her husband starts singing along to the Stones, "You can't always get what you waaant," I hoped Tess would smile, but she doesn't notice Mick's plaintive wailing, she's too busy obsessing over whether or not she should share the results of the mammogram with Will at all. He's been so distracted lately, cold, but it'd be irresponsible not to give him some warning if she's about to die. How fast does this disease move? Does she have weeks? Months? He doesn't know where she keeps the kids' birth certificates and their school reports and. . . .

She makes a kitten in distress sound.

Connie doesn't make baby-animal noises. Everyone in town thinks your husband missed the boat when he dumped her for you, mean Louise points out.

"What's the big life-threatening situation today?" her hubby asks in response to her mewling.

He's expecting her to tell him something like . . . I saw a mouse this afternoon in the attic, but it could've been a small rat, and I heard on the news about a case of bubonic plague in India and . . . and it could've snuck off one of the boats that dock in Milwaukee and then hitched a ride to Ruby Falls in a . . . a . . . truck delivering vegetables to the diner and then . . . attracted by all the chrome on the Chevy—they love shiny things—it climbed into the frame and after you parked in the garage it . . . it hopped out and—*Oh, my God!* We gotta get home and call the exterminator before it's too late!

"This time it really *is* a life-threatening situation," Tess says, a tad angrily. She lets her hand hover above her right breast like Will might need a visual aid to remember where it's located. "You know the yearly mammogram I had a few days ago?"

He checks the fur-lined rearview mirror and flicks on his turn signal. "Uh-huh."

"Well . . . I . . . I probably have cancer."

"No, you don't," he says as he changes lanes.

Now, this might seem like a steely brush-off, cruel even, but Will no longer puts much stock in her fears. He doesn't feel compelled to rush to her side and rescue his damsel in emotional distress any longer. While Tess has remained essentially the same woman he married due to her emotional challenges, he's changed. Not lately, but he can *still* be compassionate, just not like he used to be in the good old days. He's no longer the hand-holding man who had reassured her countless times over the years, "I'm pretty sure the teller with the cold at the bank didn't lick your deposit slip." Or, "I'm pretty sure that the cook at Dunkin' Donuts didn't put rat poison into your jelly-filled to get back at his wife who looks a lot like you."

When Tess would choke out, "Only *pretty* sure?"

"Real sure," Will would say with a nuzzle of her scared, sweaty neck that he loved the smell of. "Like chicken soup on the simmer," he'd told her.

These days, Tess thinks he sees her more like a middle-aged chick running through the streets screaming, "*Run for your lives! The sky is falling! The sky is falling!*"

And she really doesn't blame him for feeling that way. She *has* to put up with herself, but why should he? She can even understand why he'd go looking for nookie elsewhere. She's already damaged goods. Emotionally, spiritually, and now, probably physically. Why *would* Will want her when he could have sane and fully-breasted choir-leader Connie "Luscious" Lushman?

"And you don't have malaria or AIDS either," Will adds on after a long silence.

At the bottom of the freeway exit, he makes the turn that'll take them down the roller-coaster country road that'll deposit them back in Ruby Falls. "This is just another one of your erroneous assumptions." He'd come up with many polite terms for her fears over the years, "erroneous assumptions" was the newest.

Tess regrets telling him about the mammogram now, and reluctantly adds on, "I've got a biopsy scheduled tomorrow at St. Mary's City to confirm it."

The other reason she's been dragging her feet is she knows he's not going to take the news well. Given his current coolness toward her, she doesn't think he'll worry all that much if she's got cancer. But even if they *were* getting along, he's much too, "Keep your sunny side up, everything's going to be okay!" But, like most men, he's a wuss when it comes to illness. This disease would be particularly hard for him to deal with; his father died of bone cancer when Will was fourteen. The man has been enshrined in his son's memory, but Cyrus Blessing was anything but a saint. She's been gone many years now, but during the time that Tess tended to Mother Ruth after her stroke, the same way her gammy had when she sensed her number was up, Will's mom revealed long-held family secrets. With sad, loose lips, she told Tess one afternoon in the bedroom with the rose wallpaper how her husband had taken a fancy to one of the diner's waitresses in 1952. "Her name was Rochelle. Shelly, they called her. Willie doesn't remember, he was in kindergarten at the time, but Cy left us to be with her. He came back a few months later with his tail between his legs, but things were never the same between us after that. Pay attention to those diner girls, honey. They can sneak up on you."

Tess looks sideways at Will and wonders if unfaithfulness is coursing through his blood. Maybe he can't help but stray, it's in his DNA. He left his former fiancée for her, didn't he?

His gap-toothed grin casts a spell on my friend's body the evening he came roaring up in that old Triumph to the Arthur Murray Dance Studio, and it can still make her inner thighs tingle. She's often thought about how Connie Lushman must rue the day she'd sent him for tango lessons because she'd wanted their spotlight wedding dance to be memorable.

At twenty-three, Will Blessing was four years older than Tess, but he was far less world-weary than she for his small-town childhood had been a mostly smooth sail. With his decided slant toward optimism, she'd found him completely irresistible and more-than-a-little goofy. He wooed her with mall-store jewelry and six packs of Coke in the glass bottles because anybody who knows anything about cola knows they are the *crème de la crème*. He watched '40s musicals with her in the little efficiency apartment above the bike store, and when he proposed to her only weeks after they'd met, he was wearing a zipped-up sweatshirt with the hood tied too tight beneath his chin. He loved his mother and admired his long-dead father. He blushed when Tess cursed. "Bringing them back to their former glory," is how he described his passion for restoring old cars. She loved that. It made her feel sure that he wouldn't dump her for a newer model when she went rusty.

Had she been wrong about him? Made an "erroneous assumption"?

As they turn onto Ruby Falls' half-mile-long Main Street, Will says upbeat, "I was thinking of making ribs tonight."

He slathers baby backs in brown sugar and maple syrup. Tess is about to protest, to say something about watching her waistline, but then she remembers she probably has cancer and is probably gonna die soon, so she doesn't have to worry anymore about how fat she is.

She breathes again on the car window, draws a happy face, and tells him, "Ribs'd be great!"

Not-Such Devoted Sisters

Tess is in the sunroom, the spot where she feels most secure. Photos of the children hang on the pale-yellow walls alongside shots of wildlife that Haddie has taken since she was quite small. Even then, she showed such aptitude. She's also a runner, but Henry's the real athlete in the family. His basketball, soccer, and golf trophies are prominently displayed in the sunroom's built-in bookcases. Curtains of patterned daisy bouquets tied with green gossamer ribbon drape the floor-to-ceiling windows that remain open in the summer to allow in the smell of lilacs, Tess's and her gammy's favorite flower. Alongside the weeping willow tree—certified the oldest in town by the Ruby Falls Historical Society—stands a faded red bird feeder that Henry made in Boy Scouts when he wasn't so hip.

My friend is seated at her cherry-wood rolltop desk with her bare feet resting atop her furry footstool. She's usually quite attentive to Garbo, but she doesn't notice her tail-wagging this afternoon because she's staring at the computer that Will had surprised her with on her most-recent birthday. When she ripped open the box and expressed dismay because she's not good with anything new, especially anything technical, he said, "You gotta move into the future!" like he was so tired of her living in the past. Like she wasn't?

Tess is working hard on number five on her list this afternoon because it's Thursday—the fourth day of the week.

TO-DO LIST

1. ~~Buy broccoli.~~
2. Make sure Haddie gets the help she needs from a better therapist.
3. Set up a vocational counseling appointment for Henry.
4. Convince Will to love me again.
5. Get Birdie to talk to me.
6. Bury Louise once and for all.
7. Have a religious epiphany so #8 is going to be okay with me.
8. Die.

It's crucial that she sends the e-mail she's about to compose to her sister at 3 p.m. so it arrives at precisely four o'clock Florida time. She wishes she didn't have to write. She'd do just about anything to hear Birdie's sweet voice, but she must have caller ID because when Tess attempts to phone her, she won't pick up. And the care packages and gifts that she sends to Boca Raton are returned with a "No longer here" written across the brown paper. She'd love to believe that Birdie moved and just forgot to leave a forwarding address, but even if she didn't recognize her sister's childish scrawl, she knows that's highly improbable. To people of their ilk, change of any kind, be it location, hairdos, or eating habits, is to be avoided at all costs. Maintaining the status quo externally is crucial when your insides are a fluctuating mess.

My friend has also tried to reach her sister through her business. Ms. Robin Jean Finley has a fancy website to advertise her medical transcription services: Meditran.com. Sad to say, Tess has not found her to be "Reasonable and Rapid" the way she touts on the site. Counting today, she has attempted to contact Birdie on a 112 occasions since their mother's death. She even pretended to be a doctor who wished to use the transcription service. It wasn't until after she clicked the *Send* button that she realized she'd given herself away by signing the letter, Dr. Karen Ackerman, who was this chronic nose-pickin' kid the girls had grown up with. (How surprised the sisters would be to learn that "Boogie" Ackerman is now a well-respected otolaryngologist in Houston, Texas.)

I'm by her side, like always. Garbo can see me, that's why she's dusting the floor with her tail, but Tess can't, of course. "Imaginary friends" are forbidden to materialize unless called upon to do so, but there are always exceptions to the rules. I've appeared to her before, long ago, in another dire circumstance, and because I'm growing more and more concerned about her estrangement from Will, and her refusal to tell the children about the mammogram results, I had a little pow-wow recently with The Powers That Be. They agreed that if she didn't call upon me soon, because she doesn't have another soul to confide in at the current time other than the dog, that it'd be okay to give her a nudge in the right direction.

I'm lounging in an overstuffed chintz armchair next to her desk with my eyes closed. As she types, she speaks aloud in her throaty voice that I so thoroughly enjoy:

> "Dear Birdie,
>   Looks like your wish came true. I'm probably going to die. I'm pretty sure I've got breast cancer."

She pauses to imagine how her sister might take that news. Where was she at emotionally these days? They'd been so close as kids, practically woven together, but once they hit their teenage years, the seam that bound them began to fray. Tess loved her mother in a distant, dutiful way, but she didn't like her and never trusted her. Her rebellion as a teen was to be expected. She drank beer, skipped school, smoked cigarettes, lost her virginity, and so forth, but Birdie did no such things. She stuck to Louise's side, embedded like an embryo. Their mother did not anger her the way she had her big sister. If anything, it seemed to Tess, Louise's demands made Birdie feel needed and loved, maybe for the first time.

Robin Jean Finley would probably *never* have left the nest if their stepfather hadn't insisted on shoving her out. He'd laid down the law and refused to take her along on the move to Sacramento, California where he'd found another car job after he'd been let go by American Motors for on-site gambling. "Enough is enough already. This one ain't gonna leave on her own the way the other one did,"

Leon told their mother. "Ya gotta push her out."

Louise did not immediately jump on that bandwagon. Because eighteen-year-old anorexic and anxious Birdie couldn't hold even the simplest of jobs due to her hand-shaking panics, number-counting, and skeletal appearance, she decided that making her mother love her was going to be her life's work. From the moment the sun rose until it set, that child worked her tail off as a lady-in-waiting to Louise. Birdie would follow her around the duplex asking, "Can I get you a slice of ice cream cake roll? Wouldn't a foot rub feel good?" in her itsy-bitsy voice. "I'll get the Jergens."

Louise wouldn't miss her daughter *per se* when she moved to Sacramento, but she sure would miss being waited on hand and foot, but what could she do? Leon had drawn a line in the dirt and he was her meal ticket, so out Birdie of the nest went.

The day the moving van pulled up to the duplex, Tess arrived shortly after with a U-Haul trailer attached to Will's car. She'd been begging her sister to move in with her and her about-to-be husband into the nice, old Blessing house in Ruby Falls. When Birdie refused, Tess agreed to help her transport what little she had to call her own to a rooming house on the south side of Milwaukee that she'd pay for until her sister could apply for disability.

Birdie spent her rooming-house days pining for her mother, watching game shows and soap operas on the communal television, and playing poker for pennies with the mostly older boarders. On Christmas Eve, four months after Tess's wedding to Will, an ambulance was called to deliver Birdie's broken body to County Hospital where she was admitted to the psych ward after flying out the top-story attic window. (She had long ago stopped seeing and talking to her IF, but that's not a two-way street. If Bee hadn't moved that snow pile two feet to the left when Birdie came sailing down head first, Tess would be sisterless.)

After her physical injuries where attended to—a broken collarbone and three cracked ribs—she received intensive daily psychotherapy and was released from the hospital a month later. Despite Tess's renewed pleading to move in with her and Will, Birdie got it in her unpredictable head that a change of scene would do her good. She called and asked Leon and Louise if she could move in with them again, and when they told her again that she couldn't, she packed up her few things and hitched a ride to Boca Raton because she always did have a bit of a wild streak.

Tess writes to her sister in Thursday's email:

"Please, please forgive me. I know now that I shouldn't have taken Leon's side when Louise got sick."

Shortly before her death, their mother had been living in an apartment in the not-so-nice part of Sacramento where she'd landed after she and Leon had a final parting of the ways over a floozy named Mary Lou, the manager of the parts department at Capitol Automotive. Louise procured a job at Macy's Chanel counter to pay the rent. Her daughters faithfully called every Sunday morning to listen to her complain about her apartment that was a dump, the job that was beneath her, how the gals she worked with were jealous of her good looks, and that she got paid jack squat. Birdie beseeched her time and time again to move to sunny Florida, but Louise always told her the same thing, "Humidity is hell on my hair," and when Tess offered to bring her home and help her find a place, she'd replied, "Been there, done that."

It was the manager of the cosmetics department who called to inform Tess that Louise had collapsed at work and had been taken to the hospital. "Got your number off her application," Mrs. Lanfrey said. "She talks about you and your sister all the time. She's so proud. Are you the lawyer or the Ford model?"

Tess was brought to her knees. She had talked to her mother on the previous morning. Only thing out of the ordinary about the conversation was that pack-and-a-half-a-day smoker Louise hacked more than usual. She mentioned that she thought she was coming down with the flu, but Tess figured that she was just milking the cough to get her to write a larger-than-normal monthly check again.

Turned out they were both wrong.

Seventy-three-year-old Louise had come down with something a whole lot worse. A particular kind of pneumonia had made her lungs go hard and corrugated. (A matching set for her heart, if you ask me.)

If the Finley sisters weren't so terrified of flying that they avoided looking up when they were outdoors, they would've taken the earliest flights to Sacramento. They talked for hours on the phone about driving to California, but since the both of them had varying degrees of agoraphobia, they knew they wouldn't make it far before one of them bailed. Didn't matter. Louise lapsed into a coma and was put on life support shortly after her admission to the Kaiser emergency room.

Revolving doctors called and kept Tess up to date on her mother's condition for eight days. On the ninth, one phoned to inform her that Leon, who Louise was not officially divorced from, had decided to pull the plug.

When Tess called to pass the verdict on to Birdie, she screamed, "No . . . no . . . no . . . no . . . you gotta stop him, Tessie! You have money . . . pay Leon off . . . do something . . . I can't—"

That right there? That was the exact moment when the seed of the sisters' most-serious riff was sown.

Even if Tess *could've* convinced Leon to keep Louise alive, she wasn't about to. The doctors had made it clear that even if she did wake up, she'd spend the rest of her days on a ventilator. That's not what her vain mother would want.

Birdie, who was so accustomed to her big sister sticking up for her, interpreted her siding with Leon on this vital matter as the ultimate betrayal of their love. She yelled at her sister before she hung up, "You didn't do anything to save Daddy and . . . and now you're doing the same thing to Louise. You're a murderer. I hate . . . hate . . . hate . . . hate you. I hope you die too!"

After Louise had been disconnected from life support the following morning, Leon called Tess to report, "My little Lou-Lou is gone." There was bawling, followed by dramatic nose-blowing. "If you send me some cash, I'll take care of her . . . it . . . the arrangements. She wanted to be cremated and have her ashes thrown into Lake

Michigan. Ya know how crazy she was about the beach." Blubbering. "She mighta been a bitch on wheels, but she was gorgeous and I loved her. You and your sister too. Could you send that check right away, kiddo? Make it out to me, alright?"

Two weeks later what remained of her mother was dropped off on the Blessings' front porch by Stu the UPS man. When Tess, who had been dreading the delivery, arrived home and saw the box with the California address nestled amidst four chubby Halloween pumpkins, she locked the front door behind her and called her husband at the diner to inform him that she needed, "Help!"

She often burst into a bout of laughter in times of duress, so she giggled when Will withdrew her mother's remains from the cardboard box sent by the Neptune Society. She had pictured Louise's urn as ornate, maybe even bejeweled, but the golden cube that her husband placed on the kitchen counter was burnished and cool to the touch. (If one endeavors to select a resting spot based on the deceased's personality, I thought Leon was uncharacteristically right on the money when he'd chosen the metallic container.)

The assignment to scatter Louise's ashes brought up complicated feelings that rendered Tess all but incapable of following through on her mother's last request. Unsure how long it might take her to navigate through the flashbacks and the pain, she set the golden box on a kitchen cupboard shelf next to the bone china. She'd throw furtive glances at it throughout the day, hoping, always hoping, to experience some sense of an ending, and the courage to make the short trip to the beach.

She returns to the e-mail that she's typing in the cozy sunroom.

"You've got to believe me, Bird. I tried to scatter her."

It took her almost a month to achieve the intestinal fortitude she needed to slide Louise into an Olsen's Market brown bag for the short trip to Lake Michigan. Will offered to come with her that afternoon, but she told him, "No. This is between her and me."

A steady drizzle was falling upon the crayon-colored leaves stuck to the twisty, crumbly, asphalt path that wound from the top of the bluff down to the shoreline. In the surrounding woods, squirrels scooted up and down old-growth black-barked trees, hustling like crazy to put up supplies for another brutal Wisconsin winter. The calls of hungry seagulls mingled with the crash of waves as they fell apart on the beach below, but the sounds barely registered above the rush of blood in Tess's ears.

When she reached the stretch of sand, she heeled off her shoes, peeled off her socks, and set them on a Goodyear tire that'd washed ashore. The grit between her toes brought back the days when their sun-worshipping mother would take Birdie and her to the beach when they were kids. Louise could lie for hours on a white sheet, oiled up from nose to toes, her eyes half open to take in the admiring glances from the other beachgoers. She was a fine-looking woman with a ripe figure. A cinnamon toast tan made her downright edible.

On those late-afternoon drives back home to the

duplex after they'd spent a summer day at the lake, the smell of sun-burned skin, and songs by Duane Eddy and Bobby Vinton, would fill the woody station wagon. Birdie loved to stick her head out the back window and lap at the air, but Tess would hold her breath while she studied her mother's pale-blue eyes in the rearview mirror looking for signs of what was to come. Sure, she was in a good mood now, she always was after a day in the sun that always seemed to melt some of her anger, but what about tonight?

To her love-thirsty girls, she was an oasis that would appear and disappear at will. They could never be sure if after they got home unpredictable Louise would suddenly refuse to talk to them for no apparent reason. She often went mute, mostly for an hour or two, but there were times she didn't speak for a week. It didn't bother Tess all that much when she gave them the cold shoulder, but it just about killed Birdie to be ignored like that. She'd beg Louise to tell her what she'd done wrong, but when the only answer she ever received was a snarling, "Don't give me that. You know what you did," the both of them learned to stay out of her way until the sweet surprise that would mark their mother's mood shift appeared under their pillows.

The sisters' fingers would brush up against the corner of the prickly serrated paper of a Three Musketeers bar because that's how Louise would refer to them when she was on an upswing. Tess and Birdie would stay up most of the night nibbling, and reminding each other to profusely thank their mother for her thoughtfulness first thing in the morning or there would be a price to pay. If they didn't sound grateful enough, she might even resort to a "drop-off." She'd force them into the woody wagon and let them off at a park pond because she knew that Tess was frightened of water and if she was scared, so was Birdie. Or she might choose a back alley or a vacant lot, and off she'd go to do some shopping or stop into Lonnigan's Bar for a cold one. She'd return for the girls after she thought they'd learned how lucky they were to have her.

The particular "drop-off" that's etched in *my* mind took place on the night Louise drove furiously east through the streets of Milwaukee and left the girls at the corner of 3rd and Walnut Streets because they hadn't cleared the supper dishes fast enough. "You made your bed now lie in it," was all she told them before she drove off.

This part of the city was miles from their home and known in those days by a few different names, the politest being the "Core." Louise, who referred to black people as, "jigaboos" or "jungle bunnies," thought they'd be terrified because they didn't know any people of color in real life, only movies. The Finley sisters *were* scared, but just a smidgeon. Their love for *To Kill a Mockingbird*—the first movie they'd seen that portrayed Negroes not as scary jungle natives looking to use their blow guns on white explorers, but like regular people—soothed any ruffled feathers.

When a woman with coffee-two-creams skin and a distinctly southern drawl appeared next to the bus stop bench where they'd settled in, Tess and Birdie set their hands in hers and didn't think twice when she led them to a white wooden house up the block because there was just something about her. An Etta James album was playing in the parlor and the sound of her sweet voice drifted out of an open window. After the gal who reminded the sisters of Calpurnia from their favorite movie set them down on the front porch steps with rolled sugar cookies and two tall glasses of milk, she patted their backs and told them that there was nothing to be afraid of, that they were safe, and for the first time since their daddy's death they felt so.

Yup. The evening of August 5, 1960 was when my very first meeting with Tess occurred. She doesn't remember me, or even what transpired that night, all she knows is that whenever she hears the greatest singer of all time crooning *At Last*, for some reason she doesn't understand, she feels rescued.

My friend's voice cracks when she goes back to writing to her sister.

". . . But when I tried to scatter the ashes the way I told you I would, there were some technical difficulties."

Tessie both feared and despised Lake Michigan. Thought of it as a murderer and herself as its accomplice. Despite therapists telling her time and again that that there was nothing she could've done to save her father that afternoon after he tumbled over the side of the boat, words, no matter how wise, have a way of fading over time if not grasped deeply enough by the heart. The difference between knowing and believing is a deep chasm to cross without a safety net.

Tess withdrew the golden cube from the market bag

and cautiously approached the foamy, scalloped edge of the water. She knew she should say some parting words. She tried, but failed to think of anything nice to say about her mother before she heaved the box into the same water that had claimed her father's life.

If the sun had been out that afternoon a ray of light might've illuminated the cube before it tumbled to the sandy lake bottom, but the sky was fittingly tombstone gray, and Louise proved to be as uncooperative in death as she was in life.

Tess watched with growing horror as an east wind kicked up and the waves seemed to grow magically larger. Each crest brought unsinkable Louise closer . . . closer . . . closer . . . until the cube landed back at her daughter's toes.

Panicked, she was about to abandon Louise there on the beach, until she remembered the information on the side of the box that an employee at the Neptune Society had engraved for some unfathomable reason:

Theresa Marie Blessing
314 Chestnut Street
Ruby Falls, Wisconsin 53012

If Tess'd been anywhere else, say the Pacific Ocean or the Gulf Coast, she *would've* taken off, sure that her mother would be found by a homeless man. *Eureka!* he'd say on his way to a pawn shop where he'd make enough to buy a bottle of Thunderbird to soothe his sad heart. She could live with that outcome. She might even be able to convince herself that she'd performed a charitable work in Louise's memory.

But she wasn't anywhere else, was she. She was on the shores of Lake Michigan. For the most part, Wisconsinites are a fun-loving, God-fearing people raised on the Golden Rule. There's a bar or church on almost every corner, sometimes both. If Tess left Louise's box on the beach, she knew some Good Samaritan would eventually show up on her doorstep. *Hey, there. I'm Bob. I found this when I was usin' my metal detector down by the lake this mornin'*, the man would say. He'd be rosy-cheeked and plump, maybe a little lit up. *Ya probably been lookin' all over the place for it, eh?*

As Tess stared down at the golden box in the sand, it suddenly occurred to her that in her haste to be rid of Louise, she'd forgotten an important step in the process. She'd tossed the whole box into the water. How could she be so stupid! What she needed to do was open it and release the ashes!

With mounting desperation, she grappled in her purse for something sharp and her hand landed on her father's Swiss Army knife. She flicked open the big blade and was about to begin stabbing at the cube when an awful thought grabbed a hold of her. What if she succeeded? On a calm day that might've been all right, but with the wind coming in strong the way it was, when she tipped the box to free her mother's remains, the ashes would blow back in her face. She might inhale Louise. She'd become part of her and she'd never be free.

Horrified by the thought, Tess shoved her daddy's knife back into her lucky purse and her mother into the damp grocery bag, and scrambled up the same slippery slope she'd come down.

After she arrived home, exhausted and defeated, she didn't return Louise back to the kitchen cabinet next to the bone china. She set the ashes of the woman who still tormented her during the day, and woke her in the middle of the night with nagging criticisms on a garage shelf behind the bag of salt that Will scatters atop winter ice, which I found more poetic than anything ever written by Robert Frost.

Tess mumbles to herself as she pecks out the note.

"Please, forgive me, Birdie. I'm sick. I need you. You'd love Ruby Falls. There's a store called The Emporium that sells the kind of candy we ate when we were kids. And there's a spooky convent and cute shops and I miss you like I've never missed anybody.

Butterfly kisses,
Tessie"

Before she sends it off, she reads over what she's written through tears that all but douse the flicker of hope that this might be the *mea culpa* that does the trick.

Bellowing

Tess rolled over in bed and called Haddie first thing this morning. She was thinking she might feel better about today if she could only hear the sound of her daughter's voice, but there'd been no answer in the dorm room that she and Will paid extra for because her daughter couldn't risk exposing her gaunt body to a gossipy roommate.

Henry, who was generally disgruntled and more so at 7:13 a.m., lifted his hoodie-covered head, mumbled something about eating breakfast with his friends at the Wooden Goose Café and disappeared through the backdoor before Tess could give him the hug she so badly needed.

Will, who'd returned home last night later than usual, managed to rouse himself on this momentous morning to prepare breakfast for his wife before she took off for her biopsy appointment then settled in behind the Sports page at the kitchen table. He read a story aloud about how Tiger Woods was playing with a bad knee. "Isn't that brave of him?" he'd asked with a hitch in his voice. "To be in so much pain and keep going?"

To show compassion for a sporty stranger, but have such a hard time expressing to his family the same kindness instantly enrages Tess. Most of the time she can tame her anger and dark fantasies—both symptoms of her PTSD—using the special relaxation techniques psychiatrist Dr. Drake had taught her, but already wild with grief over Haddie's recent departure, Henry's blow-off, and her impending procedure, she imagined Will's head on a tee, hauling back, and smacking it so hard that a group of polite bystanders would say in subdued whispers, *Wow! Tess Blessing killed that!*

Thatta girl! Louise cheers.

Why couldn't Will see that Tess wanted, no, needed, him to insist that he drive her to the appointment even though she'd told him it was fine if he didn't? To punish him for not reading her mind, she pushed away the eggs Benedict he'd prepared, which took real willpower since it's one of his signature dishes and quite scrumptious.

She wishes she hadn't now. Her stomach is putting up a fuss as she turns into the parking lot of St. Mary's City.

A sexless winter-coated someone is shoveling the walk in front of the entrance of the turn-of-the-century hospital. The scraping of cold metal against cement was once a comforting sound, but as she enters through the pneumatic doors, from that moment forth, Tess knows the sound will always be associated with cancer.

"The Women's Center?" she asks the bow-tied Orville Redenbacher look-alike seated behind the reception desk.

"Down the hallway, make a quick right then a left past the gift shop. You can't miss it!"

Her mind otherwise engaged, as usual, Tess doesn't catch most of what the nice man with the loose dentures had to say, but she can't bear asking him again, so she thanks him and wanders off confused.

She is lost. Wishing she had someone to lean on. This is it! The time has finally come for me to make myself known again!

I make the adjustments necessary to actualize and swoop in behind her. Setting a warm hand firmly on her elbow, I say in the reassuring small-town Alabama drawl that's been handpicked by Tess, "Allow me to show you the way, my friend."

She startles, does a double take because I look vaguely familiar, then says with a polite Brownie smile, "Thank you," but not much else on our way to her destination. (She's much too scared of what she's walking into to form words or further wonder who I remind her of.)

The gal in her early thirties seated behind the Women's Center's glass doors is gypsy pretty. She doesn't acknowledge the handsome black woman dressed in a herringbone coat because, of course, she can't see me, but after Tess identifies herself, the receptionist tells her with an enchanting smile, "Welcome, Mrs. Blessing. If you could fill out these forms. . . ." She passes a pink clipboard over the counter. "I'll also need your insurance card."

It's never easy finding anything in that lucky black purse of hers. After she fingers past the Swiss Army knife, her copy of *To Kill a Mockingbird*, and discovers her wallet shrouded in the shards of her children's baby blankets, she leaves the Blue Cross card on the counter and takes a seat in the farthest corner of the overheated waiting area.

I ease down next to her even though we're the only two in the room. I'm emanating powerful energy that I'm having a hard time controlling because I've waited so long for Tess and me to be reunited. I'm giving her the heebie-jeebies. She doesn't like people to get too close even if they were nice enough to show her the way to the Women's Center. She could change seats, but she knows it's futile, I'd only follow her. Since she can remember, certain types of people are attracted to her. The different ones, the ones operating on another wavelength, they hone in on her. She's a big hit with schizophrenics. She wonders if she puts out some sort of vibe. Cats like her too, even though she's really more of a dog person.

She's just about completed the required admittance forms when she hears, "And how are you this fine morning, Mary Ann? Gettin' any?"

Tess's head jerks up. She recognizes the high-pitched voice. On three-inch heels, Babs Hoover has come tottering through the door of the center pushing a metal cart loaded with magazines and various sundries. Tess shrinks into the folds of her puffy red parka, brings the clipboard up to her face, and remains perfectly still so as not to garner any attention. She's vowed to keep her illness a secret and the last thing she needs this morning is the biggest blabbermouth in all of Ruby Falls noticing her and asking, *What are you doing here? Oh, no! Don't tell me you have cancer!*

Circling her emotional wagons, quick-witted Tess has already come up with a response if Babs *does* come wheeling by. She'll tell her that she has procured a position at nearby University of Wisconsin's psychology department and she's at the Women's Center to do some research on the effects breast cancer has on one's sex life.

She's sure the second Babs hears the word *sex*, whatever else she has going on in her brain will be shoved to a back burner. The gal loves to brag about how often she and her husband, Ernie, owner and proprietor of Hoover's Hardware, do the "tongue and groove."

Babs chats a bit longer with the pretty receptionist, drops off a few gift items on the desk, and says, "Well, I'm off to labor and delivery." She wiggles a pint-sized plastic champagne bottle filled with candy. "We have four ladies about to pop their corks. See you next week."

That big mouth Babs didn't notice her fills Tess with a relief that's thick enough to eat. Keeping her potential illness quiet isn't only about protecting Haddie's or Henry's delicate emotional states, she's also concerned about the family business. True, the diner has been one of the mainstays in town for over sixty years, and she'd like to believe that her sickness wouldn't affect business, but let's be honest, no matter how you plate it, cancer does not go well with a Super-Duper Blessing burger, an order of fries, and a chocolate shake. Much too real for customers who love the joint because it allows them to slip into carefree yesteryear without hardly trying. The diner suffering financially? Tess *wouldn't* let that happen. Not only for the obvious bill-paying reasons, but for the further stress it would put on her marriage. She couldn't relive those months she and Will had fought so viciously after he borrowed the money to build the diner's party room. Rationally, she realized it wasn't his fault that the room took some time to catch on. But with all the hours he worked to make sure that it did, he was barely home. He wasn't there for her and the kids, and that brought up feelings she had toward the other important person she hadn't been able to count on—her mother. She threatened numerous times to leave him. (Of course, the both of them knew she wouldn't. She could never leave anybody.)

"Theresa Blessing?" The nurse who'd come through the double doors is a smart-looking, mid-forties gal with a short, layered haircut, and muscular arms.

"God bless," I tell her as she gathers her things, but she's too focused on what she believes to be her gallows walk to let my words sink in. I need to keep an eye on her, but I can't come on too strong. She'll get scared and block me out if I do, so I artfully deactualize and follow her.

After the nurse introduces herself as Jill Larkin, Tess asks her to please call her by her nickname on their walk to a conference room where they perch in brown vinyl chairs. She used to have a bit in her stand-up routine about Nauga's and their hides and she's about to use the old joke as an icebreaker, but the nurse shuts her down with a curt, "Do you have any questions before I take you back to prepare for the procedure?"

"How big is it?"

Jill peruses the file that's lying in front of her and says, "1.4 centimeters."

That could be as small as a penny or as large as a silver dollar. Tess isn't good with numbers, better with visual aids. She asks, "What makes it *look* like cancer?" She's been picturing a Hershey's Kiss that'd been left on the dashboard of her car in August. "I mean, how can you tell that's what it is as opposed to something else not so bad?"

"The shape," Jill says. "The edges of the tumor are jagged."

That's the first time the T word has been mentioned. It makes Tess think of number eight on her To-Do List. *Die.*

She's just about to ask the nurse if she can tell by looking at the tumor how long she has to live when Jill pushes back her chair and says, "If you don't have any more questions . . . let me show you where you can change." She leads a tense Tess down a hall into a sugar and spice and everything nice locker room. Like she's giving a tour to a potential recruit, the peppy nurse says, "I'm sure you're aware that pink is the official color of breast cancer."

The disease got a secret handshake? Louise snipes.

Jill gestures toward stacks of pink robes and gowns. "When you're ready, you can take a seat in the waiting room." She points to an alcove. "I'll be back in a few minutes."

There're only three of us in the locker room. Tess and me, and an old lady with fly-away white hair who's in a stage of either dressing or undressing.

Tess says, "Hello," to the woman who reminds her of an elderly version of Miss Kitty from *Gunsmoke* because she's got this sort of Wild West look about her, and hurriedly snatches a gown and robe off the pile and slides the dressing room shower curtain shut behind her. She dressed thoughtfully this morning. Beneath the blue crew-neck sweater Will had given her this Christmas, she slipped on one of Henry's white T-shirts that reeks of the Polo aftershave he's been dousing himself in. She fingers the mother-of-pearl heart earrings that her daughter had given her on her most recent birthday. As she slips the bra straps off her shoulders, she averts her eyes so she will not see her breasts in the mirror, especially the traitorous right one.

On the other side of the pink curtain, the wrinkly woman is rambling on the way the old do because they're fully aware that people stopped listening to them eons ago.

"When I was younger," she hollers, "my cups runneth over!" She snorts. "Now my bellows look like empty saddle bags after a long dusty ride 'cross Kansas."

Tess is uncertain if the old lady is speaking to herself or to her. Or if she's speaking at all. Did she imagine that she'd just called her breasts *bellows*?

As the Finley sisters grew older, they found they had little in common with the more-carefree kids in the neighborhood and they gravitated toward a group of girls who swore, filched cigarettes from their older brothers' packs, and rolled their school uniform skirts up at the waist to show off their knobby knees in an attempt to get a boy to grin a half-crooked smile of shy interest. After their last class at Blessed Children of God School, the six pack of seventh-grade "bad girls" would convene at the neighborhood hangout—Ma's.

Overflowing bins of malted milk balls and red wax lips (Birdie's favorite) and BB Bats and gummy raisins and other earthly delights nudged one another aside in the glass cases that sat in what had once been the living room of Mrs. Alvina Malishewski, a first-generation double-wide Pole, who'd had the genius idea to turn the front half of her house into a candy store after her taxi-driving husband was murdered by unknown assailants outside the Greyhound bus station.

The kids would alert Ma she had customers by hollering

back into her kitchen, "We need candy!" until she'd come out from between the blue curtains smelling like kielbasa and mumbling "*Cholera, cholera,*" damn it . . . damn it . . . 'cause *Password* was on and she had a crush on Allen Ludden.

The group of girls would dig into their candy on the store steps as they'd talk about the things adolescent girls do.

"Holy cow, Cindy Berlman's bellows are gettin' huge. When she pledges allegiance to the flag, her hand is a foot away from the rest of her body," Tess said one afternoon as she munched on a stick of red licorice.

Gina Maniachi, a pint-sized Lollobrigida, cracked back, "Cindy's *what* are gettin' huge?"

Tess was thrilled that she'd finally bested worldly Gina, who just yesterday had explained to the girls that 69 wasn't only a number that came between 68 and 70, much to all of their disgust. "You know . . . her *bellows.*" Tess cupped her hands in front of her chest the way the eighth-grade boys did.

Gina mimicked the gesture and began laughing so hard that she swallowed her piece of Dubble-Bubble.

Tess cringed. Had she made another anatomical pronunciation error that Gina would razz her about? Last month, she had inadvertently called a vagina, a "vageena," because how was she supposed to know they were pronounced differently?

Gina snorted, "They're not called *bellows,* you *goomba,* they're called *ninas,*" and she went off in another peel of derisive laughter that made Tess feel not quite as cool as she would have liked. On the other hand, she was thinking, it was pretty dumb that Gina's bellows were named after one of Christopher Columbus's ships, but that's the Wops for you. All of 'em think the world revolves around 'em. "What the hell are *bellows*?"

Tess was too embarrassed to tell Gina that's what her gammy had taught her and Birdie to call their breasts, so she grabbed her sack of candy, her sister's hand, and slunk off those candy store steps in a disgrace that the Maniachi girl wouldn't let her forget about for months.

My friend's blast from the past is interrupted by the sound of the main locker room door opening, and Jill the nurse saying loudly and affectionately to the elderly woman, "See you tomorrow, Francis. Enjoy the rest of your day," and then she calls out loudly, and not affectionately at all, "Mrs. Blessing? Tess? We don't want to keep the doctor waiting, do we?"

Deceased and Desisted

A crisply dressed man with a broad forehead and crew cut extends his hand and says as Tess enters the procedure room, "Good morning, Mrs. Blessing. I'm Dr. Fred Bannister. I'll be performing your biopsy today."

Jill helps her onto the table, slides a pillow under the left side of her face, and asks if she's comfortable. Another nurse who identifies herself as Linda says something about mood lighting as she dims the switch on the wall. I'm there too. Tess couldn't miss me if she wanted to. I'm standing out like a slice of devil's food cake amidst all the meringue. When I give her a finger wave, she blinks and thinks, Who is that? Oh, it's the woman who showed me the way to the center and sat next to me in the waiting room. I thought she was another patient.

Dr. Fred leans over Tess and says, "The first thing I'll do is inject a numbing agent into your breast, then I'll slide a needle down to the mass and extract some cells."

She had been managing the worst of the fear so far, but the tide has just taken a turn for the worse.

She tells Dr. Fred with a quivering voice, "The anesthetic doesn't have any epinephrine in it, does it? I'm not allergic, but I can have ah . . . very unpleasant reaction to it." Since she has excessive amounts of adrenaline running through her veins on account of the PTSD, if the doctor injects more, she'll get so amped up that she'll become capable of harming one of these nice people if they try to restrain her when she jumps off the table and runs out of the room the way she did at the dentist's office two months ago.

Jill steps in to intercede. "You must be numbed. The pain would be unmanageable." She makes a move for her pocket and removes a laminated rectangular strip.

A Guide to Patient Pain Levels

Tess's eyes dart between the faces and the syringe in the doctor's hand. How could she put this in a way they'd understand without going into a drawn-out explanation. She has to say something, she doesn't feel right about not warning them. "You can give me the shot as long as you know that I could turn into a number ten with a twist."

She clamps her teeth and takes a quick inventory of what's going on in her mind as the doctor lowers the plunger. When he withdraws the needle, he asks, "Okay?"

Amazed to find that her mind doesn't feel like the scene of a heinous crime the way she thought it would, she tells him, "So far, so good, but stay on your toes," because even though she isn't freaking out right now, she knows from experience that could change in the next breath and she wants to give him a running chance.

Since I've moved to the head of the table, Tess can't see me, which is why she assumes that it's Jill who's running a satiny palm across her forehead while she coos reassuring words as Dr. Fred gets to work. He passes the bit of the tumor that he removed to the nurse who had been in charge of the lighting in no time at all. "Linda will run the slide up to pathology," he tells his patient. "We should have the results by the time you've finished dressing."

When she steps back into the locker room, the old-timey lady, who she thought would've been long gone, is leaning into the mirror over the sinks on her tippy toes spreading lipstick the color of an American Beauty over barely-there lips. Tess's gammy had a fox stole like the one she has draped over her shoulders.

"Forget something?" Tess asks the white-haired woman on her way to the bank of lockers.

"My face." She chortles. "I was halfway to the bus stop when I remembered." She snaps the lipstick back into the gold tube and is out the door again with a chipper, "Happy trails!"

That leaves just Tessie and me now in the pink room. She figures I'm there to change out of the hospital uniform I was wearing during the procedure into my street clothes.

After she slides the shower curtain shut behind her, I sit down on the locker-room bench outside the changing area and tell her, "You might want to start thinkin' about how *you're* gonna handle all this if it works out for the worst. This is one of those times that I've found hope comes in real handy."

I chose that remark because the reappearance of Francis

wearing the fox stole has brought Tess's gammy to the forefront of her mind and that's something *she* would've told her granddaughter under these circumstances. If only she was still alive, what a comfort Caroline Finley would be in the predicament my friend finds herself in.

She's not only alone and frightened, because she skipped Will's delicious breakfast offering this morning—she's starving. She could really go for one of those marshmallow and peanut butter sandwiches their gammy would make Birdie and her on the Sunday summer afternoons their daddy would drop them off to visit his parents in their little stone country house before he died.

Once they had polished off their lunch, dirt-hating Birdie would retreat into the house to play Gin Rummy with Boppa, and Tess and Gammy would get to work in the garden. Her grandmother was the one who taught her how to pull together tussie-mussies. The darling bouquets whose origins go back to buttoned-up-tight Victorian times when lovers would use them to send coded messages. Especially, the stirrings-below-the-waist type, which might explain why roses (passionate, romantic love) were such big sellers back in those days.

Alongside the large garden where flowers and a few radishes, carrots, pole beans, and wandering prickly stalks that bore pumpkins her beloved grandchildren carved into silly faces around Halloween, there was a precious plot that Caroline Finley tended in honor of her daughter, Alice, who had passed on years ago. Those who were still able to wrap their arms around their children had told her that time heals all wounds at the funeral, but she knew they were wrong. Her loss would not be diminished by the tick of a clock, if anything, its roots would sink deeper. She needed a way to tend to it. So she planted baby's breath for purity and lily of the valley for humility and shy Alice's favorite—pink peonies—drooped proudly for bashfulness. She nurtured the garden not with the expectation that it would somehow alleviate her suffering, but simply to honor her departed daughter, and mark the passage of sunrises and sunsets until she would be reunited with her again.

Of course, it being the 1950s, a time that death, and just about any other trauma was treated with a firm, "pull yourself up by your bootstraps" approach, Caroline didn't discuss her grief. She buried it beneath common sense subjects like cleaning and baking while they toiled in the garden together. But my Tess, a curious and sensitive child who had found out early in life that forewarned is forearmed, was compelled to ask, "What made Aunt Alice so sick and die anyway? Can you catch it?"

Her grandmother, who had been gathering green beans into her yellow checked apron at the time, responded to the question by dropping the whole kit and caboodle, pressing Tess to her bounteous breasts, and saying through tears that came as fast and unexpected as a spring shower, "Time to say a rosary for our dearly departed."

They left their muddy shoes at the backdoor of the ranch house, washed the dirt off their hands at the kitchen sink, and after they collected Birdie from the parlor, the three of them padded to their grandparents' feather mattress to hold their beads beneath a picture of Jesus displaying his sacred bleeding heart that was an exact replica of the one that Tess passes as she searches the hospital halls now for Jill.

Room #121 was where she'd been instructed to meet the nurse to discuss the results of the pathology report, but Tess is not having much luck staying in the here and now. The smell of disinfectant has shifted her mind into reverse again. She's being reminded of Birdie now. And how she'd cut one of their last telephone visits short because it was almost four o'clock and she needed to clean out the hinge holes in the back of her washing machine with Q-tips and witch hazel.

Her sister was born on the fussy side of the blanket, so Tess isn't exactly sure when Birdie escalated into compulsive cleanliness. She thinks it might've been about a year after their mother married Mr. Gallagher. Louise told the girls, "It's official," on the ride home from the legal adoption proceedings at the Milwaukee courthouse. "Leon's your father now. You can be arrested if you don't call him Daddy."

Being the fastidious person that she was, their mother wasn't done housecleaning. When the girls showed up at the breakfast table nine days later to jelly doughnuts and two glasses of Ovaltine, she wished them a cheery, "Happy birthday," and slowly withdrew an envelope from her capri pants and set it down next to her pack of L&M cigarettes that Tess was sure she smoked because they were her mother's first two initials. She recognized their gammy's handwriting and reached out for the card, but her mother's hand slapped down hard. "You won't be seeing them anymore. Don't call or write to them either. It hurts Leon's feelings." Louise deposited the card that Tess knew would have eleven dimes scotch-taped to the bottom into the trash can under the sink, thought better of it, and slipped it back into her apron pocket. "Think of Caroline and Al as deceased and desisted. Like your father."

At first, the girls didn't think they could face a life without the Sundays afternoons they'd spent with their funny boppa, who'd been a fireman in his prime, but now spent his days in a bank protecting money and pulling practical jokes on the tellers, and their gammy, who loved to garden and could make a mean leg of lamb. But, in time, the memories faded, and the Lord's Day became like any other. And as weeks turned into months, as summers passed and winters arrived, the sisters could barely recall anymore the way Boppa would pass out gum that turned their teeth black, or how their gammy would prepare a Nativity scene each Christmas and since she wasn't that great of a baker, the holy tableau would always come out looking like blobs of dough looking religiously at other blobs of dough.

It wasn't until many moons later—New Year's Day of last year—that forty-seven-year-old Birdie, who was still living in Boca Raton, and grappling with unresolved grief over the loss of her mother, got it into her unbalanced head that if she couldn't have Louise anymore she'd replace her with the next best thing. "We found Daddy in the cemetery, didn't we? Now I'm going to find Gammy, not dead, but alive!" she told her big sister way, way too excited on the phone call from Florida.

Birdie's resolution greatly concerned Tess. For when she failed to find Gammy, who *had* to have passed on years and years ago, she would be devastated and pay dearly. Her symptoms would ratchet up ten notches. She didn't experience the breaks with reality with the same frequency she'd once had, but when she did, they were doozies. She would call Tess, usually in the middle of the night, to report something like, "Guess who just visited Birdie? Marie Antoinette!" Since she'd always refer to herself in the third person when she was experiencing a delusion, Tess had no problem recognizing when Birdie had a meltdown, and, of course, the high improbability of the dead Queen of France dropping in on her sister in Boca Raton was also a tip-off.

Tess was stumped during the disturbing calls at first, but through trial and error, she'd stumbled upon the most effective way to reel Birdie back to the here and now. It was quite simple, really, as so many profound ideas are. All she had to do was dig a little deeper. She would say, "No kidding! Wow! Marie Antoinette? Was she speaking French?" The questions would be met with a hollow silence on the end of the line, but then her sister would say softly four times, "Birdie doesn't remember," and then Tess would tell her she loved her and remind her to take her green pills.

When the end of January drew closer and nothing more was mentioned about the search for their long-dead grandmother, she thought that Birdie had forgotten all about finding her because her OCD brain had latched onto something else, so Tess relaxed some, well, as much as she can relax.

On February 2, six weeks after she had brought up the preposterous idea, Birdie called early to make sure Tess had received her four Happy Groundhog's Day cards because commemorating every holiday, no matter how inconsequential, was one of her compulsions.

Tess thanked her four times for the cards, told her how much she loved the pictures of Punxsutawney Phil she'd included, but what about the other photo she'd sent? She asked, "Who's the old lady sitting on the sofa?" The woman was kind of turned away from the camera, but Tess thought it might be the gal who lived downstairs from her sister. They'd struck up a friendship over their mutual love for cards and anise cookies. "Is that Esther?"

"No!" Birdie replied with glee. "Surprise! Surprise! Surprise! Surprise! It's Gammy! I found her just like I told you I would!"

Tess's heart tanked. Unable to ask her outright because she didn't know when she was suffering from a delusion, she did what she always did to shut down her sister's troubled brain. She leaned back in her sunroom chair and said with a sigh, "Really? Wow! Gammy? What's her address?"

"Seventy-five-fifteen Nash Street. Apartment two."

And then Birdie babbled on about how she'd found their grandmother in the phone book only a few days after she'd set forth to look for her, and how over the last month she'd spent time with ninety-three-year-old Gammy in Milwaukee, but not Boppa, who had died of a heart attack at the bank years ago and . . . and she'd met their Uncle Raymond and they'd had a big party with balloons and liver sausage and . . . played charades.

Tess, thinking that her sister's desire to replace their dead mother was so profound that she'd taken the delusion one step beyond, quickly composed another question. She was just about to ask aviophobic Birdie how she'd gotten to Milwaukee when her sister said, "I can fly now!" And then she went on to explain how she'd been hypnotized, which didn't surprise Tess. Birdie had that wild streak, and had always been the more adventurous in seeking out fringe cures, like astrology, psychic visits, and past-life regression therapy.

As Tessie listened to her sister prattle on, she slowly realized that not once during the conversation had Birdie referred to herself in the third person, which was an absolute, without a doubt, delusion indicator. Which was why, as far-fetched as the story was, she grew more and more convinced of two things. Birdie really *had* found their gammy alive and not dead. And she'd withheld that vital information from her for over a month.

How could she?

"But . . . why didn't you tell me as soon as you found her?" a wounded Tess asked.

Birdie crowed, "Because I wanted to keep her to myself for a while. You like to garden and you don't have scars on your wrists and. . . ." She was unremorseful and wound up tighter than usual. "You got a husband, children, a nice house, and what do I have after you let Daddy and Louise die?"

Tess wanted to say, *Me, you got me, Bird*, but it was at that moment that she realized that her sister hadn't nudged her off the pedestal she'd placed her on so many years ago, she'd knocked her clean off.

Bewildered, but still somewhat hopeful that Birdie really had made it all up, Tess hung up and raced over to the address on Nash Street in Milwaukee. She was familiar with the neighborhood. Their old house and Holy Cross

Cemetery were just three blocks down.

The apartment building their grandmother was purportedly living in was four units up, four down, sandwiched on a block between a savings and loan and a Shell station. The usual stale smells rose out of the matted gold carpet that ran in front of apartment number two. Tess knocked hard, but it took some repeating to be heard above parakeet chirping and a TV commercial selling the quicker picker upper. It seemed like forever before she heard rustling on the other side of the apartment door and a voice tentatively asking, "Yes? Who's there?"

She sounded different, shakier, but the pit of Tess's stomach had no difficulty identifying her. When she answered, "Lily of the Valley stands for returning happiness," her gammy cried out, "Tessie?" and fumbled with the lock. "Sweet Jesus, Mary, and Joseph! What are you doing here? Birdie told us you were dead!"

Bottoms Up

Bulky black-and-gray medical machines hover in the shadows of Room #121 like subversives devising an end-of-the-world plan.

Jill is sitting on a three-wheeled stool across from recently biopsied Tess, who is studying her facial expressions for a hint of things to come. Did the nurse look happy? Sad? Concerned? She had learned how to mood-read early on in life because if she could figure out the way her mother was feeling, she and Birdie could get running starts because Louise was fast. Real fast.

Jill slides closer. Their knees are touching. Tess can smell her perfume, something rosy. "It's cancer," the nurse says fast, like she's pulling off a Band-Aid. "But the good news is that the tumor doesn't look very angry."

My friend is saddened, but not unduly shocked by the verdict because she's always prepared for the worst. She *is* perplexed by the way Jill described it though. "Angry?"

"That means—" she glances down at the folder in her lap. "How much do you know about the disease? I noticed on your questionnaire that no one in your family—"

"Ahhh. . . ." Since Tess hadn't really taken what she'd been told by her gammy or her uncle seriously, considering the circumstances, she kinda forgot about the whole thing until just this very moment. It might be important information for these people to have. "I just remembered that my aunt might've had. . . ."

It was only a few months after they'd reconnected that Gammy was admitted into the burn unit in the same hospital that her granddaughter was currently receiving her life-changing diagnosis. A doctor had called to inform her that Caroline's polyester house dress had caught fire while cooking bacon and she'd been engulfed in flames. Tess rushed to the hospital, where she was directed to the intensive care unit on the fourth floor. She found Gammy crying into her bandages, but not because of the pain of the burns for she'd been well sedated. "Please don't leave me here," she begged. "My Alice died in this hospital of brain cancer."

More information on her aunt's illness didn't surface until the afternoon her father's brother set the record straight during their first meeting to discuss Gammy's future. Tess had seen a few black-and-white pictures of him in her grandmother's scrapbook during her growing-up years, but Raymond Finley was quite a bit older than her daddy and hadn't played any part in her childhood. Even though he lived in Milwaukee, he never expressed interest in spending time with his brother's daughters. Tess didn't think of him as part of her family either until he stepped in to handle Gammy's hospitalization because he was her closest next of kin.

Professor Raymond, as he corrected his niece on the call she'd made to his office at the University of Wisconsin-Milwaukee, offered a Chaucer caveat when he considered her lunch invitation. "There's no workman, whatsoever he be, that may both work well and hastily," he said with a lousy British accent he'd acquired during his recent sabbatical in Stratford-upon-Avon. "I suppose I could fit you in between my upper-level English classes, but it'd have to be somewhere close. The Wurst Haus."

The Finleys were a short-in-stature family. Tess's father was five-feet-seven, and Gammy and Boppa, when they stood side by side, reminded her of imported salt and pepper shakers. Same went for Aunt Alice, who topped out at five feet. But Uncle Raymond? Fee fie fo fum! Tess marveled at genetics, and was gratified that she'd finally figured out who Henry had inherited his height from when she sat down across from him at the German pub across the street from the campus.

The Professor monopolized the conversation. Went on about the academic success he'd achieved . . . his tenure . . . his visit to Mr. Shakespeare's hometown. It wasn't until he paused to take a bite out of his knockwurst that Tess had the chance to jump in and ask a few questions. She'd never brought up the subject again after the first time she'd asked Gammy about Alice's demise, but the mysterious aunt who had passed so young had piqued Tess's interest for many years. "Your sister was a librarian before she died of brain cancer?" she asked.

He answered with a mouthful, "Alice worked at the downtown library in the reference section for many years, yes, but who told you that she died of *brain* cancer?"

"Gammy."

"Alice died of *breast* cancer, not *brain* cancer." He burped. "That's so typical of my goddamn mother. She has a tendency to screw things." The Professor lifted his glass of beer to his lips. "Bottoms up," he said, laughing bitterly at some private joke.

Tess was appalled by his anger. Sure, she wasn't nuts about *her* mother, but she thought she had some pretty good reasons to hold a grudge against Louise. But . . . how could Raymond be so ticked-off at sweet Gammy?

She didn't receive the answer to that head-scratcher until months later during one of her last visits to the St. Francis Catholic Home for the Aged, the spot her uncle had determined was the most appropriate place for his religious mother to reside after her release from the burn unit, and as much as my friend disliked the Professor, she couldn't disagree with his choice.

Religious statues and biblical pictures lined the hallways of the turn-of-the-century, three-story building. The body and blood of Christ was served every morning, and old-style Milwaukee fish fries—beer-battered cod, cole slaw, rye bread, and potato pancakes—were on Friday's dinner menu. Flower gardens clustered about a generous stretch of back lawn. From a branch of a glorious oak tree not far from the wraparound porch, a worn wooden swing hung. That's where the two of them would sit on their twice-weekly visits, weather permitting. The years had made it Tess's turn to rock.

Perhaps sensing that her end was near, Gammy was not as reserved as she'd once been. Same as Will's mother had, she appeared to delight in not only revealing, but reveling in the darkest of family secrets. Tess had gotten an earful about Louise during the visits. "I warned Eddie that he shouldn't marry that self-centered trollop," is what

Caroline said. Many times. She also had a few choice words to say about her remaining son. "Poor Raymond. He works so hard to think so highly of himself," she said with a proper tut-tut. "You ever wonder why he's so much taller than the rest of us, dear?" She took a sip of her proper afternoon tea that Tess'd brought in a thermos. "A bit of a sticky wicket that." Caroline then went on to describe the affair of which her uncle was the bastard outcome as, "My fun with Gus the milkman." Of the lanky, delivery fella who left cream in the box outside her backdoor every morning, she admitted with a vixen smile, "I never have been able to resist a man in uniform."

Tess is debating if she should continue telling Jill about Aunt Alice's confusing health history. Better to error on the side of caution, she decides. Always. "My father's sister might've had cancer," she says. "I'm a little fuzzy on the details, but it could've been brain or . . . ," she almost says *bellow*—that's how bad she wants to make the nurse quit looking at her with pity eyes—"breast."

Jill says, "Okay. I'll add that to your chart, but I doubt that it will make any difference at this point."

"Hello?" Dr. Fred waltzes in after what looks like a visit to the little boy's room looking damp, but relieved. "Any questions?" he asks Tess.

"What happens next?"

"You have to hope that it hasn't spread."

Tess had tried her hardest to know as little as possible about the disease and she'd thoroughly succeeded. She didn't know that cancer could travel. She looks to Jill for confirmation because even though the doctor appeared to be a good sort, men on the whole didn't seem that smart to her. Just about every morning Will or Henry had to be told not to leave the house without zipping up their barn doors.

The nurse nods. "It's called metastasizing."

Tess says, "Oh," then asks the doctor, "Well, how do we know if it *has* metas . . . mesat . . . what Jill said?"

"During the operation to excise the tumor, your surgeon will also remove a few lymph nodes for testing. If cancer is found, the prognosis can be, well, more complicated." He slides something out of the pocket of his lab coat and offers it to her like a parting gift. It's a holy card. She'd once had quite the collection of God's All-Star Team. Traded them with the other Catholic kids on the block, and Mr. McGinty, the caretaker at Holy Cross Cemetery. "Are you devout?" the crucifix-wearing doctor asks her.

Make a joke. Ask him . . . does the Pope shit in the woods? Louise heckles.

Despite her lack of faith, Tess doesn't want to turn down the gift card. The doc might take offense and retaliate. He might even inform her that he suspects that her breast cancer *has* journeyed to somewhere else in her body because why else would he be offering her a picture of Jude, the patron saint of lost causes? What if she only has days to live? That wouldn't give her enough time to get done what she's gotta get done.

TO-DO LIST

1. ~~Buy broccoli.~~
2. Make sure Haddie gets the help she needs from a better therapist.

3. Set up a vocational counseling appointment for Henry.
4. Convince Will to love me again.
5. Get Birdie to talk to me.
6. Bury Louise once and for all.
7. Have a religious epiphany so #8 is going to be okay with me.
8. Die.

Tess thanks the doctor, reaches for the saint picture, and slides into the little compartment in her wallet where she keeps her credit cards, and he, satisfied with a job well done, stands and says, "God bless you," and is out the door and on to his next patient.

Jill rifles through a manila folder. There are a few more items to cover. "The pathology results will be sent to your surgeon. Who do you see?"

The check-out girls at Olsen's Market. The old folks at Horizons. Garbo's vet. The customers and staff at the diner. Will and Henry. Haddie, when she's home.

Tess is about to ask Jill for a referral, when the man who coached Ruby Falls High varsity cross-country team pops into her mind. "What about Rob Whaley?" In the hostile territory she finds herself in, it's important that she surround herself with as much familiarity as possible to keep her panic at bay. She didn't know how good Rob was at his job, but he'd been great with Haddie and her teammates, his family regularly frequented the diner, and they were also parishioners of St. Lucy's. She knew he was affiliated with St. Mary's North Hospital, but she wasn't sure what kind of surgeon he was. "Does he do this type of thing?"

"Yes, and I'd highly recommend him. Dr. Whaley is wonderful," Jill says with a schoolgirl blush that Tess understands. (The surgeon is easy on the eyes going in both directions.)

"What will he . . . will he cut it off?" my friend asks.

"Not necessarily. You might be a candidate for a lumpectomy. He'd remove only the tumor and leave the rest of your breast intact, but a mastectomy *would* be safer."

As much as Tess wanted to be safe, her breasts were important to her. She loved her good old girls, and so did Will, no matter how little attention he was currently paying them. She wasn't going to let the right one end up looking like it belonged on her twelve-year-old flat-as-an-ironing-board self. The one who would walk to Dalinsky's Drugstore to peruse the large periodicals section every chance she got. She'd open an issue of *Look* magazine and place it beneath a *Playboy* or *True Detective*, so she'd look smart instead of perverted, in case somebody from the neighborhood wandered in. As she turned the pages, she'd pray that her bellows would grow as large as Miss August's, or that she'd be given the opportunity someday to be one of those "knock-out broads" in a form-fitting sweater who turns up in a gumshoe's office offering to pay for his services with anything but cash. These protuberances had power over men! The more shade they cast, the better!

Jill says, "After the tumor has been removed, the next step will be to make an appointment with an oncologist to talk about your radiation treatments."

Tess figures that bit might not be too bad, other than the fact that it would bring up memories of her sunbathing mother.

Speaking of . . . when are you going to scatter my ashes the way you promised your sister you would?

"And after radiation, you'll receive a course of chemotherapy," Jill says, "if it's called for."

Which it won't be. Not only is Tess terrified of chemicals of any kind, she's quite fond of her unruly red hair that even self-occupied Henry would notice was no longer on her head. She'd have no choice but to tell him about the cancer. He'd put on a good show, maybe even make a few jokes, but her sensitive boy would be devastated. Sure, sure, she could wear a wig during the treatments, but since she can spot fake hair a mile off, she assumes her son and everyone else can as well. Ruby Falls is a small town. Word would get back to Haddie.

"I know this is a shock and a lot to take in," Jill says. "If you think of any other questions, here's my card, and Dr. Whaley's too."

Tess thanks her, and after delivering a clumsy pat on the nurse's back, she bolts to the hospital parking lot and the relative safety of her Volvo. Woozy and weak, overwhelmed emotionally and physically, she wishes again that she'd eaten Will's eggs Benedict this morning.

As she fires up the car, she remembers that she'd told him that she'd call right after she got the biopsy results, but on a chilly exhale, she says, "Fuck it," because she's still angry with him for not making a bigger deal out of today. For not being what she needs. For changing. For maybe having an affair with Connie Lushman. And the thought of he who she holds most dear saying, *Egbok—everything's going to be okay. I'll have a slice of lemon meringue pie waiting for you when you get home,* after she tells him that she's got cancer, is more than she and her stomach can bear.

She stops at the corner of Downer Avenue and Edgewood and looks east through the black-forked trees toward Lighthouse Point Park. Considering what she's going through, it seems only right to pay homage to the site where'd she relinquished another part of herself long ago.

She turns into the park lot, switches the car's engine off, and plods through the snow toward Picnic Area 7. She knows what she'll find.

The lucky-in-love brag table has stood the test of time the way she knew it would. It'd been a high-school tradition in those days for boys to have their way with their steadies then carve the initials of the girls they'd "drilled" into the redwood. Some things never change. Tess sweeps off the snow and runs her fingers across the barely legible scratching in the upper-left corner of the table: "D.D. loves T.G."

She'd believed him.

Tess Finley Gallagher and Richard "Dickie" Detmeister started drinking early on that crisp, autumn evening of October 3, 1967. After the under-the-big-lights football game, her steady with the blah brown eyes and the nose hooked enough to hang a winter coat off of took her in his arms, told her how much he loved her, and that he would love her even more—they could even get married if she wanted to after they graduated—if she would only, please,

please, please let him go all the way.

Tess wasn't interested in Dickie's marriage pitch for she had spent many years observing double L—Leon and Louise—locked in an unending battle. It was the part about being more loved that'd convinced her. The Pabst Blue Ribbon played a role too. "Okay," she'd told him, "what the hell."

This venture being the stuff adolescent boys dreams are made of, Dickie about dragged her out of the stadium stands to the confines of his mother's beige station wagon. He laid rubber out of the Marquette High School lot so desperately excited about what they were about to do that he'd forgotten to figure out where they'd do it. He turned down the eight-track Beatles' tape and asked, "Where should we go? Lighthouse Point Park?"

Tess sucked down the rest of the cold beer, tossed the can in the backseat over her shoulder, and said, "Sure."

The thought that she'd be performing her first love act near where her father had lost his life didn't cross her mind. She rarely thought about him anymore. Her daddy only came to her in dreams that she couldn't remember and in tears that she didn't understand.

The light of a harvest moon shone through the woods of the park as she stripped by the light of the glove compartment and Dickie struggled with his zipper with slippery beer fingers. Tess watched with interest as he jerked down his khakis and his tighty-whities past his knees.

The penis that she had thus far only felt through her boyfriend's blue jeans was waving back and forth, looking the way it'd been described in *True Confessions* magazine:

"A throbbing divining rod," but when Tess moved her gaze farther south, where she was expecting to see: "Two fleshy orbs swollen with love juice," she found nothing of the sort. The boy's manhood was a figure of speech.

!

Of course, Dickie had anticipated her confusion and was prepared to field her questions about his missing testicle. "I wasn't born this way. I'm not defective or anything," he panted. "During a game four years ago, this kid came sliding into home and spiked me in the nuts. My right one blew up so bad they had to remove it." He looked scared. Like he was expecting his steady of two years to say, *Sorry, I've changed my mind. I'd rather lose my virginity to a boy who comes fully loaded.*

But Tess being Tess, Dickie's lack of sack only made her care for him more, so she told her beau in a tipsy May West voice, "Batter up, big boy."

She moans, "Ow," and looks down at the splinter sticking out from the finger she'd been running over the carved initials in the picnic table. She plucks it out and is thinking about Will and how much she misses their connubial bliss, when her attention is diverted by a woman and a young girl who have appeared out of the woods on the bluff.

They are an unusual pairing this side of the Mason-Dixon line. A child with skin so white against the hood of her pink snowsuit and a middle-aged black woman wearing a hound's tooth coat. Tess can't make out their faces, but the intense love they feel for one another is emanating from their very being in beams that melt the snow they are treading upon. The woman leans down to say something to the girl with the dark-blue eyes and deep-red hair and she nods and marches purposefully toward the picnic table. She lies down in the snow and begins to solemnly swing her arms and legs back and forth as if creating an angel is sacred work. When she has completed her task, she looks up with an expectant smile and pats the ground next to her.

It's an invitation Tess is unable to resist. She is tentative at first, then faster and faster she goes until a feeling beyond happiness swells inside her chest, growing stronger with each arc of her arms and legs. But when she draws her tear-filled eyes off the sky and turns her head toward the little girl to thank her for the indescribable gift, she finds herself alone again.

Freaks

When Tess steps through the backdoor of the house, she finds it empty except for steadfast Garbo, who greets her and me like we're pounds of ground round. She checks the kitchen clock. Henry will be home from school soon, Will is feeding the tail end of the lunch bunch, and she wonders what Haddie is doing so far from home in a place where she is known as the Yankee Girl?

After she lets her dog out to do her duty in the backyard, the two of them climb the stairs. She looks forward to the times she can visit her children's rooms when they're not home. She can touch their things, and lay her cheek against their pillows, without them asking her, "Ya ever heard of this little thing called privacy?"

Henry's bedroom walls are lined with *Star Wars* and poker posters. She'd given him the William S. Hart cowboys-playing-cards one for his most-recent birthday, and the Darth Vader and Luke Skywalker ones because they'd seen the movies together when he was a little boy and he still loved them so damn much. She runs her finger across the top of the narrow dresser she'd stained white when he was a baby, and checks on Phil, his pet snake. The garters up and die every couple of months, so if need be, Tess'll dispose of it and buzz over to the Pet Palace to purchase another before her son can discover it's passed on because she doesn't want to upset him. The boy takes loss to heart. Same as her, he still misses his GG—great grandmother.

The evening she had broken the news of Gammy's fatal heart attack to him, her son cried out, "But I just saw her on Saturday. How can she be here one minute and . . . God is such an asshole," and she did not reprimand him. Will takes the kids to Mass every Sunday. She does not accompany them unless it's one of the life-or-death holy days—Christmas or Easter. Her lack of attendance on a more regular basis has not helped her standing in the community. She regrets the discomfort it causes Will, but she's got enough reasons to feel bad about herself and does not wish to add hypocrite to her list.

Tess wanders into her daughter's room through the kids' connecting bathroom. Stunning photographs hang off the bedroom's pink walls, running trophies gather dust on the bureau, and the stuffed animals look like they're missing her girl as much as she does. They used to lie in this bed together and giggle about boys. They'd share a bedtime snack of buttered graham crackers and hot cocoa back in the days her daughter didn't care how much she weighed.

Down the hall past the linen closet is her and Will's room. They made their babies in this bed, and until a few months ago, love, sweet, love, much, much more often than other couples their age. Her husband did almost all his talking between the sheets and Tess was an excellent listener.

She flops back onto the white down comforter, thinks about Will a bit more, their ardor, and smiles a little when she recalls the Finley sisters' curiosity about the birds and the bees.

After eleven-year-old Tess was sure that Louise and Leon were too busy fighting with one another to bother Birdie and her, she'd slide their flashlight and one of their most-prized possessions out from beneath their mattress. A shiny turquoise-and-silver book entitled, *Freaks of Nature* that she'd "borrowed" permanently from the Finney Library.

The lava-spewing volcano on the cover reminded the girls how Louise's anger could erupt without warning and destroy everything in her path, so they never stared at it too long. They'd flip straight to the pages where they'd find the stories and pictures of the mysterious . . . the exotic . . . the strange. Lepers of Molokai, a six-hundred pound lady who hadn't left her house in eight years, and a legless man who got around in a Radio Flyer wagon pulled by a Shetland pony named Muffin.

Since sex education hadn't been invented yet, it made sense to trust the book—it had already taught the sisters so much about geography, nature, and how things could always be worse—to reveal answers to the subject that they'd been fervently wishing to learn more about that summer.

The girls had become fixated on "doin' it," when Tess discovered that it was so important to their mother that she get it done that she'd turned to their next-door neighbor and Elvis impersonator, Mr. Hauser, when Leon wouldn't or couldn't. She became privy to their tryst, when she'd heard Louise and Mr. Hauser going at it when she'd run out to the garage to fetch a sand bucket full of shells that she and Birdie had collected at the beach that afternoon. She followed the moaning sounds to the hedge that separated their yard from the Hausers' in time to see the mister wiggling on top of her mother who cried out, "Oh, Gary, do it! Do it! Give me your hunka burnin' love!"

Tess had heard the other kids in the neighborhood call what she'd caught them at, "having the sex," "the birds and the bees," "screwing," and now "doin' it," but how did it all work? It certainly seemed to make their moody mother happy. That would be a handy skill for the sisters to have. They needed to know more.

Semi-enlightenment arrived on one of the many nights their oaky summer-stained legs were wrapped around each other's in between the bed sheets. Birdie yipped, "I think I finally found something!" Beneath the Eveready flashlight's circle glow, her bitten-to-the-quick fingernail pointed to a scorpion resting on top of another scorpion.

Since she was still struggling with her reading skills, she handed the book off to her sister, who read aloud a short paragraph entitled: INSECT REPRODUCTION. Tess explained as she went along: "Before they mate—that means do it—the female of the species—that's the lady—performs what is known as the Scorpion Dance of Love. Once the offspring arrive—that's another word for babies—they must raise themselves and not be a burden—that means a bother—to the mother because if they are—" she swallows hard when she realized that she should've stopped while she was ahead.

Picturing Louise, Birdie said, "What does the mother do if the babies bother her?"

Tessie didn't want to tell her, but she knew her stubborn sister wouldn't let her fall asleep if she didn't and she barely got enough shut-eye as it was. "She . . . ah . . . eats them."

"*Beats* them?"

"Ummm. . . ." Tess was tempted to go with that, but while she protected her sister, she rarely lied to her. "She *eats* them."

Birdie flipped onto her back and moaned loudly, "Oh, sweet Mother of God, please save us!"

Desperate to hush Birdie up before Louise or Leon heard, Tess cupped her hand over her sister's mouth and began reading to herself the next paragraph that she'd hoped would hold much more cheerful information than mothers devouring their bothersome children.

"What?" Birdie asked after Tess slammed the book shut and rolled over.

"Nothin'."

After her sister begged in her baby voice to tell her more, Tess had no choice but to rattle out, "Sometimes after the scorpions do their love dancing, the lady eats the man too. Now go to sleep."

Birdie didn't say anything at first, but then she whispered out of the dark, "Maybe *that's* why Leon can't do it anymore." The walls of the duplex were thin, so the girls couldn't help but hear their mother berating their stepfather for his inability to become aroused. "He's too afraid that Louise is gonna eat his wiener if he does."

"She wouldn't do that."

"Ya can't know what she'll do," Birdie said with a shiver beneath the sheet.

"That's true, but. . . ." Tess imagined their mother at the kitchen table complaining how little meat was on Leon' s wiener the same way she always complained about the pork chops she got from the butcher. "She would have to cut it off first and that would make a mess and you know how neat she is." That was a fact. Louise had a place for everything. Except them.

Without the help of *Sea Hunt*, it might've taken years before the girls got a better look at what they'd been dying to learn more about. Every Thursday after school, they'd scoot up close to the black-and-white television in the duplex's living room. Goose bumps would sprout up on their thin little arms when they'd hear the ominous theme music that signaled Mike Nelson's departure over the side of the *Argonaut*.

It's not that they were enamored with underwater adventure, you understand. Far from it. Their father had drowned, after all. Tess and Birdie watched the show for one reason and one reason only. They wanted to study Mr. Nelson's wiener in his form-fitting scuba outfit. Maybe getting a gander at it would give them a clue as to why their mother wanted one so damn bad. How much did it look like an Oscar Mayer one? They'd heard from the boys at school that it could grow. Was it like one of those sponge toys you could get at the Five & Dime? The kind you put in a bowl of water overnight that tripled in size by the next day?

Since it was a sin to be sexually curious, the girls would run up to Blessed Children of God church to confess after every episode. Father John, who'd begun to recognize the sisters' voices after their many visits, was uncomfortable hearing the *Sea Hunt* sin because he also found Mr. Nelson unusually attractive. Perhaps that's why his most-recent reminder that not only *looking* at Mr. Nelson's manhood was a sin, just *thinking* about *looking* at it was so fervent. "Final warning," he said from behind the confessional screen. "Banish these impure thoughts immediately or you'll burn in Hell for all eternity!"

After he assigned their penance, Tess whispered to Birdie in between Hail Marys in the church pew, "I can't take sayin' the rosary so much. My knees are getting creaky, and I don't want to burn forever. We better stop thinking about Mike's, ya know, like Father said."

Birdie agreed at the time, but the more she tried not to, the more she thought about Mr. Nelson and his wet-suited wiener. She *had* to come up with something else to block the damning thoughts out of her mind, which is when the counting started.

Sea Hunt was on Channel 4 at 4 p.m. every Thursday, the fourth day of the week.

Nowadays, without her medication, Birdie needs to return to her apartment four times to make sure the iron is turned off and touch her clock four times before she can get in or out of bed and scrub her hands four times before and after she touches food and all important things must be said four times, 'cause besides her eating problems and delusions and other emotional maladies, she's lugging around a wicked case of obsessive-compulsive disorder. Not the kind folks tell you they have in order to sound more interesting. Birdie's condition is—as Father John had righteously prophesied—hellish.

Tess shakes off the flashback and the thoughts of her troubled sister, picks up her husband's pillow, and brings it to her nose. Tabu. He *has* to be "doin' it" with Connie, she thinks, there is no other explanation. Will's sex drive is so unusually high that she doesn't believe he's capable of not making love for this length of time without spontaneously combusting.

She nabs the portable phone off the bedside table and punches in the diner's number unsure if she wants to profess her undying love or ask him for a divorce.

"Count Your Blessings," Will answers. "Be right with you." His father had taught him that putting customers on hold was bad business in a small town, so as she waits, Tess can hear him tapping the register keys, wait staff shouting orders to the guys in the kitchen, kids playing the pinball machines in the game room, Duane Eddy wailing on the jukebox, and her husband telling a customer, "Please come again."

"Why, Will Blessing, what a wonderful suggestion!" says sexpot Babs Hoover. She must've finished her do-gooder shift at St. Mary's City Hospital and rushed right back to town in time to lunch with her friends who would lavish praise upon her once again for her humanitarian efforts.

When Will laughs at Bab's dumb joke, Tess thinks that maybe she's not kidding. It might not be Connie he's sleeping with. Maybe Babs has gotten her claws into him.

"Sorry about the wait," her hubby says when he picks up the phone. "How can I help you?"

"I've got cancer."

Will's gasp is loud and quick. *Finally*, Tess thinks with a small smile of satisfaction on the other end of the line. He'd been so sure this tumor talk had been nothing more than one of her erroneous assumptions, one of her Chicken Little moments.

He stutters out, "Are you sure?"

"Yeah."

"Okay . . . I'll . . . I'll come home and we can . . . ah . . . would a BLT hit your spot, or maybe . . . ?"

Before he can ask her if she'd rather have a Blessing burger, a disappointed-yet-again Tess hangs up and dials the number on the card that Jill the nurse had given her.

A woman with a stuffy nose answers on the second ring, "Dr. Robert Whaley's office."

"Hi, this is Theresa. . . ." Not everybody in Ruby Falls knows her, but many do. Is this woman required to keep these things to herself the way a doctor is supposed to? She's not sure, so she gives the receptionist her maiden name. "I'd like to make an appointment for a consultation."

The woman sniffles as she flips through an appointment book. "How about this Wednesday at eleven forty-five?"

Tess quickly confirms when she hears the ring of the jingle bells that hang on the backdoor of the house. She'd used them when she potty trained Garbo and had never taken them down because it made the family's comings and goings seem jollier. It had to be Henry back from another grueling day of harassing Ruby Falls High faculty.

She hurries downstairs to find him already sprawled in front of the computer in the den concentrating on Internet

Poker—Ubet. She says, "Hey," and places her hand on his long back—the one he inherited from her uncle. He still let her rub it when he was in the mood. God, she adored every inch of this boy. The way he flaunted authority might be a red flag to another mother, but not to anxiety-ridden Tess who greatly admires his indomitable spirit. She used to be so much like him when she was a kid. She tip-toes her fingers through his curls. "How was school?"

He leans away from her hand. "Do we have any chips and dip?"

She'd normally take the brush-off in her stride, but it's been a bad day and his rejection lands hard on top of the messy stack already piled up in her heart. She's this close to yelling at him, *You better let me run my fingers through your hair before they're buried along with the rest of me!*

Her mother goads her on. *Smack him one. Let the ungrateful little snot know who's boss.*

Tess has never and would never hit her children. Better to take her frustration out on Will. She calls out to him, "We're in the den," when she hears the bells jingle again.

"Hey, guys!" Her husband sets an order of fries down next to their little card sharp and waves a glassy-looking diner bag her way. "Grilled cheese and tomato?" When she shakes her head, Henry snatches the bag out of his dad's hand and returns to his royal flush.

They can't talk about the cancer in front of him, so Tess heads back upstairs, collapses onto her side of the bed, and waits for Will, who turns up a few minutes later to sit beside her. He massages his temples.

See what a headache you are? Louise gloats.

"Are you sure it's ah . . . ?" Will asks again.

"I have an appointment with Rob Whaley on Thursday to discuss the surgery."

"Great! Rob's a good guy. Wonderful family. Steady customer." When Tess doesn't respond, he asks, the way you do when you offer to help someone and hope like heck that they don't take you up on the offer, "So, ah, do you need me to drive you to his office?"

The appointment is right before the diner staff switches from breakfast to lunch, always a hectic time. "It's scheduled right around the turn," Tess says.

"No problem. I'm sure Connie would be happy to fill in."

Oh, I just bet she would, Louise says with a raunchy laugh.

"You're supposed to work lunch on Friday. Do you think you'll be up to it?" Will asks. "I could ask Sandy to cover for you."

"Don't," Tess bosses the boss. "Friday is Richie day."

Will smiles, places his hand atop of hers, pats it, and says, "Egbok. You'll see."

He'd offered her food . . . a ride . . . a corny platitude. He's exhausted his repertoire.

When he stands and jiggles the ring of keys he keeps in his pocket, Tess is struck by how defined his biceps have become. And what happened to his pudgy belly? Maybe that's what he's been doing on Wednesday nights! He's not bedding Connie, he's pumping iron at Russell's Gym! One of the women trainers must have long blond hair and wears Tabu!

Your fancy head shrinker ever mention a little concept called denial?

"Wish I could stay longer, but I've got a meeting with a new supplier in ten minutes back at the diner. Gonna be up when I get home tonight?" Will asks as he steps toward the bedroom door.

She takes a chance, and replies flirtatiously, "That depends."

"Well, don't force yourself to stay awake for me. You need your rest!" he says as he hustles out of the room.

Tess is picturing him now lying at the bottom of the staircase where he landed splay-legged after missing the top step in his dash to get away from her.

(Sad and mad can be as hard to separate as Siamese twins, can't they.)

She has just about had her fill of the male gender for one day, so she reaches for the phone to call Haddie for the third time today. Maybe her daughter wasn't ignoring her calls, she could be studying in the library, or out on a date. There was a boy in the picture now. An artist psychically named Drew.

When her call is routed to voice mail, Tess becomes so desperate to speak to a woman she loves that she lies back, closes her eyes, and makes one of her pretend calls. Post-traumatic stress disorder is horrible, but it isn't *all* bad. Thanks to her hyperactive imagination she can virtually hear her sister speaking back to her in her baby-talking way.

Birdie: Hello?

Tess: (Bursting into tears) I've got cancer and I need your help with Haddie and . . . and Will doesn't love me anymore and Henry is being such a little jerk and . . . Louise is saying hateful things in my head and I'm gonna die and I don't believe in God so I'm gonna go to Hell.

Birdie: (Bubbly) Guess who just visited Birdie?

You Catch My Drift?

Waiting tables at Count Your Blessings is the perfect job for my Tess. She gets a kick out of the staff, fills her customers' hungry bellies, amuses all with her scintillating brand of humor, and when the shift ends, everyone returns to their respective lives, no one the wiser.

For patrons around her age, the diner is a tonic for the ills of modern life. The younger set appreciates the place the same way they do the history museum. The jukebox holds forty-fives like Chubby Checker's *The Twist* and the Everly Brothers *Wake Up Little Susie*. Above the soda fountain and running the length of the walls are eight-by-ten glossy pictures of '50s movies like *The Blob* and *From Here to Eternity* that Will was given by his friend, Stan Majerus, who owns the Rivoli Movie House next door.

No matter how much Tess wishes it weren't true, she knows that their customers would be yanked straight out of those happy days if they knew that a malignant growth was flourishing inside the middle-aged, ponytailed waitress dressed in the old-fashioned white uniform with the wide black belt. She certainly is when she waits on cancer-patient Marilyn "Mare" Hanson, who used to run a little plump, but now reminds Tess of the No. 2 pencil she'll use to jot down her order. Mare also used to be quite obnoxious, but the illness knocked the snot right outta her.

(The folks that are attracted to Tess that I mentioned earlier on? I forgot to point out that a lot of them are also physically ill. She lures them like Lourdes.)

On this particular afternoon Mare, a regular, is seated at table four. She's staring out the front window of the diner with a wistful smile watching the Winter Festival visitors bustle by. The event is one of Ruby Falls' most appealing. (Doesn't take much to entertain folks who've been cooped up and staring at four walls most of the winter.) The snowman-building contest, bed races held on the river, and ice sculptures that line the sidewalks in front of shops offering sales are a big draw, and since Count Your Blessings is iconic, it'd been slammed as well.

Mare's chapped hands are cupped and lying on the red Formica table like she's waiting for something to be dropped into them. *Hope*, Tess thinks. When she delivered Will's shirts to Melton's Dry Cleaners on Tuesday, Jan told her that employee, Mare, didn't seem to be bouncing back the way she did the other times she went through chemo. "She's got three kids," Jan choked out before she slipped through the curtain into the backroom.

Tess approaches the table and says, "Hey, Mare, what can I get you today?" She is aware that it's a ridiculous question to ask in a myriad of ways. She'll order the same thing she always does, but so much of her life now is in the hands of others that my friend feels compelled to allow her choices.

"The usual?" Mare asks. "When you get the chance?

No hurry."

Tess says, "Comin' right up," plucks a straw out of her apron, and sets it down next to one of her customer's beseeching hands.

On her way into the kitchen to prepare the double-thick chocolate malt that will hopefully add more meat to Mare's bones, Tess slips on a spill and grabs onto the hairless arm of Otto von Schmidt to save herself from a nasty fall.

The dishwasher's reaction to her grab is to yell, "Whoa, Nelly!" way, way too loudly because he's wearing sound-reducing headphones. Otto, who uses Nair on his hands and arms because he thinks it makes them faster in water, is wiry and of medium height. Seems silly to describe his hair as dishwater blond, but it is, and it stands on end like he was struck by lightning on the way to work, so he always comes off quite energetic. He fixes his one hazel eye on Tess—his other is made of glass, the result of a pencil incident that occurred when he was a child that no one has ever gotten to the bottom of—and says, "Steady there, Bess."

She gave up correcting him years ago.

Despite it being the toughest position in the diner to keep filled, Will might have fired him by now if Tess hadn't pled his case. Her husband likes things to run smoothly and Otto von Schmidt is a mile of bad road, emotionally speaking. When he isn't wearing his usual heavy duty headgear, a shower cap covered in aluminum foil is set atop his head in order to block satellite communications from the CIA and the dreaded Planet Argon. And if you should strike up a conversation with him be prepared to set aside some time. Otto will go on and on, repeating every once in a while, "You catch my drift?"

Tess's heart goes out to the fragile and paranoid dishwasher because he reminds her at times of Birdie, but even she had to admit that he'd gone too far when he began "investigating" one of the young women who worked in the vintage clothing store across the street from the diner. Otto bought high-powered binoculars and kept track of the girl's every move in a black composition notebook. When just watching her wasn't enough, he purchased a device called The Ear so he could listen in on her private conversations. He also wrote a stack of letters that he hand delivered to the owner of What's Old Is New Again that went something like this:

Deer Missus of Old Close Store. sailsgirl
Debbie is hot to trot. give me her number
pronto!!!!!!!!!!!
xxx OOOtto xoxo

The mash notes stopped shortly after the owner of the store complained to Will, who had a serious discussion with his employee about appropriate behavior. Since Otto always took "The Big Boss Man's" words to heart, he forgot about the local girl and went international. He ordered himself a Russian mail-order bride. He keeps a picture of the beautiful Elena above his workspace. The edges of the photo are curling from the steam, and it's been kissed so many times that it's become worn in the mouth area. His wife from Minsk doesn't speak or understand much English, so when Otto says, "Did you hear that? That growling?" she nods and asks, "You vant I blow on your job?" and seems as happy with her big strong American as he is with her.

Tess tells Otto, "Thanks for the hand," wipes off the bottom of her shoe with a bar towel, and fetches the milk for Mare's malted out of the drinks cooler.

Connie Bushman leans into the kitchen to let Tess know, "Go ahead and double that malted order. Holly and Richie just rolled in . . . I mean. . . ."

Throughout the shift, my friend has been studying the hostess. Did Connie check to see if Will was watching when she bent over to give crayons and a coloring page to the little girl at the soda fountain? Was she showing him her cushy bottom or what a great mom she'll be once Tess steps out of the family picture? She picked a thread off of Will's shirt—a meaningless gesture of coworkers or the casual touch of intimates?

I pick door number two, her mother says.

Tess shouts back to the hostess, "Got it. *Muchas gracias.*"

Juan Castillo, who is hunkered over the deep fryer, had been teaching her some kitchen Spanish, so he turns toward her with a smile.

Tess thinks it's funny that the head cook at a '50s diner in a small Wisconsin town that serves the most American of American food is a man from down Mexico way. She's *muy* fond of Juan. He can sling hash with the best of them, and even better, he cracks her up. Unlike the two revolving cousins that he brings in as line cooks, Juan's

English is pretty good, but not perfect. The one and only time he was late for his shift, he rushed into the diner apologizing for having a flat on the highway. "And when I open trunk of car there es no asparagus tire!"

There's a team of four servers this afternoon. Tess, two other women—Jeannie and Val—and a guy by the name of Cal Fullerton. Cal is in his early thirties, but flirts with every woman no matter her age. What a favorite he is amongst the mature ladies. Courtesy of the GI bill, he's attending film school at the University of Wisconsin-Milwaukee, the same school that the Professor teaches at, and Tessie had attended in her younger years. Cal wants to direct motion pictures someday.

He reaches for a glass on the shelf above Tess's head and says, "Hey, did you and Henry have a chance to catch Scorsese's remake of *Cape Fear* yet?"

"Yup." Cal and her son are friends. Their shared passion for films bridged the age gap. The two of them love quoting dialogue to one another, each trying to top the other.

"Wasn't it incredible?" he says as he scoops ice out of the machine. "The camera angles were so inventive."

"Yeah, and the lighting was really something too," movie-buff Tess replies. She would usually expound because she enjoys this kind of discussion, but she's got an order to get out to Mare, and another to her favorite customer, Richie. God only knows how much time he has left she thinks as she pours the creamy goodness out of the stainless steel malt cups into three mugs and scoots out of the kitchen.

She drops one of the malts on her tray to Mare

Hanson, who is too appreciative, and then turns toward the table that she sets a RESERVED sign on every Friday because it's closest to the door and can accommodate his elaborate wheelchair that his children have decorated like a Rose Bowl float.

Richie Mattigan has Lou Gehrig's disease. A powerful man nine months ago, the father of two was a lawyer for the downtrodden, active in the town, and taught Sunday School classes at St. Lucy's, but these days, saliva slips down his chin and his speech is so foreign-sounding that his wife, Holly, must act as both his nursemaid and interpreter. Before the ALS hit, Richie could knock back a Blessing burger in two bites, but he lost the ability to chew and swallow solids within the last month.

Whenever Tess sets his chocolate malt down in front of him on Fridays, she always makes sure to have a bit of comedy ready, the same way she did before he got sick. He has a great sense of humor and one of those soulful belly laughs that the disease has yet to claim. She keeps the jokes simple these days.

"Hey, Richie, did you hear about the new organization Mothers Against Dyslexia?"

He shakes his head. Can't help it.

"It's called DAM."

The punch line takes more than a few beats to work its way to his diminishing brain, but when it arrives, he brays so forcefully that some of the malt comes shooting out of his nose. His wife reaches over and mops him up, which she'll do for the duration of their visit. Holly never orders food when she's in with her ailing husband because, as she told Tess one day behind her hand, "Eating in front of him seems like rubbing it in."

As much as Tess adores the Mattigan family, the hopelessness and unfairness of Richie's condition always takes a toll on her, so after a few more convivial words she tells them, "Be back to check on you in a little bit," and hurries off to make a pit stop.

The "Dolls" restroom had won an award from the Mayor's Beautification Committee thanks to arty Tess. She had papered the walls in *Look* magazine covers and other '50s paraphernalia she and Will had found at swap meets when they were still doing fun things together. The porcelain racks hold embroidered hand towels and a fifties' bureau is topped with colored perfume bottles with old-fashioned atomizers. She reaches for the blue Evening in Paris bottle and sprays a little behind her ears even though it was her mother's favorite before she switched to Chanel No. 5. Tess was, still is, and will be until the day she dies, a hopeless romantic. She'd dreamt of spending her honeymoon in the City of Lights, but her agoraphobia and inability to fly had made that an impossible.

Will was the one who came up with the idea of celebrating their vows in a more attainable Paris. They drove the red Triumph to Paris, Illinois where he'd booked the wedding suite at the Holiday Inn on the River. He ordered room service—the deluxe chicken dinner—and the lovebirds pretended they were dining on escargot and the packaged dinner rolls were croissants fresh from the oven. The murky water outside their motel window was the Seine. They danced the tango she'd taught him at the Arthur Murray Dance Studio on its banks. When they returned to the room, the newlyweds fed each other slices of cherry pie à la mode with their fingers and they rechristened Will's penis, the way young lovers are apt to. *Mr. Business* would henceforth be known as *Monsieur Pierre.*

Tess splashes cool water on her face, runs a comb through her shaggy bangs, retightens her ponytail, and returns to the kitchen to find curvy Connie leaning against one of the prep tables taking a breather from the lunch rush. She's helped herself to a glass of the pause that semi-refreshes.

"How *are* you?" the hostess with the mostest asks sweetly as she slips a straw into the Diet Coke.

Tess wonders, Does she sound solicitous? Did Will tell her that she had cancer? Is she feeling sorry for her? She gives Connie one of her stock answers, "Hangin' in there. You?"

The buxom blond closes her baby blues and sighs like she's on cloud nine. "Couldn't be better."

Tess knows there's only one feeling that could elicit that sort of response. Connie is in love. She is dying to know with who, but there's that famous saying, "Don't ask a question if you don't want to know the answer." It'd be awful if she's tired of hiding the affair with Will and comes clean right here, right now. On the other hand, she could say that she's seeing Neil the cop again.

Tess grips the edge of the silver prep table and says, "Do tell."

Connie replies with a minx grin, "Oh, I wish I could, but. . . ." She even shrugs cute. "Don't want to jinx it." She wraps her luscious lips around the straw. "You have another table, by the way. Hoover and her book club are at the six top."

Tess isn't in any mood to listen to Babs and the five other Book Babes heatedly discuss another Jackie Collins novel. She usually insists on being treated like any other member of the staff when she's waitressing, but occasionally she pulls rank and this is one of those occasions. Screw Connie and her damn table assignments. She turns her back on the woman who might be feeling so dreamy about her husband and says bossy, "Val can take them."

But seconds after Will's right-hand gal heads back to the dining room to resume her duties looking bewildered by Tess's sudden change of voice, my friend feels stupid and ashamed of herself. This could all be in her head. The affair . . . everything. Connie might not be messing around with Will at all. She didn't even admit to being in love. She might not want to jinx just about anything.

Tess knows that she needs to make amends, to tell her that she'll happily take Babs and her Book Babes after all, but as she heads toward the dining room determined to smooth things over, Otto, the man who makes it his business to keep track not only of the CIA and the inhabitants of Planet Argon, but everyone on the staff, stops her in her tracks when he begins to loudly singsong from the sink, "Connie's got a boyfriend . . . Connie's got a boyfriend."

Please Allow Me to Introduce Myself

The doctors affiliated with St. Mary's North have offices growing out of the back of the hospital like a hump. Tess's gynecologist/obstetrician is on the first floor, and their long-time family doctor, Scott Johannson, is one story up. Surgeon Rob Whaley is in Room #318.

Tess is on high alert as she comes through the doors that morning. This is dangerous territory. She treads softly, her ears pricked forward, her nose twitching. The hospital smells different than when she was here for her mammogram. What is that?

Embalming fluid. That welcoming broad hasn't moved since the last time you were here, always quick to criticize Louise snips.

When Tess skirts past the information desk because she's running late, the volunteer greeter gives her the evil eye, like she's trying to put her out of a job. (Even though Tess loathes agreeing with her dead mother, she has to concur. Poor Vivian *does* look slightly deceased.)

My friend squeezes her lucky black purse to her side. She needs the talismans inside—the children's blanket swatches, her treasured *Mockingbird* book, and her daddy's Swiss Army knife—to give her enough strength to try and pry herself out from between the rock and the hard place she finds herself wedged into. Her severe claustrophobia prevents her from taking the elevator to Rob Whaley's office, but she's so nervous about the appointment that her legs feel like Slinkies, which are designed to go down steps, not up.

You coward.

When the elevator door slides open, Tess checks her watch and takes a few tentative steps. There are times she can force herself into what she calls, "A steel coffin," but only if certain requirements are met. It's got to be roomy. The ones in parking garages, for instance, are out of the question. Mirrors are important because seeing her reflection makes her feel more real. The mirrored elevator she's considering stepping into is generous in size, so those criteria are met, but an unfortunate green-and-yellow paisley-patterned carpet reminds her of her gambling stepfather's "lucky" shirt.

When she backs up and turns to head for the STAIRS sign, I materialize just out of her line of vision, take a step forward, say, "Good morning!" and accidentally on purpose herd her inside the elevator before she knows what's hit her.

She lunges at the OPEN button on the panel, but I've made sure it won't respond, so her fight-or-flight response kicks into high gear. She's trapped, so running away is out. She balls her fists, like she's preparing to punch me in the breadbasket, which she might, if she wasn't plastered against the side of the elevator. She's terrified that she'll get stuck with the woman she just now recognizes from her recent visit to St. Mary's City Hospital. Could I be pulling an Otto? Stalking her? Another panicked line of thinking involves me being one of the ailing people who tend to latch onto her. She sneakily checks me for any obvious symptoms. When she finds none, she begins to wonder if the illness is mental, or maybe I'm fine in body and soul, but I hate white people and here she is confined in this steel coffin with an angry black woman who is about to bring up slavery or what if. . . .

I try to shove the needle off the panicking, obsessing groove in her brain by saying, "How nice to see you again," in my most soothing voice. Up to now, we've been waves crashing on the same beach. Time to formally introduce ourselves. I don't bother offering my hand on account of her germaphobia. "By the way, I'm Grace," and she has no choice but to feebly respond, "Theresa," because she's polite, but also doesn't want to irritate unpredictable me.

Now that we're on a first-name basis, I need to put her mind further at ease, which can be a challenge once she gets balled up like this. Music often soothes her savage breast. Especially the blues. (Misery really does love company.) I'm sorely tempted to take her in my arms and sing our song—*At Last*—but it's much too soon in our journey for that. I'd only scare her worse than she already is. I'll offer assistance instead.

When the elevator comes to a stuttering stop on floor three, I tell Tess as she barges out the doors, "You're lookin' a bit peaked, mind if I come along with ya?"

She's wishing I'd take a long walk off a short pier, but she says, "Suit yourself." I don't appear to be some sort of maniac or a member of the Black Panthers, after all. And she *is* feeling wobbly. A healthcare provider could come in handy. (She's decided that's what I am because I showed her the way to St. Mary's City Women's Center, sat too close to her in the waiting room, waved at her during the biopsy, and gave her advice about holding onto hope in the locker room.)

To confirm her suspicions, she tries to get a gander at what I'm wearing beneath my hounds tooth coat. She's looking for a white uniform, but today I'm wearing a royal-blue dress with half-dollar-sized red buttons running down the front, one of my favorites.

"You're a nurse, right?" she says as we walk.

I smile and say, "When necessary."

Like everyone else in the surrounding counties, she'd recently found a sleek pamphlet in her mailbox from the PR firm the hospital had hired to spread the word that the hospital is now—"Passionate about Patient Care," so she decides that I must be an RN most of the time, but on some days, like today, the muckety-mucks at St. Mary's gave me another job as an emissary at-large. A black nurse with a gregarious personality liberally doling out customer service to white folks would do wonders for the hospital's image.

Tess pauses for a moment in front of the fake potted plants set below the office numbers painted on the third-floor hallway wall. She doesn't recall doing so, but she figures that she must've mumbled out the room number, because I tell her, "Dr. Whaley's office is right down here."

Engaging with me is further depleting the strength she needs to focus on fighting back the fear, so she gives me one of her Brownie smiles and says, "I can find it. I'm sure you've got better things to do."

I say, "Actually . . . ," and show her *my* ivories, which stand out quite nicely against my ebony skin. (Tess is reminded of the Girl Scout merit badge she earned for piano playing.) "Bein' here for you *is* my job."

Wishing that this public-relations person could take a hint, she thanks me, and attempts to put some physical distance between us. She begins jogging past the identical office doors toward the end of the hall, but I keep right up, and the both of us arrive at Room #318 breathless.

As a reward for my perseverance, a quality that she greatly admires, she says to me, "I noticed that you have an accent. Where are you from?"

Oh, my.

"A small town in Alabama," I tell her.

She pats her black purse where the book is nestled amongst her other good-luck charms. "My favorite story, *To Kill a Mockingbird*, is set in a small town in Alabama."

"You don't say."

She cocks her head, studies my deep-brown eyes, slim body, and natty hair. "I knew you looked familiar, but I couldn't put my finger on it! Has anybody ever told you how much you look like Estelle Evans?"

"Who?" I say straight-faced.

"She's the actress who played the housekeeper and mother figure to Jem and Scout in the movie version of *Mockingbird*. Calpurnia?"

Neither one of us is sure that she's ready to figure out that other than dressing more modern that I don't just look like Calpurnia, I'm an *exact* replica of her favorite character in her favorite movie of all time, so instead of answering the question, I distract her by tilting my head toward the office door and saying, "I like Rob Whaley, don't you? Nice back bumper."

Tess, who's thought the same thing many times as he'd rise from one of the diner's booths, goes all proper on me. She says like she'd never stoop so low as to notice a man's behind, "Well, nice to see you again. Have a nice day," and pushes open the doctor's office door.

The curiosity and confusion she's feeling about me fades the moment she lays eyes on the deserted office with minimal decor. Just a few wooden chairs, a magazine table, and a coat rack. The closed window to the receptionist area is begging for a spritz of Windex.

Is that a tumbleweed in the corner? her mother says with a wicked snort.

Tess isn't acquainted with many physicians, other than head shrinkers, but she'd been told by medical transcriptionist Birdie that surgeons are at the top of the heap. Searching her brain for any reason to flee, she tells herself only a sawbones who has been brought up on malpractice charges many times would have zero patients waiting to see him in such a bare-bones office. Why, it'd be irresponsible to allow Rob Whaley to cut her open! She'll get the name of another more-successful surgeon from Mare Hanson. She mentioned once that her husband worked in the medical field, or maybe Jill could refer her to someone more qualified that she didn't have a crush on.

Tess is about to take her leave when the smudged reception window slides open and a woman around her age, give or take, says nasally, "Theresa Finley?"

She's unsure now how to proceed. The office is making her very uneasy, but as long as she's here, maybe she should just listen to what Rob Whaley has to say? She doesn't want to offend him. After all, he's a pillar of the community. A regular at the diner to boot.

"Please call me Tess," she says as she steps toward the window.

The woman with the permanent-waved chestnut hair has red half-moon reading glasses perched low on her nose and a name tag pinned to the chest of her smock identifies her as Patience. As a rule, the more scared my friend is, the quicker she is to resort to witty repartee, so she's about to crack to the receptionist, *What if everybody had jobs based on their names? There'd be gas station owners named Ethyl and barbers named Harry and. . . .*

"Patience," Tess says. "Great name! What if everybody—?"

"Save it. I've been working in this office for sixteen years. Heard 'em all. Insurance?" Patience inspects the card Tess hands her with a quizzical look. "It says here that your last name is Blessing. Didn't you tell me it was Finley when you made the appointment?"

She can't tell Patience that she's incognito—that sounds too paranoid. Tess castigates herself for her slipup, and then says with a self-conscious laugh, "Finley is my maiden name. Sorry. Menopause. Having a hard time focusing lately."

Patience points to a little desk fan. "I hear ya. Between the hot flashes, the mental fogginess, and the allergy meds, I feel like I'm stroking out most of the time."

After the receptionist spends time pouring over her computer, she escorts Tess to an exam room. She is much taller than she looked sitting behind the desk, close to six feet. "Undress from the waist up," she says, and then in a more intimate voice, adds on, "How are you feeling about all this?"

Like a minnow flailing at the base of a lighthouse. Wishing this woman would take her leave, Tess heels off her shoes and answers, "All what?"

Patience takes a step closer and sets a warm hand on Tess's arm. "The *cancer*?"

She had been so careful! How did Patience find out? (If the cloud of anxiety hadn't kept her from thinking clearly, she would have realized that the sister hospitals share medical files.) Tess shouts, "I . . . I have to keep it a secret!"

Patience isn't thrown by her vehemence. She's a professional and used to all sorts of wild reactions from patients. "Keeping your cancer a secret is not a good idea," she says. "You're gonna need support from your friends and family, and other women who have been diagnosed. We have a wonderful group called The Pink Ladies that meets at the hospital twice a week to share what they're going through. I'll arrange for you to join after your surgery."

The idea of broadcasting her innermost feelings to complete strangers is repulsive to Tess. Even if she was prone to "sharing," she couldn't take the chance that one of The Pink Ladies hailed from Ruby Falls. Someone might recognize her and turn into the town crier, or organize a *Spirit Raiser* like the one that'd been held at St. Lucy's for Richie Mattigan. Award-winning photographer, Haddie, would be recruited to provide heart-plucking

Blessing family photos that'd be hung on the gym wall behind the cookie and punch table. Henry might be asked to organize a basketball tournament between fathers and sons.

"Don't you *dare* tell anyone!" Tess says enraged. "I'll sue you!"

Patience takes a step back, says huffy, "Well, exc*uuu*se me," and slams the exam room door behind her.

Tess immediately regrets getting in her face. She'll apologize profusely, or better yet, make her laugh on her way out the door. She looks over at the file that Patience had tossed on the nearby counter. Something had slipped out. A pamphlet:

The Pink Ladies

There Is Hope

Hope is for chumps.

After Tess changes, she sits on the edge of the exam table, and plucks the floppy copy of *To Kill a Mockingbird* out of her lucky purse to help her calm down. She's in the middle of Chapter 28, the climax. Although she has read it countless times, she's always pulled in like it's the first. Scout and Jem are returning home after the Maycomb Halloween pageant at the high school. A storm's coming and it's grown darker than the children expected it to be on the walk back home. Scout's wearing her chicken-wire ham costume and "*Bam . . . bam . . . bam!*"

Tess jumps, half-expecting drunken Bob Ewell to come slobbering through the exam room door, but in struts the guy with the handsome face and nice back fender. He's not her type, she doesn't like a man to be prettier than she is, and with his tousled sandy hair, green eyes, and lofty cheekbones, Dr. Whaley most definitely is. "Nice to see you, as always," he says warmly.

"Wish I could say the same, Rob."

He peruses her chart with a confident grin and sets it aside. "What say we get a look at what we're dealing with?"

There is a lying of hands upon her right breast, followed by a through kneading. It's occurring to Tess that it might've been better to see a doctor she didn't know.

"There it is." He pulls away, makes a note, and comes back to explore further. "Haddie still enjoying school?"

"Yup." Tess often wonders if people suspect that her girl has a problem, or whether they admire her commitment to fitness when they see her tearing around town at the crack of dawn. "Mandy?"

"Struggling with calculus." His manipulation has caused her right nipple to turn into a Parcheesi piece. "Let's talk about lumpectomy versus mastectomy."

"I've decided to go with a lumpectomy. So could I get a local anesthetic instead of a general?" She'd feel too out of control if they put her under, and very, very afraid.

Rob pretends to consider her question. "A local is feasible, but I'd feel much more comfortable with a general."

Well as long as HE's comfortable, Louise spits out.

"Talk to Patience. Have her schedule you in two weeks," the surgeon says as he prepares to exit the room. "Oh, yeah, and could you tell Will the *rumaki* special last night was beyond perfect?"

She gives him the thumbs up, reassembles herself, and makes her way back to the waiting room. She can see the receptionist's silhouette behind the finger-printed frosted glass, but she doesn't respond to Tess's knock. Recognizing a cold shoulder when she sees one, her mother was a master, she says, "Patience? Can I get a sticker?"

The receptionist forcefully slides the window back and says, "When does the doctor want your surgery scheduled? About two weeks?"

"Yeah. Hey. I'm really sorry for losing it before. It was kind of you to offer to set me up with The Pink Ladies. *Grease* is one of my favorite musicals, by the way, but I'm super-shy in a crowd." Some phobias are more popular and therefore more socially acceptable than others. She says with a put-on quiver in her voice, "I'm . . . I'm terrified of public speaking." (As a performer, that's one of the few fears she doesn't have, but she knows it tops the list of activities that scares the hell out of "normal" people.)

An explanation and apology were all Patience needed because she visibly thaws. "I get it," she says with a resolute nod. "My husband gets a bad case of the trots when he has to speak in front of groups." She passes the appointment card through the window. "If you change your mind about joining the group, the offer still stands."

Tess thanks her again and slips out of the office door and straight into me. For the first time, my sudden appearance doesn't further throw her, and that's a good sign. She barely stiffens when I put my arm through hers.

"Breast cancer, huh."

First the receptionist, and now me. She says ticked-off, "What the ... ?" but then she remembers that I was present during the biopsy, and goes straight to wondering if nurses or ambassadors-at-large or whatever the heck I am, need to respect confidentiality the same way doctors and hopefully, receptionists do.

"Patience is right, ya know," I say as we stroll down the hall. "Cancer is a hard row to hoe alone." Thinking that this must be the hospital's party line and that I'm out to pitch the support group too, she withdraws her arm and quickens her pace down the hall. "Do you have family nearby?"

Tess nods.

"They must be takin' this real hard."

"They don't know. Well, my husband does, but my children. . . ."

(Obviously, I'm already aware of this. I'm just trying to draw her out of her shell.)

"You got anyone else that you could lean on?" I ask. "A close friend?"

She shakes her head.

"Parents?"

"Uh-uh."

"Siblings?"

"I have a sister, but I can't reach her."

"Oh, that's a real shame. Sisters can be a great help under these circumstances." I pause to let that sink in. "Speaking of which, perhaps you'll have lunch with me and mine today."

She says, "Oh, that's really nice, but I can't today," as

she rabbits past the elevator toward the STAIRS sign, but what she's actually thinking is that lunching together is entirely too familiar and completely out of the question. A passion for patient care gone amok. She flings open the stairwell door and begins her rabid flight down the steps. "I've got some important things to do."

As we fly past floor numbers two, then one, and exit into the lobby, I ask, "Like what?"

"Oh . . . you know," she says as she explodes out of the hospital doors. "Stuff."

I catch up to her at the side of the Volvo where she's struggling to insert the key into the sticky old lock. "Allow me," I say as I lift the chain out of her shaking fingers and open it easy peasy. "Maybe you could put your "stuff" off for an hour or so? We're having corn and crab bisque and bread straight out of the oven, and . . . and I already called and asked my sisters to set another place at the table. They can't wait to meet you."

As she slides behind the steering wheel, she whispers, "I love homemade bread and corn and crab bisque is my favorite. And sisters . . . ," she's become misty-eyed, "I adore mine."

"I know that, Tessie," I tell her as I settle into the passenger seat. "I know."

We were careening through the streets of Ruby Falls, almost halfway to our destination, before it occurs to her that she hadn't told me her nickname. Nobody but Birdie calls her Tessie.

Sisterland

There'd been heated discussions during numerous church coffee klatches about what to do with the abandoned convent that sat not far off from St. Lucy's Church and School. They all knew that the point was moot because the ultimate decision on what would happen to the building would be made by those more powerful than the parishioners, but that didn't keep them from arguing. Oddly, Will who loved the past, spearheaded a group that believed the two-story Gothic building should be razed. "It's an eyesore." But the aging students who'd attended school at St. Lucy's in the previous decades were up in arms about leveling the home of the Dominican nuns. "It's an historical site worthy of preserving same as the old mill and the covered bridge!" Tess agrees with that bunch because during Halloween time the parish uses the convent to stage a "Holy Haunted House!" to raise funds to buy books for the school library, new playground equipment, and field trips for the kids. The woods that surround the decrepit building are stocked with local teenagers dressed in ghoulish costumes, skeletons hanging from trees, big ol' dangling spiders, and the like. Artistic Tess contributes Styrofoam gravestones for a pretend cemetery because

Halloween is her second-favorite holiday next to Easter. (Since she spent so much time wandering around Holy Cross Cemetery as a child, she grew up feeling much more comfortable with the dead than the alive.)

"Right this way," I say as we enter the backdoor of the empty convent. I take Tess's puffy parka from her and set it down on the back of a peeling black ladder-back chair after she absentmindedly plugs in the large space heater that warms the bottom floor of the house during the Halloween festivities. Despite my offer to further lighten her load, she won't hand over her lucky purse because the location is unnerving her, even though she's the one who's selected it.

I say, "That's my sister, Hope, that I mentioned to you on the ride over," and point to a sweet-looking, thin-faced woman in a black habit who's stirring a soup pot at an avocado-colored stove. A crown of pink orchids is nestled on top of her wimple. "And that," I nod to a middle-aged roly-poly woman wearing a grass skirt over her black dress who is standing at the entrance of the dining room, "that's Faith."

Tess has a serious case of spheniphobia—the fear of penguins—but she needs the nuns in order to work on her new To-Do List, especially number seven: Have a religious epiphany, so number eight—dying—will be okay with her. But she hasn't figured that out yet, so she hides behind my skirt and says, "Your sisters are sisters? Oh, shit," as she is swept back to her and Birdie's days at Blessed Children of God School.

The Finley girls would've put their mother on the top of their fear chart, but the nuns were number two with a bullet. The women with the excellent posture and rosary beads holstered at their sides reminded Tess and Birdie of a gang of Western-movie bad guys who rode into town tall in the saddle with nothin' else but murder on their minds. And they weren't the only ones who quaked in their boots at the sight of the sisters. *All* the students at the school lived in terror of the mysterious and law-enforcing ladies who were the subject of many a recess conversation.

"I heard they aren't born with boobies and that's how they know that they're s'posed to be nuns," a kid would say during one of their numerous chats on the blacktop. "And they can't have babies either because after they sign up they get hung upside down in the bell tower and their delivering holes are filled in with cement by the Archbishop," the son of a mason would toss in. "Do you think they have hair or not?" *Not*, according to Hughie Fitzpatrick whose father owned the barbershop on 79th Street. Hughie had heard that after the nuns' tresses were shorn, the cuttings were swept up and saved in a special "hair" room located in the basement of the school until enough had been gathered to call in the midget priest from St. Cecilia's, who would spend all night weaving their locks on a spinning wheel into sharp-looking pork pie hats that got sent to pagans in steaming hot Africa as an added incentive to convert to Christianity.

My laugh interrupts her flashback. "Yup, my sisters are sisters. And that's our dog." A fine-boned golden retriever, the spittin' image of Garbo, is lying in the corner of the pretty peach-and-green dining room. A white Frisbee imprinted with purple letters—*St. Lucy's . . . we've got one heck of a Lost and Found Department*—cradled between her legs.

Sister Hope enters from the kitchen and sets an ornate soup tureen down on the pine dining-room table that's been laid out with care. Pink peonies sit in a Depression glass vase. The china pattern is a replica of Tess's, same for the silverware.

"Grace tells us that you have two children," Sister Hope says as she takes her seat.

"A boy and a girl?" chubby Sister Faith asks as she settles across the table with an "oomph."

Proud mama Tess beams. "Henry and Haddie."

I ladle out the soup and place the bowl in front of my friend, who places a pale-pink napkin on her lap, and plunges in. The corn is roasted, and the crab is fresh, like it'd been picked off a beach moments ago. The loaf of potato bread is warm on the inside and crunchy on the outside.

Sister Hope asks Tess, "Do you taste the basil in the soup? We grew it in our garden."

That's Sister Faith's cue to rise abruptly and sweep aside the chintz curtain hanging across the four-pane dining-room window. Outside, no more than twenty feet away, there's an amazingly detailed re-creation of Tess's garden complete with white picket fence. "Can you imagine what this looks like in the summer?" the nun asks her.

"Ha!" I say with a snort.

(She came up with all this, didn't she?)

Tess nods and says, "I love gardens. They're good for the soul, but . . . not always." Before she can even try to stop the flashback, the summer of '60 comes barreling into her brain.

It was the summer you couldn't go anywhere in Milwaukee without somebody saying, "Hot enough for ya?" Even in June, a month that usually took its time to warm up, the Finley sisters perspired so profusely in their duplex bedroom on 66th Street that they had to take turns sucking on ice cubes and blowing on each other's backs to stay cool.

When Tess's little feet hit the ground the morning of June 8, she was fired up. She couldn't change the fact that her daddy was gone, but she'd come up with an idea that she believed would at least help her recapture *some* of what the Indian podiatrist had mentioned. Her "passed life." After seeing *The Time Machine* movie at the Tosa Theatre, Tess wished for two things. That she had hair like Yvette Mimieux's, and that she and Birdie could leave the here and now and travel back in time to the Sunday afternoons that they'd spent with their gammy and boppa who they missed so much after their mother had struck them from the lives.

Normally, eleven-year-old Tess and her sister were inseparable, but the morning that she decided that they didn't need a fancy, futuristic machine transporting them to the past, that a garden would be just the ticket, she had to get the ball rolling on her own because Birdie and Bee had slept over at Doris Franken's house. The kid had an "imaginary friend" too, named Jane Doe, so the girls had that in common. (Doris's father was a police officer.)

Tess jotted down the details of her plan on a piece of scratch paper while she ate a quick bowl of Wheaties.

GARDEN TO DO'S

1. Get permission from Louise and Mr. Lloyd.
2. Borrow a rake and a shovel from neighbors.
3. Buy seeds from the Five & Dime.
4. Water and weed every day.

The owner of the property, Mr. Hank Lloyd, lived downstairs from them, but they rarely saw their landlord because he kept his curtains closed tight after his wife of thirty-one years got hit by a car on her way home from the Red Owl food market last year, so Tess wasn't sure how he would feel about her digging up his backyard. Her fingers were crossed as she rinsed out her bowl and went in search for her mother, who she found in the backyard hanging wash.

Louise's auburn hair was pulled atop her head like a cresting wave. She was wearing white Bermuda shorts to show off her shapely, tan legs, and her matching sleeveless blouse clung to her full breasts. Like always, Tess was filled with wonder when she laid eyes upon her gorgeous mother. She guessed that just like people said, you could never judge a book by its cover.

After she told Louise the garden idea, she quickly added on, like she hardly cared one way or another, "Just an idea. No big deal," for she had learned the hard way not to reveal her innermost desires to her mother. If she discovered what was really in Tess's heart, she would figure out a way to use it against her.

"What about tools? Seeds?" Louise asked slyly as she jammed wooden clothespins into the collars of Leon's work shirts. She was attempting to stump her daughter, and in a way she had. Tess was stunned to learn that she knew anything about growing things.

"I'm gonna borrow tools from the neighbors and they got seeds at the Five & Dime. I'll use money from my piggy bank," Tess said with a shrug.

Louise smirked and replied, "No skin offa my nose," and went back to her hanging.

Tess thanked her many times, as was required, and was sure to add on, "Could you please be sure to ask Mr. Lloyd if it'd be all right with him?"

She skipped up to the Five & Dime, planning out the rows in her mind. She selected carrots and radishes because she and her gammy loved them with a little salt. And there'd be daisies, her sister's favorite flower, and climbing morning glories would cover the falling-down fence between the yard and the alley.

When Birdie and Bee returned from their sleepover at Doris's later that morning, the three of them went looking for donations. Mrs. Jackson contributed an old shovel and Mr. Glovarnik from the next block over told Tess she could borrow one of his hoes, but to not leave out in the rain. Mrs. Wily gave her a rusty sprinkling can.

Since Tess spent half of her nights fretting over her "weird" sister or feeling guilty for not trying to save her daddy on the day he drowned, and the other half making hand shadows on the bedroom wall or singing *Favorite Things* because she needed a talent when she entered the Miss America contest, most mornings she got up on the wrong side of the bed. But once she'd sowed those seeds in the backyard? That child was joyful, and in tune with the

Creator again. She'd race to the garden, stroke the carrots' fragile green tops, and imagine them pushing their pointy orange ends down into the dirt. The fast-growing radishes were doing great, and the daisies weren't dawdlers, not like the morning glories that had barely begun to find purchase against the back fence.

When the Assumption rolled around—the important August 15 feast day when Catholics celebrate the Virgin Mary's ascension into Heaven that also just so happens to be the day of the Finley sisters' shared birthday—Tess woke Birdie up with a tickle and a joke, the same way their daddy always had on their special day. She told her, "Be right back with a surprise!" then scrambled out the back door to pick the daisies that she'd planned to set in a jelly jar on their bedroom dresser to celebrate, "Their day."

An exuberant Tess was singing the chorus of her daddy's favorite fishing song, "Merrily, merrily, merrily, merrily, life is but a dream," but as she peeled around the corner of the garage on her way to the garden the song got stuck in her throat. Where the morning glories had been doing their darndest and the daisies had been begging to be picked, a three-inch thick, six-foot square block of cement held three brand new aluminum garbage cans that were so shiny that she could barely make out the tops of the flowers that'd been crushed from the waist down.

Tess let forth a scream that was so bloodcurdling that it even managed to penetrate her mother's self-absorption. Banging out of the backdoor of the house, Louise marched toward her shouting, "Pipe down, for godssakes! You're gonna wake the dead. What's wrong?"

Tess lifted her small, quivering arm and pointed.

The beauty of the garden had been so pure and sincere that the destruction of it dented even someone as hard as Louise. She yelled, "Goddamn it," and even felt a moment of fleeting guilt for not asking the landlord's permission to create the plot the way Tess had asked her to. *Like a peasant asking a king for permission*, she'd told herself. *The hell with that.*

She grabbed Tess by the wrist and stormed to Mr. Lloyd's door.

He answered the irate knocks in shiny black pants, cracked leather bedroom slippers, and a T-shirt splotched with food stains. Grief dressed him now, not his lovely wife.

Yes?" he said like he hadn't used his voice for a while, or like he wasn't exactly sure who they were.

After Louise finished her tirade, Mr. Lloyd slowly reached deep into his pocket and gave her mother something. "I'm sorry," he said. "I . . . I didn't know," and closed the door softly in their faces.

For a moment, Tess thought Louise might cry, but she thrust out her chin and told her, "Let this be a lesson to you. *This* is what's important to people. Open your hand." She dropped into her daughter's palm what Mr. Lloyd had given her to make amends for the demise of a little girl's heaven on Earth. It was a fifty-cent piece.

Tess bolted out of the yard and threw the coin down an alley sewer along with the religious medal she wore around her neck. She didn't return home until dark. She might've never come back if she didn't need to check on Birdie.

"Tessie?" I place my hand on her arm to bring her back to the convent dining table.

"I'm sorry," she says. "Did you say something?"

"That's such a sad, sad story in so many ways," Sister Faith says as she passes the bread their guest's way.

Tess rips another hunk off the loaf that never seems to dwindle. "Yeah. Well. Took me a lot of years before I got up enough courage to try growing something again."

After Sisters Faith and Hope share concerned looks with one another, I slide back my chair and say upbeat, "How 'bout we continue our chitchat in more comfortable surroundings?"

The convent living room has been decorated with a Hawaiian motif because my friend is attempting to work out a coupla things that've been troubling her for a long, long time. It goes back to the volcano picture on the cover of *The Freaks of Nature* that always reminded her of her mother. Tess has nightmares set in Hawaii. Sexy scorpions surfing waves of lava chase her through jungles of smothering orchids. Lepers limp after her through the streets of Molokai, their begging mouths lying in their outstretched hands. Nothing quite so horrifying today, just Don Ho and his ukulele giving it their all on the pointy-legged blond hi-fi. Tiki torches burn in all four corners. Palm-tree shaped pillows are arranged on nearby armchairs. The room smells of warm sand and a large body of water, and a coconut-smelling breeze ruffles Tess's long bangs as we sit side by side on a couch the color of a conch shell.

After Sisters Faith and Hope get cozy in the overstuffed armchairs, I withdraw from the pocket of the parrot muumuu I'm now wearing a small green box that I set atop the driftwood coffee table. "The sisters and I want you to have this, Tessie."

"Really? How nice. You didn't have to," she says. Giving the moment its due, she slowly lifts the top off the gift box, carefully removes the contents, and let's it dangle from her fingers. The medallion is swinging from a lovely gold chain that's a replica of one that Will had given her on her fortieth birthday.

I ask her, "Do you remember?"

Of course, she does.

Her gammy had given her the St. Nicholas medal. "He's the patron saint of children. He'll watch over you and Birdie when I can't," she'd told her as she placed it around her neck. Tess had never taken the medal off until she tossed it into the sewer with the half-dollar on the long-ago morning her faith had been buried. A garbage can its headstone.

When the impact of holding the St. Nick medal fully sinks in, a now-terrified Tess leaps off the couch, and dashes through the dining room straight into the kitchen. She yanks her puffy parka off the ladder-back chair and makes haste for the convent's backdoor.

The sisters and I block her way. "You reap what you sow," I say as I produce a baby carrot out of thin air. "Once you plant the seed, you can't see it growing beneath the dirt, you just have faith that it is, right?" I hold up the medal in my other hand. "You think you could—"

"Cut it out!" she hollers.

I remind her, ever so calmly, "You know in your heart that faith is the Big Kahuna."

Sister Hope grins at vastly overweight Sister Faith, taps an imaginary cigar, and says, like Groucho, "I'll second that motion, little lady."

How Low Can You Go?

Tess is in the midst of a full-blown anxiety attack, one of the worst she's had in a long time. She can't go home until she pulls herself together. She can't let Henry see her like this.

She rips out of the convent lot and takes the scenic route through Ruby Falls. "Calm down . . . calm down. Breathe," she's telling herself as she passes the town park with the white band shell and stone bridge that arches over the river. The playground is empty, the swings pushed by the wind, but the ducks are out in force, chasing after the crackers a mom and a toddler are tossing into the water while the dad snaps pictures. Tessie's family had once done the same every Saturday morning, only Haddie was the one with the camera in her hands.

After my friend makes it through the rest of downtown, she drives west to the wide-open spaces off of County Road C.

What the hell were you doing with those nuns? Louise asks. *Have you finally gone completely insane?*

Tess has already come up with a few rationalizations that could explain the appearance of the sisters and me. She's juggling an enormous amount of stress, something's bound to slip, right? She had seen me around St. Mary's a number of times and I remind her of Calpurnia and that had dredged up some better-off-forgotten childhood memories and she had dissociated from reality. That's all. Yes. She's pretty sure that Dr. Drake would agree with that diagnosis. He'd done a few emergency phone sessions with her in the past when a crisis had arisen. She'd call him the moment she got home.

Dr. Drake: How nice to hear from you.

Tess: You may eat those words in a few minutes.

Dr. Drake: What's going on?

Tess: I've got breast cancer. My daughter is anorexic and bulimic. My son is treating me like I'm something nasty stuck on the bottom of his shoe. My sister won't speak to me. And I think my husband is screwing around.

Dr. Drake: I'm sorry to hear that.

Tess: And I . . . I'm seeing things. A woman.

Dr. Drake: Hmmm . . . are you taking any medications?

Tess: No.

Dr. Drake: Does this woman have a name?

Tess: Grace.

Dr. Drake: Have there been others?

Tess: Just a couple of nuns.

Dr. Drake: (Very long pause) Perhaps a visit to the office is in order. How does tomorrow morning sound? Take the earliest train available.

As she passes by the Neumeyer farm she comes up with

another possible explanation for what she'd experienced. What if she'd driven over to St. Lucy's to talk to Father Joe about achieving the religious epiphany (number seven) on her new To-Do List and then . . . then she'd hit her head on something, grew disoriented, and wandered into the convent? No, she can't convince herself of that. Father Joe is almost senile and doesn't have much to offer in the way of spiritual enlightenment these days, besides, she doesn't even believe in his brand of religion anymore.

There *had* to be another reason she went to the church grounds this afternoon. Ah, yes. She'd spent time yesterday sorting through Haddie's and Henry's outgrown winter jackets, and filled a bag to donate to St. Lucy's Coats for Kids drive. Before she could drop them off, her lack of sleep, and the sound of the windshield wipers whooshing away must've caused her to drift off in the church parking lot and she had a hell of a dream. She checks her rearview mirror to see if the black bag is still in her backseat. She touches it to make sure it's real.

Her brain, unable to allow one stone to be unturned in its blistering quest to keep her safe, has her thinking now that it could also be a simple case of poisoning that had caused her to hallucinate or imagine me, the sisters, and our Hawaii-inspired home. What had she eaten or drunk today? She'd used that McDonald's gift certificate Will had stuck in her Christmas stocking on a hot cocoa. The drive-thru girl *did* look ticked off, and like she wouldn't think twice about poisoning one of her customers to make a point.

Tess pulls up alongside Jackson Marsh and parks. She loves this place. Especially in the fall when the surrounding woods are aflame with color. She and Garbo come to walk the wood-chipped path that circles the pond that's frozen now. Snow-covered reeds are bent at their waists in supplication. Thankfully, the marsh is doing its job to calm and center her. Her breathing is slowing down. Until she spots the lone mallard swimming in a small pool of open water.

"Will," she cries.

Ducks mate for life.

When Tess finally returns home, she finds her husband hunched over the kitchen table, polishing off a triple-decker club sandwich. She hangs up her puffy parka and removes her boots in the mud room, scratches behind Garbo's ears, then reaches into the treat jar above the washer and gives her companion a grand helping of Milk-Bones.

"Where've you been?" Will calls through a mouthful of food. "I was getting worried."

See how he lost his appetite from all that worrying?

"Sorry," Tess tells him with a yawn that would further convince herself of the falling asleep in the car idea versus the poisoning idea she'd considered to explain her break with reality. Especially since she remembered as she turned down Chestnut Street that the McDonald's drive-thru girl was one Haddie had gone to school with, and really, how likely was it that Trisha Wells could get hold of curare in Ruby Falls?

You can get just about anything off the Internet, know-it-all Louise says. *Ask Otto.*

"The consultation took longer than expected," Tess

tells Will when she comes into the kitchen. "Is Henry home?"

He takes another bite of his sandwich and points down to the basement. "What did Rob say?"

"That he loved the *rumaki* last night."

"I meant . . . when did he schedule your surgery?" he asks with a grin that's trying to look less sickly than it is.

Thank the Lord that she's the one who's ill and not him. For Will, a stubbed toe is a major incident; he once insisted on going to the emergency room to have a wart removed. If he was the one about to have an operation. . . . Tess imagines a few nights before the surgery to remove his colon cancer, which would be the worst kind for him to get. (Being a regular fella is quite important to Will.) She would feel his hand shaking her awake. *This cancer is making me parched*, he'd whine. *Can you get me a glass of milk? And a piece of German chocolate cake?*

"Earth to wife," Wills says. He throws in a little static sound. "We need a status update."

Tess digs around in her lucky purse, removes the surgery appointment card, and hands it to him.

"February 13th. That's next week," he says.

This makes Tess feel like he thinks she's too stupid to notice the date that something life-ending will be sloshing her way. "No shit, Sherlock," she says snotty.

Dr. Drake's breathing exercises that she'd attempted to summon forth on the drive home from the convent hadn't worked, so Tess shuts her eyes and tries something else to put a cork in her anger. Visualization. Someplace peaceful. Water works best. She brings to mind the shores of Waikiki . . . no, that only reminds her of me and the sisters and lepers ... ah ... the south of France ... Côte d'Azur ... hold on, that won't work either, that makes Tess recall her honeymoon. Lake Michigan looms, but she vanquishes it straight off because it's bringing up her failure to save her drowning daddy, and number six on her new To-Do List—the disposing of Louise's ashes. The Atlantic Ocean reminds her of Birdie in Boca Raton. There *has* to be a body of water that will calm her to the point that she'll no longer wish to rip Will's face off. Ahhh ... there we go. The river that meanders through Ruby Falls is now wending its way through her cerebral cortex.

Slightly calmer, Tess tells her husband with an apologetic shrug, "Sorry. Tough day. Could you make me a cuppa?"

Always happy to run from a conversation, especially a heated one, Will puts the kettle on and searches the cupboard for one of her special cups. She's watching him from the old pine table. Did he make tea for Connie after today's shift? Does *she* have a special cup? Or maybe it isn't Connie that he's spending Wednesday nights with. Maybe it's pharmacist Margaret Mary Holden. She has long blond hair too, like the ones she finds on Will's shirt, and she always seems a mite too thrilled to fill the family's prescriptions. And it wasn't like Will hadn't been to Boomer's Drugs recently. She found an empty box of Grecian Formula in the bathroom trash basket. She'll try to get a whiff of Margaret Mary the next time she pays a visit to the drug store to see if she wears Tabu.

Will delivers the tea and says, "Do you want to come down later? It's Tuesday." Luau night at the diner had been Tess's idea. "Maybe that would take your mind off things." He glances down at the appointment card.

If she's in the right kind of mood, Tess enjoys watching the customers get silly during the weekly re-creation of the Hawaiian parties that harken back to the fifties. Thing is, she isn't in the right kind of mood. She's feeling abandoned by the man who she wishes would understand that she couldn't receive a death sentence a few hours ago and get a kick out of watching folks dancing the limbo tonight while bystanders shout, "How low can you go?"

She closes her fingers around the appointment card's sharp edges until they bite into her skin because new pain can sometimes erase old pain. "No, thanks," she tells him. "I want to eat with Henry and catch a movie."

She shoves her chair back and opens the basement door behind her. The video game her son is playing—Doom—is booming so she's forced to holler, "What do you want for supper?" This is somewhat of a rhetorical question. She knows it will be either pepperoni pizza or scrambled cheese eggs, and bacon, of course, goes with anything.

Haddie has begun the transition to independence, but Tess is concerned about what will become of Henry when she dies. He's smart and sensitive, but stubborn, qualities that she knows will not become gifts until he learns how to put them to good use. Will spends so many hours at the diner, and when he *is* around, he only seems to connect with his son when they're playing golf, watching a ball game, or tinkering with the Chevy.

Her hubby grabs his keys off the hook above the kitchen desk. "I've gotta stop at the party store. A couple of the grass skirts need to be replaced." He pecks her cheek. "Love you," he says before he closes the backdoor behind him.

Those two little words used to mean something to Tess, but lately they sound like the patter he passes out to the customers. "Thanks for your business. Have a nice day. Love you."

Henry shouts his order up from the basement, "I want p.p." (Pepperoni pizza.)

How will he remember me when I'm gone? Tess wonders. As a devoted mother, or the chunky woman who was only useful when he needed dough?

She slides the pizza into the oven, sets the timer, and steadies herself. The pepperoni reminded her of nipples and she suddenly feels the urge to hunt down the culprit that might end her life, the same way Rob Whaley had.

She mutters to herself, "Why should he have all the fun?" as she steps into the guest bathroom off the kitchen. She lifts her sweatshirt and bra, and explores her right breast with her fingertips until she finds the growth about an inch right of her nipple. Down deep. Like one of those sneaky sea creatures that blends into the bottom of the ocean until they explode through the water to snatch the life away from some unsuspecting crab. She isn't surprised that she didn't find it during one of her monthly shower exams, which she has to admit—since cancer didn't run in the family—she performs with about as much care as she does flossing. She wouldn't have even known there was something wrong if she hadn't had that stupid routine mammogram. Why had she gone looking for trouble? She should've waited until she saw tumors popping out of her chest to make an appointment with her gynecologist, who prides herself on her direct approach to women's healthcare. *Wow, Tess,* Dr. Sheila would say when she ran her hands over her patient's Braille bosom. *I wouldn't buy any magazine subscriptions, if I were you.*

Henry races up the basement stairs, and with a ticked-off tone shouts through the bathroom door, "Haddie's right. You *are* going deaf. Can't you hear the timer goin' off?"

Tess calls, "Be right out."

Henry is waiting for her next to the stove, drumming his fingers on his special plate, the one with the rotund cartoon Italian man dressed in chef's gear. She nudges the pizza out of the oven and cuts him three pieces. "After you're done, how about a movie?" she says. "I heard a lot of good things about this new one at the Oriental Theatre."

"Can't." He grabs a Mountain Dew out of the fridge. "I'm in the middle of a level." He stops half-way down the basement steps and shouts back, "Oh, yeah. Haddie called when you were out today."

Her daughter rarely phoned, and when she did, it was Will she spoke to first and in length. When it was Tess's turn to talk, she was careful to skirt the eating issue because it made her girl feel like she was giving her the third degree instead of caring for her so deeply, so she would barrage her with other questions like, "Are you enjoying your classes? How's Drew? Shoot any great pictures lately?" Haddie would invariably reply, "Ask Dad. Gotta run."

Tess wonders briefly if Patience got too chatty with someone in Ruby Falls, or maybe Rob Whaley told his wife and she let it accidentally slip to their daughter,

Mandy, who called her ex-teammate to sympathize. Why else would Haddie be calling if it wasn't to confront her with the cancer? Could she have been in an accident?

Rushing to the den phone, Tess punches in the oft-used numbers that've begun to look more like hieroglyphs. "I'm sorry I didn't get back to you earlier, honey. Henry just gave me your message. Everything okay?" she says after her daughter picks up.

"No big deal. Just wanted tell you that they have a new therapist at school. Dr. Chandler. She's an eating disorder specialist. I've still got a long way to go, so don't get excited and think that I'm all better, but . . . ," Haddie sounds both proud and scared, "I ate some french fries today, Mom, and they're still in my stomach."

She doesn't trust herself to reply. She can feel the tears coming and Haddie can't stand it when she cries. Any suggestion that her mother is a mere mortal is confusing. So instead of bawling, and showering her daughter with compliments as is her nature, she snorts back her tears and says, "Good job. That's a step in the right direction, honey."

But the moment my Tess replaces the phone back in its cradle?

What a crybaby.

A Few Words on the Brink of Death

During the days leading up to the surgery, Tess acted the same way she usually does. Like she was under surveillance and she was the one doing the surveilling. She traveled from Olsen's Market to the post office and to the Horizons Home, so the old folks could coo and fuss over Garbo the way they do every Wednesday afternoon. She waitressed. Mare Hanson was in with some breaking news. Her bladder cancer was in remission. "Until it comes back," she'd said with a snarl. "I'm sick of all this healthy crap. Get me some fries, a Blessing burger with extra cheddar and fried onions." Tess gave her the order on the house because she was glad that her pissy attitude had returned, no matter how short-lived.

Richie, her ALS customer, stopped in on his regular day as well. For this visit, Tess drummed up an old joke that had been a favorite of her father's. The one about the Lone Ranger and Tonto getting into a fuss with a tribe of war-painted Comanches. Clearly outnumbered, the masked man assures his faithful companion, "Don't give up. We can beat these Injuns," and Tonto looks over at him and says, "What do you mean *we*, kemosabe?" But when Tess stopped by the table to lay the joke on Richie, she saw that he had worsened. So instead of kidding around with him, she set down his malt and rubbed his shoulders, which she wouldn't have if she'd known it would make his wife hide her eyes in her napkin.

She also stepped up the e-mails to her medical transcriptionist sister:

"Dear Birdie,

For sure, I have cancer. You better come. You're going to feel guilty if I die on the operating table. You'll probably develop a phobia about dead sisters or breast cancer that could affect your work and cut into your bottom line. How will you pay your rent? Or buy witch hazel and Q-tips?

Love,

Tessie"

The night before the surgery, Tess raps on Henry's bedroom door.

"Yeah?"

Garbo and I are already sitting together on the edge of his bed on top of a navy-and-white checked bedspread that Tess covers in kisses when it comes out of the dryer. Shoes are littering the floor and laundry is scattered everywhere. He's added a new poster to his wall alongside the cowboy and poker-playing Phils. It's one of Mr. Hefner's Playmates. The glass aquarium that holds the current incarnation of Snakey sits atop the white dresser alongside a boom box playing Phish at an indecent level. Tess wonders if it might be the vibrations of the jam music that are killing the reptiles off, which she could completely understand. With a start, she realizes that she'd been so scared about the impending surgery that she'd forgotten to check on Snakey Nine the last few days. She reminds herself to come back later with her flashlight once Henry's asleep. If the snake is no longer alive, she'll push the creature into the back of the plastic cave and sneak in and remove him in the morning when he's showering. After Will drops her off at the hospital, she'll insist that he head straight to the Pet Palace to buy another so by the time her boy gets home from school tomorrow, all will be right with his world again.

(Other than his mother being dead, of course.)

Henry is stretched out in his bean bag chair doing his homework at the last minute, like always. He thrives on pressure. Believes it helps build "his poker chops."

Tess toes his sneakers into the closet, picks up a pair of dirty socks, and says, "Oh, yeah," like she just remembered. "I'm going into the hospital tomorrow to get something taken care of."

Henry doesn't look up from his copy of *Heart of Darkness*. It's his favorite. "What?"

She thinks he wants her to repeat herself and she starts to, but he cuts her off with, "What do you need to get taken care of?"

He doesn't usually ask for explanations so Tess has to think quick. If by the remote chance she should live, he might get a glimpse of the bandages so thank goodness that *Playboy's* Miss June is holding a sportily situated tennis racket. "I've got something going on in my shoulder. The doctor isn't sure, but she thinks it's a rotator cuff tear."

"Okay." He still hasn't looked up at her. "When will you be back?"

"Probably by the time you get home from school," she says, even though she knows that's a long shot. If the operation doesn't kill her, the doctors could screw up in a myriad of other ways. That's what happened to the husband of Sonya Phillips, the head librarian in town. Her husband of twenty-eight years, Dale, had gone in to have a simple hernia corrected, and an anesthesiologist, or his faulty equipment, had deprived her man's brain of oxygen for five minutes.

Tess sees Sonya sometimes steering her cart through Olsen's vegetable aisle fighting back tears.

At the breakfast table the following morning, surgery morning, Tess can't take her eyes off her son. This might be the last time she ever sees him chew, swipe the curls out of his eyes, or head out the door without a word.

She watches Henry walk down the driveway out of the living room window, finding it hard to believe that he'd refused to go to preschool and she had to bribe him to attend kindergarten. He wanted to stay home with his *Momil* to eat chocolate-chip cookies and watch cartoons. She places her palm on the window and wills him to come back to her, and then she and Garbo make their way to the sunroom. She immerses herself in Haddie's photos, pictures her in her dorm bed, pink and toasty, her hair damp at the neck and curling in front of her ears. She needs to talk to her. To say goodbye.

"Mmm . . . ?" the college girl answers after many rings.

"Hey, baby. I'm sorry if I woke you, I just wanted to—"

"Later," she grumbles before she hangs up.

There's one last farewell to be made before they leave for the hospital. Tess releases Garbo into the backyard, throws her Frisbee, and heaps kisses and praise upon her for what she thinks will probably be the last time. "Take good care of everyone," she tells a woman's best friend after Will sticks his head out the porch door and reminds her that they better shake their tail feathers.

Tess finds it sweet that he'd warmed the car up for the short trip to St. Mary's. "If I die," she says to her husband as he turns onto Lakefield Road, "promise me you'll tell the kids how much I love them and that I'm in Heaven watching over them." That would be some comfort to Haddie, but Henry would probably laugh in scorn, call God an asshole, the same way he had when the Almighty took away his great-grandmother, but it's all she can think of to say.

Will reaches over and pats her hand as he turns onto Port Washington Road. "You're not gonna die."

If she did, he'd get the news via phone. Rob Whaley had told her that after she checked in, they'd begin immediately to prepare her for surgery. Since Will believed Tess would be fine, he didn't see the point in getting down on his knees to pray in the waiting room, and she didn't see the point in asking him. Was he too frightened? Shallow? Or so optimistic that he couldn't grasp a negative outcome? Why can't she be more like him?

After she hops out of the car in the hospital's drop-off zone, Will rolls down the window and says, "Call me when it's over. Love you."

Tess had been looking forward to seeing the usual greeter, Vivian, and is disappointed to find her post being manned by a much-younger woman. Out with the old, in with the new? Seems to be a growing trend. "The check-in area is right around the counter," the new gal says with a perky smile.

Tess signs in, takes a seat in the waiting area, clutches her precious lucky purse to her chest, and tries to quiet her runaway mind by staring at a picture of Jesus leading a flock of furry animals through craggy mountains that's hanging on the wall in front of her. Sheep? Lambs? Is He saving them, or leading them to the Butcher of Nazareth? This could be *her* final hour on Earth, and she'd only fulfilled a few of the items on her new list.

TO-DO LIST

1. ~~Buy broccoli.~~
2. ~~Make sure Haddie gets the help she needs from a better therapist.~~
3. ~~Set up vocational counseling appointment for Henry.~~
4. Convince Will to love me again.
5. Get Birdie to talk to me.
6. Bury Louise once and for all.
7. Have a religious epiphany so #8 is going to be okay with me.
8. Die.

Haddie was in the care of the new eating-disorder doctor at school, and Tess felt okay about crossing out number three because she *had* set up an appointment with Henry's guidance counselor. "There's nothing wrong with being a professional poker player," he told her when he'd refused to go. "You lack imagination, Mom."

"Theresa Blessing?" A big guy in scrubs and a Hitler mustache has barged through a set of double doors to her right. "I'm Jerry, your nurse this morning," he says as he leads her to what looks like a checkpoint with a scale. She steps up and watches him fiddle with the adjusting weights. "A hundred and fifty-four."

Whale. Cow. Sow.

"This way." Jerry takes her into a room with a chair, a bed, and pleated Teflon window curtains. He motions for her to sit and slides a blood-pressure cuff over her left forearm. He smells like Band-Aids and her stepfather, Leon. They still make Brylcreem? When the nurse has gotten the numbers he needs, he steps back and says, "Cancer, eh? My wife completed three rounds of chemo."

Taken off guard, Tess utters, "Oh . . . geeze." What's the right thing to say to something like that? *Sorry? Congratulations?*

He tells her the gowns are in the bathroom, then hands her a plastic package that contains tan slippers with raised V's on the soles.

She undresses with clammy hands. She's light-headed and needs to sit on the toilet to slip off her sweatpants, tennis shoes, and socks. When she emerges from the bathroom, the nurse is gone, but Ginger, the head of the Women's Center and the original bearer of bad news, is sitting on the edge of a black chair with her ankles crossed.

After exchanging good mornings, she passes Tessie a clipboard. "A little more paperwork," she apologizes.

The hospital is wondering what course of action they're to take if they screw up. Tess checks the Do Not Resuscitate box, signs the bottom line, and hands it back to Ginger, who tells her, "I'll take you to where they'll perform your wire insertion now."

As they proceed down the hall, Tess is trying to remember what Dr. Whaley had told her about this procedure. Something about another doctor lassoing the tumor with a wire so when it was his turn to have at it he would know where to cut?

"Here we are," Ginger says to the doctor and nurse who were waiting for them.

"Good morning, Mrs. Blessing. I'm Dr. Brewster, and this is Angela, my nurse." The younger-by-at-least-a-decade cute brunette is ogling the physician in his forties. He's a redhead too, but the freckled sort. He reminds Tess of someone that she can't put her finger on.

Dr. Brewster disappears to join Angela beneath the tented white cloth that she'd draped across Tess's chest once she'd helped her onto the table. She had answered, "No, thanks," to the offer of a numbing shot before the procedure. She didn't want to go through the whole epinephrine explanation, and local anesthesia seemed superfluous when she was about to get knocked out. She regrets that decision the moment the wire slides into her flesh.

When the two of them emerge from beneath the sheet ten minutes later, Dr. Brewster smiles and says, "You'll all set," to Tess who now has something that resembles an errant guitar string protruding from her right breast.

Ginger, who had been standing at the ready, remarks as they walk through the labyrinth of hospital halls lined with the factory-produced nature prints, "I love these pictures don't you? So inspirational. This one's my favorite." She points to a picture of two spotted fawn feeding next to a winter stream and Tessie thinks of Haddie and Henry. The thought of her children growing up without her make her eyes burn.

Their final destination is a large room with many beds. Curtains cover most of the other patients, only their tan-slipper-wearing feet are left exposed. "This is Susan," Ginger says after she guides Tess down the row. "She'll be your surgery nurse this morning. God bless."

Susan appears to be in her late thirties, but she might just *look* older. Her light-brown hair is coiled into a bun at her neck and she doesn't have on a stitch of makeup on. Tess is thinking the nurse might be Amish as she helps her into the bed. Like everyone else, she seems to be treating this momentous day like it's just another Monday at the office, or in Susan's case, just another day on a farm in Pennsylvania.

"Do you have any dentures?" she asks.

My friend is distracted by a groaning, gruff-voiced man a few beds down. "Mommy . . . I want my mommy."

"Was that a no on the dentures?"

"Yes that was a no," Tess says.

"Have you removed all your jewelry?"

Tess lifts her quivering left hand from beneath the sheet.

This must not be the first time this problem has come

up because Susan reaches down to the bedside table and lifts off a strip of precut surgical tape. "You need to be grounded," she says as she wraps it around her patient's gold wedding band.

Tessie remembers how often Dr. Drake mentioned the importance of being "grounded" during their sessions. Anchored to reality. But "grounded" was also an electrical term.

The hospital has to keep their success rates up. If the surgery doesn't go well, they're gonna electrocute you and blame it on faulty wiring, Louise promises.

When Dr. Whaley comes by to say good morning, he sets a hand on Tess's foot and gives it a playful wiggle. "See ya in there," he says. "I'll be the one with the scalpel."

Susan slips a clip onto Tess's middle finger that measures her heartbeat, which sounds like a Geiger counter at a nuclear waste dump. She's shaking so hard that she's almost levitating out of the bed, when another shower-capped man shows up.

"I'm Dr. Gritzhammer. We talked last night." The anesthesiologist had called during *Murder, She Wrote*. The thought of being put under was so overwhelming to Tess that she'd tuned him out in favor of Jessica Fletcher. "I'd like to give you a valium to help you relax."

She shakes her head at the bushy-haired man. "No, thanks. I've had weird reactions to tranquilizers in the past." She must stay on guard. She must.

"I wish you would've told me that last night," Gritzhammer says perturbed. Doctors have routines and she's disrupted his.

Susan covers shivering Tess with warm blankets before she wheels her into the surgical suite. Masked people are milling about the freezing room like a gang of bad guys ready to pull off a mid-winter caper. Two of them transfer Tess from the bed onto the operating table. She recognizes the anesthesiologist's bulky brows as he leans down and tells her, "I'm going to place this mask over your face now. Count out loud backward from one hundred."

Desperate to end the panic, she pictures Will and her children, breathes deeply, and whispers, "I love you. Forever and always. Ninety-nine . . . ninety-eight . . . ninety-seven . . . eleven. . . ."

A Reunion

So this is death.

The weather is lovely.

Since it would never occur to Tess that she's ended up in Heaven, she figures she's made a layover stop in Purgatory. She'll hang out here until whosoever in charge can get caught up on their paperwork, after which, her mortal-sin-ridden soul will be sent packing to the ninth circle of Hell.

Then again, if she *is* in death's waiting room, she wonders why she feels so serene. She loves the ethereal saxophone music that's playing—*At Last* is her favorite song—but she hates to wait.

She can't be sure how much time goes by, but her number must've been called because she's on the move now. There's an immediate sense of black weightlessness, and then she finds herself barreling toward a yonder light brighter than any she's ever seen. Whatever she's inhaling smells divine. In some other way other than words, a voice that is neither male or female or young or old, informs her that the aroma is called, "Heaven Scent."

Tess laughs. Dr. Drake was right. Humor *is* holy.

When she arrives at a beach with sand the color of

burnished copper, she understands that she's supposed to enter the water that's the most unusual blue, which switches to lilac, then silver. It's not just shimmering, it's alive, and imploring her to become one with it.

Without a thought of what lies beneath, normally cautious Tess dives in, and is engulfed in a protected feeling that she never knew existed. "Welcome to the Sea of Unconditional Love," the voice informs her.

Above her, stalactite sunbeams hang off the surface, below, a school of pink angelfish with pleased starfish eyes glide through a magnificent garden of kaleidoscope flowers. Two women appear. They wave at Tess like they'd been expecting her. One of them is her gammy, standing in the middle of the blooms dressed in a pretty yellow collared dress. She is not old and withered anymore, but young and vibrant. Alice, her daughter and librarian, is looking studious by her side. Her aunt is holding a field guide to flowers in her hand. Practical-joke-playing Boppa gives Tessie a wave from a nearby gazebo where he's affixing a Kick Me sign to the back of his favorite son, Eddie. Tess shouts, "Daddy!" and when he gives her the thumbs up, she can feel his everlasting love, and when he breaks into to, "Row, row, row your boat gently down the stream, merrily, merrily, merrily, merrily life is but a dream," euphoria floods her very essence. He's absolved her. Freed her of the burden of guilt she's carried around since the afternoon she didn't save him. She feels so much lighter that she wonders if she's about to rise to the surface. She doesn't want to. She wants to stay so badly, but the guide accompanying her—his name is Frank B. Willis—objects. (I requested him because no one gives a tour quite like Frank. He's knowledgeable, but funny as hell.) He gently informs Tess, "Not yet, dear one. Now is not your time."

But what is *time?* she asks when who should come swimming by but the star of *Sea Hunt*. Of course, she can't help but check out Mike Nelson's . . . ah . . . spear gun. She's impressed. You'd think with all the time the guy spent in the water. . . . Three other swimmers appear from behind a curtain of bubbles. Sisters Faith, Hope, and me. As we draw closer, Tess senses that whatever I'm about to tell her will be the most life-changing news she's ever received other than hearing Will's matrimonial, "I do," and the wails of her newborn children.

"Theresa Blessing! Theresa Blessing!"

She cocks her head. That's not my caring, drawled voice. This one's demanding, like her mother's.

"Open your eyes! Now!"

With much difficulty—it feels like fifty-cent pieces are taped to her eyelids—Tess does as commanded. She's lying flat on her back beneath a perforated white ceiling.

"What . . . where?" she mumbles.

Susan, the plain nurse who prepped her for the operation, leans down and fills her in. "You're in St. Mary's North recovery room. The surgery went well."

Tess doesn't care. She wants to dive back to where she was. She closes her eyes and begins to fade, but Susan quickly steps in, places an oxygen mask on her face, keeps after her to, "Breathe . . . breathe . . . breathe!" and when she does, the nurse goes back to dishing with two other nurses that are gathered at the foot of the bed. One of them, a blurred blond, is railing on someone named

Penny, who only got promoted to head of the unit because, "She's a complete and utter skank."

Jerry appears from stage left, unlocks the wheels of the rolling bed, and throws his two cents into the hen party. "Breaking news. Angela and Dr. Howdy Doody got caught hooking up in the cafeteria pantry." If her throat didn't feel so sore, Tess might've snickered too because she realizes now that tumor-lassoing Dr. Brewster had reminded her of Buffalo Bob's sidekick as well.

Jerry doesn't say much during the trip back to her room. Tess figures he must be as captivated as she is by the pastoral prints hanging on the hospital walls. Why had she not noticed the gorgeous texture, the subtle shading, and the vivid colors earlier?

After he maneuvers the bed through her room door, Jerry asks, "How ya doin'?"

"I wanna . . . I wanna. . . ." When Tess sits up, the room does too.

"Not so fast," Jerry says, amused by the bewildered look on her face. "If you need anything." He sets a call button next to her hand. "Stay put until," he gives her an in-the-know wink, "you get your land legs back."

Was Jerry referring to her dive into the Sea of Unconditional Love? Was he part of some cosmic conspiracy?

She replays the watery excursion. She could still hear Frank's reassuring but light-hearted voice, her daddy's singing, and feel the joy she'd experienced when she'd been reunited with her lost loved ones, and the silvery warmth of the silver-lilac water caressing her skin. What happened? Could she have had one of those near-death experiences people claim to have had on *Oprah*? Or maybe it was some sort of religious epiphany—number seven on her list. If so, it wasn't the kind she'd had in mind. She envisioned one more Biblical in nature. A Saul on the road to Damascus sorta thing. Yet, seeing her departed family, and experiencing the powerful no-strings-attached love, did feel awfully divine. And then there was her daddy's absolution. She'd been told by Dr. Drake and other therapists that she was not responsible for her father's death, but there's nothing quite like hearing it from the horse's mouth.

The longer the scenario replayed in Tess's mind, the clearer it became to her that there was no way of knowing exactly *what* she'd experienced. No proof of any kind, other than a profound sense of well-being, but, she tells herself, that could be the drugs in her system, or just relief that the surgery was over. The only thing she's absolutely certain of is that the same way traumas are imprinted in her brain, the sacred experience was indelibly tattooed on her soul.

Still . . . she is the most mentally unreliable person she knows. Utterly untrustworthy. She'd like to bounce what had happened off somebody, but who? Can't be the children. Will? Uh-uh. He'd probably say something about her ability to make erroneous assumptions even while she's unconscious. About the only one who might understand what she's feeling is Birdie, who has had many a strange trip of her own. And then, of course, there's another who might understand what she went through. Her new best friend.

This is the moment I've been waiting for.

Tessie slowly opens her eyes when she senses my presence. "Hey, Grace," she says with a blissed-out smile.

She knows who I am now the same way Birdie knew who Bee was when she appeared in her life. And as I suspected, once she figured it out, Tess willingly surrenders to my existence without a fuss.

She asks, "Do you think that . . . ah . . . adventure or pilgrimage, or whatever that was I just had, would allow me to scratch number seven off my list?"

"That the religious epiphany one?" I ask.

"Uh-huh."

I'm not allowed to answer that question directly since she needs to piece it together herself. But a little nostalgia and a dollop of hope can go a long way. When they were kids, Tess and Birdie loved those Davy Crockett TV shows with Fess Parker, so I tell her, "As the King of the Wild Frontier would say, 'I ain't sayin' yes, and I ain't sayin' no, I'm just sayin' mebbe.'"

She grins. (When she gets more comfortable with our relationship, she'll become less compliant. Pushy even. Mark my words.)

"Now would be a good time to call Will," I tell her.

Her husband answers on the first ring, "Count Your Blessings."

The diner greeting had always felt like a reprimand to Tess, but this time it feels like a reminder. She tells Will, "You were right." Might as well get it out of the way. "I lived. Come get me."

The two of us remain in companionable silence until Jerry returns with supplies in tow. "Pain level?" Tess lies and tells him that she doesn't feel a thing before he can whip the laminated unhappy faces out of his pocket. He looks skeptical, but says, "Okay, then let me show you how to empty your drain."

Discombobulated by the drugs and the discomfort, she's sure that Jerry just said, "Let me show you how to empty your *brain*." Maybe I should've read the consent forms more thoroughly, she thinks. Had her lymph nodes been so visibly ridden with disease that Dr. Whaley followed a trail to her frontal lobe and removed some of that as well? Is that what this unfamiliar, unworldly contentment is about? She'd had a partial lobotomy?

She asks, "Did you just say . . . ? Empty my *what*?"

Jerry folds back the bed clothes so she can squint down at the shoulder-to-mid-abdomen bandage. The wide adhesive tape holding it all together has an off-putting smell. A clear tube with a black bulb is lying beside it. The nurse points at it and says, "Your drain. Some of your lymph nodes were removed for testing and the excess fluid needs to go somewhere." He pops open the top of the bulb with this thumbnail and pours the blood-tinged liquid into a plastic cup with numbers on the side. "You'll need to empty it three times a day and keep track of how much fluid there is and," he takes out a small notebook from a bag with the hospital's logo printed on the front, "enter the numbers in this diary."

Her mouth fills with nervous saliva. "Is it like one of those . . . you know, those bags that people have attached to them to collect their . . . um. . . ." She can't remember the proper medical word. "Poop movement?"

"No," Jerry reassures in his big bass voice that Tess suspects he puts on because he's a male nurse. "It's not a colostomy bag, and it isn't permanent. Once the fluid diminishes, Dr. Whaley will remove the whole kit and caboodle."

She's not concerned about coming in contact with body fluids, she's a mother, but Will is another story. When she pictures how put off he'll be when he sees the drain, the rejected, hurting part of her takes pleasure picturing his squirming, but another greater part of her that wants his love back recoils when she imagines the look of utter revulsion on his face.

Jerry checks her temperature again. "Looks good. Did you call for your ride?"

She nods.

"You feel up to dressing?"

She tosses back the covers.

"Well, then," he says with a little bow. "That concludes our business for today. Here you go. Everything you'll need until your next doctor's visit. Enjoy Valentine's Day tomorrow." He passes her a navy-blue plastic sack. "I'm bringing my wife to Count Your Blessings for lunch. It's her favorite spot. Maybe you know her? Mare Hanson?"

That about stops her heart. She'd been too jumpy to pay much attention during check-in, but she now notices Jerry's full name on his shirt badge. She knew that Mare's husband worked in the medical field, but for some reason, Tess had it in her mind that Mr. Hanson worked for a drug company.

This is *exactly* what she feared might happen. Somebody she knew finding out about the cancer. She believes that Jerry is required by law to keep today's surgery confidential, but she's not leaving anything to chance. She reminds him in her sternest voice, "I signed that Right to Privacy form."

He works every day with drugged-up patients, so he doesn't take offense. He replies with a good-hearted smile, "My lips are sealed. Scout's honor."

Despite his reassurance, and curious reference to *To Kill a Mockingbird*, Tess cannot still her panic. She can't help but think that the nurse might call in an anonymous tip to the Ruby Falls Gazette during his coffee break, or maybe he and Mare will engage in pillow talk tonight and her secret will be out!

She jerks her head my way, gives me the cutthroat sign, and frantically points to Jerry who's heading toward the room door.

Since our relationship is still new, at least from her perspective, Tess is unfamiliar with its boundaries. All IFs come with standard equipment like invisibility, telepathy, and high empathy, but it's up to our friends to bestow any other special powers upon us. (Birdie's Bee was a hell of a shoplifter, swimmer, and snappy dresser. She could also perform slight-of-hand magic, and with her telekinetic powers, she was able to move the snow drift that saved her friend's life.) And while I *do* have special talents, it's too soon in Tess's and my relationship for them to be of much help. They build on her trust in me. But even if I was firing on all cylinders, I certainly wouldn't do what she is so rabidly requesting. I would not do away with Jerry. (There are rules.)

The best I can offer her at the current time is Calpurnia-like reassurance. "Jerry's not gonna tell the newspaper or his wife or anybody else about your cancer. Faith not fear," I whisper in her ear. "How 'bout we get you dressed? Will's almost here."

Tess navigates the room floor like she's crossing stepping stones set in raging water. Arms straight out and little choppy steps. Once she makes it safely to the bathroom, she changes into her street clothes, and grows calmer after she's reunited with her purse. She fingers her babies' blankets, brushes against her daddy's Swiss Army knife, and withdraws her copy of the book that's been patched together over the years with tape and admiration.

"Could you read to me until Will gets here?" She passes me *To Kill a Mockingbird*. "From the beginning?"

I don't need to actually follow the words that Miss Harper Lee put down since we've got a lot of the book memorized, but I crack it open anyway for show. Louise didn't read to her when she was younger and it was something she'd always envisioned as the motherly thing to do. Like baking a birthday cake from scratch or placing a cool hand on her fevered forehead or caring if her child lived or died.

I clear my throat and say, "'When he was nearly thirteen, my brother Jem got his arm badly broken at the elbow.'" I'd made it through the Finch family history and had just begun the paragraph that would set the tone of the story. "'Maycomb was an old town, but it was a tired old town . . . ,'" when Will steps into the room with a young woman dressed in a navy hospital-issued pantsuit.

He kisses Tess's cheek and says, "Ready Freddy?"

The hospital girl insists that the patient get into the wheelchair before she'll take her out of the room and to the side of her husband's turquoise-and-blue '57 Chevy that's parked in the patient pick-up area, so Tess has no choice but to comply.

Will asks as he helps her into the car, "Does it hurt very much?"

Number 6. ☹

"I'm fine," Tess tells him.

Even if the pain was off-the-chart, she wouldn't admit it. She sees her ability to endure discomfort as one of the only qualities she possesses that makes her feel superior to normal Will, and she's not above lording it over him.

As they pull away from the hospital, she tells her chauffeur-husband in an uppity voice that is an almost exact replica of her mother's, "Home, James. And be quick about it."

Love Is a Tree with Many Limbs from Which to Hang One's Self

It hasn't escaped Tess's attention that despite being in a hurry to return to work, he always is these days, Will has taken the route home from the hospital that he knows she likes the best. Carver Road ribbons over the thickest part of the Ridge River south of town. As they rumble over the covered bridge, she gazes out the Chevy's window at the wide expanse of flowing water below. It'd been an unusually temperate winter, but jutting out from the right bank, a fringe of ice thoughtfully provided by Mother Nature is acting as a rest stop for a flock of geese.

Once they enter into the town proper, they're welcomed by St. Lucy's. High atop the hill that overlooks the town, the church's copper spire is standing in bas relief against a sky of a deep blue. The day Will brought her home to Ruby Falls, Tess fell for the town almost as hard as she had for him, but she's experiencing more than her normal appreciation. The downtown shops appear even more charming, the red-brick buildings and cobblestone streets reminiscent of a Dickens novel or Main Street Disneyland. As they pass Count Your Blessings, Will lays on the Chevy's horn the way he always does. *Ah . . . oo . . . ga.* Lunch is busier than usual. *Milwaukee Magazine* had featured the diner in its yearly restaurant issue and world-weary customers have been showing up in droves. Through the plate-glass window, Tess gets a quick look at Connie Lushman greeting a young couple and two tow-headed kids. Even seeing the happy, well-configured, scarless woman who Will might love more than her doesn't substantially alter her newfound zest for life. (We'll see how long that lasts.)

As Will makes a left onto Chestnut Street, Tess's heart swells with the love she feels for the home that's included in the Chamber of Commerce's walking tour. Some tourists might linger longer in front of the grander houses, but to her, the Blessings' is the prettiest of them all.

In the front window of the colonial, Garbo, who'd been keeping watch for her mistress the way she always does, barks and scrambles off the back of the couch when she spots them turning into the driveway. After he pulls into the garage, Will rushes around the back of the finned car to help Tess out.

"What can I do?" he asks.

He thinks she's hunched over because she's in pain, when in reality, it's a defensive move designed to protect her heart from the one who has damaged it the most—her mother. She's passing the garage shelf where Louise is still waiting to be scattered. Tess is preparing herself to be verbally attacked, but oddly, not a peep comes out of the golden cube. Come to think of it, she hadn't heard from Louise since the surgery. Had the anesthesia put her to sleep as well? Note to self: Send Dr. Gritzhammer a thank-you note immediately.

A sight for sore eyes, Garbo is waiting in the mud room with her Frisbee. The pain in Tess's chest and throwing arm sharpens when she bends to stroke the top of her dog's head. "Maybe later," she tells her as she steps into the kitchen that she'd lovingly painted eggshell to better show off the children's artwork on the refrigerator and walls. Her attention is drawn to a third-grade crayon drawing of Henry's. Curlicue smoke escapes from the chimney and V birds fly across the sky. The Blessing stick family is standing on their front porch. It's not the first time Tess thinks that the rendering Henry did of his sister back then is now almost accurate.

Will says, "I'll make us tea. Can you get up the stairs without help?"

She grins at me and says, "No problem."

She's always been a hard-work-pays-off person, so she feels uncomfortable when I insist she slips into her *Champs-Élysées* nightie just a little past noon. After I help her into bed, she grimaces and edges the covers down to adjust a piece of surgical tape that's pulling against her side. She's in the midst of it when Will comes in holding the promised refreshments.

He jostles and almost drops the tray when he sees what Tess is fiddling with. "What's *that*?"

She says, "My drain," and then attempts to explain what she thought Jerry had told her.

Reaching for her teacup with her left hand because her right arm feels so heavy and numb reminds Tess of the long-ago days she and Birdie would pretend they were victims of attention-getting ailments of one kind or another. One of their most creative ideas came from a newsreel they'd seen on President Teddy Roosevelt. Those little Finley girls spent days letting their legs go as lifeless as Tess's arm now feels. Once they had that crippled feeling down pat, they whiled away the good part of an afternoon attempting to fasten a jump rope around two old bike tires and a cast-off kitchen chair so they'd have their very own wheelchair. When that didn't work out, they sat on the front stoop of the duplex looking wan and courageous with a wool blanket across their legs yelling, "Bully!" at passersby with the same enthusiasm they'd seen the ex-president deliver the line. Ahhh . . . the good old days when she and her sister had wished that Jonas Salk had gone into a different line of work.

Will tries, but fails to hide his discomfort at the sight of his wounded wife. "If you're feeling okay I should get back to the diner." He rakes his hands through his hair that Tess notices again looks less tarnished. It's also fuller on the top, like he's using a product to give it more body. "I left Connie alone."

Tess is about to snippily say, *Well, God forbid Connie feels abandoned*, but the pained look on his face stops her. Is he concerned about the business? His hostess? Her? She'd ask, but he'd only give her his usual happy-go-lucky shrug.

"Mom?" Henry calls from downstairs.

"What's he doing home so early?" Tess asks concerned. "You think he was suspended again?" Henry'd already been sent home twice this semester. Once for wearing a Santa Claus costume to school and the other for lipping off to a biology teacher who he's had problems getting along with since he liberated the frogs that were about to be dissected.

Will says, "Lemme check." He kisses her on the forehead. "If you need anything you know where to find me."

On his way down the steps, Tess hears him ask their son why he's home earlier than expected.

Henry doesn't like to be interrogated. Peeved, he tells Will, "I told you this morning that the teachers are having some kind of meeting. Where's Mom?"

"Resting. Take it easy on her. We just got back from the hospital."

Henry's size elevens take the remainder of the steps two at a time. He's forgotten to put on his I-am-a-cool-teenage-boy face when he sits on the edge of the bed next to Tess. "Are you okay? How's your shoulder?"

"What—" She'd momentarily forgotten the lie she'd come up with. "It's a little sore, so you might need to help me out for a couple of days." If Haddie, her lover of Lifetime medically themed movies was here, she'd have a bunch of questions, and maybe even ask to see beneath the bandage that she has artfully arranged the down comforter over. She'd eventually wheedle the truth out of her mother, but Henry? He may love to play bloody video games, but just like his dad, at the sight of the real thing he turns the color of bone.

He knits his brows together and asks, "Do you need something *now*?"

She spoils him, she knows that. He'd used to being cared for, not the other way around. If she keeps her requests simple, he'll do just fine. Nothing complicated like, *Could you come closer so I can nuzzle your neck because I was positive that up to a few hours ago that I'd never see you again? I saved all your baby teeth in a jar that I keep in my dresser beneath the little blue knit hat you wore home from the hospital. You wanna see?*

"A Coke would be great," she tells him. "With ice."

After Henry takes off, she partakes of the only tranquilizer she can swallow—a soap opera. She asks if *General Hospital* is all right with me, but I suggest my favorite, *Guiding Light*, and she politely clicks to Channel 6.

Neither one of us gets much viewing in before the phone trills an inch from her head. She struggles to prop herself up, lands on her drain, and cries out, "Hell-ow!"

"Mom?" Haddie asks. "Are you okay?"

"Yeah, yeah, honey, I'm fine." Tess gives thanks for once that her perceptive daughter is hundreds of miles away. "I was making the bed and kneeled on . . . ," she leans down and checks to make sure she didn't do any damage to the drain, "the . . . ah . . . TV controller." She doesn't see the point in telling Haddie the shoulder surgery story, and she can count on Henry not to share it with her. He's probably already forgotten about it by now because where is her Coke?

"How are *you*? Did you get your Valentine's card?" she asks Haddie.

Tess had searched for just the right ones for her family for the better part of an hour. She had to be especially careful when it came to picking out Birdie's because cards were such a big, big deal to her. They *had* to be Hallmark ones because her sister is obsessed with Hallmark. It all goes back to those *Hall of Fame* specials the company aired when the girls were children. They really got to little desperate-for-love Birdie. The sappy melodramas imprinted themselves on her so deeply that later in life she began to use Hallmark's words of wisdom for guidance, the way Christians do the Bible, Jews the Torah, and Muslims the Koran. The walls of her Boca Raton apartment are papered with inspiring card innards like, "Today Is a Purrrfect Day!" and "Spread Your Wings!" There are also silver-lining ones: "The Tree of Life Has Many Limbs. If One Should Break ... Go Out on Another!" Or "Today Was a Cloudy Day, but Tomorrow the Sun Is Sure to Shine!" and "Be a Ball and Bounce Back!"

When they were still communicating, Tess sent uplifting cards two to three times a week. Sometimes they worked to raise her sister's low self-esteem, but sometimes they wouldn't. It's not always easy to know how a depressed, anxious, obsessive-compulsive, traumatized, anorexic-bulimic, and occasionally delusional woman will respond on any particular day—especially on one as important as Valentine's. After much running about from section to section in the store, Tess settled on an innocuous, "Love Makes the World Go 'Round" card for her sister, and a small gift—a porcelain wishing well. Before she sent them off, she sealed the package with a kiss, and hoped that Birdie wouldn't send it back unopened the way she had all the others.

The card Tess chose for Henry was a knee-slapper, he wouldn't tolerate anything tender. She almost selected a hearts and flowers one for Will, but if he *was* making love to Connie that would be so pathetic, so she went with a sad-eyed basset pup instead that suggested in a cheery script, "Have a doggone nice Valentine's Day!" Haddie received a poignant one with a beautiful drawing of a mother gazing lovingly at the chubby pink baby in her arms. Tess hoped the subliminal message wasn't too obvious.

"I loved the card and thanks for the check," Haddie gushes. "Does Daddy have anything special planned?"

"Oh, I'm sure he does. You know how much he likes surprises." Tess wonders if Connie will be on the receiving end of a box of chocolates in a heart-shaped box instead of her. "And how about you and Drew? Is there romance in the air?"

"Actually . . . *giggle* . . . *giggle* . . . I met another guy. Rock."

"I'm sorry, honey. I didn't catch that." Her hearing is fine, she just can't keep up with her daughter's motormouth. She *thinks* that Haddie just told her that she'd met a new fella named Rock. Could that be right? Tess'd noticed that on the other side of the Mason-Dixon line parents often christen their offspring after all sorts of stuff. Like guns. There was a Remington in Haddie's advanced perspective class and a Colt wandering around campus. Nature names were popular too. Lake, Coon, and Gator came up every so often in their conversations. Since it annoys Haddie to hell and back when her mom asks her to repeat herself, Tess warily asks, "Did you say the name of the boy you met is R-o-c-k?"

Regretting now that she mentioned the new guy to her mother in the first place, she says exasperated, "Y-e-s."

Henry bursts in and sets the Coke down on the bedside table like a busy car hop. "Gotta get back downstairs. Big tourney on Ubet."

Tess doesn't want to interrupt Haddie when she's finally opening up about her love life, so she mouths, *thanks*, and throws him a kiss that he pretends to dodge.

"Rock is an amazing illustrator," Haddie sighs on the phone. "And he's thinks I'm sexy."

That didn't upset Tess one whit. It was fine with her if her daughter wanted to hop in bed with Rock. She didn't get all this nonsense people were spouting lately about waiting until after marriage. Getting along in the sack is vital. To feel your separate parts coming together is not only blissful, it's crucial, but only if those parts fit right. The way hers and Will's do.

Don't you mean . . . did? Louise reminds.

What if Haddie waited until after her wedding and discovered on her honeymoon that the man she committed to until death did her part unveiled a penis that resembled a ballpoint pen? What would she do then?

Use it to write a suicide note.

Haddie says, "Well, just wanted to say hi and thank you for the card." There is no mistaking the excitement in her voice. "Gotta get ready. Rock's taking me to the sweetheart dance tonight at the boathouse."

There's a pause then, a long one. Tess is just about to say, *You still there?* when Haddie utters in her sweetest voice, "I love you, Mommy."

It was the first time in months that she'd said the words Tess had been longing to hear. Tears flood her eyes, but she sucks them back and replies with a grin that she hopes that far away Haddie can hear, "I'm sorry, honey. Could you please repeat that?"

Shiver Me Timbers

February 14 is more than a holiday for Birdie. It's a holy day.

Before they'd had their most recent riff, Tessie would've received four cards from her sister before the big day. Their postman, Art Holcomb, would always attach a small note of gratitude for the contribution to his pension on the super-sized one that he slipped under the welcome mat.

My friend, who'd fallen asleep in my arms in the chintz chair in the sunroom after one of her middle-of-the-night wanderings, is woken early the next morning by the AOL man informing her, "You've got mail."

She's sore from the surgery, but as she squirms into an upright position, her heart is doing a jig. It could be a response to her many e-mails to Birdie. She might've finally gotten through to her. It's Valentine's Day, after all!

Tess slowly eases into her desk chair and clicks on the mail icon. When an offer for carpet cleaning pops up instead of a note from her sister, her disappointed sigh ruffles the papers stacked next to the computer. The letdown is awful, but never fear, she won't allow it to deter her on her quest to reignite their relationship. She says aloud as she types:

> "Dear Birdie,
> HAPPY VALENTINE'S DAY!!!
> Did you get your present? Wishing you did;)
> xoxoxoxoxoxoxoxoxoxoxoxo"

Above her head, Henry rolls out of bed and heads to the bathroom to begin his morning prep. A half hour later, Tess can hear his clodhoppers on the staircase. She calls out to him, "Happy V-day, honey. I'm in the sunroom."

He saunters in hoodie-free and handsome as all get out in jeans and a crisp white button-down shirt. Fresh out of the shower, he smells like the entire Ralph Lauren body care line. "How's your shoulder?" he asks.

That's a surprise. Tess figured he wouldn't remember the surgery this morning, and she's a little disappointed that he did. If she's going to keep the cancer from him, she's counting on his obliviousness. "Not too bad," she tells him. "Should be tossing the Frisbee around in no time."

Henry returns her smile with one that she thinks might be responsible for global warming, pulls an envelope out from behind his back, and says, "Got you a card."

"Really?" He usually doesn't go in for this sort of thing. She opens the envelope to find it's the same funny one she'd gotten him. "Thanks, baby," she says with a laugh. "Yours is on the kitchen table, and there's something yummy in the bread box." She'd asked Will to stop at Ye Olde Bakery yesterday and pick up Henry's favorite streusel coffee cake after he dropped her off at the hospital. "Leave a piece for Daddy, and don't forget to remind your friends to be here before seven tonight."

Considering that this may be her last Valentine's Day— she may have made it through the surgery, but that was just the opening gambit—she agreed to pull out all the stops and rent a limo for the Sadie Hawkins dance. This year's theme was PIRATES! Henry and his girlfriend, Kat, and three of their close friends and dates, would be whisked away this evening to partake in music and swashbuckling debauchery in the high-school gym. Knowing that she might be feeling some lingering effects from the anesthesia, Tess arranged for the stretch to pick them up at the Blessings', which unfortunately means that she'll be expected to join the other mommies in a picture-taking frenzy before they take off. She can see it all now. In the excitement, her drain pops out from beneath her sweatshirt and someone says, *Holy cow. What's that?* If not that scenario, something equally unpredictable and distressing could occur.

My friend isn't the only woman in Ruby Falls going through the change of life. Used to be, most of the ladies' problems were fairly run-of-the-mill. Like finding just the right outfit for the Fourth of July dance at Ruby Falls Country Club, or who would be the next PTA president, but the stakes were raised as their estrogen decreased. Just last week, Tess heard that Becky Winner and Nancy Lindhjem engaged in a hair-pulling scuffle in the high-school traffic circle after Becky accused Nancy of trying to skip ahead in the pick-up line. And at Henry's basketball games nasty stuff flew out of their menopausal mommy mouths that they'd once kept sealed tighter than their Tupperware.

After Henry takes off for school, Tess drags herself upstairs to find Will singing Elvis's, *Can't Help Falling in Love* in the shower. If she could rewind time back a few months, before he began withholding all his best parts, or even to before yesterday when part of her breast had been cut off, she would've stepped in and joined him in a soapy free-for-all. She misses that good clean fun.

"Happy Valentine's Day," she says with not much enthusiasm.

Will draws a heart in the steam on the shower door and replies, "Got a special surprise for you! Should be here soon!"

She says "Oh. Thanks," in a slightly incredulous way. He's been so unresponsive that she thought Cupid would fly past their house this year and straight over to Connie's. Something special? She feels guilty now for not getting him more than the Bassett hound card and a pen-and-pencil set. She should pick him up a sleeve of golf balls, or a furry cover for the Chevy's rear view mirror when she's out doing errands, tell him later that she'd forgotten to give it to him this morning. Then again, with the way things had been going lately, the "special surprise" might be a new vacuum cleaner.

Tess tells him, "I'm gonna wash up in the kids' bathroom."

She'd been instructed to keep her chest bandage dry so a sponge bath is the best she can do. She blots herself off with a blue towel Henry had left on the floor, fastens the drain onto the bottom of a ratty old Ruby Falls High sweatshirt with a safety pin, the way Jerry had shown her in his demonstration, then shimmies up her cotton undies and stretchy-waisted pants.

She's halfway down the stairs when the phone rings. She figures it must be one of the detail-oriented mothers reconfirming the drop-off time for tonight's Sadie Hawkins dance. She snags it with her left hand on her way into the kitchen. "Happy Valentine's Day, Mom!"

"Thank you, sweetie! You too!" It was one of those great connections. Her daughter sounded like she was in the next room, and if Garbo would quit barking, Tess could hear her even better. She turns toward the mud room to scold her dog, and there . . . there in the entryway is . . . "Haddie!?"

Will hadn't agreed with her when she insisted that it was important to keep the cancer to themselves, so Tess's first panicked thought is that he had broken his reluctant promise to do so. Had he called her home to share the burden? She quickly reads Haddie's face. She looks happy, and doesn't sound like she's coming to rescue her dying mother as she runs toward her shouting, "Surprise!"

Tess hadn't laid eyes on her gaunt girl for six weeks. Her first impulse is to crush her to her chest, but if she does, she'd surely feel the bulky drain that's beneath the sweatshirt. So she sets her arms around her daughter, not in the way she normally would—like she was drowning and Haddie was a life jacket—but in the awkward way women do to prevent their breasts from rubbing against another's.

"Oh, honey," Tess says with a manufactured sniffle as she steps back. "I don't want to get too close. I have a little . . . *cough . . . cough . . .* virus."

Will saves her from further explanation when he comes bounding down the stairs, proud as hell of perpetrating the surprise. "*Gotcha!*" he says to Tess with one of his trademark winks. "Welcome home, baby!" He gives Haddie a bear hug, then gets to work doing what he does to show how much he loves his girls.

Mother and daughter get cozy at the kitchen table while Chef Will prepares the house specialty. Haddie had brought home her portfolio and was eager to show what she'd been up to. The Savannah School of Art and Design was doing a wonderful job expanding her vision. Her primary focus had formerly been nature photography, but she'd enrolled in a portraiture class this semester. Tess was moved by what she saw as she leafed through the book, and told her so. "I think you mighta found your true calling." Haddie had shot a series of pictures of grizzled black men lounging out front of a shabby café smoking hand-rolled cigarettes and playing dominoes on a card table. More than just the decentness in the men's eyes, she had captured their longing for dreams beyond their reach.

"*Voilà,*" Will says as he sets the plates of eggs Benedict down in front of them.

Tess, who is almost swooning from happiness, sedation hangover, and the grind of appearing normal, is growing more doubtful by the minute about her ability to keep the surgery a secret from Haddie. She's an artist, observant, so as much as she loves her, she hopes her daughter doesn't intend to stay long. But surely, Tess thinks as she slips a bite of eggs into her mouth, she's a good enough performer that she can keep her secret hidden during a short visit.

"How long are you home for, hon?" she asks Haddie like she wishes it could be forever."

With a grin that shows off the dimple that sits high on her right cheek, she says, "I moved some things around! You've got me for the whole weekend!"

The high-school kids show up later that night looking like they'd just arrived from Penzance. The boys are jabbing each other in the ribs, battling with plastic cutlasses, and "Yo, ho, hoing" it up. Timmy Wescoe, who has yet to go through a growth spurt, is wearing tall, black boots with heels. Billy Brown had a stuffed parrot sewn into the shoulder of a red waistcoat that looked homemade. Always hungry, Steve Mertz, is looting a sack of chocolate doubloons that is swinging from Henry's gray hook. Their wenches, donned in hoop earrings and shoulder-baring peasant blouses with swishy long skirts, are admiring their dates' swashbuckling moves.

Tess's fear of one of the picture-taking moms discovering her condition is neutralized when photographer Haddie tells her to stand back and steps into the fray. She snaps off shots of the motley crew first in the den, and then in the limousine with the Jolly Roger flag affixed to its antenna. Her daughter would also be attending the pirate soiree. Tess waved as the car pulled away and was grateful for the time apart. She was worn to the nub from keeping her guard up, and it did her heart good to know that her girl, who had inherited her mother's love of dance, would be showing the high-school kids how it's done.

When Haddie came home a few hours later, she gave Tess a thumbnail description of the evening. "Great decorations. The music was okay, some garage band. The best parts were when one of the chaperones bitch-slapped another, and the walk-the-plank game got even better after Henry spiked the grog."

The Blessings are enjoying a celebratory lunch on Saturday afternoon after Henry's basketball game at the high school. The diner staff fawns over former waitress, Haddie, and congratulates Henry and the Ruby Falls Buccaneers on their win at the buzzer. Filmmaker wanna-be waiter, Cal, pops by for another brief discussion about one of his and her son's favorite movies, *The Silence of the Lambs*. Tess is enjoying herself until Connie Lushman lands at their table. She places her hand on Will's shoulder, whispers something in his ear, and he smiles and excuses himself.

When Henry challenges Haddie to a game of pinball, Tess takes the opportunity to step into the kitchen to say "*Hola,*" to Juan and the other *señors*. They'd be hurt if she didn't tell them how delicious her burger was. Waiters and waitresses are rushing to and fro delivering and picking up orders, but dishwasher Otto is standing still and straight-backed at the sink wearing full battle gear. The picture of his Russian mail-order bride above the faucet has been defaced. Elena has a mustache covering her worn-away-with-kisses lips, a laddered scar across her right cheek, and devil horns sprouting from her forehead. She'd emptied their savings account on the way to the airport to catch a flight back to Minsk ten days ago. Otto is heartbroken, pissed off, and has been more paranoid than usual. Aluminum foil is bunched around his shower cap *and* he's wearing his noise-reducing earphones. He's also added another something new to his protective ensemble that Tess hasn't seen before. A kilt? Made out of . . . what are those things? Roof shingles?

Her heart breaks for him, but she can't commit to another drawn-out conversation about his Russian soon-to-be ex-wife that is punctuated every few minutes with, "You catch my drift?" because she and the kids, and hopefully Will, are going to catch a matinee—*Wayne's World*.

She backs out of the kitchen, sticks her head in the game room, tells the kids to meet her at the car in five minutes, and goes off to look for her husband. She finds him and Connie deep in conversation in his office. They appear startled when Tess asks Will, "Ready?"

He rubs his finger under his nose and tells her, "Sorry. I can't come. Connie and I have an urgent diner matter we need to tend to."

Tess catches herself before she can make a baby-animal noise. She shrugs, says gaily, "Oh. Okay," and heads down the hall alone. Mewling.

With her son off to one of his card-playing lollapaloozas, and Will managing the busiest dinner of the week at the diner, Tess has her daughter to herself on Saturday night.

They're snuggled up on the den couch, basking in the warmth of the fire, and watching a Lifetime movie about a crime-solving psychic. During the commercial breaks, Haddie tells tales about her boyfriend, Rock, the joys of

Asti Spumante, and how she's sure that one of her professors is coming on to her because he keeps bumping into her "accidentally" in the dark room.

Tess is lost in the joy of having her daughter speak to her in more than one-syllable words. She is hesitant to bring her eating up, but Haddie, who she'd thought had been making some progress, had only picked at her food the past couple of days. As her mother, she thinks it'd be irresponsible not to say *something*, but she doesn't want to overstep and is unsure where the boundary line has been drawn. She finally settles on a topic that doesn't take eating, or lack thereof, head on, but might lead to further discussion. "Tell me more about the new doctor you're seeing. Chandler?"

An unpredicted cold front blows in. The heart-shaped votive candles atop the fireplace mantel flicker when Haddie jumps off the couch and growls, "Don't go there," like she's warning off a stranger who dared to venture onto private property. She spent the remainder of the evening locked in her room. Tess spent it outside the door begging to be let in.

Late Sunday morning, the Blessings load up their daughter's carry-on and camera bags and drive to Billy Mitchell Field. Mom accompanies her into the airport while Dad circles. At the check-in counter, Tess starts to cry, she can't help it. Haddie huffs in disgust. She thinks her mother is making a scene because she doesn't want her to leave. While that's true, it's not the whole picture. Since Tess feels responsible for her eating disorder, she's weeping because she's relieved that Haddie would be far from her grasp so she couldn't hurt her any more than she already had, but she also desperately wants to press her daughter to her chest so she would feel the bandages and know her suffering, and those dual feelings of needing to take care of and needing to be taken care of are too much to contain.

Haddie gives her mother a courtesy hug, says, "I'll send you the pictures I took at the Sadie Hawkins dance," and climbs the steps to Concourse A, like she'd been hired for the weekend and her job had been completed.

On the drive home, the inside of the car is crypt quiet until Will hits the freeway. "You get the results of the lymph node testing tomorrow. Do you want ... ?" He almost asks if she'd like mashed potatoes and pot roast for supper tonight.

Bless his heart. How was he supposed to know that's exactly what she's craving?

Tempus Does Not Fugit

1:27 a.m.

Tess jerks awake with the *Hearse* song echoing in her head.

> *The worms crawl in, the worms crawl out,*
> *The worms play pinochle in your snout.*
> *They eat your eyes, they eat your nose,*
> *They eat the jelly between your toes.*

In a few hours she'd find out if the cancer was dining on any other part of her. Was it feasting on her liver? Gnawing on her bones? Consuming her pancreas?

She reaches across the bed to brush her lips against Will's stubbly sleeping cheek and stroke his less-silver hair, grasp his curled sleeping hand to her bandaged chest, and for a moment she feels peaceful and saved.

For godssakes, Theresa. Have a little self-respect.

1:46 a.m.

Light from their neighbor's garage is shining through the top of their bedroom window and illuminating the oil painting above their bedroom door. Tess had created it from a snapshot Will had taken when he surprised her with a trip on their twentieth wedding anniversary. He'd wanted to whisk her back to their honeymoon suite at the Holiday Inn in Paris, Illinois, but her fear of leaving home had set deeper roots throughout the years and Will had to settle for the Gay Paree Motel in Wisconsin Dells instead.

In the painting, Tess is floating on a corn-colored air mattress in the unnaturally blue motel pool. She's trimmer than she is now, and chestier than she ever was. Amusing Will is one of the ways she shows him how much she loves him, so she'd given herself astronomically large breasts with flying saucer-sized nipples visible through the skimpy swimsuit fabric so he'd cock his eyebrow and say like a French alien, *Ooo . . . la . . . la . . . take me to your leader.*

Tess had taken up oil painting shortly after she'd informed her psychiatrist that driving down to the Chicago comedy clubs to perform was taking too much of a toll on her and her family. Dr. Drake agreed, but was concerned that removing her only source of creative expression might affect her mental health. "Perhaps you could take up something that doesn't require an audience, or a dance partner." She had always loved art so she suggested painting, and Drake was all for it.

When she talked the idea over with Will, he took the bull by the horns and found an interesting class at a place a few miles up the road. Dressed in a goofy-looking smock and a beret Will had given her, she eagerly drove off the following week toward Lemon Hill, the town a few miles north. Like Ruby Falls, it was famous for its historical landmarks. Amongst them, a renowned artists' and writers' colony named Greendale. One of the other places of interest in the town was Meadowview, a posh private psychiatric facility that Tess avoided driving by at all costs.

The two-hour art class was held every Tuesday afternoon in one of the quaint cottages strewn across Greendale's grounds. The instructor was a fine-looking German gentleman named Alec Strobel. Once his students became lost in their canvasses, Alec would meander around the room sharing—in a melancholy voice that reminded Tess of Marlena Dietrich—memories of the women he had known, the women he had loved, and the women he had lost. Somehow he always managed to end each of his recollections with, "*Ach*. It is de vomen's job in life to zuffer, *nein*?"

There'd be a lot of head-bobbing in the class right about then because most of the middle-aged gals had ceased to find a sense of accomplishment in scrubbing floors and ironing. Other than the class, their only creative outlet was dreaming up excuses so they wouldn't have to, as they say in Alabama in mixed company, "Pound the snow leopard," with their equally disenchanted husbands.

Mixed in with the seven "normal" women was a psychiatric patient name of Marcy Marie Gates, a faded girl with pale skin and bleached-blue eyes, who looked like she'd been run through the wash too many times. She was younger than the rest of them, twenty-five, at most. After Marcy Marie was escorted into the cottage by a caretaker from Meadowview, she would make a beeline for Tess, (naturally), set up her easel, and ask her every fifteen minutes on the dot, "Do you like my painting, Miss Tess? Is it beautiful, Miss Tess? Do you love it with all your heart, Miss Tess?"

My friend didn't *know* what kind of awfulness Marcy Marie had had to endure, but she could *feel* the agony shoot out of her fellow student like a missile that honed in on her gut. She would tell the girl, "I like your painting *very* much. It *is* beautiful, and I *do* love it with all my heart," which wasn't true since she couldn't look at Marcy Marie's work without crossing her eyes. She was too afraid the paintings would get branded into her brain. (There were just so many shades of black the troubled girl could use before the canvas began to look like it should be framed in lost souls and hanging in the foyer of artist Edvard Munch's house.)

Tess quit the class after a few months because it'd become too difficult to paint with Marcy Marie's depression breathing down her neck. *Watch your step, Blessing*, it'd begun to whisper. *Your paintings may be pastel colored now, but I got a tube of gray in my pocket that can be put to good use."*

2:12 a.m.

I say from the chaise lounge where I'm guarding over my friend, "I think you mighta forgot to check on Snakey Nine today."

She gasps, throws the covers back, and reaches for the flashlight she keeps next to the bed. Forgetting all about the cutting that'd been done on her chest, she jogs down the hall, opens Henry's bedroom door inch-by-inch, tiptoes in, and shines the light on the aquarium. The snake is nocturnal and should be moving about.

Henry stirs and mumbles, "Mom."

She needs to come up with a reason to be in his room other than disposing of the dead reptile. She kneels on the side of his bed and whispers, "I thought you might've left your window open and I came to check." When Henry doesn't respond, she realizes that he's not awake. He called out her name because he's dreaming about her and . . . damn, that gets to her.

She's about to run back to her bedroom and hide under the sheets, but I intercede. "Instead of lying here and compulsively checking the time or having flashbacks or wondering which part of your body the cancer is consuming or riding yourself for not checking on the snake earlier or wondering if Will is messing around with Connie or doing any of the other twenty-two things you do to torture yourself, why don't we head downstairs for a cup of tea in the sunroom?"

Tess reluctantly agrees that might be a better approach.

After she lets Garbo loose in the backyard and brews herself a cup of decaf Earl Grey, she wanders into her special room. Being surrounded by Haddie's photographs, Henry's basketball and soccer trophies, and a few Georgia O'Keefe prints she loves makes her feel safer, almost loved. Will's first diner dollar hangs on the wall above the desk in a gold frame. Her children's bronzed baby shoes flank her pencil cup. Since she visits the sunroom often in the middle of the night, the desk lamp with the green glass shade is always left on.

Relaxation is more what I had in mind, but she slips her new To-Do List out of the pocket of the once-green chenille robe and smoothes it down on the desk. The paper is tear- and tea-stained.

TO-DO LIST

1. ~~Buy broccoli.~~
2. ~~Hope that Haddie gets the help she needs from a better therapist.~~
3. ~~Set up vocational counseling appointment for Henry.~~
4. Convince Will to love me again.
5. Get Birdie to talk to me.
6. Bury Louise once and for all.
7. ~~Have a religious~~ epiphany so #8 is going to be okay with me.
8. Die.

She started to cross out number seven because what she'd experienced during the surgery felt divine, but could she count it as an epiphany? Tess wasn't sure, but she almost never was. She was the prime suspect in the murder of her intuition. She needs to spend more time analyzing the experience the way she'd been taught by psyche investigator Dr. Drake. She needed to sift slowly through her thoughts and inspect them for reliability.

With head in hands, she stares down at the list. "My mother's right. I'm good for nothing. I let everybody down. Even the stupid snake."

I pluck a Kleenex out of the box on the edge of the desk and hand it to Tess, who is feeling let down by *me*. She's wishing again that I had more to offer other than reassurance, companionship, and love. Don't actions speak louder than words? What good was I if I couldn't bring the snake back to life, reunite her with her sister, give Connie Lushman a chronic yeast infection, and dispose of her mother's remains?

She's stroking Garbo's head with too much ardor and her leg is bouncing beneath the desk. Her hopped-up brain needs something to focus on other than working on her not-so-new-anymore To-Do List that isn't dwindling the way she'd like it to.

I give her hand a quick pat and say, "We'll go directly to the pet store first thing tomorrow to get Snakey Ten, I have a lot of faith in your sister, I can't do much about Connie's nether region, but believe me, you'll be rid of your mother when the time is right." Best to change the subject now. "In the meantime, how 'bout we come up with something to take your mind offa things?"

She swipes at her tears with the sleeve of her cows-sipping-*café-au-lait*-on-the-*Champs-Élysées* nightie that needed washing a week ago, and points out the window into the clear night. The light of a three-quarters moon is illuminating her flock of snow angels. "Make more?"

I wrap my arms around myself and shiver.

"Empty my drain?"

"Sounds like a ball, but I've got another idea." I stand, bow at the waist, and offer her my hand. "May I have this dance?"

The last thing she wants to do right now is trip the light fantastic, but she is far too polite to turn me down. "We need music," she says.

I follow her into the den where she thumbs through the extensive vinyl record collection. When she finds what she wants, she drops the classic Muddy Waters album onto the turntable and lowers the volume so it doesn't wake the boys. "You lead," she says.

We're waltzing to *The Thrill Is Gone*. I thought I'd succeeded in calming her some, but then she sighs, and says into my shoulder, "Will doesn't want me anymore and I don't blame him for going back to Connie."

"I wouldn't jump to that conclusion if I were you." I stuck close to him last night. I had my suspicions, but I wanted to see with my own eyes what he and Connie have been up to. The two of them *did* have their bodies pressed together. "You don't have any proof."

"What about the long blond hairs?" When she gets up enough nerve to confront him, she's planning to wave the ones she keeps in an envelope in the mud room cupboard triumphantly in his face so he can't accuse her of making one of her erroneous assumptions. "And the perfume?"

"They work together in a busy restaurant," I say as we move around the room. The heaviness that she's feeling in her heart doesn't reach her feet. She really is a lovely dancer. "They're bound to brush up against one another."

"Nice try. I work there too and I don't come home with black hair on my blouse smelling like Juan and french fries. And Otto keeps track of *everything* that goes on in the diner and I heard him singing to himself, 'Connie has a boyfriend . . . Connie has a boyfriend.'"

I come to an abrupt halt and hold her at arm's length. "C'mon, Tessie. Really? Otto? The man who wears shingle kilts and believes we're under attack from the Planet Argon?" The way a mother wishes to spare her child pain, I'd love to tell her what's going on between Connie and Will, but it's contrary to one of the most basic tenants of an imaginary's life: "**There are no shortcuts to** your friend's destination. **Do not interfere with their journey.**" (I'm aware this sounds like one of Birdie's Hallmark cards, but that doesn't make it any less true.)

"Our wedding anniversary is coming up in May," Tess says. "If the cancer has spread . . . ," I take an extra-strong hold of her, but she resists and steps back, "I need to go to the sanctuary."

The subterranean space is separated from the finished side of the basement that holds the big TV and beanbag chairs by a door to the past that she steps through often to worship the happy childhoods that are kept here. The overhead bulbs shine down too harshly upon what she holds precious, so she lights the three votive candles in red glass holders that she keeps at the ready on one of the storage shelves near the door.

Will was raised in the house, and sometimes on nights like these, when nothing else seems to work to take her out of herself, she comes down here and digs up souvenirs of his boyhood that his mother packed away in containers to keep time from nesting in them. If you don't count Birdie, Louise's ashes and her constant nagging, and the pictures Tess inherited upon her gammy's passing, there is little left of her childhood except for the reruns that play in her head.

She lifts the top off the plastic box marked **William— 1957-1960**. There's a laminated school report that his mother was so proud of with a childish drawing of the diner below the title printed in Will's little-boy hand—*My Daddy Makes the best Hamgers in the Hole World.* She digs down farther and buries her nose in his little baseball glove. Willie played shortstop.

Remnants of Haddie's and Henry's early years have been lovingly preserved as well. The blue blanket she brought her son home from the hospital in. Her daughter's lacy baptismal dress, she was so chubby. Their tiny white baby socks. Henry's *Go, Dog, Go* book. Haddie's earliest photographs of her mother and father shot from such a low angle that Will and Tess look like beneficent giants.

She thought the memories would bring comfort the way they usually did, but tonight they're having the opposite effect. She's barely able to blow out the votive candles, and says raggedy, "I can't catch my breath," as she dodges around the boxes, shoots up the stairs, and straight out to the deck of the house.

It's below zero and the sky is sprinkled with stars. Garbo is looking up at Tess, who is looking up at the northern sky. The cold air hitting her tight lungs opens up her breathing some, but she's still struggling. She points at Orion the Hunter. "Like father, like son," she gasps. "Henry doesn't need me anymore either."

"Now ya know that's not true. Henry Orion adores you. He just ain't showin' it at the current time." I'm gonna get in Dutch. I'm not supposed to do this sort of thing, but she's feeling so forlorn and what are friends for? I spin her toward the house, point up to her son's bedroom window, and say to the heavens above, "Please enlighten her."

When the lamp pops on in Henry's bedroom, she turns to me gap-mouthed. "Holy shit, Grace. How . . . how'd you do that?"

I give her a grin and point to the eastern sky. Dawn is dressed in vivid shades of peach and gold. "Lordy, how time do fly when a body is havin' fun. We better get busy in the kitchen. The boy'll be up soon lookin' for his breakfast and ya know how cranky he gets when he's hungry."

A Greater Margin of Safety

Tess, Garbo, and I are heaped together a few hours later on the plaid den couch. Will is preparing cups of fortifying tea in the kitchen. The two rooms open into one other, so Tessie picks up the den phone and enables the speaker doohickey so he can hear the dread-filled call she's about to make to Dr. Whaley's office.

"Hey, Patience." Her need for secrecy is utmost in her mind, so she considers giving the receptionist a fake name again, then she realizes that doesn't make sense. "It's Tess Blessing. I'm calling to get the results of the pathology report."

"Oh, hey. Sure. Let me pull your chart."

Kenny Rogers and The First Edition begin serenading her and Will with, "Up, up, and awaaay in my beautiful, my beautiful ballooon."

"Got it," Patience comes back and says, "lemme see."

Flop sweat, the kind that Tess had experienced when she was performing her stand-up routine in front of a particularly tough crowd, has broken out on her forehead. She picks up my hand and squeezes.

"Congratulations!" the allergy-plagued receptionist trumpets. "Your lymph nodes are clean!"

Will sets their cups on the coffee table with a smile that's just a few ticks away from a gloat. Hadn't he told her all along that everything was going to be okay? Tessie isn't that easy. It's almost impossible for her to believe that she's one of the lucky ones. Maybe Patience misheard her name because her ears are always clogged up. "That's really great, but are you absolutely, positively sure that you've got the right report?"

"Yup, and . . . wait a sec."

"What?" Tess asks.

"Looks like there's another little problem."

There . . . that's better. More familiar territory. (Tess really doesn't do all that well with joy.)

Patience says, "Looks like your margins aren't wide enough."

"My *margins*?" A fourth-grade book report comes to mind.

"Margins are the space between good tissue and bad. Yours aren't what they should be, which means that you're going to need to have them revised."

"I thought Rob cut the tumor out." Was he incompetent? Sure, everyone liked the guy. He was a great track coach with a cute behind, and a pillar of the church and the community, but she excelled at fooling people too. What did she *really* know about him? Should she drive over to the hospital and demand to see proof of the work he'd done? When Will repairs the Volvo, he always shows her the busted parts. "And what do you mean I have to have more tissue removed?" It registers then. "Wait a minute . . . are you telling me that I'm gonna have to have another surgery?" she asks. "Just like the last one?"

Patience says, "Not exactly like the last one, but yes, you'll need another surgery."

Tess moans. Any relief she was feeling about the rest of her body being free of cancer is being snuffed out by the thought of another operation. She can't picture having the strength to go through that again.

"But first things first," Patience says. "How are you doing with your drain?"

Preoccupied with the thought that she could die during this new surgery, Tess mumbles, "Just peachy."

"Good. Then let's schedule you on March eighth at seven in the morning for the margin surgery." She sneezes. "And can you come by this Thursday at two to get the drain removed?"

"Ah . . . let me get back to you."

Something is going on with Will. He's gasping for air. Assuming the tea had gone down the wrong way, Tess whacks him hard on the back, but when he turns to face her, she can see that he's not choking. He's sobbing. She's only seen him cry this hard a few times over the past twenty-nine years—their wedding night, the afternoon his mother departed to the other side of the veil, and following the births of their children.

"What's wrong?" she asks.

"I'm just so relieved that you're gonna be okay . . . and I feel bad that . . . I'm so sorry . . . but I've been going through something really hard of my own."

Tess sinks deeper into the couch cushions. This has got to be about the affair. All this time he'd been keeping it under his hat because he thought she was about to meet her Maker, but now that they've gotten the news that her death no longer appears to be imminent, looks like her husband is about to profess his undying love for Connie.

"I'm having . . . ," Will takes in another shuddering breath, "a midlife crisis."

"A . . . a *what*?" She was so sure he was about to tell her—I'm having *an affair*, that she doesn't think she heard him right. "What did you say?"

"I'm having a midlife crisis. That's why I . . . I haven't been here for you the way I shoulda been."

Tess doesn't believe she could be struck any dumber. She needs a moment to consider what he'd gotten off his chest and put onto hers. Is he telling her the truth, or is this some elaborate ruse he's devised to further cover up the affair? She'd very much like to buy into this, it'd be so much better than him cheating on her. If only she wasn't having such a hard time believing that he even knows what a midlife crisis *is*. He doesn't watch daytime TV. Won't read books. He sticks to magazines, and not *Psychology Today*. His bathroom library is comprised of issues of *Golf Digest*, *Hospitality Today,* and *Classic Cars*.

On the other hand, Tess is very familiar with the condition. It's fodder for many comediennes' stand-up routines, and a hot-button topic on daytime television talk shows. She mentally ticks off the midlife-crisis bullet points and addresses them:

- A sudden improvement in appearance.

She says, "I noticed that you've been working out more and . . . ." She touches his hair. "You're coloring it."

- Foolish purchases.

"Did you buy a little red sports car?" she asks him.

His tears turn into self-deprecating laughter. "Almost bought a '64 Triumph a few weekends ago."

It had been what he was driving the night they'd first met at the Arthur Murray Dance Studio. It'd been a warm spring, and instructor Tess had propped open the front door to allow a lake breeze in. The muffler on the sports car was hanging by a wire, so when her last client of the night roared up, there was no mistaking he'd arrived. Cupid's arrows found their mark the moment they laid eyes on one another. They could barely make it through the first tango lesson, that's how weak in the knees they went in each other's arms. They made no-holds-barred love later that night, and were married on May 16, a month and a half after Will had tripped across the studio's threshold into her teaching arms.

She proceeds with caution. "Are you sure about this?" The shoe's on the other foot now. Maybe he's made an erroneous assumption of his own.

"I had an appointment with Scottie." If Tess started having unusual symptoms her first thought would be to show up at a psychiatrist's office, but it makes total sense that if he sensed something was off, he'd head straight to his former classmate, and now their family doctor, Dr. Johannson. "He gave me a clean bill of health, and then he explained what a midlife crisis is all about." Will looks down at his family jewels. "And . . . there's something else I need to tell you."

- Affairs.

Tess re-tenses, sure now that everything he's revealed up to this point was just foreplay. He's about to confess that he's been making love to Connie every Wednesday night after all. Was it only a few minutes ago that she was feeling grateful that her life wasn't drawing to an end?

With a flush racing up his neck, Will murmurs, "*Monsieur Pierre* . . . he's . . . out of order. That's why I haven't been, ya know . . . eager."

Tess stress giggles. Is the man who possesses the sex drive of a teenage boy honestly asking her to believe that he can't get it up? That's not only preposterous, it's insulting. Like asking her to believe the sun won't rise.

Trying to keep the incredulousness out of her voice, she asks, "Are you telling me that Pierre can't . . . ?" She slowly raises her limp index finger to a firm upright position.

Will nods sheepishly.

What a crock. The Frenchman is working fine. Connie's just worn the poor thing out, her mother scoffs.

Tess doesn't completely disagree with Louise, and finds herself in another difficult position. She'd love to believe that a midlife dip in testosterone is why Will's not been going after her the fevered way he usually does. It's not that he doesn't want to make mad love to her anymore, or that he's stepping out on her, he's impotent.

Trust, but verify? How could she prove it? When Will was dead to the world tonight, she and Pierre could have a little *tête à tête*. But even if he did rise to the occasion that would only prove that he was capable of doing so when her husband was an unconscious and unwilling participant.

She realizes that she should just stop all this torturous wondering. Ask him straight out if the high-school sweethearts have fallen back in love again, but enduring another surgery knowing for *sure* that her husband is cheating on her? That would take away all her hope. And he *could* be telling her the truth.

If wishes were horses you woulda been trampled to death years ago, Theresa.

Tess knows that she needs to take some time to carefully sort through what Will has told her. If she doesn't, her mind will automatically take the low road. She'll begin thinking crazy thoughts. Something like, he's not having a midlife crisis, and now that it looks like she's going to live, Will is just stalling for time until he can come up with a way to fulfill his promise to marry Connie. He can't get a divorce because he's Catholic, so the only way he can get out of their marriage is by murdering her. He'll expertly carve up her body the way he does a side of beef at the diner, after which he'll tell everyone, including the police chief of Ruby Falls, Stu Whitehall, that he had absolutely no idea what had happened to her and everyone would believe him because he's a Blessing and apparently, so good at lying now.

She places her hand on Will's cheek and says, "I want to talk more about this, but I need a few minutes to organize my thoughts, and I gotta empty my drain. I forgot to do it earlier. Stay put. I'll be right back."

She hurries to the upstairs bathroom to consider Will's confession, lifts her shirt to perform the emptying routine, but something . . . it looks like there's a hunk of tissue blocking the flow and the backed-up fluid is about to pop the top. She's about to blow.

"Will!" she hollers. "Help!"

After he pounds up the stairs and arrives at her side, he says, "What's . . . ? Oh, geeze, that doesn't look right." He's gone green around the gills, but the backup gives his manly self something to focus on. He sinks to his knees and begins tinkering with the apparatus the same way he would if something stopped working at the diner. "Let me pull this out of the top and—" he tugs too hard and the bulb separates from the tube and the insides of Tess—the blood, tissue, and fluid—spew all over the both of them.

She is mortified, but Will doesn't pull away from her with a look of revulsion the way she anticipated he would. He tilts forward, presses his lips against the side of her bandaged breast, and says, "I know my problem can't compare to what you've been going through, but . . . I hope you know that it's been hard for me too, believe it or not."

When in doubt—joke.

She places her bare foot gently on his Pierre region and says tentatively, "Not."

When his laugh resonates in her chest, Tess bows her head and is grateful to receive the best medicine there is.

What a Trooper

My friend had been able to forget about tomorrow's margin surgery for twenty seconds at a time, but for the other twenty-three hours, fifty-nine minutes, and forty seconds of the day, the fear took over. And it brought company. Depression.

Heartened by their recent bathroom exchange, she had asked Will during his break from the diner yesterday, "After work tonight, how about we bundle up and take a walk? Like the old days."

He pulled a face and said, "Sorry, I can't. It's Wednesday. I've gotta stay late to . . . ah . . . review our food costs."

Tess was crushed, until her rage kicked in. Hell hath no fury and all that. She swore to herself that if and when she did feel stronger she'd quit pussyfooting around and discover what her husband was up to once and for all and it better not be Connie. She's already devised a rudimentary plan. She'll follow him. Like one of those dicks in *True Detective* she used to read about at Dalinsky's Drugstore when she was a kid. She might even take it one step further and get some helpful hints from the best stalker she knows—Otto the dishwasher.

She's listening to the soundtrack of *To Kill a Mockingbird* as we head south on I-43 this morning. She usually plays the *West Side Story* soundtrack when she goes on errands longer than two miles because it's her favorite musical, but singing along this morning to *I Feel Pretty* is out of the question. She's gained nine pounds in the last month, her hair has gone even wilder, and her right breast appears to have been involved in a fender bender. Her nipple—a smashed taillight.

The day after Dr. Whaley removed the bandages and pulled the drain out with a breathtaking *swoosh*, she'd begun doing the exercises he'd given her to stretch the muscles near where he'd removed the lymph nodes. If she didn't, he warned, her arm wouldn't gain back its full mobility. The stretches would also help guard against lymphedema. Because the flow of lymphatic fluid had been changed after he removed some nodes, she had to take certain precautions to keep it from draining into her arm, which would cause it to painfully swell. When her blood pressure needed to be checked from here on out, the doc told her to insist that the phlebotomist place the cuff on her left arm. And no shaving her right underarm with a razor that could nick and lead to an infection.

To Tess's questions about the need for the margin surgery, he shrugged and said, "I don't necessarily agree with the pathology report, but it's important to cover all the bases."

Patience stopped in the exam room after Tess and Whaley had finished up. "Where'd you decide to go for your radiation treatments?" she asked.

"St. Joe's."

Tess had done some field research at the diner. Knowing now that one in eight women got breast cancer, she'd eavesdropped on tables of four or more lunching ladies. A Dr. David Sherman, a radiation oncologist located at the cancer center at St. Joseph's, came up more than once in conversations. She was supposed to meet with him next week at the hospital in her old neighborhood—she and Birdie had been born there—but now, on account of the margin surgery, she'd had to push the appointment back.

Patience told her, "Dr. Sherman is highly respected. I'm sure he mentioned that you won't be able to wear your regular bras during radiation." He had. "You'll need soothing fabric against your skin." She dabbed at her nose. "The Pink Ladies would be the first to tell you that it's better to stock up on sports bras now rather than in the midst of treatment when shopping will be too exhausting."

That's why we're turning into Bayshore Mall this morning.

Sun's not out, and there's a twenty-mile-an-hour wind coming off Lake Michigan that's sending the temperature below zero. Tess would love to park the Volvo out of the elements, but in the Lifetime movies Haddie and she watch, a vulnerable woman is often attacked in a parking structure, and she'd also heard that it's the last place a person wants to be during an earthquake. (A very minor one was reported on May 6, 1947. She figures they're due.)

Since it's not the type of day many venture from their homes, she easily finds a slot, flips up her furry parka hood, and the two of us trudge through the lot toward the mall doors.

The children are always foremost on her mind, so after she picks up a *Rounders* poster that was screaming Henry's name from the front window of a novelty store, she moseys over to Boston Store's perfume counter for a bottle of Happy. She sprays a sample of Haddie's favorite on her wrists so she can more easily pretend that she and her girl are shopping together the way they had before trying on a pair of jeans became torturous. At Williams-Sonoma, she purchases a copper sauté pan that she knows Will would put to good use, and at the Barkery—she picks up a bag of chewy cookies for Garbo.

Trying to buy your children's love? Charm your husband with cookware? Bribe your poor dog with a bone?

Demons are waiting for Tess in Macy's third-floor lingerie department. When we step off the escalator, we are met by mannequins dressed in frothy, creamy underthings. She stops to finger the flimsy lace fabric like a child forever denied dessert. She wells up when she thinks that she'll never be able to wear anything frou frou again without feeling like she's trying to make a silk purse out of a sow's ear. She ends up snatching four of the simple cotton sports bras that Patience had suggested off a nearby rack.

I set my arm around her shoulders as we drag toward the down escalator with her purchases. "Remember the words of Dr. Drake," I say. "Humor is the best way to transcend the pain. Whatcha got?"

She's nonresponsive, almost limp, so I take the

initiative and tell her the joke about the Polack who got stuck on an escalator as we step on. It's one of her favorites because her daddy told it to her, but even that doesn't help stave off the black feelings.

"The song?" I suggest.

She's so tangled up inside that she doesn't even realize she's acquiesced and given voice to, "I've got something in my pocket that belongs upon my face. I keep it very close at hand in a most convenient place," until another woman with a haunting vibrato joins in, and then one by one so do the other ladies stacked up behind her. "I'm sure you'll never guess it if you guess a long, long while. So I'll take it out and put it on it's a great big Brownie smile."

By the time they reach the ground floor, the troopers are in perfect harmony.

An Encore Performance

Unlike his response to the initial surgery, Will volunteered to stay in the hospital room while Dr. Whaley completed the margin cleanup, but until Tess's questions about his faithfulness are satisfactorily answered, she thought it best to keep him at arm's length.

After he delivers her to St. Mary's North, she jumps out of the car and rushes through the hospital's double doors before he can holler an insipid, "Love you," out the car window.

"We've got to stop meeting like this," Nurse Jerry quips when he shows Tess into the room.

The accommodations are not as sumptuous as the last time. The bed has been replaced by a La-Z-Boy, and she assumes that Will was right when he'd told her, "This surgery doesn't sound like a complete engine overhaul like the first one. This will be quick. Like a tune-up."

After Susan, the Amish-looking nurse, checks off the presurgery questionnaire, off they go to the operating room where Dr. Whaley asks from behind his green mask, "You set?"

"Like a table," hysterical Tess says through chattering teeth. (Birdie had told her that joke when they were kids.)

When anesthesiologist, Dr. Gritzhammer, lowers the mask it occurs to her that it might've been prudent to apologize for not returning his call last night since he's controlling her air flow, but by her third inhalation—ninety-thirteen—she no longer gives a fig. She's got bigger fish to fry. The only way she could talk herself into the surgery was by reminding herself over and over that while she's under, she'll be reunited again with her family in the Sea of Unconditional Love.

What a cotton-pickin' shame nothing like that happened.

Tess awakens in the recovery room remembering nothing and feeling leaden and groggier than the last time. Jerry returns her to her room, fusses over her vitals for a few minutes, and warns her to stay seated.

She's relieved that Dr. Gritzhammer hadn't transformed her into a salad ingredient, but she's crushed that she'd not experienced another visit to the Land of Milk and Honey. Close to tears, she asks me, "Why do you think that is?"

I shrug and say with a smile, "One per customer?" because I can't answer that truthfully. I can only commiserate. (Another part of my job is to decide how many revelations my already overstimulated friend can handle at any particular point in time. I don't want her to short circuit.)

Upon Jerry's return, Tess tells him how glad she is that Mare's cancer had gone into remission in an overly lucid way—the way drunks talk to cops—because he won't release her if she seems too out of it, which she is.

Will shows up to retrieve her an hour later.

Back home, he helps her into bed and returns to the diner for the afternoon shift. She drifts into a deep sleep and a drug-induced dream. She and Birdie are having a picnic on the beach where Tess had tried to dispose of her mother's ashes. The girls are having a grand old time until they notice someone darting amongst the trees in the woods behind them. It takes them a few minutes to figure out it's Louise. She keeps her distance until the sisters go for a swim, but then she scuttles down to the sand and steals their lunch basket.

Tess hears herself yell out, "Stop, thief!" when she bolts up in bed drenched in sweat. Unsure how long she'd been out, she checks the clock next to the bed. It's almost five. "Henry?" she calls out. "You home?"

If he is, he isn't answering her. She didn't tell him about the early-morning surgery. She'd figured that the anesthesia would've worn off by the time he got home from basketball practice asking for a snack or complaining about some teacher.

She calls him on his cell phone because she recently discovered this is a better line of communication as opposed to face-to-face conversation.

"Where are you?" she asks.

"Bobo's."

"What're you doing?"

"Poker."

"It's getting late. Are you eating supper over there?"

"Yeah."

She hangs up and leans back onto the pillows. Other than Garbo, who is lying at the foot of the bed, she thought she was alone until she hears the toilet flush. Will usually came home between shifts, but not always. He zips up and tells her how busy lunch had been and she gives him an update on Henry.

"You hungry?" he asks.

"Uh-uh."

He kisses her on the forehead. "If you change your mind, you know where to find me."

Except on Wednesday nights, Louise reminds, before Tess drifts off again.

She wakes up a few hours later after a fitful sleep. She's in pain. Her wounded breast is aching more than it had. She rolls onto her back and lifts up her nightie to check beneath the loose bandage. "Oh, man, Grace. Look." Her good old girl is shiny and swollen, the skin stretched tightly across what feels like a piece of teakwood. "I don't think this is supposed to happen."

I agree. "You better call Will."

He has difficulty hearing her because the diner is hopping and that's good. The medical bills have already started pouring in. Tess shouts into the phone, "There's something going on with my breast. It hurts and it's hard and . . . I don't know what to do."

"Rob Whaley's here with his wife," he hollers. "Let me ask him."

Tess hopes he remembers to lower his voice. Not blurt out something about the cancer in front of the doctor's wife or the restaurant staff and customers.

Will comes back to tell her a few minutes later, "He says we need to meet him at the emergency room. He's leaving now, and I've already got on my coat."

Tess hangs up and calls Henry back. "There's

something going on with my elbow. I mean . . . ," she smacks herself in the head, "my shoulder. I've gotta go back to the hospital and get it looked at. Can you get a ride home?"

No response.

"Henry?"

"We're in the middle of a hold 'em tournament. Can I stay the night?"

He's got school tomorrow, but it might be a good idea to keep him away until she knows what's going on. "Yeah, sure."

She doesn't bother changing out of her cows-sipping-*café-au-lait*-on-the-*Champs-Élysées* nightie, just slips on her coat and boots, kisses Garbo goodbye, and waits in the mud room until she hears Will beep the horn in the driveway.

Dr. Whaley must've called ahead because an emergency-room nurse, who looks better suited for work on a loading dock, is expecting them. Will's holding Tess's hand in the curtained exam room, but it's not doing much good to keep her steady. She's barely recovered from this afternoon's surgery.

Her surgeon shows up ten minutes later wearing a leather jacket, creased jeans, and a white button-down shirt. He asks her to lie back and slides his practiced fingers across her petrified breast. "That's what I thought. It's a hematoma," he says. "You're bleeding into your breast. It's a complication from the surgery. I have to drain it."

This is the second time Dr. Cutie Patootie has screwed up. Where'd he get his scalpel? A Cracker Jack box?

Tess tells him, "Fine." She was so very tired. "I'll rest my eyes and you go fetch your drain."

"I'm afraid it's not quite that simple. Eventually the blood will be reabsorbed, but that takes time and you need to start your radiation treatments," the doc says. "You'll have to have another surgery."

She dissolves into kitten yowls.

Will asks the man who'd been sharing a romantic banana split a half hour earlier with his wife at Count Your Blessings, "When?"

"Immediately."

Tessie cries out, "Nooo!" but the wheels are already set in motion.

A little after two a.m., the Blessings return home down the empty streets of Ruby Falls. Will helps his still-woozy woman through the backdoor of the house and up the staircase. As they approach the closed door of their son's room, which was supposed to be vacant, Tess stops. She can feel Henry's presence. "He must've come home 'cause he lost big," she says. "I need to check on the snake. Could you let Garbo out?"

She tiptoes in, but throws only a cursory look at the reptile aquarium. She's really come to touch Henry the only time he'll let her. She kneels down beside his bed to stroke his long back and nuzzle his hair. He grunts and rolls away from her.

When she stands, the drugs hit her hard and she grabs onto the foot of the bed to steady herself. While she's waiting for the room to stop spinning, Henry says out of the dark, "I know ya got something bad wrong with you and it's not your shoulder. Or your elbow." A rustling of sheets, the flipping of a pillow. "And the snake croaked again. 'Night."

Four Pairs of Red Wax Lips, The Really Big Ones

Tess rose determined from a dreamless sleep. Once she gets things straightened out with Henry, she plans to set into her new To-Do List with renewed vigor.

She'll be the first to admit that her cooking is nothing to write home about, but she's a pretty good baker. Her technique isn't great, but she kneads dough with so much heart you can taste it. She's thrown together a colorful breakfast for her son this morning: Cinnamon rolls with orange cream cheese frosting and Green Mountain coffee.

Will's still asleep. Last night's emergency surgery took so much out of him, poor baby. So it's just Henry and gung-ho Tess in the heavenly smelling kitchen this morning. She's seated in her usual spot at the table. Garbo is nuzzled at her feet and, as always, I'm by her side. Henry's across from us.

Instead of tackling the big issue right off, I suggest that she breaks the ice by asking her early-morning-challenged son how cards went last night.

He paws at one of the rolls and tells her, "I won my fair share of the pots," in an assured, James-Bond-in-

Monte-Carlo way.

Tess grins. She adores every single thing about this boy, but it's his sense of humor that really slays her. She takes a sip of tea, then says as offhandedly as she can, which isn't very, "What you said last night? You're right. I do . . . *did* have something bad wrong with me, but I'm fine now." She launches into an abbreviated, untechnical version of the cancer ordeal and concludes with, "I kept it a secret because I didn't want to upset you." Henry doesn't appear to be thrown, nor does he pepper her with questions, which doesn't really surprise her. After all, the tumor was located in one of her good old girls, which he felt entirely uncomfortable acknowledging she possessed. And he's a teenage boy, with a practiced poker face. She didn't expect him to dissolve into tears the way Haddie might when she shares the news with her.

Her children have very little in common except the love they have for one another. They teased, but also confided in each other. Tess had overheard them talking while they were watching a movie together in the basement a few months back. Henry had been jamming pepperoni pizza into his face and making fun of Haddie for nibbling "hamster food," and the truth about her disorder came out.

Tess takes another sip of tea and tells her son, "You need to promise me that you'll keep all of this on the down low. Even from your sister, most especially from your sister. I know that you know she's going through something really hard of her own right now."

"Whatever," he says as he reaches for a cinnamon roll for the road. "Bobo's gonna pick me up in ten minutes. He bet giving me a ride to school for the rest of the year and he lost." Henry isn't looking at Tess. His focus is over her shoulder, on the flock of snow angels outside the kitchen window. "You sure you're not gonna . . . ya know?"

"Positive," she says, even though she's still not convinced that she won't die sooner rather than later. It appears that she licked it his time, but look at Mare Hanson and all her recurrences. "All that's left now are the radiation treatments to make sure every bit of it is gone."

When Henry pushes his chair away from the table, his eyes are shining, but he's doing a good job of pretending they aren't. "What's radiation?"

She tells her *Star Wars* fanatic, "Light-saber stuff," because that's how she's framed the treatment in her mind—Princess Tess fighting the Dark Side.

He shakes his head, says dryly, "If you're about to say, 'May the force be with you'—don't. Seriously. That's *so* lame."

Tess laughs as he proceeds toward the mud room to bundle himself against March's blustering. "Love you, Momil," he says before he slams out of the house.

With a warm, fuzzy feeling, the kind one might experience when a lost sock turns up, Tess moves on to the next items on today's agenda. She removes the new To-Do List from her robe pocket, smoothes it out on the kitchen table, and studies it.

She crosses out number seven, same for number eight.

Having a religious epiphany didn't feel important to her anymore. According to the doctors, her number wasn't up, and the way she looked at it, if she wasn't about to die in the next month or so why bother getting all holy?

1. ~~Buy broccoli.~~
2. ~~Make sure Haddie gets the help she needs from a better therapist.~~
3. ~~Set up a vocational counseling appointment for Henry.~~
4. Convince Will to love me again.
5. Get Birdie to talk to me.
6. Bury Louise once and for all.
7. ~~Have a religious epiphany so #8 is going to be okay with me.~~
8. ~~Die.~~

She skips past number four because she's not sure anymore if she even wants to convince Will to love her again. That depends on whether he's having an affair.

Number five on the list is her number one priority this morning.

Tess has been pining for her sister. Desperately needs the comfort of their shared experience. To not say to someone, for instance, her husband, "Do you ever feel like someone has gotten a hold of your mind and is using it to beat you into submission?" and have that someone, say her husband, reply, "Speaking of beating . . . doesn't an egg-white omelet sound good?" Birdie would understand. Despite the state their relationship is now in, her sister's and her connection is as powerful as two soldiers surviving a war, a bond that can't be replicated. They went crazy together.

On her walk to the sunroom, Tess reviews everything she's done thus far to open their line of communication.

Besides sending the twenty-eight smiling-suns-and-kitties Hallmark cards that she'd hoped might put Birdie into a "Today Is a Purrrfect Day" frame of mind, she'd tried a telegram—"Let's stop this. Stop." Sent a gorgeous tussie-mussie. A yellow angora sweater. The wishing well. And one hundred and forty-two e-mails, as of this morning.

When I make myself comfortable in the chintz chaise, Garbo plops down next to me. Tess is psyching herself up to write Birdie yet again, and also preparing herself for another rejection. But when she turns on her computer, much to her astonishment, her sister has already beaten her to the punch! (I mighta asked Bee to nudge her a little.) Will felt bad about how much Tess'd been missing her sister and he helped out too. He knew from her past attempts to contact Birdie that she might not pick up if he placed the call from home, so he phoned her yesterday afternoon from a number that he knew she wouldn't recognize—the diner's. She was chilly at first, but Will can lay on the Blessing charm when he wants to, and they ended up having a fairly nice talk. Not nice enough that she felt comfortable accepting his invitation to come visit in May, but the groundwork had been laid.

Tessie's eyes are locked onto the instant message from **Birdistheword** that's appeared on the computer screen. Her immediate reaction was, "Hurray!" but then, of course, her guard went up. She's suspicious of all fortuitous events, and this one really has her wondering. The timing is too extraordinary, too much of a coincidence. She'd been whining to Will more than usual lately how badly she needed to connect with Birdie and *poof*—here she is!? Which is why it's now occurring to my friend that it's *not* her sister after all, but *Will* communicating with her on his laptop upstairs. He's been slightly more attentive as of late and he might be trying to comfort her. She doesn't know very much about computers. Is it possible for him to impersonate her sister via instant messages?

If not, and it really *is* Birdie, it's just occurred to Tess that while it's so, so wonderful to finally hear from her, this conversation might not go as hoped. She's been dreaming about the loving, close relationship they'd once had, but she had to face the fact that Birdie might not feel the same way. She might've only reached out to her this morning because she's in the grips of a delusion, or she could be having one of her "Today Was a Cloudy Day and Tomorrow Will Be One as Well and Every Day after That Is Not Looking So Hot Either, So What's the Fucking Point?" days and only contacted Tess to castigate her once again for not being the big sister she'd always wanted and needed. One who would've saved their daddy from drowning, one who wouldn't have agreed with Leon about pulling the plug on Louise, one who would've kept her promise to scatter their mother's ashes.

Tess's fingertips are almost vibrating when she places them on the keyboard and pecks out:

> Tessie: Is that really you?
> Birdistheword: No. It's Boogie Ackerman.
> Tessie: LOL.

She's only laughing out of one side of her mouth though. That doesn't prove anything. It could still be Will pretending to be Birdie. She'd told him how she'd accidentally impersonated the notorious nose-picker in one of her e-mails to her sister.

> Tessie: If it's really you, tell me something that only you and I know.

When there's not an immediate response, her heart takes a dive. Goddammit. She's about to fire off a nasty note to Will when I tell her, "Give it a minute."

Forty-four seconds later this pops up:

> Birdistheword: Me and Bee.
> Tessie: :)

She'd never told Will, or anybody else, about Birdie's "imaginary friend."

> Birdistheword: I'm sorry you have cancer. I didn't mean it when I told you that I wished you were dead.
> Tessie: I know.
> Birdistheword: I feel really, really, really, really bad. I think I gave it to you. I stuck some pins in a voodoo doll.

Tess looks over at me and laughs. "I bet that's why she hasn't gotten back to me before now. She's been feeling guilty." This will be a quick fix. She's pretty good at reassuring Birdie.

Tessie: You didn't give me cancer, Bird.

Birdistheword: Okay. Did you scatter Louise's ashes yet?

Tessie: If it's alright with you, I decided that it'd better if the Finley sisters did that together.

Another long pause, during which I remind my friend of one of the most basic, but effective techniques to center herself, "Breathe." She gets three good ones in before her sister types back.

Birdistheword: Let me think about it.

Now, that could take a spell. When you're obsessive, reaching a decision on the simplest questions can take hours, months, even years, so Tess takes her time walking back to the kitchen to make another cup of Earl Grey. When she returns to the sunroom, there's been no new communication, so she looks to me for advice. "Prod her a little."

Tessie: Don't you want to be sisters again?

Birdistheword: Yes, but. . . .

Tessie: What?

Birdistheword: I don't know if I can trust you.

Tess understands her sister's skittishness, but doesn't feel the same way. She trusts Birdie implicitly. The locating of Gammy and not sharing her had only temporarily shaken her belief in their relationship.

> Tessie: What can I do to prove to you that I'm
> trustworthy?
> Birdistheword: Send me a little something. A present.

No surprise. Gifts mean a lot to Birdie because it was the only way that Louise showed her love when they were kids—a candy bar here, a hula hoop there, and balloons on their birthday. *Those* "wants" would be a breeze to fill, but generally, the more het up Birdie was, the stranger the requests could get. She might ask Tess for something so incredibly odd that no matter how much she wants to, she'll be unable to fill her request. Her sister might decide she needs an assortment of Mexican jumping beans. (She's always been partial to them.) Or a pair of genuine lederhosen. (*The Sound of Music* is her all-time favorite movie.) A Bob Mackie original. (She's nuts about Cher's way-out costumes.)

My friend clenches her jaw and types out:

> Tessie: Like what?
> Birdistheword: Go to *Ma's* and get me four pairs of
> those wax lips. The really big red ones. Not those
> small pinkish ones.

Due to her compliant personality, Birdie had always been an easier target than Tess. When their mother would do something extraordinarily humiliating to her, like the time she hung out the pee sheet off the front porch or forced her to get up on a scale during a church fair and called her a freak and "Two-ton Robin" over the PA system, Tess would inevitably find her lying curled up in their bed later than night wearing those smooth red wax lips that she'd bought at the neighborhood candy store. Only after her big sister pressed her soft lips against the wax ones four times, would little Birdie fall asleep.

> Tessie: I love you as much as the stars and the moon. I'll send the lips.
> Birdistheword: FedEx. FedEx. FedEx. FedEx.

When her sister signs off, Tess is basking in the glow of the Hallmark moment. "The Tree of Life Has Many Limbs. If One Should Break . . . Go Out on Another!" is exactly what the both of them had semi-accomplished during the chat.

She removes a pen from the cup holder on her desk and takes it to her list:

~~5. Get Birdie to talk to me again.~~

Experiencing a rare sense of satisfaction, she leans back in her chair and tells Garbo and me, "Six down . . . two to go."

The Horse Is Out of the Barn

We're waiting patiently, well, I'm waiting patiently. Tess is hugging her lucky purse to her chest and pacing in front of the bank of elevators at St. Mary's North office building because she has a follow-up visit scheduled with Dr. Whaley after her recent surgery to remove the hematoma. She's berating herself, calling herself a lily-livered chicken, a loser, fat slob, stupid, worthless, and every other name in the book all because I suggested it'd be nice if we didn't have to walk up three flights of stairs this morning.

When an opportunity presents itself, it's part of my job description to pounce on it. "Ya know that quote you love so much from the *Mockingbird* story?"

"Which one?" she asks. "I love a lot of 'em."

I nudge her closer to the elevator doors. "I was thinkin' about the one in which Atticus describes courage."

She stops pacing long enough to recite how Mr. Finch explained it to his son, Jem, at the end of Chapter Eleven: "'It's when you know you're licked before you begin but you begin anyway and you see it through no matter what. You rarely win, but sometimes you do.'"

"That's the one." I take another step closer to her. "He's right you know. All of us have to figure out a way to get past that two-edged sword. Fear is real good at keepin' us safe, but it's also real good at keepin' us from living." On my cue, the elevator door opens. "Think of all the things you've given up because you were too afraid to take a risk. Travel . . . museums . . . truffles." Of course, I already know the answer to the question I'm about to ask, but I want her to tell me because speaking aloud about our fears can loosen their hold. "Say . . . why are ya afraid of truffles anyway?"

She says to the floor, "I'm not afraid of truffles. I'm afraid of the snot that's leaking out of the pig's snout when it snarfs around for the truffles."

I give her my hundred-watt smile, take two giant steps into the elevator, lean against the back wall, and say, "Maybe you could learn to acknowledge the fear, but instead of runnin' away, just get about your business. The best way to do that is to just say, 'fuck it.'"

Tess shakes her head. "I can't do that."

"But you already *do* when the children need you to."

"That's different."

"So you can overcome terror to drive to far-off places for Haddie's art shows, and eat food that someone coughed all over at Henry's high-school basketball games, because it's for them?"

"Right."

"But when it comes to dealing with something that would benefit you, no dice?"

She strokes her lucky purse.

"I believe in you, Tessie. I know you could deal with the things you're scared of all the time with a little practice and a stout heart."

"I want to but. . . ." It's not like she's afraid of just a few things. For reasons that I'm not privy to, Tessie has been given a heavier load than most to tote. "How would I . . . I mean—"

"First thing you gotta do when you feel the panic coming is to think to yourself—what's the worst that can happen?"

"You're joking, right?"

"Let me put it another way," I say. "If you trace fear back to its roots, what do you think that folks are *really* scared of. It might seem like it's flyin' and speakin' in public and spiders and snakes, but that's smoke and mirrors. What ya 'spose is at the bottom of it?"

She toes the lobby carpet and shrugs.

The correct answer is death, of course. An inevitability that the truest part of her isn't scared of anymore. Getting a glimpse at the place people most often call Heaven when she was put under for the first surgery has taken away a chunk of her fear. (She hasn't consciously realized this yet, but that's fine, her soul KNOWS that it's paid a visit to home, sweet, home.) But earthbound Tessie, the one who's cowering and fidgeting, the one who's so thoroughly imprisoned by her brain, thinks about my question and says, "I don't know. I remember a time when the fear was something I *had*, but now . . . it's who I am. I've tried and tried, Grace, but I can't beat it."

"Damn," I say as I throw my hands up, "that right there . . . that's what you're doin' wrong, baby! You're settin' your goals too high. Nobody walks God's green Earth without stepping into the shadows. It's part of why y'all are here. To work these things out. Heck, even I've got a coupla of bad fears."

"You're just saying that to make me feel better."

I sense an opening.

"If I tell you what strikes terror in *my* heart, will you get in here next to me? Trust yourself enough to rise above your fear?"

She winces at the pun, but then, like she's approaching the edge of a bottomless pool, nonswimmer Tess inches toward me.

"Your turn," she whispers as the elevator doors slide shut behind her. "What are you afraid of?"

Before I get into that, I make the elevator lights flicker just long enough to increase her fear of getting stuck. What I'm about to tell her needs to imprint deeply into her PTSD brain and the more scared she is, the more of an impression it'll make. "My biggest fear is that I might fail to get through to you."

When the lights stop flickering and the elevator comes to a bouncy stop on floor three, Tess doesn't rush out. She searches my face, slowly exits, and makes her way down the hallway to Dr. Whaley's office. She hesitates in front of the door and asks me, "What's your second-biggest fear?"

I hem and haw a little before I admit, "I'm petrified of the Oscar Mayer Wienermobile."

Tess is laughing as she steps into Whaley's office to find Patience sorting out the magazines in the waiting room. "Well," she says to the first patient of the day. "That's music to my ears."

Into the exam room they go. Patience wastes no time getting to what's on her mind. "Now that you've finished with the surgeries, I hope that you've given some further thought to joining The Pink Ladies." She removes a Kleenex from her uniform pocket and blows her pink-tipped nose. "It's so important to recovery to spend time with others who are, or have been, in the same situation as you. You can draw strength from the other women while you go through your radiation treatments."

Sometimes Tess felt buoyed by breast cancer patients' commitment to staying upbeat, but mostly she thought their attempts came off like Birdie trying to stay one step ahead of her problems by surrounding herself with Hallmark cards. And what if during one of the meetings, she had a hyperventilating panic attack in front of the other women? She didn't need that kind of stress and neither did they. Even if she did share her journey with them, she couldn't very well ask every Pink Lady to keep her cancer to themselves. Word would get out. Henry knows now, but Haddie's still in the dark and her mother aims to keep her there for the time being.

"I know your heart is in the right place, but please, stop asking me to join the group," Tess tells Patience. "You're beginning to make me feel like I've got a life-threatening disease and need all the help I can get."

The receptionist grins, but clears her throat like she's about to deliver a speech, which she is. "You told me that you're afraid of speaking in public, but I noticed on your employment history that you're a stand-up comedian." Tess starts to explain that doing a bit in a club is not the same as sharing her innermost feelings in an intimate setting, but Patience pulls down the paper sheet on the exam table and ignores her. "Cancer can be alienating, and the psychological healing process mysterious. One woman can pull out of this illness to go on with her life with renewed hope, while another lets it take the best of her. About the only thing experts seem to agree upon in terms of treatment is the importance of keeping one's spirits up."

Tess entertains the suggestion. The idea of doing one of her old stand-up routines in front of the women's cancer group is not entirely unappealing. She truly does love to make people laugh.

Patience ups the ante. "Who knows? You might even get some new material out of the group. The meetings can get pretty funny."

Oh yeah, I bet that support group is one big yuckathon, Louise cracks.

"A while back, one of the ladies was telling the group about the first time she went swimming after she'd had a mastectomy," Patience says. "She was having one of those I-am-woman-hear-me-roar moments when she paused to catch her breath after a couple of laps and saw three kids playing keep away with her prosthesis in the shallow end."

Tess is deciding if she finds that funny or so very sad or a little of both, when there's a knock on the door and Dr. Whaley steps in. After the usual niceties, and a compliment on Count Your Blessings' meatloaf that he and the Mrs. had last night for dinner, he says to his patient, "May I see the incisions, please?"

Before Patience leaves to answer the phone they can all hear ringing, she tells Tessie, "Just think about what we talked about, okay?"

Dr. Whaley pokes and prods, and says, "Has she been

putting the hard press on you to join The Pink Ladies?"

"Uh-huh."

"Did she tell you the keep-away story?"

She nods.

"She was the swimmer," Whaley says.

Tess says, "Huh," and sees Patience in a new light. She likes that she didn't lay that on her in her recruitment speech.

The doctor, who'd been engrossed in the scar on her breast and the one beneath her arm, takes a step back, like he's admiring a stunning piece of artwork, and says, "These look really, really good."

"Like they say, beauty is in the eye of the beholder," Tess replies. "I think they make me look like a Picasso."

Dr. Whaley takes that as a compliment. "On to the next step. Have you made your initial radiation appointment?"

"I'm meeting with Dr. Sherman over at St. Joe's soon as you give me the go-ahead."

Tess could tell that he thought selecting a hospital in a part of Milwaukee where there were some terrific rib joints and nobody cared about their lawn instead of posh St. Mary's North was an odd decision, but he didn't question her choice of physicians. "Dr. Sherman is top-notch. You'll be in good hands." He closes her chart. "You'll complete the radiation regime, take your Tamoxifen every day, and with a little luck, you'll live another thirty or forty years."

"Tell me more about the Tamoxifen." She'd read about the drug in the plethora of printed material she'd been given over the past months, but she was still unsure if she needed to take it.

"It's a pill form of chemotherapy," Whaley says. "You have an estrogen-receptive tumor, so taking the Tamoxifen will be like placing an embargo on an evil dictator."

She wonders how many times he's used that line on other women. "I'm not political."

"You must take the Tamoxifen."

"No."

"Yes."

"No!" Scarred and scared, quibbling with this dishy guy over a drug she's frightened to take, shoves her over the edge and into the Valley of Tears.

"Tess," Whaley says as he sets a box of Kleenex down next to her. "You can do this. You're strong."

Before she can stop herself, she shouts, "No, I'm not!" Too ashamed, caring too deeply that people would think she was as repulsive as her mother made her feel if she let them see her symptoms, she's about to yell something that she's never admitted to anyone other than mental health professionals and Will. The truth. "I've got PTSD and OCD and . . . and agoraphobia and I can't swallow pills and . . . and I can't go to Paris and I'm afraid of pig snot and—goddamn it all!"

Now you've done it.

Had she?

Tess is stunned to find that instead of wanting to curl up in a humiliated ball the way she thought she would if someone found out that she colored outside the lines, she doesn't seem to give a rat's ass what Rob Whaley thinks. It hits her then that what I'd told her in the elevator was the truth. Somewhere along this journey, without realizing it, she must've already told herself, "Fuck it," because she doesn't feel beaten down, small, and defeated. She feels like . . . like a heavyweight contender ready to take on all comers!

In response to her outburst, the doc places his hand on her forearm and says, "I don't mean to overstep my bounds, I'm a surgeon not a psychiatrist." He gives her a look dripping with concern. "But it sounds like you might have some underlying emotional issues that need to be addressed."

When she responds to his observation by breaking into fairly maniacal laughter, Whaley tries to make it look like he isn't hurrying through the exam room door—no sudden moves around crazy people—to fetch a hypodermic full of valium.

Tess stops laughing long enough to holler after the doctor, "Hey, Rob?"

"Yes?" comes warily out of the hallway.

"Your barn door's open."

Tattooed

Lou Gehrig's disease laid claim to the rest of Tess's favorite diner customer, Richie Mattigan, last week. She'd had his joke and his table ready on his usual day, but his wife had shown up alone on Friday to break the news. In the privacy of the party room, Holly had blubbered, "If you could tell one of your jokes at his service, you know how he loves . . . I mean . . . lov*ed* them." Tess rubbed her back, told her she'd be honored, and placed an order for two hot fudge sundaes with extra whipped cream that they raised in a toast, "To Richie."

A few days later, Tess was gazing down at the standing-room-only crowd at St. Lucy's who'd come to remember the life of this extraordinary man.

After a few other friends and family members spoke about Richie's many attributes and contributions, ancient Father Jessop introduced Tess to the congregation. She stood tall behind the lectern, pointed first at Richie's wife and his two beautiful children in the first pew, upwards, and then to her heart. The joke she'd prepared was a spin on a treasured anecdote Richie had shared with her before he'd become too ill to speak.

She clears her throat and says, "During one of his usual

Sunday school classes a while back, Richie quizzed his little students on how one went about getting into Heaven. He asked them, 'If I gave a lot of my time and money to St. Lucy's would that do the trick?'"

"'NO!' the children shouted back."

"'Well . . . what if I helped paint the church and mowed the lawn and plowed out the parking lot in winter, would that get me into Heaven?' he wondered."

"Once more the group of kids answered with a loud and clear, 'NO!'"

"Richie said, 'How about if I was super-duper nice and smart and worked hard at being a great dad and husband and coached Little League and donated turkeys on Thanksgiving to people less fortunate and never once complained when I got sick with a horrible disease, would that be enough to get me into Heaven?'"

"Once again, his Sunday school pupils hollered together, 'NO!'"

"'Huh,' Richie said as he scratched his head and looked perplexed at their sweet upturned faces. 'Then . . . how in the heck *would* I get into Heaven?'"

"One of the little boys sitting in the back of the room jumped up and shouted, "'You gotta be dead, Mr. Mattigan!'"

Since the congregation was more familiar with sermons than stand-up, no one knew quite how to react to the punch line. It wasn't until Richie's wife and kids began to laugh that the rest of the mourners joined in.

Tess would later tell Will that she was certain that amongst the giggles and guffaws that'd filled the church that afternoon, she'd heard Richie's unmistakably soulful laugh. She'd know it anywhere.

A deeply depressed Tess and I are making the first of many drives we'll be taking during the following months to St. Joe's Hospital. Will offered to come along, but she'd shot him down. Losing Richie has heightened her worries about losing her own husband. Not to illness, but to Connie Lushman.

I tell her as we exit the I-43 and turn up North Avenue, "You're in a rut. You need to go someplace other than funerals, the grocery store, the diner, Henry's basketball games, the old folks' home, and doctors' offices."

"Like where?" she says flatly.

"You could get your hair done." Her mass of red curls has grown long enough to reach her shoulder blades. "It's lookin' confused."

Sitting in the Peaches and Cream salon, listening to stylist Suzanne going on about Wonder Bras, steamy television shows, or saying, *Hey, did you hear that Mrs. Johnson got so ticked off at incoming PTA president Mrs. Hoskins that she toilet-papered her house?* seems as pointless as everything else does when Tess gets down like this.

And this morning's trip isn't helping her mood any. She's well aware that spending time in the old neighborhood might ignite painful flashbacks and panic on top of everything else, so we are proceeding westward under a yellow flag.

When we are stopped by the light on 48th Street, the corner home of Dalinsky's Drugstore, I point out the window and say to her perkily, "How about a little pleasure before business?"

She's hoping they still serve their classic root beer floats as she pulls to the curb. I usher her through the door and over to the red Formica lunch counter that's so much like the one at Count Your Blessings, they could be twins. While we wait for Tess's brown cow, she checks her memory against the improvements the store has made over the decades. The cosmetic counter is still where it was, so is the magazine rack near the front door. She notices the banner of a *True Detective*, and below it a row of *Playboy*s that remind her of how she'd once dreamed of her chest growing as huge as Miss August 1962. She wonders if checking out those dirty magazines when she was a kid was why she got breast cancer. Is she paying for her sins?

"Here ya go," the young waitress says as she sets the frosty mug down.

As my friend slurps, I point out, "I know ya don't give a hoot about anything right now, but you might want to have a copy of that detecting magazine at the ready. When you feel better and decide to follow Will, you'll want to be prepared." She won't respond because she can't imagine ever feeling lighter of heart again, or caring about Will, their marriage, or anything else. Except for her children. There is no dark force within or without that could keep her from loving and protecting them.

She pays the check at the same register Birdie had once seen the postcard of the burly, redheaded fellow she thought was their daddy in Boca Raton. She gets impulsive when she gets in this mood, so as we pass the rack, Tess slips a copy of *True Detective* inside her coat.

I'm hoping her mood will take an uptick after she completes her mission as we head toward our next intended stop that's about a half mile west of the drugstore.

Will had shown her Mrs. Alvina "Ma" Malishewski's obituary and the accompanying story in the *Milwaukee Journal*, so she knew the Allen Ludden-loving candy lady had died years ago of diabetes, and that her daughter Katrina a.k.a. "New Ma," was doing her best to follow in her mother's footsteps.

The bell still tinkles on the front door of the sweet shop, and it still smells of sauerkraut, and the bins are overflowing with the identical sweets that Birdie and she had adored as kids. When the woman comes scuffling out of the back room, Tess gasps at how much she resembles Old Ma. My friend tells her she was sorry to hear about her mother, and they reminisce for a bit before she asks for the four sets of red wax lips for her sister and a Holloway sucker for herself. She runs her hand down the black iron railing next to the front steps on her way back to the car and it feels the same.

It strikes her on the quick drive to the hospital how things may get an overhaul, but at the heart of the matter . . . do they really change? Do people? How much different was she really from the mixed-up sad girl who sat on the steps of Ma's forty years ago hoping to learn more about love and life?

Since she'd dissociated during their get-together last week, Tess is having a hard time recalling what her radiation oncologist, Dr. Sherman, had told her to expect at this morning's mapping appointment. Something about receiving tattoos and that the thirty-six treatments would be painless. For sure he said, "You're going to get a little tired."

She could handle just a little tired, but barely. The three surgeries had taken a toll not only on her mind, but her forty-nine-year-old body. She wanted to take Garbo for a walk down Chestnut St. yesterday, but they only got as far as the Keller's house before she had succumbed to spaghetti legs and shortness of breath. (Some of those symptoms might not have been caused by her physical state. Strolling down the block always reminded her of how she and Will would tango down to the tree that he'd carved their initials in, and the passionate lovemaking that followed.)

"Theresa . . . Tess Blessing," she tells the itty-bitty woman at the cancer center's check-in desk. "I have an appointment to get my mapping done."

"Welcome," the gal says in a dolly voice. "I'm Marty. Dr. Whaley's office forwarded your insurance information, so you can take a seat. Someone will be with you soon."

Two chairs down from us in the fluorescent-lit waiting area there's an older, ski-pole thin, bald, black woman. Her grandbaby, who she may never see grow up, is at her feet making *vroom, vroom* sounds with a red Matchbox car.

Tess thinks of Henry and turns her head away to take in the rest of the room. Unattractive nature prints similar to the ones that dot the walls of St. Mary's North hang on the walls. The four vinyl couches are muddy brown and worn on the arms, and the room reeks of nervous sweat, perfumes, and . . . salami?

A medium-sized man with lovely white hair worn in a pompadour appears at the edge of the waiting room. "Theresa Blessing?" When she asks him to call her by her nickname, he replies in a voice that makes her think of the Shhhh sign at the library. "I'm Irwin." The smile he shares is welcoming and very white. His eyes are Paul Newman blue and Tess wonders if he's wearing contacts. "I'll be your radiation tech for the next seven weeks." He slips a lotion-softened hand around her elbow and guides her down a hall to the women's locker room because men get breast cancer too. "After you change, wait here." He gestures to six hard tan chairs lined up across from a wall TV where a cocoa-colored woman is seated. When he says, "Harriet," the woman shuffles after him in worn, yellow bedroom slippers.

Mostly, Tess selected this hospital because she's positive she won't bump into someone she knows from Ruby Falls who'd blow her cover. But that's not the only reason. The color of the residents of this part of town played a huge part in her decision. Like I mentioned earlier on, my friend has always felt more comfortable with people of a darker hue. If they should hail from the South, they get bonus points. (Which came first? Her passion for *To Kill a Mockingbird* or the passion she brought to the story? Her subconscious also remembers more than she realizes about the first encounter we'd had when she and Birdie were driven furiously to the Core by Louise during one of her drop-off punishments. My rolled sugar cookies are hard to forget.)

I say with a grin when she exits the locker room

gowned and robed, "I take it that you've noticed that you're the only white girl in the joint besides tiny Marty, right?"

She cracks a smile—the first of the day—as she tugs her spine-broke copy of Miss Harper Lee's book out of her lucky purse. She's using her new To-Do List both as a bookmark and inspiration to press on, but she doesn't stop to obsess over it the way she normally would. She dives into one of her favorite scenes in her favorite story to ground herself.

Four cars of fired up men have arrived at the Maycomb jailhouse carrying a rope they're fixin' to drop over the neck of the man wrongly accused of raping Mayella Violet Ewell. Atticus Finch has come to guard his client Tom Robinson. In answer to the rumblings around town, he's propped himself up in a chair outside the jailhouse door beneath a dark sky. Unbeknownst to Mr. Finch, his children, Jem and Scout, and their friend Dill have followed him into town. They're witnessing the drama that's about to unfold from the shadows the jail casts.

As told by Scout: "They were sullen-looking, sleepy-eyed men who seemed unused to late hours. I sought once more for a familiar face, and in the center of the semi-circle I found one. Hey, Mr. Cunningham."

Courtesy of her PTSD, she isn't just reading the story, she's *in* the story. Breathing the hot honeysuckle perfumed Alabama night air, the leftover dust and sweat on the children, the car fumes, and the rancid bloodlust covering the men who are there to do the devil's work. Atticus's integrity is touchable. Scout's voice . . . inches away.

Tess is so immersed that soft-spoken Irwin must resort

to shouting her name before she takes her nose out of the book.

She says, "Sorry," and follows him into a small room off the hallway.

"Our controls," he sweeps his arm Vanna-like across the panel of dials, meters, and flashing lights. "And that's our radiation machine." He nods through a viewing window at the metal monster. "Let me introduce you."

While Irwin is giving her the ten-cent tour around the radiation room, a muscular guy wearing tight blue jeans and Tony Lama boots joins them. He extends a calloused hand, and says, "I'm Cliff," like he's the boss around these here parts. (He's wearing a wedding ring, but Tess would bet that's not preventing Irwin from having a secret cowboy crush on him.)

As Cliff helps her onto the table below the machine, he warns, "It's *extremely* important that you don't move during the process," and then he and Irwin pick up rulers and begin measuring her breast, which is what mapping is all about. They're formulating a AAA TripTik for the radiation machine.

Irwin stomps his foot at one point during the process and tells Tess in a frustrated way, "I'm sorry this is taking me so long. Cliff is a lovely teacher, but . . . ," he shrugs, "I'm just learning the ropes."

You got the new guy . . . ha . . . ha . . . ha.

Tess feels the familiar fear bunch up in her gut, but she doesn't have the heart to request someone more seasoned, she can tell Irwin's feelings would be hurt. She focuses on the ceiling. Cumulus clouds are floating across a trompe l'oeil sky. She and Haddie used to lie in their backyard grass and search for animal shapes back when her daughter still thought she hung the moon. The memory solidifies into a tear that drips past her right temple and down onto the papered table with a *plop*.

Irwin stops whatever it is he's doing to ask, "You okay?"

Cliff takes a tougher love approach. "Hang in there. We've completed the measuring and it's time for your tattoos."

While Irwin is creating the dots across her breast with a small branding iron under Cliff's watchful eye, he repeats with every stab of the needle, "Ouch . . . I know that hurts, dear. Ouch . . . I know that hurts, dear."

Upon completion, Cliff high-fives Irwin and says, "Not bad for your first time, buddy."

It's been a lot to take in.

Tess is half-naked, flat on her back, the tattoos are stinging, and strange men are paying an awful lot of attention to her breasts. She feels like she's been kidnapped by two motorcycle gang members.

When she returns to the changing room, she bumps into me humming, *Born to Be Wild*.

"*Hardy har har*. Don't quit your day job," she tells me as she bangs the locker door open.

She's in pain, worried about the treatments, but mostly, she's fretting about Haddie, who would be home soon for her monthlong spring break. When her mother left for St. Joe's each day, she would wonder where she was going. How would she react when Tess broke down and told her? Would the news send her into a tailspin? Force her to wedge her finger down her throat after she ate everything she could find in the pantry? Starve herself?

Tess is in tears when I take her into my arms and whisper, "Need something?"

"You can't know," she says as she rests her cheek against my shoulder.

"Oh, but I can, darlin'." I run my hand down her rumpled red hair. "Trust me. I know *exactly* what you're hankerin' for."

Aloha Means Hello and Goodbye

A life-size wooden cross juts out of St. Lucy's front lawn reminding all that the time for atonement and resurrection will soon be upon us. I tell Tessie from the confines of the Volvo that she's parked on the street out front of the church, "Let's go inside and say hi."

"I gave Him up for Lent." This is not at all what she had in mind when I told her I knew what she needed. She was hoping for a hot-fudge sundae with extra whipped cream.

"Please?" I ask.

"Uh-uh."

"Quit playin' hard to get."

After I pled with her for a few more minutes, she gives in, she has to. She's got business to take care of.

As we walk up the path to the church doors together, she's gazing up at the cross and the body of Jesus Christ. "How does seein' Him make you feel?" I ask her.

"Defeated. I never noticed how skinny He is. If his mother couldn't protect and nourish *her* kid, what are my chances?"

I open the heavy double doors and slowly proceed down the main aisle with her in tow. The church is not ostentatious, the way some of them can be. Not too small, not too large, it reflects the character of Ruby Falls. It's old the way the most of the town is, and resonates with the sounds of the beginnings, the middles, and the ends of life—squalling baptized babies, brides and grooms exchanging I do's, and farewell funeral wails.

Above the main altar, a crucified Christ looks down upon his flock. On one of the two smaller side altars, votive candles are flickering beneath the feet of St. Lucy, the patron saint of the blind. The altar on the right is guarded over by St. Theresa, the Little Flower. (I arranged that years ago. Good for her self-esteem.) Morning sun streams through three lovely stained-glass windows on the east side of the church. In a few minutes, the middle window will grab Tessie's attention. It always does.

I chose a pew up front. When I go straight to my knees, Tess doesn't join me. She fidgets on the dark-blond bench behind me, pages through the hymn book, and beats out a rhythm on the wood, until she can't stand the suspense anymore.

Sidling up to me, she whispers, "What are you praying for?"

"Not what. Who."

"Okay. Who?"

"You."

"Why?"

"Because I love you, and I'm not the only one. I want you to remember that when I'm gone."

She slams back in the pew like I'd slapped her. "No! You can't go away, Grace. I won't let you. I need you! I know I crossed number eight off my list, but I did it in pencil because I ... I still might die! That ... that radiation machine could shrink me the way it did Marty the receptionist at the center who I'm sure was average-sized at one time. Or ... or cowboy Cliff could stop by during a treatment and Irwin could get distracted and set the machine too high."

"Yeah, that's probably what'll happen," I say solemnly. "And after flustered Irwin reduced you to snack size, maybe he'd offer you a Coca-Cola spiked with curare to wet your teeny whistle."

After she gives me a disgusted look, one she absorbed from her mother, her attention wanders to the stained-glass window. When she's in church for the life and death holidays, art lover Tess can't help but be captivated by the magnificent blues and greens, the umber oranges and brilliant reds, but the remarkable craftsmanship is not what draws her to this particular window. It's the subject matter. St. Joan of Arc swaddled in fire up to her neck is wearing a peaceful smile that has always annoyed the hell out of Tess.

She mutters to herself, "I don't know what she's so damn happy about. She's a freaking shish kebob."

I laugh. "True, but she's also the patron saint of all those fighting against impossible odds." I hope she makes the connection. "Joan is smiling because she did herself proud and is looking forward to her reward. Her return to the kingdom of all that is and will ever be."

Tess has given up on traditional religion, which is fine, because all of 'em are just different means to the same end—think of spokes on a wagon wheel leading to the center that holds them altogether—but try as she might, she can't deny that edging her toes into the *forever* the way she had during her surgery had given her a completely different spiritual take on things.

Less ticked, she says, "When I do . . . ya know . . . do you think I'll go back to the place I visited when I was under the anesthesia?"

"Doubtful," I say woefully as I ease back in the pew. "Wish that for you with all my heart baby, but. . . ." I shake my head low and slow. "If only you didn't have that Mike Nelson wiener sin hangin' over your head."

Her laugh echoes through the church.

I don't have time for anymore tomfoolery. We need to get to work. I put on my reading glasses—don't need 'em, of course—but they'll add weight to what I'm about to teach her. I speak to her in a calm, slow voice to let her know how serious I am. "May I see your list?"

She removes it from the zipped side compartment of her lucky purse and hands it over.

TO-DO LIST

1. ~~Buy broccoli.~~
2. ~~Make sure that Haddie gets the help she needs from a better therapist.~~
3. ~~Set up vocational counseling appointment for Henry.~~
4. Convince Will to love me again.
5. ~~Get Birdie to talk to me.~~
6. Bury Louise once and for all.
7. ~~Have a religious epiphany so #8 is going to be okay with me.~~

8. ~~Die.~~

Wanting to praise and reassure before I get down to brass tacks, I point to numbers one, three, and five. "You're excellent at picking out broccoli, and I'm proud, and you should be too, of the mothering job you're doing with Henry." I place my hand atop one of hers. "Don't worry about him so much." I'm not supposed to tell her this, but what the hell. "That boy is gonna rock the world someday." I go back to the list. "And with regards to Birdie, the perseverance you've shown in rekindling your relationship is nothin' short of remarkable. And since it's not on your list, I'm not even gonna mention what a fantastic job you did coping with all those surgeries." I give her this special love look I have that is enormously penetrating. "But . . . I'm a little concerned about number two."

She grasps onto her lucky purse. "You don't think Dr. Chandler is helping Haddie?"

"I didn't say that, did I? The doc is doing an outstanding job treating her disorder, what I meant when I said I was concerned is . . . well, the time is drawing nigh for you to tell her about the cancer."

Tess doesn't realize it, but she's just made the sign of the cross. Old habits die hard.

"She'll be scared when you tell her, but when it hits her that you kept it from her, you gotta prepare yourself for all sorts of mad."

Tess whines, "How was I supposed to know I was going to live?"

"Keeping it a secret from Haddie when you weren't

sure of your prognosis and she was struggling with the worst of her problem was a good idea, but now that you're not gonna die, and she appears to be making progress, you gotta step up."

"But what if I still—"

"No buts or what ifs about it." I cross out number eight again. ~~Die.~~ This time in pen. "You're gonna live." Much, much longer.

Tess takes a moment to reflect. There are so many repercussions if she accepts once and for all that the cancer isn't going to kill her. One of them being that she summoned me and framed our time together on the premise that she was about to kick the bucket and needed someone by her side.

Before she can strengthen her argument by bringing up a recurrence, I say, "How 'bout we discuss number seven for a minute?" I take in a deep breath; I'll need it. "It and number eight are not dependent upon one another. In other words, you don't have to be drugged up, die, or come close to it, to recapture some of the profound feelings you experienced during your brief visit to the sweet bye and bye, the afterworld, Heaven, the happy hunting ground, or whatever you want to call it."

My friend can't help herself, she's intrigued. No one could resist reexperiencing those divine feelings, least of all her. "How?"

"Well, that brings me to . . . ," I place my finger next to number six: Bury Louise once and for all.

"You gotta let go of her in more ways than just scattering her ashes. You need to say goodbye to what remains of her here." I tap her forehead. "And here." I tap her heart.

She kitten mewls.

"I know you don't think you are, but you're well on your way. Haven't you noticed that she hasn't been bugging you as much lately?"

She gives me a begrudging nod.

"Well, then, the next step is," she's not going to like what I'm about to tell her, but it's gotta be said, "forgiving her."

Tess goes as hard as the church pew beneath my behind. "That's not gonna happen."

I take on my sermon voice. "In the words of Buddha, 'Holding onto anger is like taking poison and expecting the other person to die.'"

"I don't care."

"Forgiving someone doesn't mean that you absolve them of the harm they've inflicted." If I'm not careful, she'll start singing the *Brownie Smile Song* to drown me out. "All you gotta do is acknowledge that Louise did what she did and you feel about it the way you do, and go on with your life the best your can."

An harrumph.

I point down to the list again: number four.

The resounding church bells make further conversation impossible, which is how I planned it. I don't want her posing any more belligerent questions that I'm not allowed to answer. She has to figure out how to do the last item on her list on her own—convince Will to love her again—and deep down she knows that, or she wouldn't be unconsciously releasing me from my duties.

When only the echo remains of the final bell, the

twelfth, I ask her, "You know what that means?"

"That you're about to tell me some dumb-ass parable about the Disciples?"

Lord, this girl can get attitudinal.

"Actually," I say as I pass the list back, "I was gonna tell you that the time has come to say our goodbyes."

"Nooo!" She whips my way. "I'm sorry for being snotty . . . I'm not ready! You can't leave me. Please!"

I set my hand on her shoulder and say with powerful conviction, "Trust me, you know all you need to know for now, but there *are* a couple of things I want you to focus on." I'm going to frame the advice as a list because I know that'll appeal to her. "Number one, just like Dr. Drake told you, humor is the best tool you got to get you through tough times. Number two, you are an eternal soul who is loved now and forever. Number three, remember that surrendering is not the same as giving up. And, last but not least. . . ." I reach under the pew, remove a pink orchid lei, and place it around her neck. She understands the implications. She's a little expert on Hawaii. "If you could show yourself an ounce of the compassion that you show others that'd be a good start."

"Grace . . . don't go . . . PLEASE!"

Too late. I've already deactualized, but just because I can't resist having the last word, I whisper in her ear with breath that is redolent of an eternity of hellos and goodbyes, "Aloha, Tess Blessing."

What If I Start Yodeling?

Over the past weeks, Tess has reflected often on our heart-to-heart chat in the church. She hasn't radically changed—these things don't happen overnight—but she *has* noticed that she's become a tad untethered to the person previously known as Theresa Marie Blessing. Her PTSD symptoms haven't disappeared, there is no known cure, but they're becoming more manageable. When she gets depressed, color her gray instead of black, the panics are not as frantic or frequent, and the flashbacks seem fuzzier. Her dead mother is still harping, but every so often she's being replaced in Tess's brain by the kinder, drawling voice of you know who.

Big picture? She's experiencing warm feelings that you'd think she'd welcome, but instead of reveling in the benefits of our hard work, she's questioning her essence—*God almighty, who the hell am I? What's happening to me? Am I becoming chipper? What if I start yodeling?*

She tells Will through the bathroom door, "Time to abdicate the throne."

As promised by Dr. Sherman, the radiation treatments have taken their toll. Tessie is so damn exhausted that she drops into their bed each night thinking that she's *finally* found the cure for her insomnia. Radiation poisoning. She doesn't trust herself to drive to herself to the treatment this morning, so Will will be sliding behind the wheel of the Volvo.

He's been sweeter, more sensitive to her needs since she's started the treatment. Tess wants to believe those are signs that he's gotten a handle on his midlife crisis, but that's a stretch for one as pessimistic as she. (She received his permission to talk to their family doctor and Scottie confirmed the diagnosis.) Especially since her husband still hasn't shown any interest in making love to her. She overheard one woman telling another woman in the cancer center's waiting area that her husband walked out after she got sick because he no longer found her sexy. Could that be the problem? Or is he just saving himself for Connie?

The receptionist at the cancer center looks up from her computer to say, "How are you today, Tess?"

"Well, I don't know if you've heard, but I've got cancer and I'm undergoing radiation treatments, so I am not doing all that well."

Miniature Marty rewards her with a sunny smile that has done Tess's heart good over the past few weeks. "Irwin's on his way out."

She drags back to the waiting area and says to Will, "I just remembered that I have an appointment with Cappy after the treatment, so instead of sitting around here and absorbing the fantastic ambience, do you want to head over to Starbucks?"

He folds up his newspaper, hops out of the plastic

chair, and tells her, "Call me when you're finished." She hasn't seen him move this fast in years. "I'll bring you back a hot cocoa and a scone." As she watches him hightail it through the center's doors, she doesn't want to, but all she can think about is how much she loves him. Squeamishness and all.

Irwin gently calls to her from across the waiting room, "You're up."

As he helps her onto the table the same way he has the previous seventeen times, she asks him how he'd spent his weekend because she's grown very fond of him.

"I cleaned the house, baked three cherry pies for the church bake sale on Saturday, and after Mass on Sunday, I dug around in my garden." Irwin positions her arms in the holders above her head. "The Farmer's Almanac predicted we'd have a warm spring and how right it was." He slaps the plate into the radiation machine. "My daffodils are already up."

"Yeah, mine too." She'd gasped when she spotted their unfurling yellow heads out of the sunroom window this morning. They reminded her that Haddie would return home in a few days to start her spring break.

Irwin is puttering with her breast. Pushing it this way and that, until it lines up perfectly with the radiation machine. On his way out, he reminds her, the same way he always does, that there's a microphone in the room. "If you need me, just yell."

After the initial round of whirring and click-click noise, he comes back, makes some adjustments, minces out, and the machine gets busy again.

Bzzz. "Okay," his tinny voice announces a few minutes

later through the nearby speaker. "You can rest your arms now, Tess." *Bzzz*.

Upon his return to her side, he helps her into an upright position and asks, "That wasn't so bad, was it?"

"That was perfect," she tells him, like always. "So, what are you planting this year?"

"Flowers that bring joy to the parishioners." He lives on the grounds of St. Boniface, a Catholic Church in Richfield, a town west of Ruby Falls. Tess pictures a cottage with a thatched-roof and talking bluebirds flapping about the dormer windows. "Daisies, sunflowers, and I absolutely adore pink peonies, don't you?"

Resisting a double entendre that might offend pious Irwin, she says, "I certainly do." She thinks of Will's *Monsieur Pierre*, and how in the language of flowers, peonies stand for bashfulness. She hopes that's the case.

Irwin, already busy changing the paper sheet on the radiation bed with a whistle, tosses out his parting line as Tess opens the door to the room. "See you tomorrow, hon. Same time, same setting!"

She takes a deep breath, thinks of me, says, "Fuck it," and steps into the elevator to travel three floors up to the office of the medical oncologist on her team—the one who'd come up with her treatment regime—Dr. Cappy Anderson.

She had liked the mid-fifties man right off. There was gentleness inside his big bear of a body that made her feel safe, and a cut-to-the-chase sensibility that Tess appreciated. When she's led back to his office by Jennifer, his receptionist, the doctor greets her with, "Morning."

"Brilliant observation, Cappy," she says with a smile.

That's the worst comb-over I've ever seen. If the man can make a serious grooming mistake like that, how dependable could he be?

Tess disagrees with her mother. The part that Cappy makes an inch above his left ear is so touching that nothing he did could make her trust him more.

"How's the Badger State been treating you?" she asks as she settles in on the other side of his desk. He'd relocated from Upstate New York shortly before she'd begun seeing him.

"The food's hearty, the people are helpful, and there's so little traffic, but . . . I miss waterfalls. I'm a watcher from way back." Tess has never heard of that hobby before, but if she was a doctor who dealt with death all day long watching cascading water might make her feel brand new again too. "Would you like to do the exam in here today? Patients tell me it's more comfortable."

It's a typical doctor's office, nothin' special, but anything's better than the sterile room around the corner, so she opens her gown to give him easy access and tells him, "Have at it." (To any woman cancer patient who is shy about displaying her breasts, Tess would say, "Get over it, sister.")

"Well," Cappy says as he's staring at her chest. "The right one is still quite a bit smaller." She knows that and doesn't care. She's begun to find it as endearing as the runt of the litter or the scraggliest Christmas tree on the lot. She's about to close up the gown when the doctor surprises her with a new move. He leans in, closes his eyes, and places his hands lightly on her breasts. "But they feel similar, so that's good."

Tess hadn't even considered how they might feel to Will.

Cappy has sworn to first do no harm, so even though she's made her wishes abundantly clear, he asks yet again, "You sure I can't interest you in a round of chemo?" like it's an after-dinner cocktail.

She knows he has her best interests at heart and is not offended. "No, thank you."

The oncologist smiles and says, "Enjoy the holiday."

"Thanks, you too. See you in a few weeks."

Tessie sounded chipper enough during the visit, but as she walks down the hallway outside Cappy's office, she's not imagining the family Easter egg hunt, dark chocolate bunnies, or even Will's scrumptious maple ham and sweet potato casserole. She's thinking about how much she's dreading telling Haddie about the cancer.

She slows, then stops in front of the elevator, takes a deep breath, and asks another patient waiting to go down, "Excuse me. Do you know where the stairs are?"

Bad Timing

TO-DO LIST

1. ~~Buy broccoli.~~
2. ~~Make sure Haddie gets the help she needs from a better therapist.~~
3. ~~Set up a vocational counseling appointment for Henry.~~
4. Convince Will to love me again. (What about Connie?)
5. ~~Get Birdie to talk to me.~~
6. Bury Louise once and for all. (With Birdie.)
7. ~~Have a religious epiphany so #8 is going to be okay with me.~~
8. ~~Die.~~
9. Tell Haddie about the cancer.
10. Prepare the guest room for Birdie.

Tess is feeling somewhat disheartened. She'd had to make additions to numbers four and six on her list, and now there's a nine and ten.

She's working on number ten on Good Friday morning, and not doing a great job. She's phobic about cleaning products and doesn't even know what the heck half of them are used for. That was her sister's area of expertise. Now there's a gal who knows her Lysol from her Clorox. Birdie would be here soon and Tess could barely contain herself.

Four days after she'd sent the package off, she received this message:

> Birdistheword: Thanks for the lips. I'm coming.
>
> Tessie: Hurray!!!! When?!
>
> Birdistheword: May 13-20.
>
> Tessie: xoxoxoxoxxoxxoxoxoxoxo!
>
> Birdistheword: First thing, straight from the airport, I want to visit the old houses. Go to the cemetery to see daddy. Get candy from Ma's. Have the funeral for Louise. It's got to be in that order.
>
> Tessie: Ok.
>
> Birdistheword: And did Will say that your wedding anniversary is on the 16th? Should I pack a party dress?
>
> Tessie: About that. I'll explain when you get here.

She can't very well celebrate thirty years of wedded bliss if she discovers that she's the only one who feels that way.

She's on her knees planting geraniums in the front garden mulling over how she was going to deliver the news to Haddie, when she startles at the sound of the Chevy's classic *ah . . . oo . . . ga* horn as Will pulls into the driveway. She waves at her daughter as she gets out of the car and calls, "Welcome home, baby!" She thinks Haddie looks slightly more filled out. That could change after she told her about the cancer.

Henry, who'd been playing poker on the computer, hears Garbo's happy yipping and comes strolling onto the front porch to welcome his sister home. "Yo," he says. "What up?"

After Tess had told her son about her illness, he'd made a small turnabout, the same way she has. He still spoke to his mama much of the time like she was deaf and dumb, but in a more polite way. And when she suggested they make Thursday "their" night, he'd agreed. He even let *her* pick the movie, and grumbled only mildly on the drive to the East Side of Milwaukee to participate in the midnight showing—exhaustion, be damned—of the musical comedy, *The Rocky Horror Picture Show*. (She wanted to wear her packed-away Janet Weiss costume, but it didn't fit anymore, which was for the best. Henry would've refused to sit with her.)

Tess believes that her boy's sporadic thoughtfulness is the opening gambit of a more grown-up Henry. Someday he would show his true colors. (She's right. Years from now, he'll settle down after he gets into a couple of scrapes with bookies in Las Vegas. He'll turn his back on cards, move to Los Angeles, and after many years of paying dues will receive kudos, not only for the documentary films he and his partner—waiter Cal from the diner—write and direct, but for his humanitarian efforts to feed the homeless, which will make his movie-loving mother and foodie father inordinately proud.)

After Haddie had gotten unpacked and settled in, Tess asks Will and Henry if they'd change the oil in the Volvo, so she and her daughter can have, "A little girl time," which is code for: *I'm about to break the cancer news to her so you might want to seek cover.*

On the back porch deck, a relaxed Haddie informs her tense mother that she dumped boyfriend Rock. Her new beau is a boy from Chicago named Kevin Scanlon, who is an "awesome watercolorist," and then she moves on to how much she's getting out of her therapy with Dr. Chandler, the eating disorder specialist. A little nervous, a little proud, she asks, "Can you tell? I've gained two pounds." And then she launches into how once school is over, she'll need to prepare for her trip to New York to work the summer as an intern for *National Geographic* and . . . and. . . .

She sounds far away, like she's talking from the bottom of a wishing well, because Tess's mind is otherwise engaged. She's remembering the conversation they'd had the morning of her routine mammogram appointment four months ago. How'd she reassured her daughter that it was nothing to worry about.

When Haddie takes a break from her excited chatter for a sip of tea, Tess unearths her courage, and says, "Honey, I've got something really important to tell you."

"What?" she asks with a sunny smile.

"Ah . . . I. . . ." It'd been so long since she'd seen her daughter so happy. It'd be cruel to burst her bubble. "I . . . I love you. It's so good to have you home."

The weather had been so great that the Ruby Falls

Country Club opened the golf course early, so Will and Henry took off on Saturday to play nine holes between the lunch and the dinner rush, while Haddie took herself and her camera to the Easter festivities in town.

There was a parade down old-fashioned Main Street with marching bands and baton twirlers and merchants advertising their shops. High atop the last float, the Easter Bunny—Stan from Olsen's Market—tossed candy to the kids who'd lined up on the sidewalks with baskets.

Afterwards, most everybody adjourned to the park alongside the river to partake in an egg hunt, all-you-can-eat pancake and sausage breakfast, and the opportunity to have their children's picture snapped with the Easter bunny. This was the third year that Haddie had volunteered to be one of the photographers. The proceeds from the sale of the pictures would go to the Ozaukee County Humane Society, a cause near and dear to the Blessings' hearts. It's where they'd found Garbo.

Not up to all the holiday hubbub, Tess stayed home and filled the kids' baskets, planned out the logistics of her sister's visit, topped off the bird feeders, and napped on a backyard bench. Garbo woke her by dropping a muddy Frisbee on her face.

On their way back into the house, she hangs her gardening clippers on the peg in the garage, and then, instead of sneaking past the golden box the way she usually does, she pauses in front of the shelf that holds her mother's remains and says, "Birdie and I will be burying you soon."

It's about time.

(Truer words were never spoken.)

Easter morning, Will and the children oohed and aahed at the wicker baskets overflowing with treats. Henry stuffed himself with Emporium candy, but Haddie only ate a couple of jelly beans. "I'm saving my appetite for supper," she said.

It being one of the life and death holidays, Tessie donned a white frock and yellow pillbox hat that she'd spotted in the window of What's Old Is New Again and joined her family at the ten o'clock Mass at St. Lucy's.

Henry, who was kneeling next to his mother, elbowed her when she welled up. "Bored to tears?" he whispered.

That wasn't it at all. Instead of being put off by the St. Joan stained-glass window the way she used to be, she remembered our parting talk and felt humbled and inspired by the young woman who was willing to die for what she believed in. Tess dared to hope that tonight after she broke the cancer news to Haddie that the both of them would be capable of summoning the necessary faith and courage *they'd* need to soldier on.

"*Mmm . . . mmm . . . mmm,*" Tess and the kids take turns telling the chef. "The best ever!"

The windows are wide open and the tantalizing aroma of budding life fills the peach-and-green dining room where Will had elegantly served the Blessings' Easter dinner—strawberry and brie salad followed by honey and maple-sugar encrusted baked ham, sweet potato casserole, brussels sprouts sprinkled with bacon bits, homemade applesauce, freshly baked potato rolls served with butter in the shape of a lamb, topped off by lemon meringue pie.

Henry and Tess licked their plates clean, and Haddie took a few bites out of every dish.

The conversation had been lively. Golf and school talk. The soccer schedule. Haddie's upcoming one woman show when she returned to campus. Town gossip. There'd been another altercation between two of the menopausal mommies at a recent school orchestra concert that started with name calling and concluded with a wrestling match on the gym floor.

My friend had spent most of the dinner studying Haddie, and wondering if her decision to explain the illness to her on a walk beneath Chestnut Street's old-fashioned street lamps was the wisest one.

When father and son get busy clearing the table, that's Tess's cue to say to her daughter, "It's such a beautiful night, let's take Garbo for a walk."

"Good idea." She pats her concave tummy. "I could use the exercise. I'll grab her leash."

After the three of them come down the front porch of the house, Haddie turns left toward town, but Tess tells her, "Let's go this way instead," because she has a specific destination in mind. Garbo stops a few times to pee before they arrive at the three-story gingerbread Victorian halfway down the block.

Tess says, "I need to talk to you about something important and there's no easy way to—"

"Are you leaving Daddy?" Haddie says alarmed. "Is the diner having money problems again?"

My friend is completely thrown. "Why would you ask if—?" But then . . . out of the blue . . . Haddie's questions spark the illuminating insight that Tess had been dying for.

Talk about bad timing.

Tess wonders if it would be best to deal with both topics in one fell swoop, but quickly decides that she can't tell her daughter about the cancer *and* discuss what she thinks now might be at the root of her eating disorder, it would be much too much for the both of them to deal with at one time.

"No, I'm not leaving Daddy," she tells Haddie.

What if he's cheating on you? Louise asks. *Then what?*

"And the diner is doing great." Already worn-out but the day's festivities and her fear, Tess leans against the tree in front of the Thresher's house for support. "While you were at school. . . ." How many times had she rehearsed this moment in her mind? Agonized over the consequences. "I . . . ah . . . shit." She swallows back the bile in her throat. "I was diagnosed with breast cancer."

Haddie is standing directly beneath one of the old-fashioned street lights so Tessie has no problem seeing the pain ripple across her face. "Oh, Mommy. No!" She throws herself into her mother's arms and bursts into a round of violent sobbing. "Are . . . are you gonna . . . die?"

Tess coos over and over into her daughter's hair, "I'm fine, honey," until the fear quiets some. When she feels Haddie stiffen, she steels herself.

Her daughter pulls out of her arms and shouts, "But why didn't you . . . ? I'm so pissed at you for not telling me sooner!"

"I'm sorry. I . . . I kept it a secret because you're going through some serious problems of your own. I was trying to protect you. I didn't want to add—"

"Fuck you!"

Knowing all too well what it feels like to be emotionally hijacked, Tess doesn't take Haddie's anger to heart. She knows what's driving it. Fight or flight. She snags her daughter by her arm before she can take off. "I know you're scared, but—" She points to the backyard of the Victorian that she'd purposely stopped in front of. "Remember Thunder?"

When she was four years old, Haddie was terrified of the Great Dane that'd lived in the house. The dog's owner was an emergency-room doctor who often worked a night shift at St. Mary's North, so he'd turn the dog out in the fenced yard before he took off for the hospital. The beast would howl until it wore itself out, but not before badly scaring Haddie when Tess was trying to tuck her in for the night.

Will and Tess talked to their neighbor and he empathized, but Thunder needed to be outdoors to do his duty while he was doing his.

Tess thought that if Haddie could meet the beast, it'd help reassure her. An opportunity arose a few evenings later. After the two of them arrived at Dr. Kellogg's house, she picked up Haddie's hand and tugged her toward the backyard, but she dug in her heels in and screamed, "No, Mommy! I too scared!"

Nobody knew better than Tess that fear cannot be reasoned with, so she told her, "Wait here," and edged down the driveway toward the dog and his massive howling mouth. She resorted to a little prayer when she reached over the chain-link fence to pet him. The force of his wagging tail lifted her bangs and he settled right down. Hoping that her plan had worked, she turned and called back to her daughter, "See? There's nothing to be afraid of. He's a good boy, just a little scared too. Come say hi."

Haddie shook her head and stood steadfast, but when Tess returned to her on the sidewalk, she threw her little sweaty arms around her mom's neck, gave a pint-sized shudder, and told her, "Mommies are such bravery."

Things weren't perfect after their close encounter of the Thunder kind, he stilled howled occasionally, but Haddie wasn't as scared when he did.

Maybe that's all anyone could hope for when confronting fear. Not perfect, just better, Tess is thinking when she takes in the scowl on her daughter's face that's informing her that the visit to the Victorian hadn't had the inspiring effect that she had hoped it would.

"Thanks for treating me like a child," Haddie growls. She yanks her arm out of her mother's hand, races down the sidewalk, up their front porch steps, and doesn't look back.

After my depleted Tess and Garbo make it back to the house, she finds her daughter exactly where she was afraid she'd be. Locked in the upstairs bathroom. Tess hears the telltale sound of the toilet lid clanking against the tank. Haddie was waiting until her mother returned to drive home her point.

Tess places her forehead on the door and says, "Baby, we need to talk."

"Go away!"

She takes a couple steps down the hall before she has a change of heart. Time to implement Plan C. The cancer plan.

"Please don't take that tone with me," she comes back to tell Haddie. "Open the damn door."

There's silence, then the sound of running water, the jiggle of the lock, and the door opens a slice.

"I'm getting a radiation treatment tomorrow morning," Tess tells the empty space. "Like it or not, you're driving me. Be ready by eight."

After Haddie listened to Tess explain the surgeries and the goal of the radiation treatments on the drive to St. Joe's the following day, she asks, "How many more do you have to do?"

"Surgeries—none. Treatments—ten."

As the old silver Volvo turns into the cancer center lot, Haddie asks the same thing she had when Tess told her she had the appointment for her routine mammogram months ago, "Does it hurt?"

"Not during the treatment." Tess wonders how much she should tell her. She doesn't want to pile on too much information—like the burn on her breast and the utter exhaustion—but she doesn't want to lie to her either, so she says, "But afterwards . . . you know how you feel after you sit out in the sun for hours?"

"Yeah."

"It's kinda like that."

After they take seats in the cancer center's waiting room, artistic Haddie, who's always been deeply affected by her surroundings, gets twitchy. She narrows her eyes at the manufactured nature prints on the walls and says, "Those are *sooo* hideous. They should hang something more ... uh ... ," she steals a glance at her mother, "hopeful."

When Irwin shows up to collect Tess, she introduces attractive Haddie, who he lavishes with compliments. "How nice you've come to support your mom," he says. "You can watch the treatment on the television screen in the control room with me, honey."

This is one Lifetime movie your kid should have done without, Louise criticizes.

When the radiation machine is done doing its thing, Tess hears the static click of Irwin's microphone switching on, but this time it isn't him telling her breezily to relax her arms and that he'll be right in, the way he always does. It's Haddie who comes through loud and clear.

Bzzz. "Mommies are such bravery." *Bzzz.*

Back to the Future

On day thirty-six, Tessie brought along a loaf of celebratory chocolate chip-banana bread she'd baked to thank the crew at the center, but her daughter had far outdone her.

Haddie had secretly gathered twenty of her most awe-inspiring nature photographs and hid them in the trunk of the Volvo. When Tess returned to the waiting room after the last treatment, she unveiled the collection. Tess cried as the staff accepted the donation with praise and gratitude, especially Irwin, who cut himself a healthy slice of the homemade bread and promised to oversee the immediate removal of these, "Hideous Holiday Inn prints," and the installation of her daughter's "hopeful" ones.

(He selected two flower shots for the radiation room. Pink peonies in full bloom.)

Haddie is on a run, Henry at soccer practice, and Will is delivering flowers to waitress Jessie Burke who'd delivered her baby girl last night. The respite in the action has given Tess much-needed time alone.

Now that she's completed radiation, it's time to get down to the other pressing business at hand. She's in the sunroom, working so intently on her revised To-Do List, that she barely notices the damp earthy smell that reminds her so much of her daughter coming through the open windows.

She crosses out number nine on the list: Tell Haddie about the cancer. But adds a number eleven: Deal with the part you played in Haddie's eating disorder.

Tess dreaded the conversation she'd have with her as much as the one they'd had Easter night. Getting breast cancer was the luck of the draw, and if she had it to do again, she would still keep it hidden from her vulnerable girl. What she needs to discuss with Haddie now is the insight she'd had during their walk after dinner. When her girl asked, "Are you leaving Daddy? Is the diner having money problems again?"

Before Tessie can beat herself up, she refocuses on her list and what she *has* accomplished. Tells herself to keep her eyes on the prize. By tonight, number eleven will be history. And it won't be long before she'll also be able to run her pen through:

4. Convince Will to love me again. (What about Connie?)
6. Bury Louise once and for all. (With Birdie).

Her sister will be here in a few days and the agenda is set and ready.

She's not sure how it will go with Will. Unless he's more Machiavellian than she'd ever imagined, he still seems to care about her. He's been cracking jokes, and he left a love note in the bread box and cooked a heck of a pot roast last night. So other than making passionate love, their life seems to be approaching normal, which has left Tess even more puzzled. What if she'd just imagined his possible straying with Connie Lushman after all? Made one of her "erroneous assumptions" and her PTSD brain ran with that. After all, he'd explained his lack of interest in bedding her. It was a midlife crisis, that's all. And that long blond hair she'd found on his blue shirt and his smelling of Tabu . . . had I been right when I'd told her— "They work together?"

You're stupid enough to fall for a gypsy siding scam, Theresa.

Then again, all the extra lovely touches lately could be expressions of Will's guilt. But why had he smiled impishly when he told her before they turned in last night, "Thirty years. The pearl anniversary. Love ya."

Tess wasn't much on Bible verse, but this one popped unbidden into her head as she lay it on her pillow:

> Do not give what is holy to the dogs;
> nor cast your pearls before swine,
> lest they trample them under their feet,
> and turn and tear you in pieces.

Louise was quick to add on a loud *Amen to that sister.*

Ruby Falls is ramping up for the Spring Festival this weekend. Flower baskets hanging from the old-fashioned street lamps perfume the air. Fluttering banners and sales signs top the shop marquees. More than a few of the visitors have remnants of The Emporium's famous fudge smeared on their lips and a Count Your Blessings' malt in their hands.

While taking a turn through the town is an antidote for all the time Tess'd spent cooped up over the last couple of months, the walk is serving another purpose. The same way she'd discovered that it was easier to communicate with Henry on the phone, she found that Haddie was more receptive when they were on the move.

After they drop the dry cleaning at Melton's, they pick up a few odds and ends for Birdie's arrival in a few of the adorable shops that line Main Street. Tess had done the best she could to freshen up Will's mom's old room with sweet-smelling candles, a new quilt, and flickering bulbs in the antique lamps. An extra night-light if Birdie forgot hers. A new bottle of witch hazel and a carton of Q-tips was waiting in the bathroom cabinet, should the need arise.

As they approach Count Your Blessings, Tessie asks Haddie, "Hungry?"

She shakes her head, looks pensive, and switches everything up by dropping the bomb that Tess was about to unload on her as they make the turn off Bridge Street toward the park. "Dr. Chandler keeps asking me if I can remember anything traumatic that was happening around the time I started to have my problems," she says. "I don't, so she asked me to ask you."

Of course, Tess can remember. Perfectly.

Back when the diner had been experiencing critical cash-flow problems on account of the addition of the party room, Tess blamed Will. She couldn't stop herself from tearing into him in the backyard or the basement or garage. In front of the children, she was careful that they appeared to be who they always had been—devoted to each other. The picture of domestic bliss. Or so she thought. The second Haddie asked her on the Easter night walk, "Are you getting a divorce? Is the diner having money troubles again?" she knew she'd failed miserably at keeping the scorching battles from her. She's disgusted with herself for inadvertently subjecting her daughter to the same kind of ugly fights that her mother and stepfather had exposed Birdie and her to, but she's also feeling a glimmer of hope. A silver lining. She may have *finally* found a key that fits the lock she's been trying to open for years. If her daughter ends up hating her for opening this Pandora's Box, so be it.

When they come around the corner of Main and Park, Tess asks her, "Do you remember a few years ago when Daddy and I were fighting all the time after he opened the party room? About money and . . . other things?"

When her daughter's chin starts to quiver, Tess realizes that Haddie's emotions are much closer to the surface than she'd imagined. "You mean when you told him you were gonna leave him?"

"Yeah," Tess says on a heavy exhale. "I think I might've unintentionally made you feel as frightened and powerless as I was feeling at the time and . . . and I think you started starving yourself and binging and vomiting to give yourself a sense of control that you couldn't get in any other way." It must have been so scary for her to hear Will and her going at one other. "And the fights . . . they might've triggered your problem, but I think it's more complicated than that." Tess had spent years researching eating disorders. "Being a teenager is hard. Your body is changing, there are so many insecurities to deal with and . . . ," she tries to center herself. "I don't want to shift blame, but I also think the way Dad shows his love with food, the air-brushed models in magazines, and you're over-achieving personality may be contributing factors."

This was difficult for Haddie to hear, harder for Tess to say. "I'd give anything to take away your pain, sweetheart, but other than loving you and being here for you . . . I don't know what else to do."

Haddie nods, fists the tears off her check. "I know you've been trying to help me all along, but I wasn't ready to get better," she says. "I am now. With help from Dr. Chandler. We've already talked about some of the body-image stuff you mentioned, the pressure society puts on us to be thin, and . . . and what you just said about you and Dad fighting? I think that's gonna be helpful." She slow smiles at her mom. "Talking about it with the other girls in the group also helps me realize that I'm not the only one struggling with this. Not having to hide it from at least a few people takes some of the pressure off too."

Tess considers all that she'd hidden for so long and how those secrets had compounded her problems. She stops, places her arms around Haddie, and says, "I'm so sorry for whatever part I played in your pain. Sorrier than you'll ever know."

Haddie hugs her back and says, "I've been so confused and mad and sad and . . . I'm sorry for the way I treated you. I'm so, so glad you're not gonna die. I love you. I don't know what I'd do without you."

Exhausted emotionally and physically, Tess says, "I

love you too, baby," and points to the green wooden bench that overlooks the Ruby River. They've made a trip to the park because Haddie wants to take her yearly pictures of the baby ducks. She's been doing it every spring since she was eight years old. "Let's look on the bright side." (Did she really say that?) "We have a lot to deal with, but we're already getting better at talking about things. And I think Birdie's visit is going to be a real help to both of us."

Haddie squats, brings her Nikon up, and squeezes off shots of the duck mother and her five fluffy babies. "What's Aunt Birdie like?" Over the years, she and Henry had received cards from their Hallmark-loving aunt, talked to her on the phone too, but the Finley sisters went through so many ups and downs that Tess didn't want the children's feelings hurt, so she told her sister that it'd better if she wasn't involved in the kids' lives anymore, too confusing, and she agreed. "Does she have the same kind of problems you told me about?" Haddie asks.

During their many evening walks with Garbo, Tess had given her a somewhat sanitized version of her emotional struggles. She was surprised by Haddie's reaction. Instead of the depressions, panic attacks, phobias, and flashbacks scaring her the way she thought they would, when her daughter realized that she wasn't the only one in the family grappling with tough stuff, it forged a bond between them that's similar to the one Tess feels with her sister.

"In some ways Bird and I are a lot alike, but in others . . . not so much." She opens her lucky purse and withdraws the leftover dinner rolls she'd brought along. She tosses a few to the feathered family gliding by. They're making it look easy, but below the water, their little feet are paddling like mad. "She cleans. A lot. And counts and . . . ," she stops when she realizes that she's not sure what kind of problems her sister has been dealing with recently. "I'm hoping this visit might help her put some of that stuff to rest."

Haddie takes her head away from the back of her Nikon and asks, "How?"

Tess can't go into all the details, but in the spirit of their new-found open communication, she says, "Well, like we talked about today, the past is a powerful place that can hold the answers to a lot of questions. Birdie and I are going to travel back in time and take care of some unfinished business."

"Can I come?"

Tess believes that could be helpful to her in a lot of different ways, but she doesn't want her along when Birdie and she scatter Louise's ashes. She says gently, "I'd love for you to spend as much time as possible with your aunt and me while she's here, but there's one thing that Birdie and I have to do alone," she says. "You understand?"

Haddie takes a few more shots of the ducklings. "Is it a sister thing?"

"Exactly."

Unearthing

Henry and Will wanted to come along for the ride, but Tessie thought it might be better if it was just Haddie and she who picked up Birdie from the airport early Sunday morning. Less overwhelming.

Her sister is thinner than she should be; she looks like a coat hanger for her stylish clothes, but I could see by the look on Tess's face that it feels so good to hold her in her arms.

On the walk to the baggage claim, Birdie tells her, "When I first came off the plane, I thought . . . ," she shivers, "you're starting to look a lot like Louise."

Tess would have to agree that the likeness is uncanny. She didn't possess her mother's outrageous beauty, but their coloring was the same. Sometimes when she caught her reflection in a shop window, it scared her too.

Honoring her sister's demands—"First thing, straight from the airport, I want to visit the old houses. Go to the cemetery to see daddy. Get candy from Ma's. Have the funeral for Louise. It's got to be in that order," Tess made sure they got right down to it.

Haddie drove so the sisters could sit together in the backseat. Tess is hovering, asking Birdie every few minutes, "Still good?" as the streets of Milwaukee whiz by. Her sister hadn't been back in a while, and then only to reunite with their grandmother. No telling what memories might be drudged up when they hit their old haunts.

"I'll be okay," Birdie baby talks, "but if I'm not . . . you know what to do."

Out of her lucky purse, Tess pulls an Olsen's brown paper bag—a hyperventilation buster. She's also brought along a bottle of Maalox if her sister's delicate tummy starts acting up. And Pepto too, if the other end stops cooperating.

"Turn right here," Tess tells Haddie.

They slow, but do not stop in front of their "cemetery house," the one they were living at when their father died. A dark-skinned, corn-rowed girl is playing with a one-legged doll on the sagging front steps. A piece of graffiti-filled plywood covers the front window. As they slow down to get a better look, the little girl jerks her head up like she's expecting the worse and runs inside the house.

Birdie says, "Sad," and Tess echoes that sentiment.

When they reach the end of the block, the formal entrance to Holy Cross Cemetery looms. Tess remembers the amazing night she and little Birdie had climbed the black iron fence to search for their daddy's pretend grave. She hasn't been back to visit the graveyard for years and she wonders now why not. As they enter through the imposing gates, she says, "I'm sorry. For some reason . . . I can't believe . . . I don't remember where Daddy is buried."

Birdie does.

Tess shakes out the tan blanket she'd brought along and sets it next to Eddie Blessing's stone. Upon her gammy's death, my friend had been left a shoe box full of family snapshots. She'd brought along the best to show her sister. "A little present for you," she says as she hands Birdie a black-and-white photo of their daddy and them on the merry-go-round at Kiddie Land circa 1957. In another, the three of them are in a row boat in the lagoon at Washington Park. Birdie is smiling her adorable head off, but Tess is gripping onto the sides for dear life. The last shot was taken at Lonnigan's. The Finley sisters are sitting on top of the mahogany bar beside a small Christmas tree decorated with tinsel and bottle caps. Their bartender daddy is in the background wearing a Rudolph red nose and beaming at his girls.

Birdie stares especially hard at that last picture. "I remember that night," she tells Tess.

"You do?!" As a result of either the powerful drugs she'd taken over the years to relieve her anxiety, OCD, and delusions, unlike Tessie, her sister's childhood recollections are spotty and rare.

"Yeah," Birdie says. "It was taken on Christmas Eve. We were eight and seven. Daddy was supposed to take us to midnight Mass and we ended up at the bar instead. We were having a great time. Christmas carols were playing on the jukebox and Daddy was telling Polack jokes and making everyone laugh and you and me were drinking kiddie cocktails with maraschino cherries until . . . until Louise showed up."

The fascinated look that Haddie'd had on her face

when the sisters were limping down Memory Lane turns to one of concern when her aunt bolts up off the blanket and begins to pace amongst the headstones. Tessie has minimal physical manifestations of her anxiety, but Birdie had not been as fortunate. She cannot hide the supreme effort it takes to hold back the fear that quakes inside of her. She trembles and shakes, and her breathing becomes tortured.

Haddie scoots closer to her mom and asks, "Is she okay?" She isn't alarmed the way some people might be while watching another person fall apart before their eyes. Not only had Tess prepared her for Birdie's symptoms, the child had grown up with Otto at the diner dressed in full paranoid regalia going on about the CIA and the Planet Argon.

Birdie was leaning against the sooty-looking Gilgood mausoleum about fifty yards away. Tess hands Haddie the brown paper bag and she jogs over with it. They look alike. Blond hair and those eerie light-blue eyes. Thin, like drinking straws. Tess watches proudly as Haddie pats her aunt tentatively on the back after she plunges her head into the bag.

When her daughter rejoins her on the blanket, Tess holds her close and reiterates what her girl already understands, "Feelings are not for sissies."

"I remember the stub of whiskers on the back of his hands and the muscles in his arms and beer on his breath and how he'd call me tweetheart sometimes and . . . and before we fell asleep at night how he would come into our room, give us a hug, and tell us, "I love you two as much as the stars and the moon," Birdie stutters as they get back into the car.

Tess considered that seeing all the familiar places might free up her sister's repressed memories as it seems to be doing. She also considered that could be helpful and work out really well, but then again it might not. She asks her again, "You sure you're okay?"

"I cut back on my antidepressants before I came," Birdie says. "I thought I was ready, but. . . ." She turns her head to look out the window at the kaleidoscope of streets that the girls had once raced down on their red twenty-inch Schwinn, perhaps thinking about a time when she could still kid herself.

When they arrive at Birdie's next requested destination, Tessie shows Haddie where to pull in. Unlike their rundown cemetery house, the duplex off of Center Street looks scarily the same, except for a little wear on the roof and the paint that's been changed from white to beige.

"You sure you want to keep going?" Tess asks her sister. "We could come back tomorrow."

Birdie shakes her head and gives her an unexpected, almost peaceful smile.

Tessie could think of nothing about being back at the duplex that could make her feel that serene. "Who or what are you remembering?" she asks.

Birdie opens the car door and says, "Bee."

"Who's Bee?" Haddie asks.

Birdie says, not bashful at all, "My imaginary friend."

When Haddie makes an oh-boy-what-have-I-gotten-myself-into face, her aunt grins and says, "A friend in need can be a real saving grace, right, Tessie?"

She had mentioned her relationship with me during their online chats, so Tess says, "Indeed," as they brush past the peony bushes that line the sidewalk that leads to the backyard.

Dented aluminum garbage cans are leaning against one another on the concrete block that had crumbled on the edges and cracked down the middle since Tess had last seen it. She flashes back to the morning she'd raced down from their bedroom on their birthday to find her garden buried beneath its weight.

"Remember how we'd play Red Light, Green Light with the other Blessed Children of God bad girls?" Birdie says as they double back to the front of the house. "That's kinda like what we're doing today. Coming out of our hiding places and getting captured by the ghosts." She tilts her head back, looking up to the second floor of the house. "And there was that summer when it seems like all we ate were popsicles and potato chips and . . . and that time Louise didn't talk to us for two weeks because we forgot to take out the garbage and . . . and . . . when she dropped us off in the Core and when she hung the pee sheet on the front porch and. . . ."

She is talking way too fast, twirling her hair. Tess is getting a really bad feeling about what might come next.

"I need to go inside," her sister announces amped up.

"Ahhh . . . I don't think that's a good idea. We don't want to bother people on a Sunday morning," Tess replies as calmly as she can. "Let's go to the park or drive past the Tosa Theatre or—"

"I'm doing this," Birdie says, "with or without you. I *need* to."

Obsession is a shared problem, so Tess knows there's no point in arguing with her.

Dreading the awful effect the inside of the house might have on the inside of an already-agitated Birdie, Tess tells Haddie, who she feels has partaken of enough weirdness for one day, "Why don't you take a little jog around the block, honey? This shouldn't take long."

Haddie has on her running shoes. They're worn down in the heels from the fast and furious five miles she ran every day with her running partner, her pain. "Okay. Be back in twenty minutes or so."

Birdie rings the duplex doorbell four times. It makes the same sound it had when they were kids. Through the filmy door curtains, they watch a handsome young man in khakis and a plaid shirt hop down the steps. "Yes?" he says when he opens the door.

"Good morning. Sorry to bother you, but we used to live here when we were kids," Birdie says with a darling, dimpled smile. "We'd like to come in and look around for a few minutes for old time's sake."

It was more of a statement than a request. Birdie has that get-out-of-my-way-buster look in her eyes. She was normally pretty docile, but she had that unpredictable wild streak. When they were kids, Birdie dove off the high dive at the neighborhood pool and she wasn't even that great a swimmer. She cracked Dennis Patrick in the back with a rock when he attacked Tess in an alley. She rang Mr. Johnson's doorbell—he was the Lutheran that all the kids in neighborhood said would stuff you like the deer he had hanging on his living room wall if he caught you playing ding dong ditch. She liked to stick her head too far out of the window of a fast moving car.

Tess was becoming very frightened that the guy with the friendly face would have it rearranged by her sister's fist if he didn't allow her into the duplex.

Thankfully, after he gives the two middle-aged women standing on his front porch the once over, he says, "My family's at Mass and I'm just puttering. Why not?"

Tess can think of a hundred reasons.

She tells her sister, "You go." She doesn't want to stir up the past and doesn't understand why Birdie does. One of them had to stay as close to the present as possible. "I'll wait out here."

Birdie leans in to the handsome man like she's telling him a secret. "She's shy," she says with a wink. "Give us a minute." She pushes Tessie to the side of the porch and begins to softly sing in a demanding way, "All kinds of weather, we stick together. The same in the rain or sun." The *Sisters* song from the '50s musical *White Christmas* is one of the girls' favorites. They used to perform it up at Lonnigan's for their daddy and all the customers on special occasions. "Two different faces, but in tight places, we think and we act as one."

Tess can't resist when Birdie locks her arm through hers and drags her back to the nice young man to tell him, "We're the Finley sisters."

"Nice to meet you. I'm Dave Trilby. Come on up."

Birdie quietly counts the sixteen steps that deliver them to the small landing in front of the entry door.

Dave escorts them straight into the living room and there he is. Leon, on the old flowered couch in his boxer shorts, glued to the boxy black-and-white Zenith, a

THE RESURRECTION OF TESS BLESSING

Swanson's fried chicken dinner on a metal TV tray in front of him. A snubbed-out Lucky Strike is jammed into what's left of the gummy brownie.

The three of them proceed through the dining room that holds few memories since the sisters never once remember using it.

The blue paint on the girls' old bedroom has been replaced with a color that's almost the same as the pink in Haddie's room. Someone had tried repeatedly to patch the long crack in the ceiling that Tessie used to stare at night after night, waiting for it to burst open and the world to fall down upon them. "This is my little Natalie's room," Dave says. "The ceiling is a work in progress."

Birdie steps into their old room and says, "I love what you've done with it," but Tessie remains mum. The memories are coming fast and hard. Birdie rocking. Birdie wetting the bed. The two of them huddled together with the pillows over their heads to muffle the screaming on the other side of the wall. Shadow puppets.

"The bathroom," Dave says a tad embarrassed as he walks past.

Tess peeks in. She can smell the Dutch cleanser they used to scrub the tub and their mother's Aqua Net hair spray.

Dave steps to the right, into Louise and Leon's former bedroom, and says, "Speaks for itself."

Indeed it does. A cacophony of double L's arguments are bouncing around in Tess's brain. Birdie admires the bedspread, and then elbows her sister to say something polite, so Tessie closes her eyes and sticks her head in. "Hasn't changed one bit."

Dave leads them into the kitchen where the lovely Louise is standing in front of the stove complaining about cooking or her useless children or threatening to throw a pot of boiling water at Leon when she finds out he gambled away his paycheck again.

As Tess had feared, Birdie hadn't anticipated how being in the duplex would affect her. She tells the guy, "Thanks so much for taking time out of your day," puts her arm around her now-quivering sister, and guides her down the front staircase. Dave's face is puzzled as he locks the door behind them.

On the familiar front porch stoop where the Finley girls sit hand in hand to await Haddie's return, Birdie says in her littlest-girl voice, "Oh, heck, Tessie, I'm having a cloudy day." She sets her head on her sister's shoulder. "I need some candy."

On the short drive over to the third destination, Birdie insisted they stop at a Mobil station on North Avenue so she could clean off the Volvo windshield and check the oil. Four times each.

Tess calls to her out the car window, "You could get a freakin' job here it looks so good. Please get back in the car."

Birdie flaps her arms and says, "We've gotta run it through the car wash. Get off *all* the filth . . . filth . . . filth . . . filth."

"Wow," Haddie says from inside the car. "She reminds me of Otto."

Tess, who has often thought the same thing, says, "Me too."

Birdie leans through the Volvo window while they wait

for the customer in front of them to run through the cycle. She pants, "I got the super-duper version."

Tess grabs ahold of her. Birdie lets her for a moment, then pulls back, and says as she gets back in, "Just get the fucking car washed."

Wanting to make her sister feel better about her looniness, as the car is sprayed and soaped, Tess tells her and Haddie about her deep-seated fear of a greasy man watching her from a cracked window in a gas station washroom. How he'd wait for her to leave the car to pick up a Three Musketeers bar in the minimart so he could spike the Coke in her cup holder with curare.

Not exactly sure how to react, Haddie snorts.

But Birdie says perplexed, "I get being afraid of a greasy guy. "The Peeker" up at the Clark Station was always bugging you when we were kids, but curare? Where the hell did *that* come from?"

When Tess says, "*Freaks of Nature*. Those pygmy cannibals?" her sister laughs.

Back on track, at least for the moment, Tess gives Haddie the directions to Ma's as they exit the service station. Birdie is bouncing around in her seat now, giddy with delight. "You have no idea how long I've been waiting to do this!" By the time they make the turn onto 63rd Street, her car door is halfway open. She runs up the stairs, yanks open the door of the house-shop, and yells out, "Ma, we need candy!"

Tessie had told her about Little Ma taking over the business after her mother passed away, so Birdie isn't thrown when her successor comes out from behind the curtain. After they make their delicious selections, the three of them snuggle together on the steps out front.

Tess catches sadness flit across Haddie's face as she watches her aunt dig into her bag of sweets. Her daughter can't eat sugar without feeling guilty. Tess shakes out a few M&M's into her hand, offers them to Haddie, and says, "Baby steps, right, Bird?" and she nods in agreement.

They talk and eat their goodies until the Blessed Children of God church bells ring out twice. According to the schedule Tess had devised, it was time to fulfill their last order of business for the day. She stands and grabs onto the iron railing for support, smiles wanly down at her little sister, and says, "Ask not for whom the bell tolls, it tolls for we."

The Edge

Will greets them in the mudroom and takes Birdie's suitcases out of her hands. The last time he'd spent time with his sister-in-law was at Tessie's and his wedding. Soon after, she had relocated to Florida. He's unsure if he should hug her, so he comes off like a diner owner greeting a customer who hasn't frequented his establishment in a while. "Good to see you again," he tells her as he takes her hand in his and gives it a firm shake. "Hungry?"

Birdie says, "No," but that's the extent of her chit-chat repertoire.

Tess leads her into the den where Henry is playing online poker, oblivious to all but his full house. She calls him on his cell phone. He doesn't pick up. "You are so gay," he says with his killer smile. "I love you too," she says. "Don't forget we're having supper together night as a family. Turn around and say hello to your aunt."

Just like Birdie had with Haddie, she and her nephew quickly find common ground. Like him, she has always loved cards. Solitaire when they were kids, and Gin Rummy, when she got older. A few years ago when her agoraphobia got so bad that she couldn't leave the house for a few months, she became addicted to one of the first online poker sites and made a small fortune. When Tess steps back into the kitchen to touch base with Will, she can hear her sister sharing betting strategy with Henry.

Will whispers to his wife, "I drilled a hole in the box and covered it with an adhesive flap so you won't run into the same problem you had the last time you tried to scatter them. I'll show Birdie how to open it, so you don't have to, okay?"

A still-recovering Tess sighs; she's so very weary. "I'm not sure how long this is going to take." She looks over at her skinny sister deep in conversation with Henry. "If we're not back by five thirty. . . ."

Will gives her a hug and says, "Supper will be waiting."

Birdie wants to hold the golden box as they descend down the beach path, but they hadn't planned anything else out funeral-wise. Tessie's only priority is to be rid of her mother once and for all, but her sister looks sad and solemn. She doesn't feel the same bitterness toward Louise that Tess lugs around, which was hard for the both of them to understand after the way their mother had treated her.

After they wend down the crumbly asphalt path and arrive at the shore, they sit in the sand, slip off their shoes, and dig in their toes. They study the thrown-away and lost items that've rolled up onto the beach. Down the beach, a flock of seagulls are arguing over a carp.

When Birdie stands and walks to the water's edge, Tess joins her. Puffy clouds are rolling across the sky, pushed by a wind that's not coming off the lake, but at the girls' backs. Tess points up and says, "It's your color. Robin's egg blue."

Birdie tries a smile. "I was just remembering all the time we spent at the beach with her when we were kids. How beautiful she was lying on that white sheet." She begins to cry. "I know you didn't so much, but I really loved her, Tessie. I never gave up believing that if I worked hard enough, lost weight, got smarter, that she'd love me back." She turns to face her sister. "The day you agreed with Leon and let them pull the plug, you killed my hope too."

"Oh, Bird. I'm. . . ."

"I know." She leans into Tess. "I'm sorry too. I know now that you only did what you thought was right."

The girls slide into one another and lock in place until Birdie steps back and says, "I'd like to say a few words." She may not understand Birdie's devotion to Louise, but Tess is humbled by the sincerity of it. She bows her head in respect.

> *The Lord is my shepherd.*
> *I shall not want.*
> *He maketh me to lie down in green pastures.*
> *He leadeth me beside the still waters.*
> *He restoreth my soul. . . .*

When Birdie finishes reciting the entire Twenty-Third Psalm by heart, she shrugs and tells her sister's amazed face, "I've been reading the Bible. It's not as bad as it used to be. Do you want to say something?"

Her knee-jerk reaction is to repeat one of her mother's

favorite expressions—"That's the way the cookie crumbles"—but she'd been working on forgiving Louise the way I'd suggested she should. Tess knows that if a woman wasn't loved by her mother, she'll go one of two ways when she herself becomes a mom. Either she'll make it her life's work to bestow upon her children the love she never received, or she'll treat her babies the same harsh way she'd been treated. Louise took route two.

Tessie was just seven years old at the time. She'd come home crying from the park with a bloody cut below the knee. She was still young enough to hope, like Birdie, that *this* would be the time that her mother would tend to her the way she saw the other mommies in the neighborhood tend to their kids. Louise would express dismay, sit Tess down on the edge of the bathtub to ever so gently wash off the boo-boo with warm water, brush it with iodine, and cover it with care and a Band-Aid. Give her a little kiss maybe, and tell her how brave she was before she sent her on her way. But when Tess came wailing to Louise that afternoon, her mother was in the midst of scrubbing the kitchen floor. She glanced up at her daughter's bleeding leg and barked out, "You think that's bad? When I was a kid, I fell off the monkey bars at school and broke an arm and a leg. I laid there for two hours until a nun found me and called my ma who told her I was supposed to be home doing the wash and shouldn't have been playing on the monkey bars in the first place." Louise wrung out her rag in the bucket. "Sister Elizabeth found me and dropped me off at the hospital. I was in traction for a month. When Ma finally came to visit, she bitched the whole time about the bill." Tessie got only a glimpse at the profound pain in

Louise's eyes before she told her, "You know where the Band-Aids are," and went back to her scrubbing.

Tess looks at the golden cube in her sister's hands and decides to recite an Atticus quote from the book that means so much to *her*. "'You never understand a person until you consider things from his point of view—until you climb inside his skin and walk around in it.'" It was the best she could do.

When the two of them step into the icy water, Birdie kisses the golden box before she lifts up the adhesive flap the way Will had showed her. She remains dry-eyed when she tips the box and says, "Dust to dust . . . ," but Tess finds herself welling up when the water claims what remained of the woman who never loved them.

The house emptied shortly after a feast of pork chops, apple sauce, mashed potatoes, and steamed baby corn, carrots, and green beans. Henry's playing poker at Teeter's house. He has a sister that Haddie is friends with so they drove off together. Will is plying his trade. The Finley girls are in the kitchen, busy cleaning up. Like the old days. With a twist. Birdie rinses the dishes *too* thoroughly in water so steamy that it curls her pixie-cut, dyed blond hair as she scours stains off pots that Tess had thought were permanent. She shoves her hand down the garbage disposal to scrape the blades clean with a lemon. Attacks the sink with the Dutch cleanser until it shines.

She pauses at one point to tell Tessie, who's been drying the pots and wiping down the yellow tile counters, "Almost done here. Where are the rest of your cleaning supplies? Your powder-room sink needs work."

Tess needs to intervene or her sister might stay up half the night cleaning. She places her hand on Birdie's back and says, "But I've been so looking forward to the two of us cuddling and talking. How about you leave the sink 'til tomorrow? Can you do that?"

A fine sweat breaks out on the side of Birdie's nose.

"Don't make me play the cancer card," Tess says. "Go upstairs and take a shower." She doesn't tell her sister to relax. That's what people who don't know any better tell people like them. "Please? I'll be right behind you."

Birdie's arms start to shake. She's fighting the compulsion, but the effort to overcome the tug of war is monumental. She chews her lip, looks at her sister, and then back at the powder room, and then back at her sister, and chews her lip harder.

Tessie removes the sponge from her sister's hand and tosses it in the sink. Birdie picks it up and puts it in its proper place, adjusts it three more times, and says with clenched fists, "Fine. Fine. Fine. Fine. But if you love your family, you'd post an out-of-order sign on the powder-room door. That sink is a breeding ground for malaria," before she stomps toward the staircase.

After Tessie lets Garbo out, she makes two cups of Ovaltine and brings them up to the guest room that she's readied, she hopes, to her sister's liking. Her suitcases have already been emptied, her foldables put away perfectly in the oak chest, or hung in the closet on color-coded padded hangers that she'd brought along. She is quite the clothes horse.

Birdie pads into the bedroom in a pretty, frilly nightgown, still damp from the shower. She throws back the new quilt that covers the brass bed, points at the sheets, and says, "Get in. Age before beauty."

After Tess gets cozy beside her, they sip their Ovaltine and talk nonstop.

When Will comes home after work, he knocks on the bedroom door, pokes his head in, and says, "Good night, girls. Love the milk mustaches," and shuts the door behind him.

Birdie says, "He smells like fried onions and he's stupidly cheerful, but I like him."

Tess says, "Yeah, me too," and resumes describing her cancer ordeal to her medical transcriptionist sister, who, of course, wants to hear every little detail and see her scars. When she lifts up her cows-sipping-*café-au-lait*-on-the-*Champs-Élysées* nightie, Birdie inspects Dr. Whaley's handiwork and says, "I've seen worse, a lot worse."

Tess wants to know more about her work and asks, "Do you enjoy it?"

"It's a mixed bag. I think I have half the diseases I'm typing up, and most of the doctors have God complexes, but I can do it from home and I'm really, really good at it."

Tessie doesn't doubt that. Birdie can't help but be insanely thorough. "And how's life in Boca Raton?"

"Not terrible. But I still wake up every morning feeling like a stranger in a strange land. Palm trees are weird, and palmetto bugs were created by Satan."

They compare symptoms next. It's one of the ways they bond.

Birdie's tells Tess that the delusions had disappeared with cutting-edge medication, that she'd learned to manage her struggles with food years ago, but, "As you saw today . . . the OCD and panic attacks are still a problem."

Tess tells her how Louise's belittling voice is not as loud as it used to be, and that her flashbacks—other than the one she's having now about the many nights the Finley sisters spent doing the same thing they're doing—seem to be less frequent, but she still deals with depression, and panic attacks too. "But I haven't dissociated in a while."

"At least, you don't think you have."

Tess laughs. She'd forgotten how funny her sister could be when she feels secure.

The subject changes to talk of friends of the imaginary sort. Birdie grins and says, "Do you think Bee and Grace are buddies? I bet they are."

("Out of the mouths of babes and sucklings.")

"I'm making an effort to be more social," Tess confesses, "but I'm not good at it. I'm awkward. Not like you." When she's on the right medication, Birdie is more at ease around what the girls call, "NPs"—Normal People.

"My shrink says it's important that I get out of the house and mingle if I don't want to exacerbate my agoraphobia, so I take night classes at the community college near my apartment. That's fine, until we go out afterwards for coffee. I don't have much in common with people who don't need to count or clean or do things four times or always sit as close as possible to an exit." Birdie gulps down the remainder of her Ovaltine. "Esther? The old woman I told you about who lives in the apartment below me? She taught me how to play Mahjong and I clean her apartment for her once a week, so sometimes I can convince myself I have a real friend, but I don't, not really."

"You have me, Bird."

"I know, Tessie, I know."

"You could move back."

This was an ongoing request in their on-again-off-again conversations throughout the years. Whenever she'd brought it up in the past, Birdie was still dealing with her rivalry issues and she'd flat-out refuse. Tess hopes they're beyond that now. It would be wonderful to know she could be at her sister's side quickly if she needed to be, and vice versa.

"You have your poker winnings and you can do your transcribing from anywhere," Tess says. "And you wouldn't have to worry about finding somewhere to live right off. You could stay with us until you found a place of your own. You could be the weird aunt!" She ruffles her sister's hair so it's sticking out every which way. "Our Humane Society is top drawer, so there'd be no problem when it came to adopting cats. The resale shop carries lots of strange outfits, and you . . . might even meet the man of your dreams! One of the best psychiatric facilities in the country is right up the road. Maybe they host a happy hour on Friday nights!"

When Birdie playfully smacks her with a throw pillow, Tess laughs, but it's tinged with sadness. As wonderful as the moving-home scenario was, they're both wondering how long they can maintain this closeness before one of them gets their feelings hurt and puts the brakes on the relationship until they can gather up enough courage to try again.

Birdie says, "Enough about me. So what's going on with you and Will?"

After a tearful Tess shares her suspicions with her, Birdie hugs her and says, "Men. Bah. You can't live with 'em, and you can't move furniture without them." That was one of Louise's old gripes. "Are you *sure* he's cheating?"

"No, not positive." Tess blows her nose. "I've been all over the place. When we stopped making love, I thought, at first, he was just sick of me and all my problems. I didn't suspect he was having an affair until he started giving me lame excuses about why he was coming home late on Wednesday nights. Then a month or so later, he blurted out that his lack of interest didn't have anything to do with me. He told me he was being so distant because he was having a midlife crisis and that he was impotent. He had a lot of the classic symptoms, so I wanted to believe that, but now . . . ," she starts to well up again.

"Do you suspect someone?" Birdie asks.

"The hostess at the diner. Connie Lushman."

Birdie purses her lips. "Why does that name sound so familiar?"

"Will was engaged to her when we met at Arthur Murray."

"Ahhh . . . right. You have any proof they're messing around besides him not coming home late on Wednesday nights?"

Tess tells her about the smell of Tabu and the long blond hairs she finds on Will's shirts, and then she asks the one who knows her like no other, "Do you think I'm just being paranoid? Or as Will likes to say, making one of my erroneous assumptions?"

Birdie takes a minute to consider all that Tess has shared with her. She knows that her opinions matter to her, especially the medical ones. "A midlife crisis *can* be disabling, and they're real individual in nature. I've typed up reports where men have affairs like it's their job, and others who experience a radical downswing in their love life. There could also be other reasons why Will might be holding back."

"Like . . . ?"

"Stress. Or he could think of you as too fragile. That happens a lot in cancer cases. Husbands get afraid they'll break their sick wives. Or maybe he's a little nervous to try again after such a long time. What if he failed?" Birdie runs the tip of her tongue across her top lip and connects with the milk mustache. "Or you could be right and he *is* messing around. Have you tried talking to him?"

"He's not big on conversation, never has been. I tried a couple of times to draw him out before I got sick, but he would suddenly need to go to work or start snoring, and when I had to have the surgeries and then radiation I stopped trying because what if he admitted he *was* having an affair? I couldn't face knowing the truth, not then."

Birdie takes Tessie's hands in hers and says, "All I can tell you is that when he looks at you, there's love in his eyes. And no offense meant, but . . . he doesn't seem smart enough to pull off an affair. That takes timing, execution, and attention to detail. His barn door was open when he left for work tonight."

Tess had noticed that as well, but how many times can you remind a guy?

Birdie regroups. "Besides the hair and perfume, which is totally circumstantial, by the way, you got any other proof that Connie's makin' a play for Will?"

"The girls at the diner talk about their love lives all the time, but Connie doesn't, and I know she's involved with somebody. I overhead Otto say that she has a boyfriend and he's the kind of guy who doesn't miss much of anything."

"And Otto is . . . ?"

"The dishwasher." Tess fills her in on his obsession with the CIA and the Planet Argon, his dedication and fondness for Will, how he'd stalked the girl from the resale shop, and finally, his heart-rending breakup with his Russian mail-order bride.

"Other than the obvious paranoia, he sounds romantic, like a take-charge kind of guy," Birdie says a little dreamy, like Tess had just described the dashing lead character in a Barbara Cartland novel.

"I don't . . . I can't keep. . . ." Tess rolls onto her back and tugs the covers over her face. "I have to find out if Will's cheating on me. Time's running out."

It's Tuesday. Friday is their wedding anniversary. He must've planned *something*. If for no other reason than keeping up appearances in front of the kids. Dinner out, probably. It's not often the Blessings get the chance to paint the town, but when they do, Will makes a reservation at The Edge of Town. A popular supper club in the forties—it was once a favorite amongst Chicago gangsters—the abandoned building had fallen into disrepair until family friend and fellow restaurateur, Tommy McMann, bought it five years ago and renovated it. Besides offering the best prime rib on the North Shore, he'd brought back crooner-type live music, a parquet dance floor, and hat check girls. Same as the diner, it's the kind of establishment that attracts folk who are hungry for the good old days.

Birdie asks, "So how're you gonna do that?"

Lost in her thoughts, Tess asks, "What?"

"Find out if Will's cheating on you."

"I was thinking we'd follow him tomorrow night."

Her sister bolts up and yanks the covers off Tess's face. "We're gonna *tail* him?"

Like her, Birdie is a mystery buff from way back. The girls had spent much of their childhood tracking down answers to life's little mysteries. They were lovers of Nancy Drew and any and all television crime or whodunit shows. They spied on people in the neighborhood. During those summer nights out on the stoop, they'd even talked about having their own detective agency when they grew up. Tess's natural abilities led her to ballroom dance and then comedy, but Birdie seriously considered becoming a gumshoe after she moved down to Boca Raton. Private detection is a good job for the hypervigilant. They like being alone for long periods of time without stimulus, excel at puzzle-solving, and are superb at spotting dangerous situations. Barely anything escapes their eagle eyes. Conversely, they lack patience, can get sidetracked by their emotions, and cars can be claustrophobic, which is why Birdie decided to become a medical transcriptionist instead.

She eagerly says, "What's the plan?"

It'd been a momentous and monstrously long day, and

Tess feels too pooped to participate one minute longer. She reaches over and switches off the bedside table lamp and says, "I'll tell you all about it tomorrow, okay? I'm beat."

She spoons Birdie, who a few minutes later, confirms, "So we're going sightseeing and shopping in the morning, eat lunch at the diner, and we'll have pepperoni pizza for supper, and then follow Will around to see if he's cheating on you with Connie Lushman." She's organizing tomorrow in her head. She *needs* to know what she'll be doing every minute because her idle mind is the devil's workshop. "Right?"

Already half-asleep, Tess mumbles, "Uh-huh. 'Night, Bird."

Moments later, "Tessie?"

"Yeah?"

When Birdie rolls over to face her, she has the red wax lips stuck in her mouth.

After Tessie gives her four kisses, the Finley sisters drift off in each other arms to sleep the sleep of the ones that were lost and now are found.

Loose Lips Sink Ships

When they were kids, Tessie called her sister, who tended to rise the same time the sun did, "Early Bird," and the nickname still holds true.

When my friend came down to the kitchen the next morning, it was to find that Birdie and Will had whipped up breakfast together. Now that she was used to him, Tess could tell that her sister found her husband charming, but everybody did. Despite her doubts about his fidelity, *she* did. She couldn't help it if he still made her heart beat faster and her inner thighs tingle.

Tess says, "Morning!" and offers to help, but they push her out of the kitchen. "Sit," they say. "Your tea's coming right up."

From her place at the pine table, she can't hear what Birdie and Will are talking about while they bustle about preparing pancakes. It feels almost conspiratorial, but that's ridiculous, she tells herself. She's allowing her paranoia about Will to color the most innocent of exchanges. What's next? He slipped curare into the Log Cabin bottle? Birdie blended Ebola into the butter?

Spring vacation is over for Henry, so after the six of them, including Garbo, chow down, he heads outside to wait for his ride over to Ruby Falls High. Haddie, who had eaten a silver dollar-sized pancake and didn't pay a visit to the bathroom afterwards, is spending the day in Chicago at the Art Institute with her boyfriend, Kevin, so she left with her dad, who'll drop her off at the train station in downtown Milwaukee before he heads over to the diner.

As Birdie loads the dishwasher with the breakfast dishes, she says to Tessie, who's cleaning up batter flecks on the stove, "I really like the kids. I feel bad about not playing a larger part in the lives. Haddie is sweet and so talented, and Henry is a lot like you, but a much, much better card player. I'm still holding a Gin Rummy IOU from 1961, by the way. A dollar and a box of Jujubes. I'd appreciate payment at your earliest convenience."

Tess chuckles and says, "The kids still have a lot of growing up to do and you could be a part of that." She wants to add on, *Up close and personal*, but she's got to be careful. If she pushes too hard, she'll scare her. Same as Tessie, more than anything Birdie wants to be wanted, but grows suspicious when people do.

When the kitchen duties were a fait accompli, Birdie, still in her pretty pajamas with frills, put on her rubber gloves and got right to work scrubbing the powder-room sink that she'd wanted to tackle last night. She says very seriously to Tess, who's sitting on the toilet lid keeping her company, "I spent some time thinking about it, like two or three hours, and I'm pretty sure I figured out why Will doesn't want to do the Scorpion Dance of Love with you anymore."

All ears, Tess says, "Why?"

Birdie points at the ratty cows-sipping-*café-au-lait*-on-the-*Champs-Élysées* nightie and says, "Talk about a penis shrinker."

Tess grins and goes back to staring at the To-Do List that's become so worn and creased that it looks like it should be kept under glass at the Ruby Falls Historical Museum.

Birdie glances over and asks, "One of your lists?"

Tess holds it up and points to the last item to be crossed out—number four. Convince Will to love me again. (What about Connie?)

Birdie shrugs, resumes scrubbing, and says, "Things seem really good between you two other than the hoochie-koochie stuff. You sure you want to follow him tonight?

Tess considers all the Wednesday nights Will's told her that he'll be home late because he was doing the books or meeting with a supplier or reviewing an employee, but would come home smelling like Connie's perfume. "Wish I didn't *have* to know what he's up to, but I do." She couldn't give her heart to him any longer if she wasn't certain that she could trust him. She's always felt that wives who turn a blind eye and the other cheek are not virtuous, just slow learners. How would he respond if she catches him red-handed tonight? Would he blame his midlife crisis? Her emotional instability? Something else entirely? Whatever his reaction, the marriage would be over. They'd keep living together, for Henry's sake. If he noticed that she was sleeping in the guest room, she'd make a crack about his dad's snoring. But once he left for college, she would . . . what? Leave Will? A life without him is unimaginable.

Tess replaces the To-Do List back in her nightie pocket, inspects the sink, gives her sister a thumbs-up, and says, "Time to get the show on the road."

Birdie surprises her by not putting up too much of a fuss. She strips off her Playtex gloves and throws them in the bucket. "Fine, but I'm not through here. Your tile needs caulk . . . caulk . . . caulk . . . caulk. Can we stop at a hardware store when we're out?"

Birdie attended her sister's wedding at St. Lucy's, but all she'd seen of Ruby Falls was the inside of the church, and the ballroom at the country club where the reception had been held. Given how much she loves and intimately knows the town, Tessie is an extraordinary tour guide. She takes Birdie around to the historical spots first—the covered bridge, the granary, and the falls. They even swing by the old convent where Tess gets her up to speed on the rest of the adventures she'd had with Sisters Faith, Hope, and yours truly before they hit the downtown stores. Birdie *loves* to shop. She tries to talk Tess into buying a new purse at one of the many boutiques, but only as a joke. She knows her sister would rather die than surrender her lucky black one. Birdie is especially knocked out by the sweets section at The Emporium. She left the old-fashioned store with a pound box of chocolate-covered cherries, her all-time favorite.

Uptown, Tess points out Peaches 'n Cream, the salon that she so rarely frequents. Birdie, who takes enormous pride in her appearance and is meticulously well groomed, like their mother was, talks her into a walk-in visit. "Your hair . . . God. And I could use a manicure." She steers her sister toward the salon door. "Let's see if they have any openings."

Tess doesn't resist because she knows they won't. The salon is the busiest in town and the chance of her popular stylist being available is nil.

But when the Peaches 'n Cream receptionist, Katie, checks her computer, she tells them, "Wow! Talk about luck. We have a manicure opening *and* Suzanne just had a last-minute cancellation." (The events that unfold later this evening will be imprinted forever in Birdie and Tessie's brain. When they flash back to tonight's showdown, it'd be nice for them to look their best. The manicurist was already available, but I went ahead and flattened the tire on Ellie Thompson's car, which opened up the spot in Suzanne's schedule.)

Once they've completed their beautifying treatments, Birdie who had her nails painted purple, pokes fun at risk-adverse Tess's new do. "What'd Suzanne take off . . . a sixteenth of an inch?" and then she reminds her for the fourth time that before they head over to Count Your Blessings for lunch, they *need* to swing by Hoover's Hardware.

After Birdie finishes obsessing over the different colored caulks—"I should've dug some of the old stuff out and brought it with me for comparison"—bawdy Babs Hoover rings them up. As she suggestively slips the white tube into the sack, she asks Tess, "You and the hubby doing a little crack-filling tonight?" followed by one of her air-raid siren laughs that sends both girls running.

There's a sign taped to the front door of Count Your

Blessings. CLOSING AT 7:00 TONIGHT.

"That's not gonna mess up our plan is it?" Birdie asks Tess.

"No. Will's only closing to the public at seven. One of the cooler motors has to be replaced. It was supposed to happen this Sunday, but then the health inspector. . . ." It's too long an explanation. "He and the staff are going to do inventory until the usual closing time. (That's what he told her anyway.)

Birdie, who was fussed over by Will when he shows them to a table near the window, is predictably captivated by the diner. *Johnny Angel* is playing on the jukebox, and the '50s decor and food really is fantastic. "It's like being a kid again and having lunch at Dalinsky's Drugstore!" she says.

Tess is famished and orders them both today's Blue-Plate Special—a Blessing Burger, fries, and a chocolate phosphate. She thought her svelte sister would only pick at the food, but her appetite must've been whetted by the nostalgia and excitement over tonight's adventure, because she wolfs down her burger. She dips the last of her crispy fries into the ketchup, then tilts her head to the left when she hears, "Welcome to Count Your Blessings. How many are in your party?"

Birdie whispers across the table, "Is that her?"

Since Will had seated them, Tess'd thought that Connie Lushman must've taken the day off to rest up for her tryst with him tonight, but she must've been on a break. My friend finishes off the remainders of her phosphate and says, "The one and only."

"Holy shit. No wonder you're freaking out. She's hot."

When Tess kitten mewls, Birdie removes her foot from her mouth and adds on, "I mean, ya know, only if you like alabaster skin, naturally blond hair, and geeze, I think her bellows are real."

Tess can't fault her for thinking the same thing she is. She tosses the napkin onto her plate and says, "If you're done. . . ." They have to get a move on, they have a timetable to stick to. "Let's get the spy equipment from Otto."

Will gives Tess a kiss on the cheek and winks at Birdie when they approach the cash register. "Lunch good?" he asks.

Birdie says bubbly, "Best I've had in years," because she's already figured out that there is no better way to compliment her brother-in-law than by lavishing praise upon his vittles.

Will grins at the kudo, then pulls Tess aside and says, "Sorry, but I won't be home for supper after all. I forgot that I've got to empty out the cooler and move everything into the other ones during the break." Lester Holt, the county health inspector, had paid a surprise visit during Monday's dinner shift. The temperature had dropped another degree in the meat cooler and Lester *insisted* that Will get mechanic, Frank Morton, to come in and replace the motor *immediately* rather than Sunday night as planned.

Just to make sure what she told Birdie was true, she asks Will, "But you're still going to call it quits around nine?"

"Hope so," he says. "I'll let the staff go then, but I've got to stick around until Frank is finished working on the motor. You know how pokey he can be."

She puts on her Brownie smile and says, "I'll see you when I see you." *Which will be sooner than you think, you big fat liar.* "I'm gonna give Birdie the tour."

Even more determined now to expose Will's dallying, she returns to the cash register, picks up her sister's hand, and tugs her into the kitchen.

"Behind . . . behind . . . behind," she says as she steers through the chaos of the busy shift. On their way to the sink, she introduces Birdie to Juan and his cousins, who are overwhelmed in front of the deep fryers, and then to waitresses, Sandy, Nancy, and Alison, who are darting about filling and placing orders. After she calls out loudly to the dishwasher and he doesn't respond, she taps Otto on his shoulder to get his attention.

He turns, dries his hands off on his apron, removes his aluminum-foil-wrapped headwear, and says, "Oh. Hey, Bess, and. . . ." He focuses intently on Birdie, with his good eye anyway. The one he lost to the pencil accident stays as still as a Buckingham Palace guard. "Who's your friend?"

After she introduces her sister, lovelorn Otto clicks his heels together, bends at the waist, lifts Birdie's hand to his lips, and says, "*Enchanté.*"

"Oh, boy," Tess mutters because she can see where this is going. She steps between them, and asks Otto, "Did you bring the night-vision binoculars and The Ear like I asked you to?"

Still giving Birdie the goo-goo eye, he says, "They're in my locker."

"Great. What's the combination?" Tess asks him.

"That's on a need-to-know basis."

She knows trying to convince him to give up the combination won't work. He's too paranoid. "Okay," she says as she glances over her shoulder at Will to make sure he's still busy at the cash register. "We'll come with you to the locker room to get it."

"Negative." Otto is about to put his headphones back on and resume his duties. "The Big Boss Man wouldn't like it if I abandoned my station."

She thinks fast. "You saw me talking to him at the cash register a few minutes ago, didn't you?" Otto nods. He doesn't miss much. "I was asking him if it was okay if you left the sink for a few minutes and he said sure, but we have to be quick about, so *vamanos*!"

With Tess in the lead, the three of them hurry out of the kitchen's side door and down the long hall that leads to the room in the back of the building where the staff can store their personal belongings during their shifts, grab a smoke, or just get off their feet for a few minutes.

After Otto checks to make sure the room is empty, he moves ninja-like to the bank of utilitarian gray lockers that line one of the walls. Tess tries to peek, but he uses his taut, muscular body—he does the Royal Canadian Air Force exercises every morning—to shield the combination from her.

To the best of her knowledge, no one else on the staff decorates their lockers, but Otto has taped on the inside door an eight-by-ten glossy of Julie Andrews playing Maria in *The Sound of Music* that Stan Majerus, owner of the Rivoli next door, must have procured for him. Birdie yelps in delight, "It's my favorite too!" But the hills are alive with something other than von Trapps that she doesn't seem to notice. Bigfoot photos (a government conspiracy) and UFO newspaper clippings (another government conspiracy) also hang on the locker door that Otto withdraws his spy equipment from.

Tess holds out her hands and says, "Thanks," but Otto doesn't place The Eye and the binoculars in them. He grasps them to his chest and asks, "What time are we rendezvousing?"

She smiles and tells him, "I really appreciate the offer, but this is a two-person operation."

"Where my equipment goes, I go. For all I know, you could be using it against me," Otto says.

Around a year ago, he'd overheard one of the waitresses say that she was working at the diner to save enough money to attend the CIA—The Culinary Institute of America. She asked when the time came if Tess, her boss, would write her a letter of recommendation. Tess tried to explain the conversation to Otto then, and many times since, but he won't believe her.

"For the hundredth time, I'm not a deep operative sent by the CIA to spy on you. My sister and I just want to—"

"Do a little snooping on Connie," Birdie says coyly.

Tess immediately sees where her sister's going with this. "Yeah," she says to Otto. "You mentioned that she has a boyfriend and she won't tell me who it is. I know she meets him on Wednesday nights so we're going to follow her home from work tonight to . . . um . . . satisfy our curiosity."

"That killed the cat." He reaches into his locker, withdraws a fancy-looking camera, says, "Cheese," to

Birdie, and squeezes off a shot. "And you don't need to follow Connie. I know already know who her boyfriend is."

Dare she? The answer could save Tess the anguish of discovering them together in bed. She grits her teeth and asks him, "Who?"

"That's classified information," he says as he carefully replaces the camera and slams his locker shut with a bang that makes both jumpy girls jump. "I gotta get back to the kitchen."

Birdie steps in front of him and bats her eyelashes. "We would never ask you to reveal your sources, so maybe this should be a three-person operation, after all." She drags her finger up his sinewy arm. "Would you consider joining us tonight? We could use a big strong spy man's help, right, Bess?"

"Ahhh . . . I—"

"Well, when you put it so nice like that. . . ." Otto is practically drooling. "Meet me behind Rivoli's dumpster at nine hundred hours. Wear black." He gives the sisters a small salute. "And remember, loose lips sink ships. You get my drift?"

Tess would've missed the opportunity to follow Will if compulsive Birdie hadn't decided that they had to show up two hours earlier at the stakeout than expected. They have a full view of the diner's parking lot from behind the theatre's dumpster. Count Your Blessings closed for service at seven the way Will said it would, but mechanic Frank Morton's well-marked pickup hasn't shown up, and neither has health inspector Lester Holt's menacing black van.

Tess shifts nervously next to her sister when at 7:33 p.m., the staff, who was supposed to be counting beverage bottles and dry goods, files out of the diner's backdoor toward the parking lot. Will and Connie bring up the rear of the procession. They laugh as they stroll toward the '57 Chevy together. Tess thought she heard Will say something that sounded like, "After all this time . . . secret."

She crushes her lucky purse to her chest and whispers to Birdie, "What the hell is going on?"

Her sister shrugs. "Ask Otto."

The dishwasher is lingering in the lot until he's sure that his coworkers are snug in their cars before he trots next door and crouches down behind the movie theatre dumpster with the girls. He's brushed his electric hair flat, and is wearing a cologne that smells like a combination of bacon grease and Ivory soap.

Tess has more-pressing questions, but this is a first—she's never seen him without his aluminum-foil-covered headphones. She points to his head and asks, "Where are your—?!"

"As an operative of the CIA, you know better than that. The streetlights would reflect off the foil and make too easy to pick up on a satellite," he says brusquely.

"Weren't you and the rest of the staff supposed to be doing inventory while the meat cooler was being repaired?" Birdie asked. "What happened?"

Otto does an about-face, and tips his black baseball cap to her. "Don't remember hearing anything about an inventory. We closed up at seven like we were supposed to, then after we broke down our stations, Mister Will told us to enjoy our evenings and gave us the rest of the night off." He smiles at Birdie. "You look very fetching in black."

"Why, thank you, kind sir."

Tess groans. "Do you have the equipment, Otto?"

He unzips the dark gym bag he's carrying, shows her what he's got inside, and asks her, "Where's your vulva?"

Birdie gasps, but Tess doesn't. She knows he means her Volvo. Otto's vocabulary is fluid, and dependent upon what's currently occupying his mind. Tonight, it appears to be her sister's private parts. When he was still together with his Russian mail-order bride, he referred to her car as, the "Volga."

Tess tells him, "I parked it in the Rivoli's side lot."

He nods in approval. "Go get it. Me and your sister will wait here and see what direction Connie and the Big Boss Man take out of the lot."

It concerns Tess that he doesn't find Will and the hostess leaving together remarkable enough to comment on. Is this a repetitive behavior that he's witnessed many times over the past few months?

Give the little lady a Kewpie doll," Louise says with a carny laugh.

Tess's courage completely deserts her. This is way too much for her handle. She makes her way to the car thinking what a stupid idea this was. When she gets back to the lot, she's going to call the whole thing off. Go home and lick her wounds.

"What took you so long?" Otto snaps as he and Birdie pile into the backseat of the car when Tessie pulls alongside them. "Go north. Step on it!"

"But . . . I . . . I. . . ." All of her nerve endings are firing at the same time and it feels like she's under attack from a barrage of gunfire, so rather than tell Otto that she's changed her mind and wants to abort the mission, she does what she's told and squeals out of the lot in hot pursuit of Will's car. She locks onto the Chevy's distinctive headlights seconds before it makes a turn down Oak. That's the street Connie lives on.

Otto says over Tess's shoulder, "Slow down after you make the turn. Wait at the top of the block until you see Mister Will park, then get a little closer, but not too close, then pull to the curb, and douse the lights."

Once they've settled into position, Birdie leans forward and asks, "Can you see them?"

The view to the front door of Connie's sweet, Craftsman bungalow is partially blocked by a tree, so Tess wasn't able to witness them leaving the car. She can see them now, though. They're approaching the front porch. Will has a garment bag over his arm, but still manages to open the door for Connie. So gallant. She'd been hoping that he had simply given his hostess a ride home, so she says downhearted, "The eagle has landed."

Otto checks his fancy military watch. "Sun's gonna set soon. Better to wait a bit and sneak up on them under the cover of darkness."

After the fifteen minutes that seem like fifteen hours passes, Tess tells herself, *I can't stand this. I've got to know now!* She resolutely places her hand on the car door handle seconds before Birdie, who is sticking her head out of the window to get a better look, says, "They're coming out."

Otto wolf whistles from the backseat. "Looks like a hot time on the old town tonight!"

Tess feels a sudden surge of hope. She says to her sister, "Pass me the binoculars."

Enough time hadn't passed for them to make love and get all duded up to boot. Wham, bam, thank you, ma'am, is definitely not her husband's style. He must be whisking his floozy somewhere first to wine and dine her because he's changed out of his work clothes. He looks so handsome in the black pin-striped suit and pearl-gray shirt she'd bought him for his birthday, and Connie stuns in red four-inch heels, seamed nylons, and a cream dress that hugs her dangerous curves. Ruby earrings dangle to her luscious bare shoulders. The honey blond hair she keeps in a tight bun at work streams down her back in perfect waves. Tess can smell her Tabu.

Otto commands, "Fire up the vehicle, but hold steady and wait for my command." The three of them hold their breaths as Will pulls away from the curb. "Go!"

This is all the evidence Tess needs, no use prolonging the agony. She leans back and tells her sister, "Let's call it a night. I've got terrible heartburn. I . . . I need to go home."

Birdie pulls out a pack of Tums and hands her sister two. "Quit imagining the worst," she says, like that's doable. "All is not lost."

"A course all is not lost," oblivious Otto says with a snort. "I got the bead on 'em. Turn left on Pleasant."

He's so insistent, and Birdie's so excited, and Tess is feeling so dispirited that she doesn't have the strength to argue. She follows Will's car through the town streets, and then down the two-lane blacktop on the outskirts of Ruby Falls. Where are they headed? The only thing out this far is. . . .

She kitten mewls.

"You need another Tums?" Birdie asks.

Tess shakes her head and says, "I think they're going out to dinner at . . . ," her and Will's special place, "The Edge of Town."

"Copy that, Bess," Otto says when the lights of the Chevy turn into the supper club's full-to-the-gills lot. "They turned left, you go right. Park over there." He's jabbing his finger towards the part of the lot farthest from the entrance.

Now what? Tess wonders as she switches off the car's engine with shaking fingers. Should she barge in there and accuse Will with a slap across his face, or wait until the lovebirds finish dinner and trail them back to Connie's?

Birdie leaps out of the car and says, "Showtime!" and Otto is right there with her.

Tess doesn't budge. She can't bear to see Will and Connie seated at one of the white table-clothed tables next to the dance floor, or cuddling close in one of the leather booths. Maybe sipping a shared martini. Nibbling on the olive. Seeing them in such an intimate way, it'll haunt her till the end of her days.

Tess shouts to Otto and Birdie's retreating backs, "Go ahead. I'll catch up."

Her sister knows her too well.

Birdie sprints back to the car, sticks her arm through the car window, grabs the keys out of the ignition, and sticks them in her jacket. "Comb your hair and . . . here." She pulls a tube of lip gloss out of her black jeans pocket, sweeps it across her sister's lips, and says, "Put on your Brownie Smile and get out of the goddamn car. Time to face the music."

Blurry-eyed Tess can barely make out her accomplices weaving through the parked cars toward the restaurant entrance. She recognizes Stan Olsen's Cadillac that's butted up to Jack Loudon's beat-up Jeep Wrangler. Both men are on Will's bowling team. Is that why he and Connie are here tonight? Are The High Rollers having some sort of awards banquet tonight? Is she really the last to know?

The entryway to the supper club is lavish and period-correct. Two massive potted plants sit at the base of a maroon awning. At the end of a carpet of the same color, there stands a burly doorman dressed in a regal-looking black coat with epaulets.

Roger Turnbull smiles and says, "Good evening, Tess." When he opens the door, she can hear the band tuning up. People laughing and clinking glasses. "Have fun tonight."

When Birdie and Otto disappear into the darkened entry, Tess isn't hurt by their obvious excitement. Her sister is wild-streaking, and Otto has successfully completed his mission.

She tells Roger, "I need a minute."

The band has eased into the opening strains of *Hernando's Hideaway*. It's her and Will's song. The one played during their wedding dance, the one she used to hum to him before they tangoed up Chestnut Street as their prelude to making love. Had he requested it?

Tess is devastated, and intends to make a break for it. She'll have Roger call her a cab. "Would you mind . . . ?"

It appears that the time has come to pay another visit to my friend.

I come up behind her, say, "Fancy meetin' you here, sugar," and shove her through the supper-club doors.

I Know a Dark, Secluded Place

The house lights had been dimmed, and it takes a few seconds for Tess's eyes to adjust, so when the "SURPRISE!" comes barreling at her, she ducks.

She's not given enough time to orient herself before Will comes rushing toward her, Haddie and Henry too, and Birdie is clapping her hands and bouncing up and down. Otto looks as stunned as Tess and has assumed a warrior stance, but the rest of the diners are on their feet and the band is still playing *their* song.

Tessie says, "What . . . ? Will . . . ?"

"May I have this dance?" He leads his stunned wife onto the floor. "Happy anniversary, *ma chérie*" he says as he takes her in his arms and proceeds to lead her in a passionate and thoroughly professional tango.

Tess is not only bowled over by the party, she's amazed by her husband's dancing. When did he get a right foot?

When the last notes of *Hernando's Hideaway* fade, he dips his wife of thirty years, and bestows a deep kiss upon her lips. "I told you I had a little something planned," he says cockily.

Folks are clapping and gathering around the Mr. and Mrs. Blessing and shouting, "Happy thirtieth anniversary,

Will and Tess!" The staff from the restaurant, some of the old folks from Horizons, Richie Mattigan's wife and kids, most of their regular diner customers, including crabby Mare Hanson and Nurse Jerry, Irwin, Cliff, and little Marty from the St. Joe's Cancer Center, and loads of Ruby Falls neighbors who haven't registered yet are whooping and hollering above Garbo's barking.

Haddie and Henry hug Tess and Will, and when Birdie comes in close, she gives her sister a mischievous grin and disappears back into the crowd.

The lights . . . the noise . . . the swarming crowd. Tess needs to retreat to someplace quiet to pull herself together. She smiles at Will and tells him, "I'll be right back. I . . . ah . . . need to powder my nose," but as she turns and steps in the direction of the ladies' room, Connie Lushman materializes in front of her with a storybook handsome dark-haired man.

"Tess? This is Rod Albright," she gushes, "my boyfriend." By the looks they're giving one another, it's plain to see that these two have it bad for one another. "I've been dying to tell you about him, but I knew you'd ask me what he did for a living and I'm the worse liar and . . . I thought you might figure out what Will was up to if I told you that Rod's a dance instructor." She smiles at him like he's the bees' knees. "The best in Milwaukee."

Tess is so dumbfounded that she can't even tell Rod that it's nice to meet him.

"Will wanted to surprise you on your anniversary by recreating the tango you did at your wedding, only a lot, lot better," Connie says. "He needed a partner." She'd never said anything to Tess about how he had left her standing at the altar. She had always been friendly and there has never been any rancor in her voice. "Will knows how much I like to dance and asked if I'd help him out. He arranged for Rod to drive up from the city and teach us at my place every Wednesday night."

So . . . *that's* how one of her long blond hairs got onto Will's blue shirt. Why he smelled of her perfume. They *had* been spending time in each other's arms.

Will, who's been hovering behind Connie and Rod, sweeps in and says, "Excuse me. I need to have few words with my bride." He picks Tess up in his arms and whisks her to one of the high-backed leather booths that line the dance floor.

Once she settles in, she notices the French-themed decorations spread haphazardly throughout the club to commemorate the Blessings' honeymoon. A plastic Eiffel tower here berets there. Instead of their usual '40s gun-moll uniforms, the Edge of Town waitresses are wearing can-can costumes. And Haddie must have raided the family album. Blown-up pictures of Tess and Will taken throughout their many years together are taped to the walls and bar. Henry playing soccer. The award-winning photo of Garbo sailing through the air with the Frisbee in her mouth. A beautiful summer shot of their home and gardens. Tess decides that Will must've chosen the decorations because there's no underlying theme other than their enduring love.

She tells him, "I can't believe you managed to pull this off. You're not usually this. . . ." She checks beneath the tablecloth to see if his barn door is zipped up.

"I had lots of help," Will says. "The kids, Connie and

Rod, even Birdie pitched in."

"Birdie *knew*?!" Tess flashes back to the scene in the kitchen yesterday when she and Will were flipping pancakes. She hadn't imagined it. They *had* been conspiring. Probably working out the details about tonight.

Will gives his wife his irresistible gap-toothed grin. "I wanted to clue you in after she told me that you suspected Connie and me were fooling around, but she made me promise not to, and she can be pretty persuasive with or without a butcher knife in her hand."

Tess feels horribly guilty for ever doubting him. "I'm really sorry for—"

"Don't be. I get it. First there was my midlife crisis, and then I lost my confidence, and you got sick and I was afraid I'd hurt you, and between planning the party and running the diner . . . I dropped the ball." He looks so contrite that Tess doesn't make a joke about his turn of phrase. "But," he nibbles on her earlobe, "I'm sure you noticed while we were doing the tango that the *monsieur* has made a rousing comeback."

She had. A standing-at-attention Pierre was pretty hard to miss.

"We hit a rough patch," Will says as he places his hand tenderly atop hers. "But it's over now." He withdraws a long velvet box out of his suit coat pocket. "They're from Hawaii."

"Oh, Will," Tess says as he fastens the black pearls around her neck.

The kiss that follows is faith-restoring.

Hours later, after the cake from Betty's Bakery was served and the champagne toasts made and the band packed up their instruments, Tess ambushed Birdie at the bar. She gets her around the neck and gives her a noogie for the part she'd played in perpetrating the surprise.

Birdie laughs and says, "*Gotcha!*" the same way their daddy would've if was here. (He is.)

"Take the Vulva," Tess tells her. "I'll ride home with Will."

Birdie looks over at Otto, who is eyeing the corners of the supper club with his night-vision glasses. "Don't wait up for me," she says. "You get my drift?"

"Roger, that," Tessie says with a parting hug.

After Will left to bring the Chevy around, and while the children are finishing up with their good-byes, my exhausted, but exuberant friend, steps outside to breathe in the night air. No one else is around, but she's not alone. She can hear the refrain of *At Last* and she feels me beside her.

"Grace," she says with a bow of her head. "You, little rascal, you."

On the drive home, the Blessing family is abuzz with the excitement of the occasion, and the children may have had one too many glasses of the bubbly. Especially Henry. Even Garbo's smiling.

After Will pulls into their driveway, he tells the kids, "Your mom and I need some private time when we get home. Make yourselves scarce."

Henry and Haddie can't wobble into the house fast enough.

Hand in hand, Mr. and Mrs. Blessing stroll beneath the old-fashioned streetlights that line the sidewalk in front of their sturdy home. Tess makes him laugh, and Will tells her a few more details about the intricacies of planning the surprise party, and the reason why it was held two days before their actual anniversary instead of the day of. "I'm taking you back to the Holiday Inn in Paris for a second, no . . . third honeymoon. We leave first thing in the morning."

"Well, maybe not *first* thing." Tess gets that hooded look in her eyes and begins softly singing, "I know a dark, secluded place. . . ."

Will takes her in his arms and they recreate the expert tango they'd performed earlier, up the block and back again to the ancient oak tree that he'd carved their initials into the same way his father had his mother's. He presses Tess against the rough bark and cups her breasts in his hands, lays his lips against hers with insistent tenderness until she feels him rise to the occasion.

They didn't make it up to the bedroom.

P.S.

I found *this* crumpled up in the pocket of Tessie's green chenille robe this morning after she and Will took off on their trip to Paris, Illinois.

TO-DO LIST

1. ~~Buy broccoli.~~
2. ~~Hope that Haddie gets the help she needs from a better therapist.~~
3. ~~Set up vocational counseling appointment for Henry.~~
4. ~~Convince Will to love me again. (What about Connie?)~~
5. ~~Get Birdie to talk to me again.~~
6. ~~Bury Louise once and for all. (With Birdie.)~~
7. ~~Have a religious epiphany so #8 is going to be okay with me.~~
8. ~~Die.~~
9. ~~Tell Haddie about the cancer.~~
10. ~~Prepare the guest room.~~
11. ~~Deal with the part you played in Haddie's eating disorder.~~

12. Beg Police Chief Whitehall to release Otto and Birdie on their own recognizance.
13. Figure out if Henry has a drinking problem.
14. Speak to Will again about talking more in a standing position.
15. Work up a routine for The Pink Ladies.
16. Buy broccoli.

Acknowledgments

The past year has been the most difficult and devastating of my life. With deepest gratitude, I thank all who loaned me their strength, gave me a shoulder to cry on, and were there for me in tender ways that I never even knew existed.

My family: my eternally sweet, mischievous, talented, and daring boy, Riley, whose kindred spirit never leaves my side. Casey, my best friend, daughter, and hero. Our southern man, John-Michael, an exceptional father and husband, whose love for my girl and their children is boundless. And the glue that holds us all together . . . our joyful little ones, Charlie William and Hadley Ann Orion.

Publisher, Crystal Patriarche, and the team at SparkPress: kudos for making publishing a truly cooperative effort.

Editor, Wayne Parrish: heartfelt thanks for your patience and infinite wisdom.

My literary agent, Kim Witherspoon, and everyone at Inkwell Management: your belief in me never ceases to amaze.

The James E. and Rebecca Winner Foundation for the Arts: thank you for so graciously and generously contributing to my efforts.

My sister writers and early readers who held my hand during the writing and beyond, I am beholden: Becky Winner, Sandy Kring, Emily Lewis, Kerry Tanner, Lenore Buss, Bonnie Shimko, Beth Hoffman, Laurie and Nora Clark, Nancy Lindhjem, Jean Oly, Meagan Harris, and Eileen Sherman.

And to you, dear reader: your startling kindness and sweet words of encouragement have deeply touched me. I cannot thank you enough for your continued support. I can only hope that Tessie and Birdie have become as dear to you as you are to me.

Also by Lesley Kagen

The Undertaking of Tess

Whistling in the Dark

Land of a Hundred Wonders

Tomorrow River

Good Graces

Mare's Nest

About SparkPress

SparkPress is an independent boutique publisher delivering high-quality, entertaining, and engaging content that enhances readers' lives, with a special focus on female-driven work. We are proud of our catalog of both fiction and nonfiction titles, featuring authors who represent a wide array of genres, as well as our established, industry-wide reputation for innovative, creative, results-driven success in working with authors. SparkPress, a BookSparks imprint, is a division of SparkPoint Studio, LLC.

To learn more, visit us at sparkpointstudio.com.

CPSIA information can be obtained at www.ICGtesting.com
Printed in the USA
BVOW07s0001181114

375517BV00001B/1/P